Reckless Law

Copyright © 2023

All rights reserved.

No part of this publication may be reproduced, stored in a retrieval system, or transmitted, in any form or by any means without the prior permission in writing of the publisher. This is a work of fiction. Any resemblance to any person, living or dead, is purely coincidental.

Published by Bucklesby Press. First Edition.
Cover design by Talon Clemow.

Reckless Law
The Hamptons Killer

J.P. Lincoln

Bucklesby Press

For Riordan
May your freedom be more magnificent than you dreamed.

CHAPTER 1

The tires of Robert Coleman's brand new bright-yellow Mercedes came to a slow and measured halt on the crunchy gravel of his Long Island driveway. He turned off the ignition and, as the engine faded, let out a small relaxed sigh—home at last. For a moment he sat in silence outside his sprawling property, a pause to acclimatize after the long commute from Manhattan to Great Neck and another hard day in the office. He took a deep breath, savoring the fragrance of pristine leather upholstery as he pondered what lay ahead. He could almost feel his wife's warm embrace, the taste of a homecooked meal, and the waltz of bubbles on his tongue from his favorite beer, all waiting for him on arrival.

He smiled. Life was good.

From out of nowhere a clenched fist smashed through the window, shattering it into a thousand tiny fragments that showered Coleman with a hailstorm of chunky glass. Adrenaline exploded inside him, stampeding through his system as his heart rate shot to red alert. Panic and confusion set in, his mind racing, trying to comprehend the sensory overload exploding all around him.

A hand yanked at the locked door handle then thrust toward him, grabbing wildly for his neck. He pulled back on instinct, just out of reach, as a muffled sound escaped from his depths, part yelp, part fear-laced cry of protest, stifled by his own short rapid breaths that had him panting like a dog after a long hot run. Only there was nowhere for Coleman to run tonight.

The hand reached further and grabbed again, seizing the lapel of his five-thousand-dollar suit, yanking him toward the now gaping hole that moments earlier had been a window. The lapel ripped loose. Coleman tried to scramble backward, arms and legs flailing like a man on the edge of a cliff with a perilous drop below, but his seatbelt held him fast, secure in an unwelcome embrace.

"Sons of the hounds, come here and get flesh!" a voice yelled in a thick Scottish accent, evoking the traditional battle cry of Clan Cameron.

It could mean only one thing—Alfie Rainbird.

Rainbird's enraged face thrust through the broken window. With both hands he secured a lasting grip on Coleman and heaved with enough force to uproot a small tree, partly dragging him into the cold night air, while the rest of him remained tethered, rooted to the seat's tan leather upholstery by the buckle around his waist.

Rainbird heaved again. And again. Five heaves in total, each punctuated with an incensed growl from the heaver and a terrified cry from the heaved.

It was a messy job, an unwinnable tug of war that left Coleman in a ragged tatter of torn clothing, before Rainbird got his prey. Coleman, desperate to get free, popped the release on the buckle himself.

Click. He was out—and instantly regretting it.

With a final heave, Rainbird dragged Coleman wholesale though the window, dumping him on the gravel of his own driveway.

Coleman cowered on the ground, his suit and shirt hanging in pieces, exposing a slack and hairy bare white belly.

"What do you want, Rainbird? What do you want from me?!" spluttered Coleman in terror.

"Justice!" yelled Rainbird, leaning in close with a pointed finger that jabbed at Coleman's face. "I want justice! Don't you understand?"

Rainbird raised his fist into the air, ready to offload all the anger and frustration, all the grief and despair that had eaten away at him since his wife's death.

Coleman closed his eyes and tensed.

"Ahhhh!" yelled Rainbird into the night sky, as he launched his fist toward its target.

The impact was colossal. Sickening in its ferocity. He struck again and again, one violent thrust after another, until the knuckles on his fist were a bloody mess and the side panel on the Mercedes was beyond repair.

A moment of silence passed before Coleman opened an eye, just one, only a crack at first, then the other, enough to see Rainbird standing with his head in his hands. Distraught. Broken.

With slow reluctance, Coleman got to his feet, the lapel of his suit flapping down like a crow with a broken wing, rendering hours of precise and dignified tailoring obsolete.

Rainbird looked his way, his eyes scanning up and down at the sorry state in front of him. "Clothes do not merely maketh the man, the clothes are the man, and without them he is a cipher, a vacancy, a nobody, a nothing!" snarled Rainbird. "Mark Twain said that, I say you're a coward and a liar, Coleman!"

He spat out Coleman's name like it was something rancid in his mouth, well past its expiration date, best rejected and consigned to the trash.

"God's sake, Rainbird, I did what you asked! I did get you justice. I got each of the victims' families half a million dollars!"

"No amount of money is justice for a life, for my Abigail. Those bastards should be locked away for what they did, rotting there for eternity. You told me they'd pay dearly for what they did, not a token pittance that'll be covered by a goddamn insurance company. They got away with it. *You* let them get away with it!"

His voice was strong and clear, but his accent was beginning to wane, ever so slightly. It was a good sign. The Scottish always came to the fore when he was angry. But right now, little cracks of east coast American were beginning to show through. Twenty years in the United States would do that.

"There's nothing more I could have done, Rainbird. I got you, and the other families, a good result. Come on, you know the drill, we do the best for our clients, the very best we can, but we're not miracle workers. We're lawyers."

Rainbird looked at him and shook his head in disgust.

They were both lawyers, that much was true, but they were each cut from very different cloth. Robert Coleman had trodden a privileged, predictable and well-worn path to success: Exeter boarding school, Harvard law school, associate in a prestigious law firm, then senior associate, partner, and finally senior partner. No one would ever raise an eyebrow to hear that someone like Coleman, with his background, had become a lawyer. Whereas Rainbird, well, things were somewhat less conventional.

The front door of Coleman's house burst open, and standing there, with a bewildered look on her face, was Coleman's wife, Laurie.

"Alfie, what are you doing here?" she said, looking from Rainbird to her husband, then back to Rainbird again. "Are you OK?"

"Is *he* OK?!" protested Coleman. "Look at the state I'm in!"

"Oh, what on earth have you both been doing?" she scolded, in the voice of a schoolteacher reprimanding two wayward pupils, apportioning blame equally.

Rainbird remained silent, contrite. He was old school, men could sort their problems out themselves, but the moment a woman got involved, he was all respect and civility.

"I heard about the verdict," Laurie continued softly to Rainbird. "I'm so sorry. No amount of money can make up for the loss of a loved one."

Coleman was dumbfounded. Speechless.

"Come on, let's get you inside for some good food and a drink, Alfie."

"Are you serious?!" objected Coleman.

"Of course I am, after everything he's been through."

"What about my new Benz?!"

"What, the banana mobile? I told you before, it's not endearing to have a midlife crisis."

Rainbird suppressed a smile.

"The two of you need to put this to rest, is that understood? You've got to work together, for crying out loud."

It was a bitter pill for both of them, but they knew she was right.

"Now shake hands."

They both looked at her with the same incredulous reluctance, this was a step too far.

"Shake on it!" she demanded.

A few shuffles and mumbles, awkward looks at the ground and protesting exhalations, but before they knew it, their hands were clasped together and they were shaking.

"Are we good?" asked Coleman.

Rainbird nodded.

"Yeah, *we're* good. But I'll never forgive the people who did this to Abigail, and someday I *will* get my revenge. And may they burn forevermore in the hell fires."

Coleman and Laurie looked toward each other concerned.

The last time Rainbird went looking for revenge, his and many other lives had fallen apart—a body ended up in the morgue and an innocent man found himself in court, and then the bowels of the prison system.

But was he really innocent?

Only one man truly knew the answer.

The former prisoner himself—Rainbird.

CHAPTER 2

Mitch Owens took a deep breath.

The sea air was damp and heavy, but he felt lightheaded and excited, giddy even.

He knew he was taking a risk, maybe that was part of his kick, but he didn't realize just how big a risk it was.

It was a perfect location to rendezvous. Surrounded by a wire security fence and obscured from the road above by its location at the water's edge, the old boatyard remained hidden from any prying eyes. A lone security light shone in the complex, the only illumination in the darkness, casting a murky halo that perished ten feet beyond the bulb, consumed by a thick sea mist amid the endless black beyond. As he began to descend the old concrete steps leading to the boatyard, the words spoken to him thirty minutes earlier played once more in his head.

"Tread carefully, Mitch," his roommate had warned him.

Mitch's breathing quickened, anticipation building inside him with every footstep taken. He hadn't seen Stephanie in over a week, but he'd thought about little else. Her thick wavy auburn hair, her catwalk figure, her delicate ever-so-slightly freckled nose, and her trance-inducing blue eyes. Stephanie was one of those girls you might call classically beautiful. The sort of girl who looks stylish and sophisticated even in a t-shirt, jeans and sneakers. Not that this was her normal getup; her usual style was more like Audrey Hepburn most of the time. She was also smart and quick witted. Mitch and Stephanie shared a self-deprecating sense of humor which, for him, was the cream on the strawberries. But most of all, they made sense to one another.

Mitch had first met Stephanie a year beforehand when working as a deckhand on her father's superyacht, *Eleni*. The other high society crowd on board had treated the hired help with the usual condescension, but Stephanie was different. She and Mitch connected from the start and soon Stephanie was displaying an uncharacteristic interest in yachting, finding any excuse to take to the water again in *Eleni*, to see the dark-haired deckhand who she used to joke looked like a more rugged version of Orlando Bloom from the shoulders up, and a less rugged Chris Hemsworth from the shoulders down.

That they were on different rungs of the social ladder was of no concern to them.

That Stephanie's father was Magnus McLean was of grave concern to both.

As Mitch reached the fence he stopped and looked behind him, back up the steps toward the road above. The sound of a lone car approached. It seemed to slow, although he couldn't be sure. It was out of sight but for its headlights dancing on the trees along the roadside. He held his breath and wondered if it was about to pull over, before the beam faded from the trees and the vehicle continued past. He exhaled, as nearby bushes rustled in the wind.

He didn't have to worry about the car. Not that one anyway. He'd missed the one parked further up the road with its lights off. The one with the four men inside.

Mitch turned to his right, moving along the fence line toward a loose section where the wire had broken free from the ground. He pulled the wire up, just like he'd done several times before. The gap was just big enough for him to clamber through on his hands and knees. He scrambled to his feet inside the compound and headed to the metal roller door of a large boat house. It was closed but unlocked, just as they'd left it last time. It was impossible to do the next part stealthily, and he cringed in anticipation at the noise he was about to unleash. Mitch heaved upward on the old roller door, its horizontal slats coiling up above his head, releasing a hideous groaning sound as rusty metal ground against rusty metal.

Mitch checked his watch: 9:35PM, he was early. He left the door open for Stephanie and stepped into the darkness, making his way among old fishing floats and coils of ropes, while sidestepping multiple winches dangling from the wooden rafters above. He knew the boatyard well, having worked here for Stephanie's father too, offloading the precious cargo from his fleet of fishing vessels. Mitch knew the fleet's schedule and that no one would be here; the next arrival wasn't for another five hours.

Mitch made his way toward a back room, squeezing past a large wooden rowboat, his hand running along the cold steel trailer on which it sat. He smiled to himself as he reminisced on the last time Stephanie and he had met here. He had set up a picnic in the back room, complete with candles and an old record player, and there he and Stephanie had dined on lobster and shared a four-thousand-dollar bottle of Chateau Letour 82, swiped from her father's cellar. That night they had reunited after two months apart. Mitch had been away touring the country as a roadie with a local band and had returned with a head full of ambitions and dreams. He'd been invited to do an apprenticeship as a sound engineer when the band toured Europe in the fall. His one hesitation was leaving Stephanie for so long. But she encouraged him to follow his dreams and jumped at the chance to join him in Europe. As the perfect end to a perfect night, they made love by candle light to the tune of *Moon River*.

The roller door rattled closed behind him. Slamming hard onto the ground with great force. He jumped and spun around.

"Jeez, Steph, you trying to give me a heart attack?"

There was no answer.

"Steph?"

Footsteps approached in the darkness—several sets of footsteps.

He froze like a dead man. His mouth dry and heart racing.

The beam of a powerful flashlight cut through the darkness, bouncing around, highlighting random contents, until it found its target.

"There he is!" boomed a male voice.

For a moment Mitch hesitated and froze, screwing up his eyes against the blinding light.

"Get him!"

He bolted for the back door, crashing through boating equipment in the darkness as panic overwhelmed him and he tried to escape. His legs felt heavy, like the dream he used to have as a child where he was being chased but struggled to lift his feet off the ground.

He tripped over an unseen object and stumbled forward, hitting his head hard on a protruding shelf. An internal explosion of light and dancing stars erupted inside his head. It was a serious blow but he barely felt a thing, adrenaline anesthetizing him like a shot of morphine.

Mitch powered forward, only to trip once more, his legs falling out from under him as he hit the ground. In a wild panic, he staggered to his feet as his pursuers closed the gap.

He was at the door now but he never stood a chance.

That it would be locked was inevitable.

He tried to kick it but the heavy metal bolt held it firm.

A second time he raised his leg, but before his foot could connect with the door a body slammed into him, knocking him sideways and smashing him to the floor with enough force to compress the oxygen from his lungs.

He sucked at the air as blows rained in.

Kicks or punches, he didn't know which.

And then the gun came out, the cold barrel thrust hard into his temple.

"Stay where you are, Mitch. Don't move!"

He tried to move, tried to fight until the end, but he was outnumbered and there was nothing he could do.

They say your life flashes in front of you the moment before you die, but for Mitch, lying there with that gun pressed to his head, it was an image of Stephanie that flashed before him. But then she was his life. That he would die for her was never in doubt, that the end would come so soon after they got together was the tragedy. He closed his eyes and waited for the inevitable, focusing hard on the image of Stephanie so as to hold onto something perfect and pure before the bullet wiped everything away. A long moment passed as if drawn from a clock frozen in time, before an audible *click* cut through the silence—the click of a light switch. Mitch kept his eyes closed tight as a bulb faltered, then flickered on the edge like an engine struggling to tick over, before finally illuminating the room.

"Get this useless piece of trash to his feet," thundered a voice, that somewhere in the dark recesses of Mitch's subconscious was familiar. A new face flashed before him, the database of his mind matching spoken word with image.

As he was yanked upward, Mitch opened his eyes and there he was in front of him—Detective Vernon Bruce, in all his obese glory, an arrogant smile on his face, like a trophy hunter posing for a photo with a downed lion.

"What the—what the hell is going on?" spluttered Mitch, as he looked from Detective Bruce to the other three police officers, then back to Detective Bruce again, the sight of cops at once filling him with relief and confusion.

"Don't play innocent with me!" yelled Detective Bruce, right up in Mitch's face, so close that Mitch could almost taste Bruce's pungent breath, which assaulted him like a noxious fog.

Detective Bruce scowled, his heavy-set face ransacked by the deep markings of time and aggravation, features etched with a constant frown that reflected the attitude he brought to his job. Detective Bruce threw a punch into Mitch's stomach, folding him over and sending him down, only for him to be yanked back up again by several arms.

"Take him to the station. We'll get answers out of him."

Mitch's arms were wrenched backward and the cuffs went on, squeezed as tight as possible for maximum discomfort, before the metal clicked in place, cutting his flesh and compressing the bones of his wrists.

"What have I done?" protested Mitch. "Can someone tell me what the hell's going on?"

"Oh, well that would be my pleasure," said Detective Bruce, a smirk spreading across his big round chubby face. "You'd better get yourself a good lawyer Mitch. You're under arrest for the murder of Lachlan Denoon."

CHAPTER 3

TWO DAYS EARLIER
Lachlan Denoon, the new golden boy of literature, was the first of the authors to arrive outside the historic BookHampton store in East Hampton, stepping from his chauffer driven BMW into a sea of anticipation. The air buzzed with an electric charge, as members of the public, press and local dignitaries milled around outside the bookstore's grand arched entranceway waiting for the event to begin. Lachlan indulged them for a moment, posing for photographs in a sort of nerdy chic of waist coat, bow tie and obligatory reading spectacles. He looked like he was desperate to be taken seriously, that he wanted to downplay his youthful good looks, and, more than anything, that he wanted to put his former celebrity to rest. With a parting smile, he ducked into the store, flashing a set of teeth that could have been used for a paint chart under the description High Reflective White. Not that Lachlan would get to brush and floss those gleaming kitchen tiles he had in his mouth for much longer. Little did he know that before the event was over, he would lose not only his two front teeth, but also his life. Right now, though, he was blissfully unaware of his impending demise.

None of those gathered outside BookHampton noticed the lone figure taking photos on the bench across the street. Why would they? There were plenty of photographers and journalists at the event itself— only his interest was altogether different to theirs. Positioned beneath the foliage of a gnarled old sycamore tree, its welcoming branches cast a dappled shade onto the sidewalk below his feet, providing a concealed vantage point from where he could watch proceedings unfold. He'd been staking out the location for the last hour, waiting for the literary luminaries to arrive at the historic store.

Held annually, the *Bucklesby Book Fair* comprised a two-part event, launched by the late great author Roger Bucklesby, now run in his honor by his widow Mavis. The first part was open to the public and this year's venue was the BookHampton store, featuring a standard fare of author readings, book signings and a lively Q&A. The second part was a prestigious invitation only writers retreat held over several days at Mavis's grand old Hamptons property for authors who could demonstrate a connection with the area.

Mavis Bucklesby stood outside making small talk with the event sponsor, business magnate Magnus McLean, whose immaculate suit stood in sharp contrast to the aged bricks of the historic store. Dubbed *The Pie Man* by *Forbes Magazine* who featured him on the cover, Magnus had acquired his popular nickname on account of him having his hand in so many different business pies. His empire stretched from real estate to publishing, from fleets of fishing boats to television production, and plenty more besides.

While half listening to Mavis, Magnus scanned the bustling street with a predatory gaze as the crowds flowed around him, oblivious to the calculated strategizing churning inside his head. Magnus himself was oblivious to the lone figure on the bench across the street who logged his and Mavis's presence from his obscured location. As the other authors arrived, the lone figure photographed them one by one, taking special interest in two in particular, before they disappeared inside the building.

*****

An abundance of dangling pendant lights infused the interior of the bookstore in a warm glow that seemed to pay homage to the untold pages held within. On its polished hardwood floor, multiple rows of chairs had been arranged, all occupied and facing a makeshift stage at the back of the store, where five authors sat. For literary events it was unusual, not in its setting, the Hamptons had hosted plenty of them, but in a small, although not insignificant, section of the crowd it attracted. Some of the attendees sitting in the packed store looked like they'd never read a book in their lives—and that this might, until recently, have been a badge of honor. But they listened with rapt attention to the twenty-five-year-old local author, currently answering a question on stage, doing his best to look like a master of this literary domain: pensive, thoughtful and intelligent, despite some of his fans being anything but.

"They say politics is showbusiness for ugly people. In which case, writing is showbusiness for shy people," said Lachlan Denoon. "Despite my previous dalliance into what might charitably be called reality TV, I'm fundamentally an introvert. I find solace between the pages—Theroux, Dickens, Hemmingway—not in front of the camera. That world is vacuous and empty. Trust me, I know. I lived it and reject it emphatically. The world of literature is bursting at the seams with vibrancy and fulfillment, and I feel very lucky and privileged to be part of it. In writing, I've truly found my home."

A couple of airheads in the audience, clutching his book between their glitzy nails, nodded to each other enthusiastically.

They knew him first from the television, as a popular and memorable, if ultimately unsuccessful, contestant on several reality TV shows. He'd started out on a survival show, then moved on to a dating show, before trying his hand on smash hit business show, *The Rookie*, where he'd shown himself to be smart and cunning, with a real flair for marketing. His next endeavor was to capitalize on his television notoriety, as a social media star, an "influencer" with millions of followers on all the big platforms. Endorsements, sponsorship, and product lines flowed his way—he even once had his own fragrance, *Bravado*. Tall, broad-shouldered and with the sort of good looks that attracted attention wherever he went, he'd now rebranded himself as something very different, ever since his first book had taken off. That a TV and social media star would market a book was not unusual, the shelves were full of vainglorious "celebrity" autobiographies that screamed "look at me!" and little besides.

But Lachlan Denoon had penned a work of fiction.

His debut book *False Gods and Acid Fruits* was actually good, very good; some hard-nosed critics were even calling it superb. He might have once dipped his toe into the lower end of the television market, and ruthlessly exploited social media to promote himself, but his writing was thought-provoking and nuanced, and the old guard of the literary world were paying Lachlan his dues with the conservative panel of the prestigious McIntyre Award presenting him with Best New Fiction, some were even saying he might be shortlisted for the Booker Prize.

Standing proud and tall on the long table in front of him, displayed like a flag of conquest, was Lachlan Denoon's McIntyre Award, its shiny metal surface fashioned in the crescent shape of a yacht's sail with an upright pointed mast. Seated at the end of the table was historian Professor Benjamin Aris, a Rhodes scholar in his seventies who'd just completed an anthology on the life of Franklin D. Roosevelt; sandwiched between him and Lachlan was Patricia Parry-Jones, a glamourous thirty-two-year-old bestselling author of controversial self-help book, *Harness the Power of Hate,* the central thesis of her wildly popular work being to embrace, not suppress, your hatred of other people, to channel and cultivate this hatred, envy and resentment in order to gain the sweet satisfaction of revenge, in business and in life. On the other side of Lachlan was Audrey Adams, the wheelchair-bound grandmotherly children's author and illustrator of the acclaimed Sweetgum Grove book series; next to whom sat forty-six-year-old British travel writer Stamford Williamson O.B.E., who had the ridiculous sort of face that only the English aristocracy can produce, a cross between Mick Jagger and a thoroughbred racehorse, only with bigger teeth, or at least that's the way it seemed. Stamford had made his name writing about his hitchhiking adventures in war zones, before cashing in on his literary notoriety by producing his own travel and survival TV shows, the latter of which Lachlan Denoon had first cut his teeth on as a contestant. Last, and definitely least, was Cathleen Miller, poor Cathleen, the only panel member yet to be asked a question, not surprising given that her last work of any commercial merit was over twenty years ago, but she'd been involved in the event since its inception and, for this alone, was invited to return year on year.

At the back of the hall were the traditionalists of the literary world: publishers, critics and literary agents, including Henry Hunt, the man who'd first taken a chance on Lachlan Denoon's writing. At thirty-five, Henry was young to have his own agency. He'd inherited it from his father after his death in a boating accident and had really shaken things up, cutting away a lot of dead wood to make room for new talent, and Lachlan Denoon had risen to be the biggest of the lot. His cull had put a lot of noses out of joint, one-time big names with whom his father had formed personal friendships were cast aside with a callous indifference. People like Cathleen Miller, who was severed from the agency with the exactness of a surgeon's scalpel. Not that Henry cared; his only loyalty was to the bottom line. Cathleen's value had been diminished to a figure on a balance sheet, and it was negligible. There was money in books alright, if you got your hands on the next big thing, but the truth was the real money came from television and *Netflix* adaptations of books, and Henry had recently secured a huge TV deal for Lachlan, and by association himself.

"Question for Stamford," said a man standing up at the front. "I know you don't like to talk about yourself, but could you tell us a little about your recent award? I believe you had a royal title bestowed on you, an O.B.E.? Can you tell us what it stands for?"

Stamford smiled and rolled his eyes with a sort of "*aw, shucks*" fake embarrassment. "Look, I don't normally like to highlight the award as not much has changed, I'm still regular Stamford really, but yes, I was recently honored to receive an O.B.E. at the palace. It stands for: Order of the British Empire. The letters now appear after my name, so officially it *is Stamford Williamson O.B.E.*" he said, emphasizing the last bit with a little too much insistence. "It was in recognition of my work in the Scouting movement, of which I'm a patron. But, like I say, please, just call me Stamford. Although, I am happy to sign books later with my *full* official title."

Lachlan leaned in close to Patricia Parry-Jones, covering his mic with his hand, only for hers to pick up and broadcast his words to the room, "Jeez, talk about planting a questioner in the crowd. He's such a douche," said Lachlan, removing his hand from his mic, inadvertently releasing a squeal of feedback from the speaker.

Several members of the audience laughed, some more subtly than others as Stamford went a shade of scarlet. He forced a smile but the look he threw Lachlan was full of venom.

Henry Hunt's hand froze half way toward a tray of finger food, held by one of several servers offering snacks to the room, his eyes going from Lachlan to Stamford with concern.

"Now, now, Lachlan," said Audrey as she gave Lachlan a quick smack on the arm. "Don't give away our little secrets. We can't all be lucky enough to have a solid fan base from our reality TV days to carry us through."

"Indeed, Audrey, very true," chimed in Professor Arris. "I'm afraid my many hours of research count me out of such pursuits, but…"

"—Yes, well, I'll keep that in mind when casting the next series of *Williamson's Will To Survive,* Professor," Stamford put in with a broad smile, attempting to regain the room.

"If it gets another series," muttered Patricia before addressing Stamford. "Perhaps you should try focusing your hatred in a more appropriate direction. *Harnessing the power* of it, if you will. I can recommend a book for that."

The crowd laughed.

Henry relaxed with a satisfied smile as his new star signing was singled out, yet again, for the next question. But then a young woman at the front stood up and Henry's face dropped. She was dressed in what looked like the female equivalent of Lachlan's own outfit, a sort of wannabe glamorous librarian, complete with her own "academic-esque" reading spectacles, almost certainly non-prescription.

"Lachlan, is it true you once dated your fellow contestant on *The Rookie*, Julie Swanson?" she asked. "And I was wondering if there's anyone special in your life just now?"

Lachlan peered over the top of his own spectacles, fixing her with a stare.

"I'm here to talk about my work, not any past romantic liaisons I may or may not have had or my current relationship status. Honestly, if this is the level of your thinking, I suggest you leave and attend a different event; may I suggest a Sesame Street convention?"

Laughter filled the room.

She looked embarrassed and offended.

"Next question," announced Lachlan without missing a beat, as the woman headed for the exit, clutching her copy of Lachlan's book to her chest.

All eyes were back on Lachlan. All except for Henry's, who stared at the woman with disdain as she left the building, tracking her until the moment she disappeared outside.

"Matilda Wolf, literary and theater critic for *The New York Times*, question for Lachlan."

Lachlan nodded his approval.

"I'd like to ask you about the character Charlotte in your book. She was very popular with many of the readers, a lot of whom were shocked to hear she will not be included in the upcoming television adaptation of your work. Could you explain why this was?"

"Great question, Matilda. Look, literature and television are two very different mediums; with television you've got to whittle it down to the people who really matter, who are central to the story you are trying to tell. Charlotte was always a peripheral character to me anyway, and the producers and I both felt she was rather superfluous, and that it was stronger without her. Charlotte won't be back, and that goes for book two as well, which, I'm sure a lot of you will be pleased to hear, is now very nearly completed," said Lachlan, flashing his familiar Hollywood smile. "Now, does anyone have a question for Cathleen? She's been patiently waiting this whole time with the rest of us hogging the limelight."

Lachlan looked out across the room.

There was some awkward shuffling but no one spoke up.

"Oh Lachlan," said Audrey, breaking the uncomfortable silence. "I know you're a bit of a newcomer in the literary world, but surely you realize Cathleen hasn't actually produced anything recently to talk about."

"As a matter of fact Audrey, I have been embracing the modern digital era and channeling my skills into blog writing."

"*Bog* writing, you say," replied Audrey. "I don't think I've heard of that genre. Is it some sort of post-modern murky prose?"

"Or just something to be read on the bog?" said Stamford with a laugh. "As in, the toilet—for my American friends unfamiliar with British slang."

"Perhaps for use as toilet paper," replied Audrey.

"Audrey, dear, I think your public persona is slipping," said Patricia. "How many glasses of champagne did you have before we got started?"

"I am just channeling the inspiration gained from your book, Patricia. If only this panel was filled with genuine talents, then I'm sure I would have a lot less frustration to deal with."

"Ah, Audrey, you really are too funny." Lachlan placed his hand over Audrey's microphone to prevent her from saying anymore. "I think you missed your calling as a writer of satire. And on that note, it must be time for us all to enjoy another bubbly beverage. Thank you all for attending."

At the back of the store, staring at Lachlan with poorly disguised contempt, stood a server, all dressed up in a waiter's outfit, holding a tray of half-eaten canapes. If there was bad blood between the authors at the event, it paled into insignificance compared to the ill will between Lachlan Denoon and the server—his former roommate and one-time best friend, Mitch Owens.

CHAPTER 4

Rainbird threw his keys on the kitchen table and surveyed his surroundings—an old fisherman's shack, weathered and durable, nestled among the sand dunes just beyond the water's edge. Somehow it had escaped the rampant development elsewhere in the Hamptons, which saw similar traditional homes bulldozed and replaced with huge waterfront palaces, planted in the sand as soulless testaments of status. It wasn't grand, but there was an authenticity to its faded wooden planks and the old buoys and nets in the yard that felt real and genuine to Rainbird. Just like him, the shack displayed the passage of time—in its case the constant attrition of the salty air; in his, the scars of incarceration. It made him feel an affinity with the place. He stood in the kitchen and gazed out toward the ocean, dazzling in the distance like some holy apparition. He liked the view and acknowledged its charm, but no matter which way he cut it, being here still felt like a form of house arrest.

Rainbird's arrival in the Hamptons was not unlike his arrival in the USA. Both were a banishment of sorts, preceded by a period of volatile unrest best left forgotten. However, they also offered the kind of opportunities that only new beginnings can bring, even if, right now, Rainbird was blind to them. As lawyers go, even among the most flamboyant and unconventional, Alfie Rainbird was unique. That a former maximum-security prisoner was to become one of New York's top courtroom lawyers was a quirk of fate that no one, not even Rainbird himself, could have seen coming.

The fallout with Coleman had caused great anxiety at the law firm where they both worked. It was undeniable that Rainbird was an asset to the firm. He had a superb understanding of the law, but more importantly, he understood the game of law, and the power that it held, how to play it, inside court and out, to the media, to the ever-powerful court of public opinion, to a judge, but especially to a jury. Rainbird had won what seemed like doomed cases on several occasions. There is a fine line though, between asset and liability, and Rainbird had danced on the razor's edge for too long, cutting himself and others in the process. The board's unanimous decision was that if Rainbird wanted to remain at the firm, he would have to take a forced sabbatical, to get himself together again, and put this whole sordid business to bed. The beach house was offered by a former client, Daniel Hunter, as a suitable location, a place his family had owned and vacationed at for years.

Rainbird accepted.

But the board had another condition—Rainbird would have to see a psychiatrist.

For a man like Alfie Rainbird, this was a punch to the gut. He was not the sort of person to talk about his problems, let alone bare his soul. Every fiber of his being rose up in protest against it. His Scottish heritage had taught him to value and respect stoicism in the face of adversity, not this modern proclivity for therapy, hugging, back patting, and wearing your heart on your sleeve. As far as he was concerned, that was fine for other people but not for him. He wanted no part of the current cult of victimhood. Even if, to the outsider looking in, he'd had more than his fair share of trauma. Rainbird had spent years bottling it up, to unearth it now would remove his shield and leave his wounds reopened and bleeding. If he had to see a shrink, then so be it, but that didn't mean they'd be able to pry him open and spill his contents out onto the table to be analyzed, dissected, rearranged and then stuck together again in an acceptable manner of their choosing. There'd only ever been one person Rainbird could really confide in. Just one person to whom he could open his soul. But she was gone. And not coming back.

Rainbird had met Abigail within just two weeks of arriving in New York from Scotland. Two years later she was dead. Soon after, Rainbird was sentenced to life in prison for murder. Not hers, but the man many said bore the main responsibility for Abigail's death.

With an American father, albeit one he'd never met, Rainbird was entitled to full US citizenship, and so, after jumping through the usual logistical hoops, he enthusiastically did what countless forbearers had done in centuries past—crossed the Atlantic in search of a better future: life, liberty and the pursuit of happiness. That, and to escape the escalating trouble he'd gotten himself into in Scottish city Glasgow with some of the local criminal fraternity, which looked like it might come to a head any day, and with dire consequences.

He loved America and New York from the moment he arrived. The can-do attitude that permeated the air like a pulsating energy. The sense that dreams weren't distant illusions, but were real and tangible, if only they were grasped and pursued. New York was like a beacon of promise that lit in Rainbird a spark of unwavering optimism for what lay ahead. It made him feel at home. At ease. That his decision to move to the country and become American himself was unquestionably the right one. He was proud to be Scottish, but right from the start, he was proud to be American too.

The first thing that got Rainbird's attention as he glanced through the window of the upmarket art gallery in downtown Manhattan, was the complimentary food and alcohol being served by several waitresses, milling around with canapes and drinks among the well-turned-out guests. He'd been exploring the city on foot, reveling in the vast canvas of possibilities that stretched before him, as he strolled from district to district, soaking in the vibrancy and energy of a place he'd gazed at pictures of since childhood. It had been a long day on his feet, and for a moment he pondered whether or not to go inside and sip wine, eat crackers with little bits of shiny orange fish on them, and stare at pictures he couldn't afford. Then music struck up and, as if on cue, he saw her for the very first time—the red-haired violinist of the string quartet, playing the opening of the gallery.

Without question, he stepped inside.

From the beginning he made her laugh. And they would talk. How they talked. Endlessly they talked. It was as if they'd been separated all their lives but had found each other again and were now making up for all the time apart. Two happy years passed as if they were two weeks, before her health deteriorated. They married on her deathbed, a heart-breaking romantic gesture, a final confirmation of the depth and meaning of their relationship, that saw the two of them united as husband and wife for a brief two days, before she slipped away.

"Our precious time together is sacred," whispered Rainbird as Abigail's coffin was lowered into the earth. "We have no more, but you and I, my darling, are forever bound up in the scheme of things enduring and eternal."

Within a week of her funeral, John Tofield, the CEO of PrimaChem, the chemical company implicated in the involuntary manslaughter of Abigail, through the toxic poisoning of the area where she grew up, was found beaten to death.

The man charged with his murder—Alfie Rainbird.

That Rainbird was convicted was unsurprising. The evidence against him was strong. That he would one day have his own conviction overturned, and the way in which he did, was a surprise, maybe even to himself. But then, Rainbird was to go on to become the most successful jailhouse lawyer that New York's notorious Attica Correctional Facility had ever seen, with countless victories for his clients—fellow inmates. While incarcerated, he threw himself at the law, studying with an obsession and commitment unmatched by even the most diligent and gifted Ivy League scholar. Though as Rainbird liked to say: commitment is a bit like bacon and eggs—the pig's committed, the chicken isn't. And if anyone had skin in the game it was Rainbird himself. Soon his abilities to assist inmates with legal matters relating to their sentence became the stuff of legend. Shorter sentences, stays of execution, acquittals, appeals and pardons, all made Rainbird a man in demand, both respected and admired. He became a source of hope in a world of despair. His skill unlocked the impenetrable metal doors of Attica for so many, before they finally opened for him.

CHAPTER 5

Crouched among the swaying grasses of the sand dunes, a figure watched the vague silhouettes moving around within the Bucklesby mansion, highlighted in the fading light of dusk by the illumination of several chandeliers. Veiled in the shadows, he blended with the dunes, his eyes gleaming with a mixture of determination and anticipation, as he focused on the mansion that loomed before him. It was hard to decipher what was going on with the naked eye, but when he used a telephoto lens it was almost as if he was inside among them, sipping wine in the grandiose surroundings, which attempted to downplay their opulence with token rustic embellishments: lobster pots and driftwood-framed mirrors, glass fishing floats and decorative oars, just to emphasize that you were by the coast, as if you needed to be reminded, as waves crashed beyond the expansive courtyard. His target was there, mingling like the rest of them, oblivious to the danger that lay ahead or that they were being observed.
*****
"I have to say, Lachlan, it's certainly *unique* for a dedication at the front of a book: *'To myself. For believing in me when no one else did.'* Couldn't you have thought of something a little more gracious or magnanimous?" asked fellow fiction writer Cathleen Miller with a patronizing smile, as she sipped her fourth glass of champagne for the evening within the Bucklesby residence.

Henry Hunt stood nearby and rolled his eyes, he looked like he'd heard enough, that it was all getting tedious, and, what's more, he had better things to do than listen to authors bickering.

"Enjoy your discussion, everyone," he announced, with a forced smile, swigging the last of his whiskey and abruptly heading outside.

His departure left six of them in total, all authors now, spread throughout the spacious living room. The undercurrent of mutual disdain between Cathleen Miller and Lachlan Denoon had built throughout the afternoon. With the advent of alcohol, it was bubbling to the surface. If Lachlan had experienced an easy ride at the question-and-answer session when surrounded by his sycophantic fans, the session at the writers retreat was something else, not that much in the way of actual writing ever took place there, but the squabbling, posturing and jealousy between the attendees more than made up for it, even if it was, for the most part, concealed behind a veneer of intellectual civility.

"It's a fair dedication because it's true, Cathleen," responded Lachlan. "I *was* written off by everybody when I first announced I would be writing a novel. Thankfully, I didn't believe them. I retained belief in myself. They laughed at me. But they're not laughing now. Three million copies sold will do that."

"No one would ever argue your book isn't *popular*, Lachlan."

"Oh, Cathleen," said Lachlan. "You say 'popular' like it's a betrayal of principle. Like being a commercial success is somehow to be avoided. You sound like one of those tiresome people who makes a big song and dance of the fact they liked a particular band's early music long before they were *popular*, when it was cool to do so and they were only playing in their garage and at small venues, but, of course, the moment they hit the big time and were playing stadiums, you were no longer interested, because they didn't seem edgy and niche enough. Don't be that person, Cathleen. No one likes that person. I believe that every author, including those in this room, wants their work read by the highest number of people possible. From my experience, the public always recognizes true talent, and the only people who turn their nose up at the notion of being 'popular,' are those who aren't, but desperately want to be."

"Well, McDonald's is the most popular restaurant in the world, but that doesn't mean the cuisine it serves up is particularly worthy of culinary praise, now does it?" countered Cathleen. "And as for the public, one thing they do recognize is a sell-out."

"Ha!" scoffed Lachlan. "You couldn't even be accused of selling, let alone selling out. Whereas my last book did, in fact, literally sell out."

"Sales have always been secondary to me. It's authentic literary acclaim that really counts. Need I remind you that the best of them all wrote an endorsement of my first book."

"Trust me, there's no need for you to remind any of us. You're always dropping that little tidbit into the conversation. Yeah, we all know Roger Bucklesby threw you a bone a lifetime ago. Please do give it a rest. It's only because the two of you were at the same agency—not that you're there anymore. Whereas independent critics have actually drawn parallels between my work and his."

They'd been goading each other all evening. Taking pot shots at each other's work and integrity. It was a messy business—the bad blood between them—and Henry Hunt was the cause of much of it. Rumors swirled around the role Lachlan had played in persuading Henry to drop Cathleen. Some said it was even a precondition to him signing with the agency. Whatever the truth, Henry had dropped her with the same degree of concern as someone depositing a bagged-up offering of doggie doo into a dumpster, and she'd failed to find representation since. At one time the big publishers were knocking on her door, but nowadays she had the indignity of signing with whoever would accept her work, which she had to submit herself.

Not that they were the only ones with animus between them in the room.

"When I was first invited to the event, I tried to get myself a copy of everyone's books," said children's author Audrey Adams, joining the conversation. "I'm afraid I didn't manage to find any of yours, Cathleen, so I looked up your little blog instead and read one of your posts there, on the medicinal use of cannabis, of all things. It's not the sort of thing I normally read, but, despite a few shortcomings, I actually found it something of an eye opener. And a strong argument for the full legalization of cannabis."

"Er, thank you, Audrey," said Cathleen, uncertain whether or not to be offended.

"Yeah, well, I've got to pick you up on a couple of points," said Stamford Williamson. "This flawed notion that cannabis is somehow not a dangerous drug, that it doesn't cause very serious mental health problems, and that there's no downside to it is, I'm afraid to say, disingenuous at best and downright folly at worst. I mean no offense, Cathleen, but problem drug users cost the taxpayer countless billions a year. That's the reality."

"You want to talk about reality, or the lack of it?" scoffed Cathleen. "That's something you know a thing or two about, isn't it, Stamford?"

There was an awkward silence. Everyone knew what she was referring to. Recent accusations had been made in the press against Stamford, claiming that his own work was not quite as authentic as he portrayed, that often when he said he was roughing it on the road and living on the edge, he was doing anything but, staying in five-star hotels and visiting exclusive spas, and that scenes of his spinoff documentary series had been faked to make them look more dangerous and dramatic.

"Unsubstantiated claptrap!" snapped Stamford, going crimson in the face. "My lawyers have knocked a firm line in the direction of those tittle-tattle merchants."

At this moment the ever-affable Mavis Bucklesby entered the room, carrying a cheese platter for her guests.

"Uh, this all sounds a bit, erm, *enthusiastic*," she said diplomatically, with a smile that tried to conceal her concern. "Cheese and crackers, anyone?"

There were a couple of takers, Professor Benjamin Aris and Patricia Parry-Jones.

"So, what are you working on next, Benjamin?" asked Patricia, as she chowed down on a thick wedge of artisan brie, treated with the aromatic smoke of apricot wood, apparently.

"Writing the history of little-known US island, Attu. It was the site of the only land battle in World War Two that was fought on US soil, after the Japanese invaded and for a while occupied, this island off the coast of Alaska."

"I've never heard of that," remarked Lachlan, joining the conversation. "How very interesting."

Whether he was really interested was hard to tell. He'd been sucking up to the professor all evening, like he wanted some genuine academic credentials to rub off on him, bestowing legitimacy through association. As the professor elaborated for Lachlan, Mavis scurried off to fetch some smoked salmon, olives, pickled artichokes and assorted antipasti. By the time she returned to the room, Lachlan Denoon and Cathleen Miller were arguing again and going at it full throttle.

"Don't 'young man' me, blogger woman!" said Lachlan, raising his voice, as he jabbed a finger in Cathleen's direction.

"Showing your true colors now, Lachlan? Shouting and screaming. This isn't reality TV, you know. In the writing world, the big boys and girls can formulate well-reasoned arguments. Continue like this and you'll be right back there before you know it. In fact, statistically speaking, it's actually the most likely outcome," said Cathleen, turning now to Professor Aris. "What was it you were telling me earlier, Professor, about first time authors and the statistical likelihood of them having a flop with their second book?"

"That was a private conversation!" protested the professor, near choking on a mouthful of water cracker smeared with an artichoke dip. "And discussed in the broadest possible terms. It is certainly not indicative as to my expectations for you, Lachlan."

Stamford Williamson walked over and joined the fray, trying his best to project a superior air of authority, like a high-ranking army-officer.

"OK, everybody stand down. As you know, I've been in a few conflict zones myself, and, speaking from experience, I think it's best we all take a step back from our dug-in positions," he gestured using the back of his hands in that annoying way politicians do, moving them in unison away from his body in a little stepping manner. "And then, let's reflect."

"That's it?" snorted Patricia Parry-Jones. "That's your wisdom from the world's conflict zones? To tell everybody to... take a 'time out?'"

"Oh, you pompous British prick!" said Audrey Adams.

"Well, I'm not going to stand around here being spoken to like that by people of your standing—a pseudo psychologist of hatred and a little kiddies author," said Stamford, storming out of the room.

"Oh really, Audrey. That was uncalled for," said Lachlan.

"You leave her alone, Denoon," snapped Patricia Parry-Jones. "She only spoke the truth."

And so, it went. It wasn't long before the whole gathering had disintegrated into disarray, and Mavis Bucklesby was clearing away half eaten bits of cheese and olives from the empty room.

As the lone figure on the dunes lowered the telephoto lens, he chuckled at the outright bad blood and bitterness on display in the room. The prospect of an evening on the cold sand was not something he'd looked forward to, but it was proving more entertaining than anticipated. His ultimate task was of the utmost seriousness, but that didn't mean he couldn't take a little pleasure from it along the way.

CHAPTER 6

As Lachlan Denoon strode through the sunny courtyard on day two of the event his eyes lit up. He had spotted Mitch Owens, all dressed up in a waiter's outfit, carrying a tray of drinks toward the pool area.

"Mitch!" exclaimed Lachlan, with utter glee, clicking his fingers as if summoning a servant. "How very nice of you to fetch me some refreshment."

Mitch did his best to appear unfazed, like he didn't care and it was no big deal, but truth was he'd been dreading having a face-to-face encounter with Lachlan at the event. Mitch had spotted Lachlan earlier at the bookstore when floating around with a tray of appetizers, but, with all the crowds, he'd managed to blend into the background and avoid him. In the house, it was only a matter of time. Mitch had heard Lachlan would be there before he took the job, and so had hesitated in accepting the gig in the first place, but he needed the work, any work, if he was ever going to pursue his dream career. Right now, financial necessity trumped his personal pride. He took any employment he could get his hands on: waiting, gardening, deck handing, you name it. He wasn't in a position to pick and choose.

Lachlan swiped a glass from the tray and, drinking in the manner of an experienced wine taster, took a small tentative sip.

"Mmm, absolutely delicious. Have one for yourself and cool down, why don't you? ... Oh no, you can't, because you're *just the hired help*."

He said the last bit with real needle and smiled, goading Mitch to respond. He wasn't to be disappointed. Mitch might have been one of several waiting staff brought in for the event, but he wasn't going to take that, not from his former best friend.

"Screw you, Lachlan. It wasn't that long ago you were cutting grass, mending fences and serving drinks yourself. But the moment you got yourself a bit of money, you quickly turned on all your former friends, you complete and utter Judas."

"Touch of the green-eyed monster there, I'd say. Jealousy is a terrible thing, Mitch, but you've only got yourself to blame for your current predicament. You were always a dreamer. Some people dream of success, others wake up and work hard for it."

"You'd have never even got that first television gig if it wasn't for me. You and I both know the truth"

"Oh please, it was only a matter of time before I hit the big time. I've found my niche and, by the looks of it, so have you. It suits you, you know, Mitch, the outfit and the job, you're a good little worker, it's the right fit for your skill set. So, well done you."

Mitch was about to respond, was about to take the bait again and lay out the reality of the situation, but what was the point? Lachlan might have screwed him over in the past, he might be a celebrity with tons of money now, and he might be rubbing Mitch's face in it, but so what? Mitch had the girl of his dreams, a girl who made his heart swell with the sort of upbeat optimism that Lachlan couldn't even fathom, and all his money and perceived success couldn't buy that or take it from him.

"Enjoy the event," said Mitch, with fake sincerity as he tried to move off, determined to be the bigger man.

"Fetch me a sandwich."

"You're not my boss."

"Actually I am. Fetch me a sandwich."

"I don't think so."

"I am your boss and you *will* get me a sandwich."

Mitch shook his head.

"Do you want me to have a word with the host about you? Now go fetch me that sandwich, waiter. Go on, fetch!"

"You do what you want," said Mitch, turning and starting to walk away.

"I heard a little rumor about you on the grapevine," called out Lachlan behind him.

Mitch kept going.

"That you're playing around with Stephanie McLean."

Mitch stopped in his tracks and whipped his neck around, eyeballing Lachlan.

"When I heard that I was shocked," said Lachlan. "Wow, I thought, that's either brave or stupid. Then on reflection—stupid. She's a nice bit of eye candy, mind you, but she'd have to be pretty dumb herself to want anything to do with a loser like Mitch Owens."

That was it. Mitch saw red.

All the anger he'd suppressed for so long exploded in his gut, filling him with a purple fury that was about to be targeted on Lachlan.

Job or no job, Lachlan was about to get what he deserved.

When the two of them were growing up together in their teens, Lachlan had been into soccer, whereas Mitch Owens had been into football. On the soccer field Lachlan was well versed in crying murder whenever, bless him, someone merely tapped his foot and gave him a sore toe. He would dive to the floor and roll around with a fake injury, wincing in apparent excruciating pain, in the hope of getting a free kick or a penalty from the referee, before making a miraculous recovery thereafter. Mitch Owens, on the other hand, had played cornerback, arguably the hardest position on the field, where real men tested their heart and nerve and sinew against linesmen often a hundred pounds or more bigger than them on sweeps, or running backs in the open field.

It didn't bode well for the acclaimed McIntyre Award-winning writer.

Mitch dropped his tray of drinks to the ground, the sound of glass breaking on the floor tiles of the courtyard like a concerto of broken dreams—Mitch's dreams that Lachlan had stolen from him. There was a collective gasp, as the attendees in the pool area held their breath as one, all watching the approaching storm ready to unleash its fury. Time seemed to stall as Mitch paced toward Lachlan with bad intent, his eyes burning with rage. Denoon went white, rapidly realizing that he'd gone too far, that he was about to get his ass handed to him, and that it was too late for apologies.

Mitch got within range, paused for a fleeting moment and then erupted, firing off a short left hook that connected hard with Lachlan's mouth and jaw. The thudding impact of bone-on-bone contact reverberated through the courtyard, serving as a brutal display that animal urges lie dormant under even the most cultured facade. As Mitch's knuckles sank into Lachlan's jaw and shook his brain, he dropped to the ground—luckily the hard floor tiles broke his fall.

Lachlan lay in a semi-conscious heap at Mitch's feet with a deep cut on his lip.

"Speak like that again and I will kill you!" he said, turning on his heels to make his departure from the property, only to spot something mid-stride out of the corner of his eye. He changed direction, heading toward another server nearby, from whose tray he reached out and grabbed something.

"Enjoy your meal, sir," he said, tossing a sandwich into Lachlan's face, which broke apart on contact.

As bits of buttered bread, a slice of floppy ham and a garnish of salad lay on and around Lachlan, Mitch made his way toward the gates, leaving a crowd of shocked onlookers and chaos in his wake.

Audrey was first on the scene, scooting over toward Lachlan at high speed in her motorized wheelchair, inadvertently running over his foot in the process. Moments later Professor Aris and Patricia helped a dazed Lachlan up from the ground. Henry and Stamford arrived soon after, followed by a stunned looking Mavis.

No one could quite believe what had just gone down.

The event had encountered its ups and downs over the years, but nothing like this. Not that a punch in the face was to be the end of it.

Before long all hell would break loose.

CHAPTER 7

The shouts emerged from out of the darkness, piercing the still night air as a voice yelled over and over, panicked and afraid.

"Someone help! Someone call an ambulance!" yelled Professor Aris with raw intensity, until his voice was hoarse and pulse racing in a fury.

Maybe it was the grand size of the property, or a reluctance from the others to leave the comfort of the pool area or their living quarters—beautiful self-contained guest cottages in the grounds that each of the authors had been allocated—or maybe it was just the Professor's own distortion of events, but time seemed to stand still before anyone else arrived.

Tying a bathrobe cord around her waist as she walked, Patricia Parry-Jones was the first to investigate, making her way toward the shouting, emanating from the open door of Lachlan Denoon's accommodation.

"Oh, my God!" she gasped at the gruesome sight before her.

Lying on the carpet, blood seeping into a bright red halo around his head, was Lachlan Denoon, his features frozen, eyes wide, staring into the abyss in a haunting mask of horror, his McIntyre Award on the floor beside him, now bent and covered in blood. Nearby on the carpet were what at first glance looked like two shiny pieces of porcelain, but on closer inspection were Lachlan's front teeth.

"We have to call an ambulance!" exclaimed Professor Aris. "I can't detect a pulse!"

Patricia squatted down and reached toward Lachlan's neck just as Mavis stuck her head into the room and let out a scream capable of bursting eardrums at fifty feet. Patricia flinched, toppled over and landed on Lachlan, her knee digging into his ribs, releasing a blast of stale air from his inactive lungs. From here everything was a blur. Fear, confusion, and a whirlwind of chaos took over, as Cathleen, then Stamford, arrived on the scene before, finally, Henry turned up and restored order, getting a quick handle on the situation and dialing 911.

Blood splattered much of the room, on the bedding, on the furnishings, on the walls, its distinctive metallic aroma, imbuing the room with the rank smell of a slaughterhouse. One moment Lachlan was on his front having a washcloth thrust against a wound on his neck, the next he was forced into the recovery position, then placed on his back so he could have his chest pushed up and down a bit—briefly, mind you, and with little enthusiasm—no more than ten seconds before this was abandoned after it seemed a little too much like hard work, but at least it could be claimed they tried. By the time the EMTs arrived on the scene, feet had trampled through blood, hands had picked up and put down the McIntyre Award, and pretty much everyone had disturbed and contaminated the room.

"Stand back, everybody. Give us some space," demanded the first of two EMTs to the group of morbid onlookers. The crowd parted to reveal the body of Lachlan Denoon, and within seconds he was pronounced dead.

As the cold realization of what had occurred began to sink in, a hush descended upon those assembled. Before anyone had a chance to speak, a new figure barged into the room.

"Get the hell outta here!" barked Detective Bruce, slamming his fist on a countertop and glaring at the gathered spectators, who he shooed outside. "This is a goddamn crime scene and I'm calling the shots!"

They stood outside huddled together in the darkness.

Detective Bruce glanced around the crime scene before joining the others in the open air.

"Anybody touch anything?"

There was an awkward silence.

"Who found the deceased?" demanded Detective Bruce.

The Professor spoke up. "Well, that would be me."

"You've got blood on you!" said Detective Bruce, his eyes lighting up. "How'd that happen?"

"I was trying to help him," protested the professor, fidgeting with his watch.

"Were you now?" Detective Bruce stared menacingly in an attempt to force the professor to crack. "First on the scene, now covered in blood, well, you can see how that might look to someone investigating a murder."

Professor Aris shifted uncomfortably, glancing shiftily around the room as all eyes turned on him with questioning suspicion.

"I, well, um… so does he!"

The professor pointed at Stamford Williamson.

"Look here, now," replied Stamford. "The professor and Patricia were all over Lachlan when I arrived. Covered in blood. Maybe they're in it together!"

Patricia looked at the professor with alarm.

"I was just trying to check his pulse, when I lost my balance. I never intended to fall on him. It was Mavis coming through the door that startled me."

"Surely you're not suggesting Mavis had anything to do with this?" Cathleen cut in, putting an arm around their obviously shaken host.

For a moment, everyone looked from one disheveled figure to the next. All sporting blood smears and the wild eyes of the shocked or guilty.

Henry Hunt stepped forward, arms out in a calming gesture.

"Detective, I would like to apologize for the chaotic disturbance of the crime scene. As you can understand, it was a great shock to find Lachlan this evening and we were all desperate to help, resulting in the mess you now see us in. So, unless you suspect we were all in this together..."

Detective Bruce's eyes widened at the prospect, as he looked from one blood splattered suspect to the next.

"Well, obviously it wasn't any of us," piped up Stamford Williamson. "It was the server. The one we all saw attack and threaten to kill Lachlan."

Detective Bruce's curiosity was piqued, and soon the group had unburdened themselves to the detective, laying out the dramatic events that had gone down earlier that day. When word then spread that Mitch had been spotted by Stamford sneaking back into the property after his altercation with Lachlan, the search was on to find him.

CHAPTER 8

The stilettos of her Jimmy Choos sank annoyingly into the sandy ground, pinning her feet down like tent pegs, requiring an almighty yank to free them before it happened all over again.

    Step. Sink. Yank.
    Step. Sink. Yank.
    Several failed attempts along the pathway and she aborted the effort. Climbing out of her shoes and carrying them underarm, she walked barefoot toward the beach house, the warm sand squirming around her manicured painted toes, while the sweet smell of brine drifted on the breeze.
    "Mr. Rainbird, are you in?" she called out, knocking on the door. "Hello, Mr. Rainbird?"
    There was no answer.
    With both hands against the dusty glass, she peered through the window.
    Nothing.
    She checked around the back.
    Still nothing.
    Just as she was about to give up and get back in her convertible BMW with its sun warmed upholstery, she spotted a commotion out in the shallows of the ocean.
    Lying on a giant surfboard, paddling, splashing, or maybe it was some form of ritualistic drowning, was a figure flailing his arms and legs around, expending a massive amount of energy, but creating very little in the way of forward motion. Whatever he was doing, it certainly didn't resemble what most people would consider surfing, but then the individual taking part didn't exactly resemble a surfer either, sporting not so much the classic perma-tan of a seasoned beach goer, but the pale, white, goosebumped skin of a middle-aged Scotsman.
    Give him his dues though, Rainbird was taking a stab at it.
    And for that, Stephanie McLean couldn't help but smile.

*****

The Hawaiian t-shirt and Bermuda shorts he'd found in the closet of the beach house didn't suit Rainbird in the slightest, but at least he was getting into the spirit of coastal living. He placed a cup of coffee on the rustic kitchen table in front of his guest, who murmured a "thank you" as he sat down to join her with his usual cup of double strength Scottish breakfast tea with a "wee dab" of milk, inadvertently revealing the crude prison tattoo on his lower right arm in the process—a stick figure of a bird standing in diagonally slashing rain.

The sharp tang of coffee filled the air, but there was something else detectable to Rainbird's acute senses—desperation.

Stephanie wrapped her fingers around the warm mug and leaned in close to blow on the hot drink. She inhaled a deep breath of steam before speaking.

"I'm so sorry to turn up on your doorstep and ambush you like this. But I'm in dire need of legal help, and everyone says you're the best, Mr. Rainbird."

Rainbird shrugged modestly. "What does it concern?"

Stephanie looked up and locked eyes with Rainbird.

"Murder. First degree."

Rainbird raised his eyebrows and looked at his visitor with renewed interest.

"Oh, not me. My boyfriend. My boyfriend, Mitch, has been arrested for murder."

Stephanie looked like she was about to cry, like she was struggling to hold it together, and might crack at any moment. She took a sip of her coffee to compose herself, her hands shaking.

"Mitch has been arrested for the murder of Lachlan Denoon," she said, her voice quivering, as the last of her resilience threatened to crumble.

Rainbird had seen the papers.

"House of Horrors" screamed one headline, *"Waiter arrested for Lachlan Denoon murder."*

Rainbird looked into Stephanie's eyes and saw a love held dear, tarnished by the slur of allegation.

"OK, let's take it one step at a time," said Rainbird. "Firstly, and I'm sorry to say this, but I'm not supposed to be practicing law right now. I'm on a sabbatical. However, I can certainly put you in contact with other very capable counsel from my firm."

Stephanie shook her head.

"I don't want anyone else; I want the best. And by all accounts that's you."

"That's very kind but, if truth be told, it's not just a sabbatical, sort of unofficial disciplinary action, really. I'm probably not the best person to help you or your boyfriend."

"Please Mr. Rainbird, I'm begging you. I'm not naive to these things, I know how important good counsel is, and I know you're the best. In fact, I've been in court and watched you before."

"Really, when?" asked Rainbird, surprised.

"When you represented Daniel Hunter against my father."

Rainbird gave a small sniff. "Your father is Magnus McLean?"

Stephanie held Rainbird's gaze with her piercing blue eyes.

"He is. And it's the only time he's lost. If there's one thing my father doesn't like to do, it's lose. He was livid with you at the time, probably still is, but he was in total admiration of your abilities. He said to me then, and I remember his words clearly, 'That man is the greatest litigator I've ever seen. Next time, he'll damn well be on our side!'"

Rainbird paused to process this. Magnus McLean, AKA *The Pie Man*, was no joke, no joke at all. Officially worth a cool eight hundred million, although probably far more if the tax authorities could ever become acquainted with everything he'd stashed away in the Cayman Islands or Bermuda, he had a reputation for getting what he wanted and for making the rules up as he went. McLean cultivated connections, political, judicial, even some serious players in the underworld, and he was rumored to swim in a sea of dirty money. The case that Rainbird won against him had been an interesting one, to say the least. McLean's former business partner, Daniel Hunter, had sued for his fair share of a real estate development that the two of them had set up together, only *The Pie Man* had tried to cut Hunter out of his rightful slice of pie, tried to palm him off with a miniscule sliver in the form of a finder's fee, instead of the agreed equity percentage, a fifty-fifty split. There was big money involved and a lot on the line, including reputations, and reputation meant a lot to McLean. Allegations of jury tampering had dogged proceedings, resulting in a mistrial and the whole process had to be scrapped and started again from scratch. Not that this meant the underhand tactics ceased. Three witnesses clammed up so tight on the stand, changing their previous stories and crucial details therein, that it seemed clear enough, at least to Rainbird, that they'd been intimidated or bought behind the scenes by some of Magnus's "strong arm" boys. However, ultimately, it didn't matter. Rainbird won the case for Hunter and the press had a field day.

"*Pie on his face!*" shouted the headline of one. "*Greedy Pie Man left with crumbs,*" said another, "*Pie man looks like a clown,*" said a third, accompanied by a mock-up of Magnus himself as a pie-carrying clown from a circus.

Hunter had played it up on the steps of the courthouse, posing for the press with a big toothy grin, while taking a satisfied bite of tasty-looking cherry pie.

It hadn't gone down well with Magnus, but with all the press attention on him and Hunter there was little he could do but swallow hard on the unpalatable result.

"I don't want to work for your father," said Rainbird, after due consideration.

"You wouldn't be. Mitch would be the client, and I would pay whatever fee you charge. My father would know nothing about my involvement—couldn't know anything about my involvement—he doesn't know about Mitch and he wouldn't approve. He'd hate him, in fact. He's hated all my former boyfriends, but especially those from what he describes as the "lower rung." Mitch hasn't been to what my father would consider the right school nor does he come from what he would consider the right family, but Mitch is a loving, hardworking man with character and principles, and I don't believe for a second that he's guilty. Please help him. Please help us."

Rainbird knew that if he took on this case he would be advancing into hazardous terrain, but in Stephanie he recognized his own devotion to the truth.

"I'm not promising anything," said Rainbird, noncommittal. "But I'll make some inquiries with my firm, see what they say."

"Thank you, Mr. Rainbird," said Stephanie, a flicker of hope in her eyes.

"Call me Alfie."

CHAPTER 9

Born to a Scottish mother and an American father, Rainbird's parents had met when his father, Captain Charles G. Rainbird of the US Army, was stationed in Scotland. They'd had a fling, he'd flown on to a different posting elsewhere in Europe, and only after he was long gone had his mother discovered she was pregnant. And so, the young Alfie Rainbird was raised alone by his mother, with the keepsake of his father's last name, in the sprawling Scottish city of Glasgow, in one of the roughest parts of town.

His mother was poor, so poor that she had to put the young infant Rainbird to sleep every night in the open drawer of her bedroom cabinet, to save the precious money it would have cost to buy a crib. There'd been no fancy education for Rainbird, but he had a brilliant mind nonetheless, and a tongue that could tie you up in knots, placing you in mental checkmate before you even realized you were in the game. It was a skill he'd learned, developed, and honed to a high degree of mastery, not in the classroom of some sterile debating society, but somewhere far more effective—as a boy street hawker, selling fruit and vegetables at his uncle's pitch at Glasgow Fruit Market. In a way, it was the first place he held court. And hold it he did, with a natural theatrical flair, Rainbird could captivate a crowd and have them handing over their hard cash for what was, at best, very mediocre produce. As a teenager, he'd gone on to hawk just about anything he could get his hands on: clothing, cigarettes, electrical goods, cookware. He even once successfully sold Christmas trees in summer. You name it, Alfie Rainbird had sold it. Customers would walk away from his stall with their newly acquired goods, which, moments earlier, they had no intention of buying and, within about ten feet, they'd pause, bewildered, unsure of what had just happened to them—Rainbird had happened to them. To the other traders, it became known as the "Rainbird effect."

He'd navigated some tricky sells in the past—most notably convincing the New York Bar to admit him, a former felon, as an attorney. Rainbird had passed their character and fitness examination in part due to his full exoneration, but also because of his extraordinary oratory skills and ability to win them over. In a different life, these skills might have seen him on the stage or television, maybe even as a politician. But he would need to employ them to their full extent to emerge victorious today—to persuade the board of the Manhattan law firm he was on a sabbatical from to give him the Mitch Owens case.

All the big players were there, seated around the polished boardroom table. Their eyes fixed upon him, the weight of their expectations heavy in the air, mixing with a lingering scent of concern and mild anxiety. Not concern for Rainbird's wellbeing, but for the firm's reputation and whether they could risk it once more in his volatile hands. Rainbird had dressed for the occasion, swapping the Hawaiian shirt for his sharpest suit and a crisp navy-blue shirt, ironed to perfection and garnished with his trademark silver cufflinks featuring images of little thistles—the national flower of Scotland. He radiated a sense of confidence that demanded and received immediate respect. That Rainbird wanted the case was unquestionable. He needed forgiveness and another chance. But more than that, he needed to work. It made him tick. Whenever he got his teeth into a difficult new case, his energy was focused on it, instead of inward where he would be stewing over all that had gone down in the past.

"And so, in conclusion," said Rainbird, bringing to close a passionate and eloquent argument on the merits of him representing Mitch Owens. "This high-profile case is not only the perfect fit for me, but actually for the firm itself."

There were a couple of little nods from the attendees. Not that this could be read as a sign that they were all in overall agreement with him or his request, more a case of a subtle acknowledgment that his presentation contained many pertinent facts.

A silent intensity hung in the air.

"As always, Alfie, you make a powerful argument. But surely the whole point of a sabbatical is to stay away from work," said Chairman of the Board Michael Brennan, in a voice that exuded authority and control.

"I know: on a break, take it easy, unwind, go fishing, surfing—"

There were a couple of raised eyebrows at the last bit.

"—And stay away from the law," interjected Brennan. "I believe those were the board's exact words."

"That too, and believe me, I planned to. I wouldn't have considered it, not this soon afterward anyway, except for the client approaching me, literally turning up on my doorstep."

"I think it's fair to say that we wouldn't even be considering this request were it not for that and you being in the vicinity of the murder," said Brennan.

Brennan steepled his hands, weighing up the pros and cons, while Rainbird did his best to read the reaction of the man who possessed the final deciding judgement. He wasn't easy to decipher, Brennan always kept his cards close to his chest and, in truth, Rainbird thought it could go either way.

Brennan turned to Rainbird's former sparring partner Robert Coleman.

"How do you feel about this, Robert?"

"Well, since the side panel of my Mercedes has now been replaced," said Coleman, with a distinct air of virtue. "I'm willing to let bygones be bygones."

To Rainbird, Coleman sounded like he wanted to wrap himself in a magnanimous cloak of righteousness, like a king pardoning a subject, but Rainbird nodded his appreciation nonetheless. "Thank you, Robert."

"By the way, Alfie," added Coleman, glancing from side to side optimistically in readiness to deliver what he hoped would be a killer punchline. "Thanks for footing the bill, otherwise I was going to get my attorney to draft you a letter."

He smiled to himself at that one and looked at his colleagues again expectantly, but his delivery was flat and there were no takers, although Rainbird threw him a bone in the form of a little polite, though wholly manufactured, smile, even if his colleagues couldn't be bothered.

"Very good, Robert," said Michael Brennan, with more than just a hint of disapproval, unwilling to indulge him. He turned to Rainbird. "It's all very well for Robert not to have an issue with it, but as a reputable law firm we have zero tolerance for the sort of behavior you displayed at his property. Make no mistake Alfie, you are an asset to this firm while you're winning cases, but your value has been put in serious jeopardy by your behavior. You need to rescue your reputation and the firm's. You spoke with great eloquence and frankness a moment ago. Well, let me dispense with eloquence and just speak frankly to you: this is your final chance. Win this case and you may return to the firm. Lose it and you're out on your own. Do we understand each other?"

"We do."

Brennan looked around to the other members of the board. "Does anybody have an objection?"

There were some stoney stares and a few pursed lips but no one raised a protest.

"Well then, I guess the Mitch Owens case is now yours."

"Thank you, Michael," said Rainbird

"Make sure that I don't regret it," he said, fixing Rainbird with an uncompromising glare. "You'll need an investigator to assist you, of course. William Boyce?"

"Georgina Patterson," stated Rainbird emphatically.

"Is she available, though? Anybody know?" asked Brennan, glancing around his colleagues.

"She's been assisting us on the Gravity Drinks case," stated number two at the firm, Emma Carlson.

"Oh, well that's practically wrapped up," said Brennan. "I'm sure we can spare her."

"Thank you," said Rainbird.

"I believe that concludes everything then."

"Not everything," piped up Carlson. "The issue with the psych."

"Oh, yes," said Brennan.

"Reports from the last shrink were far from favorable," said Carlson. "Dodging appointments, no shows, not forthcoming with information, that sort of thing. We expect you to take this seriously from now on. No more evasion. No more of your normal shenanigans."

"Yes, of course," said Rainbird, lying, albeit convincingly. "I have an appointment next week. Mark my words, I will make the effort."

"See that you do," she said without warmth.

*****

It was during his first foray into the law, when deep within the prison system working as a jailhouse lawyer, that Rainbird met Georgina Patterson. With procedural restrictions in place for what jailhouse lawyers like Rainbird could and couldn't do during the legal process, the normal protocol was to team up with a conventional attorney on the outside who would handle any aspects that Rainbird was prohibited from doing. Often these attorneys worked pro-bono, good people giving their time and expertise for free to assist inmates in their appeals. Sometimes they came with their own legal investigator in tow, a dogged individual, whose task was to dig into the case and uncover any facts or information that could be useful to the attorney representing the case. Georgina was an investigator, and had made a dramatic career path change becoming one, having spent several years training as a semi-professional athlete, a judo competitor who once qualified for the Olympic trials. She was good, very good, and determined that next time around she'd join Team USA, but she busted her knee about ninety degrees the wrong way and missed her window, forever dashing her dream of representing her country. Never one to wallow in self-pity, after extensive surgery and physical rehabilitation, she brushed herself down and took on a new challenge—training to become a legal investigator.

Rainbird liked Georgina from the moment they met. He recognized the fighter in her. She gave a damn about and cared for her clients. And she cared about justice. True justice. Not the Mickey Mouse version of it that had been handed down to those she helped. Not that she was some bleeding-heart liberal who saw everyone as a victim. Far from it. There were plenty of the genuinely guilty who deserved to be behind bars too, those who did merit rotting away inside never to be released, and she recognized the difference. She evaluated everything and everyone on a case-by-case basis. When she fought for you, she believed in you, and a person with belief is, as the old saying goes, equal to ninety-nine people who only have interests. That's what made her so formidable.

She and Rainbird became firm friends and colleagues during his incarceration. Their skills and styles complimented each other to the point where they had an intuitive understanding, like an elite pair of mixed-doubles tennis players, who blended into one another, playing deft set ups, feints and draws, frustrating their opponents, until the big smash at the end. As individuals they were superb. Together they were an unstoppable force.

*****

"Alfie!" she exclaimed, jumping up from her desk on spotting Rainbird in the open plan section of the office.

She gave him a big hug.

"Are you back? I mean, really back?"

"For the time being," said Rainbird with a warm smile.

"That's superb news. Have they given you a case?"

"Sure have. Murder, first degree. Client asked for me personally, which I think is what swayed the board."

"I'm not surprised they asked for you, you've built up quite the reputation," she said, adding with a wink, "even if it is unfounded."

"No arguments here," said Rainbird. "Thing is, I'm looking for an investigator. Don't suppose you know anyone?"

Rainbird gave her a cheeky grin.

Georgina's eyes widened at the prospect of them working together again.

"There's no way I can argue a big murder case like this without support. So what do you say? Shall we put the old team back together again?"

CHAPTER 10

"I need to speak to the officer in charge of the arrest of Mitch Owens," stated Rainbird with authority, at the front desk of the Suffolk County Sheriff's Office in Riverhead.

"And you are?" asked the female duty officer behind the desk.

"His attorney."

"Please take a seat, someone will be with you in a moment."

Five minutes later, a side door to the waiting room flung open. There, standing in the door, which he practically filled, was a familiar face—Detective Vernon Bruce. A scowl rested on his face, amplifying the deep creases of his forehead that bore witness to the perpetual underlying anxiety under which he existed, a mixture of aggression and dissatisfaction with his lot in life. He was an odd-looking individual, dressed in jeans and an ill-fitting black t-shirt that hugged his fat rolls, accentuating them to the point where they looked like they might be pool noodles wrapped around his waist concealed beneath his clothing. His brow shone with a coating of sweat, a reminder of the constant war he fought with the blubber that looked likely to devour him. There were bits of food in his teeth. Tiny little worn-down teeth. Too small for such a big squishy face. And his hair was thinning—in patches. By the looks of it, it bothered him. He had a terrible combover, which attempted, and utterly failed, to disguise his bald patch. Probably spent a fortune on regrowth hair products, concluded Rainbird. He was tall too, much taller than Rainbird. But then Rainbird had a presence that was many times his size—a "big wee man," as they say in Scotland—that oozed strength and authority. Detective Bruce looked like he was slouching on the couch eating pizza even when standing upright.

"Well, well, well, if it isn't jailbird, Alfie Rainbird," stated the talking pudding in the doorway, laughing to himself at that one—laughing hard, too hard—as if only a man of superior wit and intellect could have come up with such brilliance, a man like him. "So very pleased to see you again," said Detective Bruce, with an over-the-top sarcastic smile.

"Oh, the pleasure is all yours," replied Rainbird.

Their paths had crossed before, when Rainbird had represented Daniel Hunter in his case against Magnus McLean. Between the first and second trials, Hunter had found himself arrested on trumped up charges of soliciting prostitutes. Nothing had stuck and he was clearly set up by Magnus as an intimidation tactic, but the story of his arrest and questioning had hit the press, which seemed Magnus's whole intention.

"Bar never should have given you a license with your record, Mr. Loophole," grunted Detective Bruce in a self-important voice that was more drill sergeant than police officer.

"For the *record*, I don't have a *record*, with a full exoneration. Best leave the law to us professionals, Vernon."

"That's Detective Bruce to you."

"Sure, Vernon."

"You know your boy's got previous, criminal damage. Makes sense, you know," he scoffed. "Couple of ex-cons. The ex-criminal with his ex-criminal, *criminal lawyer*. Birds of a feather and all that—" he paused, then took an excited intake of breath. "*Jail*birds of a feather stick together. Hah!"

Rainbird shook his head, unimpressed, but he could almost see Detective Bruce punching the air in his imagination with that one.

"Very good. Any others?"

There was a pause. He was trying.

"Where's my client?" demanded Rainbird.

"Look here, you son of a bitch, you're on my turf now and I'm the boss. Don't think I don't know all about your past, Rainbird. You might be some hotshot lawyer nowadays, who the public have taken to heart, but I know what you got away with. Not the fairytale version of it most people believe. And there ain't no amount of quick talking, clever legal maneuvering that's gonna help your boy, not this time. He's guilty, all right. And I'm gonna make sure he does the hardest time there is to do for killing that big-time book writer."

"You should try reading a book yourself sometime," quipped Rainbird. "*An Idiot's Guide to Policing*, perhaps."

"Any more of that and you'll be in a cell yourself."

"Horror!"

"You want a book? I'll give you a book, all right, in fact, I'll throw it at you, and it's the only one that matters around here—the law book, and it ain't gonna be a signed copy!"

"Hilarious. I'll catch your stage show," said Rainbird. "In the meantime, I'd like to speak to my client, alone. So, if you wouldn't mind…" Rainbird gestured with the back of his hand for the detective to shuffle on his way.

"He ain't getting no preferential treatment, you understand?"

"Are we going to stand here all-day long flirting, or are you going to take me to my client?"

Detective Bruce mumbled something to himself, then stared at Rainbird, fixing his nasty little eyes on him, doing his best to intimidate. But he was an amateur, and Rainbird had played this game with much better opponents in the past.

"Follow me," barked Detective Bruce, trying to make it sound like Rainbird was complying with his authority, not the other way around.

Rainbird gave a mock salute and clicked his heels together. "Yes, sir."

Harsh fluorescent lights flickered overhead, as they made their way along a corridor lined with a sticky linoleum floor that clung to the soles of Rainbird's polished shoes, making little squelching noises as he walked. Down a flight of stairs, along another corridor and they arrived at a thick metal door.

"You've got ten minutes," grunted Detective Bruce, yanking open the door with his meaty fingers.

Rainbird stepped inside and Detective Bruce slammed the door behind him. There, in a small, cold, windowless holding room with no furniture, was Mitch Owens, standing with his arms folded and leaning against the wall.

"My name is Alfie Rainbird, I'm your lawyer," said Rainbird, thrusting out a hand.

As Mitch locked eyes on him for the first time, he saw in Rainbird an unwavering resolve, a determination to fight for justice and truth no matter where it took him.

"Thank God, you're here," he said, shaking Rainbird's hand. "Mitch Owens."

In that moment, a spark of hope was kindled in Mitch that offered support amid the chaos that had swamped him. "How's Stephanie? Did you speak to Stephanie? Is she OK?"

Rainbird admired this. Mitch was incarcerated and staring down the barrel at a life sentence, but his first thought was not for his own predicament but for his lady's. A man like that had character, and Rainbird admired character more than anything.

"She's fine and is staying strong. She asked me to pass on her love and to tell you that she'll be fighting for you all the way. She wouldn't take no for an answer from me and that's the sort of person you want in your corner."

"I need to see her. Please, I've gotta make bail. No way I'm gonna survive on the inside. Do you think you can get me bail, Mr. Rainbird? Stephanie told me you're the best, that you can make charges disappear like a politician's pre-election promises."

"You haven't been charged yet, only arrested."

"But I will be charged, won't I?"

"I'm not going to lie to you Mitch, they'll most likely charge you today. Any bail hearing comes afterward. But can we beat their charge in court? That's what's important. Tell me, have you spoken to the cops, did you say anything to them?"

Mitch shook his head. "Not a word. 'I'm saying nothing till my lawyer gets here,' that's what I told them."

"Good man," said Rainbird. "The important thing for today is that we admit to very little. Precise details can come out at trial, and we don't want any of those specifics that we rely on later contradicted by our recorded statement today. Even if your actions are within the law, we cannot, under any circumstances, have your statement take you outside the law. You are convicted more on what you say than on what you do. Understood?"

Mitch nodded.

"So answer their questions as shortly as possible. I'll take the lead, you follow me."

There was something about the tone in which Rainbird spoke to Mitch that put him at ease. Even though the situation he faced was perilous, with Rainbird by his side, speaking with authority and experience, it didn't seem so bad, and for the first time he felt a sense of hope, a hope that whispered of salvation and deliverance, that maybe, just maybe, justice would prevail in the end.

Rainbird had gleaned the basics of the charges and the run up to them from Stephanie; what was alleged and how it supposedly went down. What's more, by now he was also vaguely familiar with Mitch's background, so he wasn't starting from scratch.

"Let's start at the beginning. I believe you knew the deceased, that you were former friends, is that correct?"

"That's right. Lachlan and I were best friends for a long time, lived around the corner from each other and went to the same high school. He was good fun, outgoing, always a laugh. We got up to all manner of mischief as teenagers. Nothing serious, you know. After high school we were roommates and did random jobs together to pay the bills, usually when the big rich society set are summering in their fancy houses. Sometimes we'd be mowing their lawns, other times fixing fences, serving drinks at their parties or deck handing on their yachts."

"What led to your falling out?"

"I took a job gardening for Stamford Williamson—you know, the author and survival guy from TV—at his summer house. Lachlan wasn't there, never met the guy, was working on a construction site elsewhere at the time. Anyway, Stamford and I got talking, he was sort of interesting, had been all over the world and seen places I'll never get to go. So I listened as he told me about his exploits, in-between me pulling up weeds from his flowerbed. He told me about a new reality TV show he was working on, which he was going to present, where contestants would battle it out in the wild, taking on different survival challenges each week, with a contestant eliminated at the end of every show, until there was only one man or woman left standing. That went on to be the hit show *Williamson's Will to Survive*."

"The series Lachlan first made his name on?"

"Yeah, that's right. Anyway, I finished the job and wished Stamford well with his series, but before I left, he asked me if I was interested in more work, which I took to mean gardening. I said I was and he told me he'd be in touch, and that was that. But the very next day, when I'm out working at a different house, Stamford Williamson's production company called the landline at the apartment Lachlan and I shared, asking for me."

"A landline?" asked Rainbird, surprised.

"Yeah, part of the telecom service package; was cheaper than getting internet alone. Anyway, Lachlan takes the call and offers to pass on a message, and the woman on the phone says that Stamford Williamson is offering me the chance to try out for his show tomorrow at a studio in Manhattan, after one of the confirmed contestants pulled out with a broken leg earlier in the week. She said it was urgent, that they could only fit me in tomorrow, what a great opportunity it was, and all the rest of it. And so, Lachlan, the total snake that he is, says that I'm ill and have gone off to stay at my parent's place and won't be available. But that he'd be delighted to take my place, and could make it to the studio tomorrow."

"How did you find out about this?"

"Stamford Williamson himself told me the following summer, after his show had aired and Lachlan had become famous, when I was back pulling out weeds from the same flowerbed."

"That's motive there, alright. How many people know about this?"

"Quite a few."

"But not the police?"

"Maybe not yet, but with a bit of digging someone will tell them the whole sordid tale."

"Detective Bruce mentioned you have a previous conviction?"

"Yeah, it's from a long time ago and it's ridiculous. I got fined for criminal damage."

"What happened?"

"I did a job erecting a fence on a property in New Haven, and after I'd completed the work, the owner refused to pay, said they were unhappy, not with the work I'd done but with the style of fence; said it clashed with the house. But here's the thing, they'd chosen the type of fence in the first place, not me. It took over a week of solid work, so when it became clear they weren't going to pay, I went back to the property and dismantled it. Left all the fencing there, didn't damage anything, but they used their influence and got me charged, even spent a night in the cells. I thought, no way is a judge going to side with them, but their smartass lawyer twisted everything and got me fined. I had to complete a community service order picking up trash, and now I have a record too."

Mitch said the last bit through gritted teeth. The injustice of it still stung. However, he had more pressing matters to consider. Premeditated murder in the first degree was a whole different ballgame—and they didn't hand out fines and community service orders for that. Be in the wrong state and they handed out a death sentence. Be in the right state and they handed out a virtual one, where you could kiss goodbye to any life worth living, and would spend the rest of your days in a cramped little box, sharing it with a cellmate whom you didn't get to interview for the position. If you were lucky, they didn't have pre-existing violent tendencies. If not, well, good luck sleeping. In short, somewhere your hopes and dreams would be snuffed out just as effectively as any electric chair could do the job.

"I want you to tell me about the day of Lachlan's murder and your interactions with him."

Mitch took a deep breath, composing himself.

He knew it didn't look good.

"I saw him at the Bucklesby mansion. I was a server handing out drinks to the guests, of which he was one, big bestselling author that he is now."

"Was," interjected Rainbird.

"Yeah, was," said Mitch in a considered manner.

Rainbird searched Mitch's face for truth in the midst of a sea of uncertainty, studying his every gesture. He was a master of observation, and his first impressions of Mitch were favorable.

"I guess it was inevitable that our paths would cross there, and when they did it didn't go down well. I tried to get on with what I was there for, to have as little as possible to do with him, but he had to play it all high and mighty, and rub it in my face. I know it doesn't look good, Mr. Rainbird, but it ended up getting physical. He insulted me repeatedly, and, at first, I didn't lash out, but when he insulted Stephanie, that was the final straw, and I'm afraid to say we came to blows."

"You say blows, did he hit you?"

"Well, no. I hit him. Only once."

"But it was enough to do the job, right?"

Mitch gave a solemn nod.

"How many witnesses saw this?"

"Pretty much everyone there."

"And did they hear the preceding argument when he was goading you?"

"I don't know. Maybe. Probably not."

"OK," said Rainbird. "What happened next?"

"I left the property, got in my car and drove home. That night when I'd planned to meet up with Stephanie at one of her father's boatyards, a team of cops stormed in and, after roughing me up, arrested me for Lachlan's murder. I've been in here since. That's all that happened. You've got to believe me. I didn't kill anyone."

Rainbird reserved judgment. He had learned through hard experience that no matter how credible a narrative, he must proceed with carful intent and to trust his gut. His gut told him there was a lot more to this business than met the eye, but then it didn't look good for Mitch on paper. He had a motive alright; people had seen him arguing with, then assaulting Lachlan. And there was the hostile history between them. It seemed likely the police had more damning evidence on Mitch that they would present during the interview; question was, what?

The door burst open and there was Detective Bruce, accompanied by another cop. A woman, approachable looking, a bit like a kindergarten teacher, polite, meek, and wholesome. The sort of person who might be into knitting or embroidery, not the cut and thrust world of law enforcement. Or so she wanted to appear.

"My name is Detective Rebecca O'Brien. Please, follow me."

"No prizes for guessing who'll be playing good cop," whispered Rainbird to Mitch with a smile, as they followed them back into the depths of the police station. "Remember, answer as briefly as possible, and I'll take the lead."

As they walked deeper along the corridors, walls stark and bare, Mitch tried to calm himself in readiness for what lay ahead. A door, thick and heavy, stood at the end, a gateway to the interview room, a chamber where lies fell apart. The door creaked open, revealing another windowless room, with a dull uninviting glow and a noticeable scent of disinfectant. It smelled like a morgue, only this room wasn't decked out with a slab but a metal table, four faded plastic chairs and a recording device.

"Take a seat, please," said Detective O'Brien.

Rainbird and Mitch sat down, pulling their chairs forward ready to begin, the cold metal of the table chilling their palms, amplifying the gravity of the situation. Good Cop followed their lead, while Detective Vernon Bruce stood, hands resting on the back of the chair, glaring at them both, exuding arrogance from every sweaty pore of his being. Finally, he pulled the seat out and sat, his fat ass spilling out over the sides of the plastic seat that looked like it might give way at any moment.

"Bear with me a second," said Detective O'Brien to Mitch with a warm smile, as she fumbled with the recording device.

"Don't say anything important until my colleague has got the recorder running," demanded Detective Bruce.

"I killed him! It was me!" blurted Rainbird with a grin, holding out his hands as if to be cuffed.

"What?!" exclaimed Detective Bruce, his eyes almost popping out of their sockets.

"Joking," said Rainbird, gesturing to the inactive recorder.

Even Detective O'Brien couldn't contain a small involuntary smile at that one. It was all part of Rainbird's plan, to subtly disarm her from the get-go.

Detective Bruce glared at Rainbird.

O'Brien pressed the right configuration of buttons and the recorder sprang into life.

"I'm Detective Rebecca O'Brien, joined by Detective Vernon Bruce, this is in reference to case number 150523/5505, the time now is 1:55PM on Monday the fifteenth of May. Would you please state your name for the record?"

"Mitch Owens."

"Thank you, Mitch. I'd like to start by asking you about your time at the Bucklesby residence. What were you doing there?" asked Detective O'Brien.

Mitch glanced over to Rainbird, who nodded.

"I was working there, at the annual writers retreat."

"What work were you doing there?"

"I was a waiter."

"And while there, you had a heated argument with the deceased, Mr. Lachlan Denoon?" said Detective Bruce.

Rainbird answered first. "Any argument or antagonism was directed from Lachlan Denoon toward my client. And not the other way around."

"Bull!" barked Detective Bruce, emitting a blast of spittle across the table. "We have multiple witnesses who say Lachlan Denoon and you argued. That right, Mitch?"

Mitch was about to answer but Rainbird cut in.

"We dispute that interpretation. My client was the aggrieved party, Lachlan Denoon tried to draw my client into an argument, which he resisted."

"It takes two to argue."

"No, it doesn't. If I stand here arguing with you, shouting and insulting you but you don't respond or you do respond but in a civil and reasoned manner, are you arguing with me? No, you're not. Debating, perhaps."

"This is ridiculous. An argument is an argument. A debate is a debate."

"Would you please define the two for me?" asked Rainbird.

Detective Bruce paused for a moment, the cogs in his mind turning, confusion etched on his big circular face.

"No," he grunted. "I won't. And I'm the one asking the questions, got it?"

There was a pause—then Detective O'Brien asked a question.

"What was your verbal exchange with Lachlan about, Mitch?"

"—As well as her," cut in Detective Bruce. "She's asking questions too, of course," he conceded, looking rattled.

While Mitch elaborated for her, in a nonspecific way, Rainbird began staring at Detective Bruce's thinning hairline, as if he'd just spotted something peculiar there. Occasionally he'd glance down, so Detective Bruce and he were eye to eye, but always he'd look up again, almost inquisitively at that unfortunate bald patch. Rainbird had a knack for spotting people's insecurities and, if necessary, exploiting them. He wanted to rattle the detective. Put him off his game and disrupt his flow. Detective Bruce started to go red. With his left hand he smoothed his hair down. While Rainbird was playing with him, he kept monitoring his client: what Mitch said or didn't say, poised ready to jump in the moment it was necessary.

Rainbird had to give Mitch credit, he was smart. He kept it short. Spoke in generalities. And used "to the best of my recollection" instead of dealing in absolutes, so as to give him wriggle room later if necessary. He might have over done that bit a little, but still, he covered his back and that was the main thing.

"And after your verbal exchange, you hit Mr. Denoon, didn't you?" said Detective O'Brien. "Hit him in the face with such force as to knock him to the ground." She turned to Rainbird. "Please tell me you're not going to dispute that interpretation of events?"

"My client acted in self-defense."

"That ain't gonna cut it," said Detective Bruce. "He hit him first, that ain't self-defense."

"Common misunderstanding of the law which is, in fact, quite clear on this matter. If physical harm is imminent then the law absolutely allows you to use reasonable force to prevent an attack by acting pre-emptively. There is no requirement in law to wait until struck by another to have acted in self-defense."

"So you're saying Lachlan Denoon was about to attack him?"

"I'm saying my client acted in self-defense."

"So you're saying he was about to be attacked."

"I state again, my client acted in self-defense."

Mitch could see what Rainbird was up to, and what's more so could detectives O'Neil and Bruce, but that didn't matter, what mattered to the cops was how much incriminating information they could get Mitch to reveal in his statement. What mattered to Rainbird was the opposite. Rainbird was fighting for every inch of the argument, even if his stated interpretation of events didn't match the actual reality of them as they unfolded. Lachlan wouldn't have swung at Mitch that fateful day, but right now that was irrelevant. He needed to sow that suggestion. The strategy was to admit nothing and question the police's interpretation of everything, providing them with very little in the way of specific information. Specifics would be what preparing a defense for trial was all about, and that would come later.

"Tell me what happened after your run-in with Lachlan, Mitch," said O'Brien.

"I left the premises and went home."

"So, to be clear, you didn't return to the Bucklesby property?" asked O'Brien.

"No."

"What did you do when you got home?" asked Detective Bruce.

"Read a book."

"You read a book?" scoffed the detective, as if this was a very odd thing to do. "Did you read the book while you soaked your blood-stained t-shirt in a lukewarm bucket of detergent? Yeah, we found that, wanna tell us why Lachlan Denoon's blood was all over your shirt, Mitch?"

"It was from when I hit him."

"That's a hell of a lotta blood for one punch," said Detective Bruce, raising an eyebrow.

"And we have a witness," added O'Brien, softly. "Possibly two, in fact. We're following up with a second. But the one we have is saying that they saw someone matching your description running from the property over the sand dunes later on, after your altercation with Lachlan Denoon. I'm guessing they'll pick you out of a lineup too, so why not just make it easier for yourself and admit it. The judge will be more lenient if you do."

"But I didn't do anything."

"Wanna tell us about the stolen property, Mitch?"

Mitch's eyes widened as shock crept across his face.

"Your little keepsake from the murder scene in your bedroom," said Detective Bruce, reaching into his pocket for a sealed bag containing a bright red fountain pen.

He placed it on the desk.

"Oh," said Mitch. "That's my pen. Lachlan swiped it when he moved out of the apartment we used to share. He always liked it. I saw him signing books with it at the bookstore, and so the next day, when I was working at the retreat, I took it back."

"When?" asked O'Brien.

"On the second day, around lunchtime, when I delivered some fresh towels to his room."

"Was Lachlan there when you did this?" she asked.

"No."

Detective Bruce scoffed. "I'll tell you what I think went down," he said. "I think you attacked Lachlan Denoon in a nasty red mist of rage—and yeah, I'm saying you attacked him in an unprovoked way—and then you hightailed it out of that big expensive writer house. Only that red mist stuck around; it didn't go away. I think you sat in your car stewing on it all, getting angrier by the minute. I bet it felt good throwing a fist into that pretty face, but you wanted more, much more, and you were damn sure you were going to get it. So back you went, sneaking in over the dunes. Then you found him in his room, and stabbed him in the neck with the nasty pointy bit of that book award trophy thing of his. Not that you left it there. Forensics say he was struck on that handsome high cheek-boned face of his too, two teeth were recovered at the scene, so it's not a crime of passion, is it? No. That's something altogether more sinister. Any jury is gonna see that. But then you either panic and steal something to try and make it look like a botched robbery or just pocket yourself a twisted memento of the event. Plenty of killers do it."

"I didn't kill him. I swear it."

"You *swear* it?" asked Detective Bruce with mock sincerity. "Oh, hell! Why didn't you say so earlier? If that's the case, then I guess it couldn't have been you." He stood up and looked over to Detective O'Brien. "Come on, Detective, our case against this guy has fallen apart. Just when I thought we'd found our man too—seen arguing with the deceased, placed at the scene of the crime at the time of the crime with a motive to kill and with the deceased's blood on him too. But he swears it wasn't him. Not *says* it wasn't him. Not *promises* it wasn't him. No. He *swears* it. Guess it's back to the drawing board for us."

Detective Bruce slammed his fist on the table, the impact reverberating around the room like a shock wave, as he eyeballed Mitch.

"You're gonna have to do a lot better than that, sonny!"

"Veritas is an absolute defense," responded Rainbird.

"Veri-what?"

"Veritas—the truth—is an absolute defense. Your case has more holes in it than a Swiss cheese factory, Detective. There were multiple other people in that house, multiple people who could just as easily have killed Lachlan Denoon. And plenty of them with more motive too, no doubt."

"That's a long shot and you know it, Rainbird," said Detective Bruce.

"You don't have anything, detectives."

"The hell we don't!" barked Detective Bruce, getting to his feet again. "Let's make it official, Mitch Owens, you are hereby charged with the murder of Lachlan Denoon."

CHAPTER 11

Rainbird had only been there a few weeks but already he'd met half the village. He was that sort of person, the sort who strikes up conversations with strangers, pleasant motiveless conversations, about the weather, about the tide, about what sort of bait a fisherman is using. Conversations that introduced him to the community, and in no time, he was fending off invitations for coffee, cake and cookies from several residents, in particular the elderly women of the neighborhood, who really took him to heart.

"Need anything from the shop, Barbara?" called out Rainbird, to his retiree neighbor, who began struggling to contain her black Labrador's excitement on spotting him.

"Could you get me the paper, Alfie?" she asked, as the dog broke free of her grasp and bounded over to Rainbird in a manic ball of enthusiasm. "Oh, he's got so much energy."

"Hello, Fenton!" said Rainbird, nuzzling in close to the dog, giving him a flurry of pats and strokes. "How are you, boy? Been cooped up all morning?"

He turned to his neighbor. "I could take Fenton with me if you like, burn off a bit of energy on the way?"

"Oh, if you wouldn't mind."

Rainbird had loved dogs since his first visit to the Scottish Highlands as a young boy, where he once spent a week with his mother at an old farm, visiting an elderly relative. At the farm were two beautiful Border Collies, and from the get-go Rainbird and they were inseparable. Off he'd go with those dogs, running through the countryside that was so different to the city he was used to, so clean, expansive and serene. Only when it started to get dark would he return, exhausted, covered in mud and bits of bush, but always so very content. When they returned to Glasgow, he pestered his mother to get a dog, but with no garden and so little money it was hopeless from the start. Still, the happy memory of those Border Collies had remained with him ever since.

Rainbird set off for the village with Fenton, his tail wagging methodically and soft paws compressing against the warm concrete of the sidewalk. The sun shone bright and a calm wind blew as they approached a small marina, alive with the flutter of nautical flags and sail lines pinging against hollow aluminum masts. A shifting kaleidoscope of light pulsed on the water's surface that lapped at the gleaming hulls of yachts. The air was heavy with the smell of salt. Rainbird took a deep breath and smiled. He felt an affinity with the ocean from the start. The world was crazy and unfathomable but the ocean made sense.

After purchasing a paper from the historic village store, Rainbird took an outdoor table at his favorite café and ordered his normal double-strength black tea with a "wee dab" of milk, something that always raised an eyebrow from the server. Before leaving, he couldn't resist picking up a little doggie treat for Fenton, which he near wolfed down in one bite.

"You liked that didn't you, boy?" said Rainbird as he ruffled Fenton's ears, adding with a sigh, "Time to face the music, I suppose."

Rising from the table with an air of resignation, Rainbird headed down the street to a nearby office and rang the intercom buzzer.

"Dr. Hobart's office, can I help you?"

"Yes, hello, this is Alfie Rainbird, I have an appointment."

The disapproving tone in the receptionist's reply was impossible to miss.

"Mr. Rainbird, you are fifteen minutes late already. OK, I'm buzzing you in."

Rainbird rolled his eyes as he entered the building, but he had his apology ready as he approached the desk.

"I'm very sorry, I was caught up…"

Before he was even through the door, the receptionist stood up behind the desk.

"Mr. Rainbird, I must stop you. You cannot bring a dog into the appointment room, or even into the building. We have health and safety regulations, and other patients to consider."

Rainbird feigned surprise as he looked from the receptionist to Fenton and back again.

"Ach, no, ain't that a shame. I guess I'll have to reschedule."

"Well, you could just leave him outside."

"No, no, that's OK," called Rainbird over his shoulder as he departed. "I'll be in touch."

Rainbird chuckled as he gave Fenton a pat on the head. Fenton barked with unabashed delight, his glossy coat shining in the sun as he looked up at Rainbird with his big brown eyes that held a steadfast loyalty.

"Well done boy, I think a long walk down the beach with you is better than therapy any day, don't you?"

CHAPTER 12

Work began straight away on the strategy for Mitch's bail hearing, scheduled to take place at the end of the week. It was a tight deadline but Rainbird liked it that way. The best came out of him when the pressure was on.

"It's crucial we secure Mitch bail," said Rainbird to Georgina in the kitchen of the beach house that had become their makeshift office. "This kid's in real danger if he's thrown inside until trial, high-profile prisoner like him, in a case all over the media, that's almost a neon sign above his head inviting attack from every crazy who wants an easy bit of notoriety."

"Add to the mix his girlfriend is daughter of *The Pie Man* and you've got a recipe for disaster," said Georgina, blowing out her cheeks. "If Magnus McLean hears Mitch has been, to his mind, messing about with his little girl, he's not gonna be happy. And we both know his connections stretch far and wide, including inmates and prison staff."

"No kidding."

"But will he find out?"

"Oh, he'll find out, alright," said Rainbird. "Prosecution will bring it up. They'll argue Mitch is a flight risk because of his financial means through association with Stephanie, and that her friends abroad could facilitate him having it away on his toes."

"And they'd be right."

Rainbird bobbed his head. "Well, of course they'd be right. We'll counter that his strong family and community ties make this highly unlikely. That him taking flight is in the realm of fiction."

"Nice. Get some literary references in there. Media will like that."

"I thought you'd think so."

"If he gets bail, it's not going to be chicken feed. Not for the murder of someone of Lachlan Denoon's notoriety," said Georgina.

"You better believe it. Let's hope Stephanie has clear, unimpeded access to that trust fund."

"Yeah. She's gonna need it."

Rainbird glanced at the clock. "Another cuppa, George?"

"Sure. I'll do it."

For a moment Rainbird hesitated. He was normally a stickler for making his own "brew" but today he yielded. As Georgina made a coffee for herself and a Scottish Breakfast tea for him, Rainbird opened up Lachlan Denoon's Instagram profile on his computer.

There was something about it he found cringeworthy. The perfect lighting that fell on those sharp features of Lachlan, and that head of hair with not a single strand out of place that looked, for all the world, like he had a stylist on hand at all times, poised, ready to jump in and save the day, with a brush and a bottle of hairspray, should an unwelcome gust of wind upset his perfect locks. Those poses that were meant to appear natural and spontaneous, but to Rainbird's eye looked all too stage-managed and manufactured. The fake smiles and the laughter. The steely far-off gaze. The poignant reflection. And the settings, they were all so cliché: supposedly deep in thought in a historic library, having a pensive saunter through the campus of an Ivy League university—somewhere Lachlan Denoon had never studied; enthralling some ultra glamorous fans at a book signing in a small exclusive bookstore, fans who looked like they'd been booked from a model agency, which, in all likelihood, they had. Even the profile picture on the back of his book seemed calculated: sitting in front of an antique typewriter in a manuscript-strewn office, wearing a patterned gentleman's flat cap. It was as if he'd thought to himself, how can I look traditional and established?

It reeked of BS.

And Rainbird could smell it a mile off.

Lachlan Denoon was as much a product as a writer. Something to be consumed and aspired to.

Question was, could Rainbird and Georgina separate the fact from the fiction?

"I'm not surprised someone wanted to kill him," said Rainbird with a smile as Georgina brought the drinks over. "He's a bit nauseating, is he, no?"

"Oh, I wouldn't say that," said Georgina, looking at the image of Lachlan open on Rainbird's computer. "He's pretty easy on the eye."

"Not anymore he ain't."

Georgina pulled a face.

Rainbird stared up at the beginnings of a murder map on the wall that he and Georgina had put together, linking people of interest, their connection to one another, as well as key locations and anything else of interest. More often the preserve of detectives investigating a crime, Rainbird was a firm believer in the value of murder maps to the legal process, especially in complex investigations where there were multiple people and locations involved.

Staring out from the middle of the chart was a photo of Lachlan, a publicity shot from his author period, looking at the camera, head low, eyes looking over his spectacles, with his hands steepled in front of him like some wise old sage. Links came off in every direction, radiating from the deceased to the outer edges of the wall—people he knew, people he had commercial connections to, people who benefitted from his death, people he associated with and what those associations were. Georgina had been adding information she'd dug up: basic stuff reported in the media prior to Lachlan's death about his career and personal life, in particular anything that mentioned someone with a grievance, be it personal or professional, toward him, as well as people who'd criticized him or he them. There was no shortage of material.

"What do you make of my latest intel?" asked Georgina, looking up at the chart.

"The TV rights?"

"Yeah, looks like Mr. Denoon became seriously wealthy. Sold them to the tune of several million dollars. But he put a lot of fans' noses out of joint by allowing the producers to mess around with the original story, pretty much doing as they pleased, changing the backstory of characters like Marion Ryan, and even killing off popular characters like Charlotte Renée, until it bore little resemblance to the book he wrote, all to suit the TV format and how they wanted it to look. It's yet to be released but, by the sound of it, the purists aren't going to be happy. There's already been plenty of backlash on his fan pages, some of it pretty intense, and they haven't even finished filming yet."

"Hardly comes as a surprise," said Rainbird. "Denoon seemed the sort to dispense with integrity in favor of the almighty buck. Based on what we've seen of him so far, I'd say market forces were his main driving factor, despite his obvious talent in the writing department."

"Agreed."

Rainbird drummed his fingers on the table. "All this wrapping himself in academia, it seems more a deceptive facade than a legitimate reflection of the true him. I'd say, at his core, Mr. Denoon was a self-obsessed self-promoter and a sellout. A man without true values who'd turn on a dime and find new ones if it became advantageous to him. Bit like the old Groucho Marx quip: 'These are my principles. If you don't like them, I have others.'"

Georgina laughed.

"But being unpalatable and cliché is one thing," said Rainbird. "It's enough to maybe make you roll your eyes and 'tut-tut', but it's hardly enough to put a man in the ground. So, what was?"

"Having a color coordinated bookshelf?" said Georgina with a grin, looking at a picture on screen of Lachlan in front of his home book collection. "I've never liked that."

"Good point," laughed Rainbird. "But did anyone have genuine bad blood with him? Not a disagreement or a rivalry but genuine animosity—other than Mitch, of course."

"Yeah, we need to do some digging."

"And we need to act fast. Right now, they're all suspects, everyone in attendance at the Bucklesby mansion. They were all at the scene of the crime when it went down. We rule nobody in and nobody out, any of them could be the murderer, but we need to prioritize who we're going to interview. We need someone who's familiar with the greatest number of suspects, and that's got to be the host herself, Mavis Bucklesby."

"If anyone was privy to bad blood between attendees it's gotta be the organizer of the event," said Georgina. "She'll hear all the gossip from everyone present. She's been running it since its inception, so let's get the ball rolling with her."

Rainbird reached for his drink. "Let's take five."

As he raised the steaming mug to his mouth, Georgina flicked on the small television in the kitchen.

There on screen, addressing the media outside the ornate gates of the Bucklesby residence, was Stamford Williamson.

"Having spent a good deal of time in conflict zones, I've seen plenty of dead people before, so I didn't panic. I knew what I was dealing with from the start. Death is, in many ways, very much part of life. But coldblooded murder? Well, that there, is something very different."

He gazed poignantly into the camera.

The case was all over the news and Stamford Williamson was doing his noble best to milk it for all the publicity it was worth, talking to each and every journalist covering the story, emphasizing that he was there, on hand, and had attempted to stem the bleeding, then assisted the EMTs, but alas, despite all his efforts, and theirs—yes, they too, had played a part, he was good enough to acknowledge that—it had all been in vain. Oh, and did he mention he had a new book coming out? *Zen and The Art of Hitchhiking to Iraq*, which, in its way, also dealt with death, of sorts...

Yawn.

Georgina hit the off button on the remote.

"We need to meet this Stamford character too," said Rainbird. "See what he really knows. And what the truth is behind his media friendly soundbites."

CHAPTER 13

Mitch wasn't just nervous, he was outright scared. His face was so drained of color that he looked physically ill. He was also exhausted—big bags hung heavy around his eyes, testament to the sleepless nights in the run up to today. Grueling nights where his mind refused to switch off and it feasted on his sanity, flashing hideous images of what might soon become his reality on an inescapable repeat loop. Images of being handcuffed. Images of being taken down and strip searched. Images of being beaten. But mainly images of a small dark room. A box with no windows. And no human contact whatsoever. Solitary confinement. A place where only fear could ever grow. A silent void filled with an all-embracing evil vibration, where he would disappear forever and his soul would wither and die.

He sat next to Rainbird on a hard and uncomfortable wooden bench in a cell within the criminal court complex in Riverhead. He'd been in court before for the criminal damage charge, but last time he'd sat in the corridor beforehand. As a murder defendant he was held in custody right up until the moment of his bail hearing. A prisoner was a prisoner until bailed. He'd been nervous on his first visit to court, but this time the stakes were of a different order of magnitude. Mitch rocked back and forth, staring at the floor, waiting to be called in to see the judge, in whose hands his immediate fate rested. He'd been shuffling around and fidgeting for the last twenty minutes and had been to the bathroom three times. On the last visit he'd vomited into the wash basin.

"What's the judge like?" asked Mitch. "This Teresa Kilpatrick, does she have a good reputation?"

"There's no point in me sugar coating it for you, Mitch. She's no joke. She's tough, although considered fair. But if you keep your chin up, treat her with deference and respect, I believe I can get the result you're after," said Rainbird. "But don't worry too much about today's judge. She's only here for the bail hearing, the trial judge, the one who really matters, will be announced soon."

A guard approached in the corridor outside the cell.
"You're up next."

Mitch sprang to his feet, his heart pounding in his chest, as the guard unlocked the cell.

"Just relax, Mitch," said Rainbird. "I've got everything under control. I'll see you inside."

Rainbird and Mitch headed in different directions along the corridor. As Mitch was led toward a holding room by a side entrance to the court, he glanced back in Rainbird's direction but he had already disappeared from sight, up a flight of stairs that led to the lobby and the courtroom's main entrance.

Georgina was waiting for him in the lobby. She wasn't counsel so she couldn't be involved in proceedings or sit up front, but he wanted her here today to familiarize herself with the case.

"Ready for battle?" she asked.

"Once more unto the breach, dear friend," said Rainbird.

As Rainbird stepped into the bustling courtroom, a surge of animated expectation coursed through him. With an air of authority, he strode toward the defense table and sat, eyes fixed on the heavy door where Mitch would soon emerge. Time seemed to stretch before the door swung open and Mitch appeared. With his first step inside, the low drone of whispered conversations ceased and an eerie silence permeated the air. Mitch tried to focus straight ahead toward the defense table, but he could feel the collective weight of eyes fixed upon him. He glanced around the room, spotting Stephanie in the public gallery, her smile, like a beam of radiant light cutting through the darkness, carried an unspoken message of hope, optimism and the promise of a brighter day. He returned her smile and took a deep breath as he was led over to Rainbird.

"Sit here. Have a glass of water. And *relax*. Got it?" said Rainbird, exuding an unyielding confidence.

Mitch gave a compliant nod and tried to settle in.

It wasn't the biggest of the 19 courtrooms in the Arthur M. Cromarty Criminal Court Complex in Riverhead, but it was still overwhelming. The place was full to capacity, packed with both supporters of Mitch and Lachlan Denoon's family, while journalists and court reporters made up the rest. Several cast hostile stares Mitch's way, bad vibes hanging in the air like a toxic smog. In the public gallery, sitting up front, was the woman Lachlan humiliated at his Q&A event. Here she was again, dressed in much the same academic couture as before, staring at the back of Mitch's head with bad intent, willing him to glance her way so she could impart a bit of it on him face to face. She didn't look interested in a trial. She looked interested in a hanging. Georgina recognized her face from her own preliminary research into Lachlan—Rosina Pavlova, an obsessive Denoon fangirl who, at the time of Lachlan's reality TV fame, had a temporary restraining order placed against her by him, before having it overturned on appeal.

Mitch tried to be positive, but to him the courtroom felt like a gladiator's pit, and he the unfortunate soul about to be torn apart by lions for the amusement of others. An unnerving intensity filled the air, to the extent that even the police officers and security staff looked tense and jumpy.

In stark contrast to Mitch's turmoil, a calm and composed-looking woman entered the room, her gaze resolute, carrying a red case file under her arm—Prosecution Counsel, Rachael Mears. With a courteous nod she greeted Rainbird, then sat, bolt upright, poised, ready for action, next to a male colleague already waiting in place. At first glance, Mears looked like an honest and fair sort of person. Professional, but the type who, although doing a difficult job, played it by the book, and took no pleasure in wielding her power. It was a persona that had lulled countless victims into a false sense of security. She had a soft voice and did everything behind a congenial smile, something akin to a doctor's bedside manner, reassuring to the point that people trusted that she had their best interests at heart. Then they let their guard down, and let their mouth off the leash until it had blabbed out everything Mears wanted. That's when she bared her teeth, when she'd unmasked their duplicity and lies and they were on the ropes, exposed and vulnerable. Then she would turn on them and attack. Hitting home point after point. She was ruthless. Bloodthirsty even. Rumor had it a defendant once suffered a cardiac arrest under the weight of her questioning and keeled over mid-sentence in court.

Maybe it happened, maybe it didn't, and no one had verified it to Rainbird, at least to his satisfaction, but, regardless, her reputation was ferocious and you underestimated her at your peril.

"All rise. Court is now in session. The honorable Judge Teresa Kilpatrick presiding."

As the court got to their feet, in came Kilpatrick, the woman who'd decide whether or not Mitch could walk free until a verdict.

If Kilpatrick was feeling the pressure, she didn't show it. In fact, if anything, she looked downright uninterested in the whole affair, like her mind was on something else, perhaps the round of golf she intended to play in the afternoon, or the type of wine she'd select when she could settle down later to a nice lunch.

"Mitch Owens, petition number 155/50," announced the Court Clerk.

"Be seated," stated Judge Kilpatrick, after she'd settled in and was good and comfy. "Counsel, would you identify yourself for the record," she said, with an air of apathetic boredom at the dull repetitiveness of protocol.

It didn't so much start with a bang as a whimper.

But this was it. The game had begun.

Up stood the prosecution.

"District attorney Rachael Mears for the State, Your Honor."

Rainbird rose next.

"Alfie Rainbird for the defendant, Mitch Owens. Good morning, Your Honor."

Kilpatrick lowered her head. "As to preliminary matters, I have received written filings in connection with the application for bail from both the defense and the State. So let's move on to opening statements, shall we? I'll hear first from the, erm—" Kilpatrick paused, bouncing her head from side to side, weighing up which way she wanted to go. "—the State."

"Thank you and good morning, Your Honor," said Rachael Mears, rising again. "Your Honor, the State is going to ask the court to refuse bail in this case, for the accused to be remanded in custody until the time of his trial."

There were murmurings from the public gallery.

Kilpatrick cast a swift stern glance their way, bringing them back in line.

Mears continued. "There are numerous very powerful and valid reasons why this is entirely appropriate. The defendant is charged with first-degree murder. This is as serious a charge as there can be. Another man's life has been taken in this case. A much loved, respected and admired person, an acclaimed author, whose life has now been extinguished in his prime. First-degree murder is a charge that, if convicted, will likely result in the defendant spending the rest of his life incarcerated. That, or an imposition of many decades behind bars. Under circumstances such as these, the defendant has the strongest possible incentive to skip bail, to avoid court and flee from the justice system by absconding abroad. I would point out too, that the defendant has not only the incentive, but also the means to do this. His girlfriend is a wealthy woman. His girlfriend is Stephanie McLean, daughter of business tycoon, Magnus McLean."

There it was, out in the public sphere.

Stephanie smiled encouragingly at Mitch, as did he at her. This revelation would cause serious issues for both of them, but there was also a sense of relief that it was now, finally, out in the open. It had only been a matter of time before the prosecution discovered their relationship. That they'd use it to their advantage was inevitable. There was no need to hide anymore, the dice had been thrown, how they would settle was out of their hands.

"She is a wealthy woman and very connected, as is the defendant by association. Does she have friends abroad? Yes, many. Does he now? Quite possibly. It is therefore not unlikely that he is familiar with people outside the country who could facilitate his flight abroad."

Kilpatrick listened in earnest.

"In addition, the defendant has a prior criminal conviction, for willful destruction of a homeowner's private property. He himself is not a property owner. Although he is from this area, he appears to have spent a lot of time recently living something of an itinerant existence, traveling across the country, residing at various addresses and undisclosed locations, for, as far as I can tell, very short periods of time. This is cause for concern."

Mears began to sit down as if she'd finished her piece but then abruptly stood up again, as if having just remembered one final pertinent point. Not that she had, of course, it was all part of her theater aimed at the judge.

"Oh, and of course, the defendant has previously breached bail."

She paused, letting that one sink in.

"Yes. Actually, breached the conditions of his bail," she said it again. "When the defendant was first bailed in relation to the aforementioned criminal damage offense, his first court hearing had to be canceled due to a failure to appear. Given this, and all the other concerning circumstances, the State requests in the strongest possible terms that the defendant be remanded in custody. Indeed, it is only right and proper that he is."

Now she sat. Proud and straight like before. It was a strong performance.

Rainbird rose, a look of quiet determination on his face. He had his work cut out for him.

"Your Honor, my learned colleague makes a powerful argument. A very powerful argument—so long as you ignore the facts, that is. And the facts of this case are overwhelming. My client is charged with a serious offense, but as we will prove at trial, he is innocent of this charge. To say the case against him is flimsy is a gross understatement. It is downright ridiculous. My client poses no danger to the public. His previous conviction does not relate to violence. Quite the contrary, in fact. It relates to a garden fence, yes, a garden fence of all things, as well as two garden gates, erected by my client and then dismantled again by him, following a refusal to pay by the person who commissioned him to erect it all in the first place. It's not exactly high criminality or conspiracy. It's hardly *Fencegate,* now, is it?"

Judge Kilpatrick chuckled to herself at that one, as did several others in the court.

"This is not a moot point. For the State would have us believe he is a hardened criminal. He is anything of the sort. His community service file, following the aforementioned *Fencegate,* is exemplary. It is one of the best records I've seen—zero reprimands, flawless attendance, always on time, always polite, always hard working—it's all here in the file, Your Honor. Hardly the actions of a thug, is it? Not only did he get his head down and carry out his community service, but he paid his fine, in full and on time. My client is a hard-working self-employed man. He does live locally, with very strong ties to the community, he has numerous family and friends nearby, many of whom are sitting in this court today and are willing to act as a surety. To claim otherwise has no basis in fact or law."

Rainbird picked up a piece of paper from the table in front of him with some scribbled notes.

"The State claims that my client, and I quote: 'appears to have spent a lot of time recently living something of an itinerant existence, traveling across the country, residing at various addresses and undisclosed locations.' This is, like the case against him, quite untrue. Mr. Owens was working as a roadie for a local Hamptons-based band, traveling across the length and breadth of our great country, playing at various venues along the way. He stayed in hotels and at the homes of friends near to these events as a matter of necessity. How this is presented by the State as an issue of concern is beyond me. I mean, really, is the State arguing that he should have purchased a property and then registered this as his permanent residence at every location the band visited along the way?"

Judge Kilpatrick smiled. It was a good sign.

"The State seems to have taken leave of itself with this one. I would go so far as to say that the State's portrayal of my client's accommodation requirements as being somehow nefarious, when they're entirely reasonable, is borderline dishonesty in court. As is their invoking of his supposed 'no show' during his first trial. No action was taken against my client at the time because, as was proved in court, he was driving his critically ill mother to E.R. The State knows this. Once again, it's all in the file."

Rainbird picked up a weighty court file and held it aloft for a moment. Maybe it contained what he spoke of, maybe it didn't, and neither did it matter. It was captivating nonetheless. He released it from his grasp, letting it fall onto the solid oak table with a resonating boom, causing those sitting nearest to flinch with surprise.

"But they choose to present it differently for their own expedience. If they can't be trusted on this, at the bail hearing, what then can we expect from them at trial itself? It was Einstein who once remarked, 'Those who cannot be trusted with the truth in small matters, should not be trusted with it in big matters.' How true. But I'm afraid the State's approach to this bail hearing is indicative of their approach to this whole case, and the preposterous charge my client finds himself facing. The State has come up with a theory—a nice, simple, convenient theory about my client. But as the old saying goes: 'For every problem, there is a solution that is clear, simple, and wrong.' In this case, *dead wrong.*"

Rainbird paused, the silence underlining his words as he adjusted the lapels of his jacket.

"My client is not a flight risk because he is an innocent man held on the flimsiest of pretexts, a hodgepodge of circumstantial evidence, and it is in his best interest to fight these erroneous charges and establish his innocence before this court and his family and friends. That the prosecution has failed to establish any ground for refusing bail, is quite clear. And I hereby request that my client be granted full, unconditional bail."

He sat.

Judge Kilpatrick mulled things over, as the courtroom held its collective breath. It was unclear which way she'd go, which way the scales of justice would swing. She scribbled some notes, looked at a couple of court documents and took a little sip of water, just enough to wet her lips, before finally she spoke.

"Thank you for your submissions. I've given them careful consideration," she said in a slow deliberate manner. "I am satisfied Mr. Owens should be granted bail—at a million dollars."

Relief washed over Mitch but for the moment he didn't let it show.

No one in the public gallery dared speak, but the cumulative sound of bodies shifting in their seats, of people breathing out in relief or drawing breath in with surprised disquiet, was enough to illicit a reproachful glare from Kilpatrick.

"However, this will be conditional bail, subject to several measures being put in place to mitigate the risk of the accused failing to attend trial. Bail, as I said, will be set with a bond of one million dollars. As for non-monetary conditions, Mr. Owens will be required to submit to electronic monitoring. If Mr. Owens violates the terms of the electronic monitoring, the monitoring company will notify the court. In addition, Mr. Owens will have to reside locally at an address agreeable to this court. He has three days to notify the court of this or he will be transferred to a permanent facility until trial. And he is to have no contact with persons associated with this case, directly or indirectly, including all fellow attendees at the Bucklesby writers retreat, as well as family members of the deceased. Are there any objections from the defense?"

Rainbird rose.

"We have no objections to the bail conditions, Your Honor."

"And from the prosecution?"

Mears whispered a few words to her colleague, the two of them going back and forth over some unheard matter.

They reached a consensus and she rose.

"No objections, Your Honor."

"Good. As such, bail is granted," stated Kilpatrick.

She turned to Mitch. "You are free to go," she said, hitting her gavel down hard.

Rainbird leaned in to Mitch. "That was a good result."

Mitch smiled, then turned to Stephanie, the tension that had hung heavy on his face evaporating like a morning mist under a rising sun as she smiled back at him, their connection stronger than ever.

"Can I?" asked Mitch to Rainbird, gesturing to the public gallery.

"Sure, go see her."

As Mitch went over to see Stephanie and documents were collated and shuffled by officials, Georgina made her way over to Rainbird's side and leaned in close. "Now we need to discover the truth of all this—who really killed Lachlan Denoon and why?"

Rainbird gave a solemn nod and cast his eye around the courtroom, taking particular notice of the attendees in the public gallery. He knew that the list of suspects was long, that he was going to have to work fast, and that there was more than likely trouble ahead.

CHAPTER 14

Two iron gates opened up electronically, allowing passage to a grand gravel driveway beyond, which wound its way toward a huge light-blue house with beachside grandeur written all over it—the Bucklesby mansion, scene of Lachlan Denoon's murder.

Rainbird drove his prized, although obscure, American classic car, a sky blue 1963 Studebaker Avanti—a vehicle he'd spent years renovating from a wreck—through the manicured opulence of the gardens toward the towering structure ahead.

He turned to Georgina with a smile. "I think we're in the wrong business."

"No kidding," she replied.

Rainbird parked at the front of the house and, as they got out, surveyed the surroundings. Uninterrupted views of the ocean on one side, beautiful grounds more akin to a botanical garden than a backyard on the other; and then the property itself: triple story with huge sweeping balconies that capitalized on the view from every angle, a lighthouse-esque tower on the left side of the house, which, by the looks of it, contained a spiral staircase between the floors. An obligatory swimming pool resided on the grounds, stretching its way toward the ocean, and off the main building sat separate servants' quarters and several self-contained guest cottages.

They made their way to the front door, but before they arrived, it opened and there she stood, Mavis Bucklesby, wearing an apron around her waist and a thick pair of oven gloves.

"Do come in," she said. "Just doing a spot of baking. Do you both like brownies?"

"Err, yeah," said Rainbird, taken aback.

"You betcha," answered Georgina. "Thank you."

"Not at all. Follow me."

She turned on her heels and, before they could introduce themselves, she'd trotted off through a vast entrance hall, where a broad staircase rose upward toward a central landing on the floor above, splitting in two like tributaries of a great river to the east and west wings of the property. She continued through the hall, leading them to a doorway on its far side. They stepped through and entered a cavernous kitchen, into which light streamed through multiple French windows that stretched from floor to ceiling on the far side of the room, where they opened up onto a courtyard overlooking a calm and sparkling ocean.

"They've only got a minute to go," said Mavis, looking through the window of a polished stainless-steel stove to her chocolate treats cooking away inside. "I'm a stickler for doing things by the book, they don't come out until we hear—"

A buzzer rang.

"—Ah, and there we go," said Mavis with a smile, as she opened up the oven and retrieved a baking tray full of brownies, placing it on the kitchen's marble-topped island.

The aroma of hot melted chocolate and sweet doughy goodness filled the room.

"Mmm, those *do* smell good," said Rainbird.

"They taste even better," said Mavis. "But we'll give them a minute to settle."

"Thank you for agreeing to meet with us Mrs. Bucklesby. I'm Alfie Rainbird, pleased to meet you," said Rainbird, holding out a hand.

"Not at all, it's the least I could do, and, please, do call me Mavis."

Mavis took off her oven gloves and gently shook Rainbird's hand.

"Georgina Patterson. Lovely to meet you, Mavis," said Georgina, extending a palm.

"Oh, I do like your nails," said Mavis, looking at Georgina's fancy French manicure as they shook.

"Thank you, Mavis."

"I'll get us a plate," said Mavis, arranging three brownies on a delicate gold-rimmed plate. "Let's have them in the courtyard, shall we?"

They headed through the French doors and stepped out onto the grand stone paving, alive with the splendor of luscious foliage that erupted from huge decorative ceramic pots. A gentle sea breeze blew, soft and charming, as they took a seat at a large glass-topped table.

"Don't stand on ceremony," said Mavis, gesturing to the brownies.

No further encouragement was needed. Rainbird was normally a gentleman, a ladies first kind of guy, but today he let that one slip and reached in before Georgina.

"Goodness," he exclaimed, taking his first bite. "That there is the best brownie I've ever tasted and no mistake."

"Delicious," enthused Georgina. "What's your secret?"

"Beetroot."

"Well, I never," said Rainbird in disbelief. "Beetroot in a brownie, who'd have thought?"

Rainbird's culinary tastes were what you might call unsophisticated. Growing up in one of the poorest parts of Scotland, his staple had consisted of the unappealing foodstuff his mother had appropriately named, stodge. Stodge was a sort of thick, savory, dough that his mother would serve up for both main course and dessert, achieved by way of the crafty inclusion of one of two additional foodstuffs—mince or raisins, respectively. It tasted terrible, looked as bad, and its nutritional value was practically void, but stodge was filling and, most important of all, it was cheap. The genesis of stodge was flour, water and salt, mixed up together and thrown in a baking tray. What came out of the oven thirty minutes later was the foundation, ready to be garnished with desiccated vine fruit or ground up bovine. Other than that, he and his mother would dine on big Scottish bags of "chips" from the fish and chip shop, or "chippy" as it was known. They rarely had enough money to compliment these with the actual fish, so instead opted for the next best thing the chippy had to offer: a bag of batter bits on the side—excess bits of left over batter scooped from the deep fat fryer that were served in a cone of old newspaper and topped with salt and vinegar. By the time you got halfway through, your batter bits were stained inky black from the print of the paper, and the roof of your mouth was coated in a thick film of fat. To wash it all down they'd share between them a can of bright orange soda—'Irn-Bru,' a soft drink for hard men, or so his mother used to say.

"You know, you're quite the talent, Mavis," exclaimed Rainbird, taking his second bite of real food.

A sheepish smile crept across her face, but one that also held a dash of unsurprised expectancy. She knew her brownies and abilities in the kitchen were good, better than good, and was proud to show them off. In Rainbird she'd found a more than appreciative audience.

"Have you lived here a long time?" asked Georgina, trying to steer things toward more pressing matters.

"Twenty-two years. A lot has changed in that time."

"And how long have you been running the writers retreat?" she asked.

"My husband and I started the retreat twenty years ago. Back then it was a lot more low-key and could last for several weeks. Now it's only a few days. More of a get together. After my husband Roger died, I decided to keep it going. Partly in honor of him and his work, but also because I just like doing it. But before this year's event I decided it would be the last. My time doing this sort of thing is coming to an end. I will miss it. I enjoy entertaining and the social side of the retreat. Although I've got access to staff at the house and for the event, I help out and do the catering myself. Or should I say, I *especially* do the catering."

"I can see why," said Rainbird, chomping on another mouthful.

"How many people attended this year's event?" asked Georgina.

"Well, let me see. There was the professor; that's Professor Benjamin Aris the historian. Lovely man, great conversationalist, and so knowledgeable on such a wide range of different subjects, a veritable encyclopedia. There's very little he doesn't know at least something about. Then there was Audrey Adams, the children's author. You know, the Sweetgum Grove book series, such gorgeous illustrations, which she does herself, you know. Most people think she's only the author, but she does the illustrations too."

"Does she?" asked Georgina.

"Oh, yes. Not many people can do both. Beatrix Potter was the most famous, of course. And I have to say, I think there's a similarity between the two of them, you know, the quality of work. Nice, soft muted colors, nothing garish or computer generated. A return to elegance, if you will."

Rainbird gave a precise approving nod.

"Then there was Patricia Parry-Jones the, well, you know, that ghastly hatred book. Why, oh why, would you want to write and promote such a thing? Quite appalling. Whatever happened to using literature for the promotion of ideas and values that inspire and enrich? Although, to be fair, she wasn't unpleasant in person. But her book? I don't approve."

Mavis shook her head with a look of distaste.

"Why did you invite her then?" asked Rainbird.

"Professor Aris nominated her to attend. Same publisher I think. He's been to many events so I was happy to oblige. Then there was Cathleen Miller, fiction writer, quite high end, her books, or at least they were. Hasn't done much of late, but she's much more to my taste. They get you thinking. There was also Henry Hunt, the literary agent. His father was pretty much part of the furniture around here until his death. He represented a lot of big names over the years, including Cathleen."

"Does Henry represent her now?" asked Rainbird.

"Oh, no. Henry went through his father's list of authors and chop, chop, chop."

She mimed using a pair of scissors. "Cathleen was one of the first to go. She's never forgiven him or Lachlan."

"Why Lachlan?" asked Georgina.

"I don't know if it's true, but rumor is that Lachlan insisted on Cathleen being dropped before he'd sign with Henry."

"Why would he do that?" asked Rainbird.

"Not sure. Some people say he thought her image was too staid and boring for an agency he was attached to and so insisted she go first. But whatever the truth, Cathleen saw being dropped as a betrayal from Henry. And I can't say I disagree with her. Not after everything she did to help his father in the early days. She was one of his highest earning clients back then, but those days are gone."

For a moment Mavis paused and reflected wistfully.

"Then there was Stamford Williamson, funny-looking travel chap from England. I know I shouldn't say it, what with it being an English stereotype and all—but his teeth! My, what teeth! They're so gap ridden he looks like he could eat a tomato through a tennis racket. Or floss with one of those thick old fashioned jumping ropes."

Georgina and Rainbird laughed.

"Oh, and there was Magnus McLean, the sponsor of the event. He popped in after lunchtime, didn't stick around long, busy man, you know. He's been involved for the last few years. Such a helpful soul, especially with promotion for the publicly attended Q&A at the bookstore. His media image is one thing, but I have to say I've always found him charming in person. There's a charity component to the event these days and he's always very generous."

"What cause were you fundraising for?" asked Rainbird.

"This year there were two. The Star Legacy Foundation, which is dedicated to stillbirth education, research and awareness, and the American Cancer Society. Poor Lachlan also made a substantial donation. God rest his soul. I can't remember how many people that was now, five, maybe six?"

"Eight, I think, if we include yourself, Mavis," said Georgina.

She nodded. "Eight, it is."

Rainbird swallowed down the last of his brownie and leant in a little closer to Mavis. "The prosecution is likely to make a big deal out of Lachlan Denoon and Mitch Owens having an argument on the afternoon of his murder. Did you see this happen?"

"Oh, yes. They argued, all right. And then he punched him. Right in the face."

"Did anybody else argue with Lachlan during the event?" asked Georgina.

"Most everybody at one stage or another, although Mitch Owens was the only staff member to do so," said Mavis, in a matter-of-fact way. "There's a common misconception that authors are all polite and agreeable, but nothing could be further from the truth. There's an awful lot of petty jealously and resentment in the literary world that comes to the fore when behind closed doors at an invitation-only event like mine. To say that it can get heated is a huge understatement. They're not shy about speaking their mind, especially about each other's work, so tempers can flare. Even Lachlan and Henry argued."

"Henry Hunt? His agent?" asked Rainbird.

"Yes, that's right. In this very courtyard. Can't say I know what it was about, but they had a very heated discussion after lunch about something. I walked out with some cheesecake—raspberry, homemade, on a crushed cookie base, I can give you the recipe—and had to turn around and excuse myself they were going at it so strong. I'm afraid to say the language used was a little bit rich."

Rainbird gave a sympathetic tut.

"That did surprise me a bit, what with them working together. Normally those two are at least very amicable."

"Who else argued with Lachlan?" asked Rainbird.

"They all had their moments, disagreements though, nothing more. I wouldn't place too much importance on them. And I don't want to say too much, but Stamford Williamson, well, soon after he and the other authors arrived, he and Lachlan had a falling out over politics—at least I think it was politics—that somewhat soured the mood, for a while, at least."

"Can you remember the specifics?" asked Georgina.

"Oh, I'm afraid I can't. I try not to get too involved in that side of things. You'll have to ask him yourself. I should warn you though, he can be quite opinionated, that man, not that that's a bad thing. My late Roger held strong opinions too, and he didn't suffer fools gladly. What he'd have thought of the goings on last week, I shudder to think. I'm pleased he didn't have to see that."

"Mavis, would it be possible for us to see where Lachlan's body was found?" asked Rainbird.

"I can show you outside if you like, but I'm afraid it's still an official crime scene. That's what Detective Bruce told me, so I'm not to go in or let anybody else in there. He even put some of that bright yellow tape across the door like they do in the movies," said Mavis, getting up from her seat. "Come on, I'll take you."

She led them out through the courtyard to a little walkway that meandered past two elegant guest cottages, the second of which, the one closest to the sand dunes and the ocean, was draped in crime scene tape.

"This is it," announced Mavis.

"No CCTV around here?" asked Georgina, glancing about.

"Just around the house itself, I'm afraid."

"Is it only external, or are there internal cameras too?"

"Only outside, I can't abide cameras in the house. I know it's a valuable property, but it's also a home, and I wouldn't feel comfortable with that sort of thing indoors. It just wouldn't feel homely, at least not to me."

"Could we get a copy of the footage from the night of the murder? There might be something the police have missed."

"I suppose so. The police have already taken the tapes, so I imagine there's nothing that will help you, but it's all backed up. I'll get one of the staff to do it for you. Philip, I think, he's good with computers."

"Thank you."

"Practically on the beach," said Rainbird, almost to himself, as his eyes traced the path of the walkway toward the dunes and the ocean. "Could anyone walk in?"

"Oh, no," said Mavis. "There's a private property sign on the dunes."

"Err, yes, but if someone was to ignore that."

Mavis looked shocked at the suggestion. "Well, there's a gate."

"Locked?"

"Not always."

"During the writers retreat?"

"The guests like to come and go."

"Mmm," pondered Rainbird, glancing about, looking from the beach to the house, then from the nearby servants' quarters to Lachlan's accommodation, trying to piece together the scene.

"Did you see the body, yourself?" asked Georgina.

"I did. And what a sorry sight it was. Poor Lachlan, lying on the carpet in a pool of his own blood. Such a nice man, would even lend a hand in the kitchen, and at the beginning of his writing career. He held so much promise, and now it's gone. His poor family and friends."

"Can you tell us how you happened upon the scene?"

"Well, I was in the kitchen when, all of a sudden, I heard a great commotion, a big old hullaballoo, shouting and screaming and whatnot. I didn't know what to think or what was going on, so I got up and made my way toward the noise as fast as I could."

"Weren't you scared?" asked Georgina.

"Of course not, I thought a pipe had burst or something. I'm the host, it's my business if there's a problem, so I needed to know what was going on so I could remedy the situation. Not in a million years did I think that someone had been, well—" she paused, as if saying the word was difficult, "—*murdered*."

She looked at them both with distress in her eyes for the first time.

"Oh, Mavis," said Georgina, grasping her by the hand and doing her best to reassure her.

"I'm sorry. It's been quite an experience," said Mavis, a tremor in her voice.

"Of course, it has," said Rainbird. "We won't take up much more of your time. Though, can I ask you about Mitch Owens before we go? Do you think it's possible someone else, someone other than Mitch who was at the property, could have killed Lachlan Denoon?"

"Oh, no, I don't think so, not one of the attendees. I mean, I know he's your client and all, but he had real hatred in his eyes that boy did. Never seen anything like it, smashing all that glass—expensive glass too, cut crystal, difficult to replace—and the way he yelled at him, not to mention when he struck him, punched him he did, good and hard. Knocked him to the ground and continued yelling—threatened to kill him. I saw that with my own eyes and it was quite a shock, I can tell you. The police told me he came back onto the property afterward and this is when they think he killed him. Said Lachlan and him had some sort of history together and that this was the source of their argument. I know you've got a job to do and you have to look into it, but…" Mavis trailed off with a pessimistic shake of the head.

Minutes later Rainbird and Georgina were making their way toward Rainbird's car with a doggie bag of brownies each. As Rainbird eased into his familiar seat and Georgina settled in next to him, he deftly slotted his key into the ignition and the engine rumbled into life. With a final wave farewell to Mavis, they headed back through the grounds along the winding driveway, gravel crunching beneath the tires as they went, toward the main entrance.

"That's a lot to digest," said Georgina, as the gates parted and they pulled out onto the open road. "And I'm not talking about the baking."

"Yeah, there's no shortage of people with opportunity and even possible motive," said Rainbird, casting a final glance back at the towering property behind him. "But I don't think this was just an argument that went too far. I think there's more to this, but what, I don't know. Our first line of inquiry is the agent. I need to know what that argument with Lachlan was about."

CHAPTER 15

Her throat was dry, her heart pounded in her chest. She glanced at the old grandfather clock on the opposite side of the immense room. He was late, and likely on purpose, just to make her squirm until his arrival. She took a sip of water, her hand shaking as she placed the glass back down on top of the long reflective mahogany table. The smell of beeswax polish lingered in the air. On the wall were portraits of her relatives, oil paintings of her late great-grandparents and their parents before them, all staring down at her, stern and judging. Pride of place in the center of the room was the biggest painting of them all, a solo picture of her grandmother, Magnus's late mother, Nanette McLean, the woman Magnus had lionized in story, almost to the point of myth, looking down at Stephanie with what today seemed like disapproval in her eyes. She gave the painting a weak smile and checked the clock again.

The furnishings of this room, of this house, and the actual historic property itself, were a contradiction. Magnus often railed against the old money East Coast establishment and made much of his humble upbringings, that he was a self-made man, not some blue blood born with the advantages of wealth, but secretly a part of him was desperate to be one of them. All these antiques and the contrived old-world portraits adapted from the tattered remnants of a box of family photographs, were his manufactured attempt at joining the club, albeit by default.

Stephanie had been going over in her head what she was going to say, how she would stand up for and defend Mitch to her father. The problem was, everything she saw as a positive character trait in Mitch, her father would see as a flaw. Everyone he'd previously encouraged her toward was the same: a mini-Magnus. Money and power obsessed nobodies, soulless and devoid of any charm or humor—investment bankers, hedge fund managers, corporate executives, even the son of a congressman. They all blended into one another and she had no interest in any of them. They all thought the same, spoke the same and acted the same.

"Daddy!" Stephanie jumped to her feet as the heavy wooden door in the corner of the room swept open. Then, regretting being taken by surprise and allowing her father the upper hand, she cleared her throat and attempted a more restrained greeting.

"Hi, Dad."

"Stephanie," Magnus's response oozed patronizingly, "my little princess."

He strode across the room with a confident gait, projecting his expectation that this meeting was between a wayward child and her benevolent guardian—he was here to usher her back into the fold of his protection.

Upon reaching Stephanie, Magnus lifted his hands and rested them on her shoulders. Stephanie felt her insides recoil and had to fight the urge not to crumple under his will. He'd brought her up sheltered from discomfort and difficult decisions, and it would have been easy to bow to his authority, but she also had his blood in her veins, and Stephanie could be just as strong-willed as Magnus. She took a deep breath and looked him in the eye, tensing her muscles in readiness for the confrontation to come.

"I know that look," Magnus said with a low laugh. "When you were a toddler, it was accompanied by a foot stamp." Magnus gave Stephanie's shoulders a squeeze that was a little firmer than just reassuring, before dropping his hands. "I'm proud of the strong, independent woman you've become, Stephanie, but you must recognize that I've seen more of the world than you, and there are still times when I know what's best for you—better than you can see for yourself."

With a sharp intake of breath, Stephanie started to respond, but Magnus held up a hand to stop her. Despite boiling at the gesture, she knew that to interrupt her father now would make him more hardheaded, so she released the air from her lungs and resolved to bide her time, hear him out, then talk him around. He might know her well, but she also knew him, and she'd had him wrapped around her little finger since she was two years old.

"Sweetheart," Magnus began, as he gestured that she should sit back down in her seat at the head of the table. He, however, remained standing a moment longer, looking down at her, before choosing the seat to her left and lowering himself to her level. "Would you like a drink? I can ask Emma to bring us some soda, if you like. Perhaps some cookies to go with it. She still makes your favorite—peanut butter crunch."

"No thanks, Dad, I'm OK for now," was Stephanie's subdued response. Inwardly, she urged her father to get to the point, to stop putting off the inevitable, no matter how much she was dreading it.

Magnus reclined and crossed one ankle over the other leg.

"Well, Stephanie, you know why I asked you to come visit today. You're putting on a brave face, but even you must have been shocked at Mitch revealing your relationship at the bail hearing. I can see it in your eyes. Clearly that was not something he'd prepared you for, no surprises there," said Magnus, twisting the reality of the prosecution revealing this information not Mitch. "I want you to know that I am here for you. I can look after you until this madness dies down. It would probably be best if you moved back home for the time being. We've the best security system money can buy, security guards patrol the neighborhood and Emma and the rest of the household staff consider you as dear to them as any of their own children. If Mitch or the press try to hassle you, they will see them on their way. And if there's any trouble, I have the personal phone number of the chief of police."

Stephanie sat in silence for a moment. So, this was how her father planned to play it, treat her as the foolish child, masking his anger with false paternal concern. Well, they were both adults now, and it was time to acquaint Magnus with that fact.

"I don't need anyone to protect me from Mitch," Stephanie began softly. "In fact, I love him."

"Love him?" Magnus responded, incredulous. "Mitch is not a person to be trusted, let alone loved. He's a murderer."

Stephanie's eyes narrowed with anger, "Innocent until proven guilty, Dad." The last word was uttered through gritted teeth. "And there will be no 'proven guilty.' He didn't do it, I know that, and I'm pretty sure you do too."

"Guilty or not, he clearly can't be trusted. He's had you sneaking around behind everyone's backs—I'm sure you found that exciting to begin with, but it's no foundation for a genuine relationship." Magnus paused to assess Stephanie's reaction, seeing a flicker of doubt cross her face, then pushed on. "You seem to forget that I've known Mitch as long, no, longer, than you have. He was my employee, and I can't say he left me with a good impression of his character."

"Did you even notice his character? I doubt you even remember him as an employee, just another faceless number in the account books. Or perhaps not even in the books. And the reason we were 'sneaking around' was because we knew, I knew, you would object and try to come between us."

"Ha! Do you think anything goes on in this town that I don't know about?"

Magnus sat up straighter and checked his phone. "Stephanie, enough of this nonsense. It's time to end this little delayed teenage rebellion. Just let the boy down gently, I'll even let you keep paying his legal fees, what little good that will do. The evidence is all against him, it's an open and shut case. The only reason he made bail is your good name behind him and the fact the judge considered him too dumb to be a flight risk."

Stephanie's anger flared out of her control. She got to her feet and started pacing to diffuse some of the energy before turning back to her father.

"He's not dumb. He's just a regular, nice guy. He's not out to be the richest, or the most powerful. He has ambitions, but nothing that you would consider worthwhile. He just wants to earn enough to enjoy a comfortable life, with time to spare to be with me, with his friends. He's thoughtful like that. And funny. And caring. He makes time for me when I need him. He never brushes me off on someone else." She was glaring at Magnus but stopped to take a calming breath, her eyes warning Magnus she wasn't finished yet. "Of course you knew, I've seen your gofer Dave loitering in strange places, outside my gym, at my favorite café. Oh, and I bet you were behind those waitresses trying to get Mitch to go with them for a threesome. I should have realized, he said it was weird how persistent they were, I thought he was just being humble, but no doubt you paid them not to take no for an answer."

Magnus just shrugged and stood up. "I'm not going to pander to your little paranoias, Stephanie. You know perfectly well you could do better than Mitch, you're just being stubborn because you don't want to admit I'm right. And trust me, I'm also right when I say Mitch is a gold digger after your money."

"That is so unfair, and untrue! When he told me he was saving up to do an unpaid apprenticeship as a sound engineer, something he's passionate about, I offered to help him out, but he turned me down flat, wouldn't take a cent, insisted he was going to do it all off his own back."

"A *sound engineer*? Oh, please. You'll acknowledge one day that I'm right, but maybe I could speed things up by putting a freeze on your trust fund. I can't have you wasting my hard-earned money on a lost cause."

Stephanie looked hard into her father's eyes. "You wouldn't dare," she said, then turned away from him with a sigh. "Not that it would matter if you did. I paid in full upfront, I guess deep down I suspected you might try to interfere. So go ahead, freeze it, cancel it, I don't care. Money isn't that important to me."

Magnus snorted. "Now you're just being childish."

Stephanie started to walk toward the door, it was not the result she wanted from today, but at least now she knew where she stood. She'd no doubt that her father would welcome her back into his fold eventually, she would ride out her time in purgatory knowing she'd done the right thing and in time Magnus would realize that Mitch was loyal and caring, and that those qualities were all that mattered.

Magnus' voice followed her to the exit, causing her to falter as a cold chill rippled through her body. "If you're going to stick by him, you'd better warn him—if he's going to play with the big boys, the big boys don't always play nice."

CHAPTER 16

From the look on Rainbird's face, whoever was on the other end of the telephone wasn't someone he wanted to talk with. It sounded like someone he'd tried to duck, someone who'd flown beneath the radar and had unexpectedly got through, and now Rainbird was having a conversation he neither wanted, nor had intended to have in the first place. Although Georgina could only hear half of what was being said, it was clear whoever was on the line was getting on Rainbird's nerves. Normally he kept his cool, but today his voice rose as the conversation progressed, and they were succeeding, to use one of Rainbird's expressions, to get his blood up.

"That's not possible," said Rainbird to the caller in a firm manner, as he paced about the makeshift office in the kitchen of the beach house. "We'll have to reschedule. To say I'm flat out at the moment is a gross understatement. What I'm working on right now is of far greater importance than the prearranged and preordained waste of time you have penciled in for me in your diary."

Georgina smiled to herself as she watched Rainbird from her side of the room. He was always fun to watch in action, fun to observe as he exchanged verbal blows with an antagonist. Most of the time his opposition was outgunned and found wanting, but today whoever it was seemed to be getting under Rainbird's skin.

There was a long pause from Rainbird, while he listened to the response from the caller.

Georgina could see the cogs turning in his head.

"What? You'd really do that?" said Rainbird, with a look of consternation. "Ridiculous."

There was another pause.

"Fine," snapped Rainbird. "If that's the way you want it, then so be it."

He hung up.

"Everything OK?" ventured Georgina.

"Everything is *not* OK," said Rainbird with a palpable exhalation. "That was the brand new shrink that the firm's booked for me after the last one quit. She says I'm refusing to meet with her, that I'm stringing her along, that I've canceled too many appointments already, and if I'm not in her office in the next thirty minutes she's going to call the board and tell them I'm in breach of my agreement with her and, more importantly, with them, by refusing to attend."

"Any of that true?"

"Of course, it's *all* true," said Rainbird. "That's the problem."

He drew in a long breath, then let it out in a slow exasperation.

Georgina suppressed a smile as Rainbird swiped his overcoat from a hanger.

"Hold the fort. I'll be as quick as I can."

Moments later he was on his way out the door.

It was a short drive to reach the shrink, but to get there in time Rainbird had to take it at speed, weaving in and out of traffic, speeding up and then slowing down as he approached the construction zone speed cameras he knew about along the route. As he pulled up out the front, he glanced at his watch—two minutes to go.

He sighed, a mixture of foreboding and frustration.

There was no time to go looking around for a parking space, so he just stopped in front of the office and abandoned his Avanti where it was. If he received a ticket, so be it.

With his head lowered and eyes fixed ahead, Rainbird marched to the office front door where, with an aggressive finger, he stabbed at the button on an external intercom, releasing a contorted electronic retch from its depths.

Silence, then a female voice came through the speaker.

"Dr Anna Hobart," stated a matter-of-fact voice. "Who's there?"

"Alfie Rainbird," announced Rainbird, as much grunt as spoken word.

"Come up to the second floor," stated the voice as the door buzzed open.

In through a dim entranceway he strode, past an unstaffed reception desk and up a narrow flight of stairs toward a frosted glass door at the top, but before he could reach it the door swung open, stopping him in his tracks. There she was, arms folded, looking down over her spectacles at Rainbird below, with a look that was more scornful school principal than clinical psychiatrist. She wasn't what Rainbird had expected. Of average height but above average appearance, she was undeniably good looking, attractive even. She was well turned out in a professional kind of way, and sported a jaunty bobbed hair cut straight out of a 1920s period drama, the color of which matched her big brown eyes.

She glanced at her watch.

"And with a full thirty seconds to go. Congratulations, Mr. Rainbird."

He said nothing.

She turned her back and walked through the door, leaving him to follow behind.

"You were right to take me at my word, you know," she stated with a cold glare as Rainbird walked in. "A second late and I would have placed the call to your superiors."

She smiled, insincerely.

"Please, do come in and take a seat."

Still Rainbird said nothing. Already she was very different to the shrinks the firm had set him up with before. They'd been easy to delay, dodge and dismiss, but right from the start Dr. Hobart was taking none of Rainbird's nonsense.

There were two large comfy chairs in a humble office that was minimalist by design, so as to provide little for the mind to focus on, to encourage it to go inward instead. The room's lone window had frosted glass to prevent a view, next to which sat a heavy-looking cherry wood desk, with a laptop and an open file of papers. And that, pretty much, was it. There were no books, no plants, no pictures, no framed certificates, or any other decorations, not even a clock. It was all business and zero presentation. But that was fine by Rainbird, he was never an aesthetics kind of guy anyway, with the exception of his tailor-made suits and classic car, that is. If things were too fancy and without substance they were, in Rainbird's vernacular, "all a bit ice cream and wafers."

He took a seat and waited.

He'd already decided to be a counter puncher this time, happy for her to make the first move, for him to bob, weave and slip; then counter with the metaphorical big right hand when the opportunity presented itself.

Dr. Hobart picked up the file from the desk then sat opposite.

"Mr. Alfred Rainbird, mmm." she said, mulling over its contents, flicking pages here and there. "Aren't you the enigma—or, at least, that's the way you want it to appear."

This annoyed Rainbird, the inference that a part of his persona was something other than genuine. In particular, that it was something crafted for the consumption of others. But he knew what she was up to, she was trying to get a rise out of him, throwing out a falsehood from the get-go in the hope that he'd bite and let his guard down. He let it pass without reaction. The other shrinks had gotten nothing from him, and the new one would know this; she was clearly trying to provoke a response, to get things in motion, by hook or by crook.

"Born: 1976, Glasgow, Scotland, to an American father and Scottish mother. Raised alone by mother in tough conditions. Many occupations, including street hawker—much acclaimed, apparently. Moved to New York as a young man, prompted by fallout with local gangsters in Glasgow. Married once. Wife deceased after—"

"—OK, I get your point," interrupted Rainbird.

Rainbird hadn't intended to say a word, but already Dr Anna Hobart was proving good at pressing his buttons and was a far more capable opposition than the long list of amateurs he'd been assigned before her. She also knew a lot more about him than he expected. She'd done her research, and for that he had to give her credit, but where she'd gotten the information from, he didn't know. Regardless, it gave her a distinct advantage. And he didn't like that.

"Charged and convicted of the murder of John Tofield, Chief Executive Officer of PrimaChem. Served ten years inside. The first two in maximum-security prison Allenwood in Pennsylvania, the final eight in New York facility Attica, a prison you were transferred to following a string of disciplinary problems in the former. Conviction overturned thanks to own skill and aptitude as a jailhouse lawyer, also acclaimed. On release began practicing law with great success, marred by a string of unprofessional incidents culminating in a recent altercation with a colleague, which saw you take a forced sabbatical, a contractual condition of which—" She paused and smiled. "Is to *compliantly* participate in therapy sessions with me."

Rainbird, raising an eyebrow.

"Yes, against my wishes, I've been assigned yet another psychologist."

"No, you most certainly have not!" Dr. Hobart retorted. "I'm a clinical psychiatrist, thank you very much. *Not* a psychologist. For the record, psychiatrists are qualified medical doctors with at least eleven years of training, usually far more, as is the case with me, if you were wondering. We also have to do at least five years training in the diagnosis and treatment of mental illness. Psychologists on the other hand, like the ones you were assigned before, receive their qualification through a university degree and limited supervised experience."

"So they've rolled out the big guns this time?"

"Oh, you better believe it."

Dr. Hobart flicked through the file pondering papers here and there.

"Your prison record makes for interesting reading."

"How the hell did you get hold of that?" snapped Rainbird.

"Mr. Rainbird, don't be surprised that I'm thorough. To assist my clients, I have to understand my clients, and to do so I need a full picture of their situation and background. From what I understand after extensive discussions with the previous *psychologists* you've seen, you haven't been the slightest bit forthcoming about your problems. 'Not so much a closed book,' one of them told me, 'as a chained and padlocked box under constant armed guard.' Under such circumstances, I have to go looking for information elsewhere—your physician, your prison records, your work colleagues and superiors."

Rainbird folded his arms across his chest and contemplated Dr. Hobart with a frown. He didn't like the sound of this. Damn it, he didn't like any of this. Talking about himself, hearing about himself, this self-centered, self-indulgent claptrap. What good was any of it? There was value in looking outward not inward, in burying the past, leaving it dead in the ground, not digging it up to examine like some morbid pathologist. Why relive the past a second, third, or fourth time around, when once was more than enough in the first place?

"Your prison records show a recurring theme—serious anger management problems. Constant flare ups and aggression. You recognize this, presumably?"

"No. Anger under such circumstances is a completely natural, even healthy, response. The great Indian philosopher Krishnamurti once noted, 'It is no measure of health to be well-adjusted to a profoundly sick society.' Same goes for prison, it is no measure of good health to be well-adjusted to the injustice of unfair and barbaric incarceration."

Dr. Hobart wouldn't be drawn on this.

"Your file doesn't read that way. One prison doctor describes you as a pressure cooker, they note that your deep frustrations, resentments and anger build over time, until the inevitable happens and you explode, in a manner out of all proportion to the stimulus that caused it."

"Oh, please! Don't confuse anger with righteous indignation. You see that's the problem with people like you, with your fancy doctorates and pieces of paper to say how clever you are. What you don't seem to realize is that anger has a positive value. Anger gives you energy, it can motivate you, drive you to endure, to overcome and to succeed. People should be angry. Anger, in the right circumstances, is good."

"How so?"

"Think about it, you don't believe everything in the world is all fine and dandy, do you? That everything in the world is just and fair? Of course not. The world is riddled with injustice, cruelty and despair, you know that. In which case, this lack of fairness and justice should make you angry. To feel otherwise would be to have lost your sense of empathy for others, to have sold your soul and become calloused and unfeeling in the face of other people's suffering. Or to have given up your own fight to change the injustice of your circumstances. You may choose capitulation, but I don't and never will. Not only is anger a good thing; it is a healthy thing."

"Tell me more."

"As a great Scotsman once said, 'Anger is like electricity, electricity can kill a man in the electric chair or it can keep a baby alive in the incubator.' Like electricity, it is the direction that anger is given that determines whether it is, if you'll pardon the pun, positive or negative. Anger used to harm the innocent, to stir up hatred against the weak and oppressed, is reprehensible. But anger used as fuel to fight for the weak and oppressed, anger focused and channeled into a laser beam of righteous indignant rage on their behalf, is not only a good thing, it is the only right and decent thing to feel. There's nothing wrong with the bit of steel and sharpness anger provides."

Without missing a beat, Dr. Hobart was straight back at Rainbird.

"But losing your temper is different to being angry and feeling justifiable outrage. I'm referring to you losing your temper, not a righteous indignation, as you put it. Your file shows again and again a person who, at times, is not in control of their anger, a person who has lost control of it on several occasions, most recently with your work colleague Robert Coleman, whom I believe you dragged through a broken car window, a window that you yourself smashed with a bare fist. I ask you, does that sound like a reasonable response from someone in control of their anger, or is the anger, in fact, in control of them?"

At first Rainbird didn't answer. Problem was, he knew Dr. Hobart was right. He had lost control, and the person who'd suffered the most was him. This wasn't always the case. The vast majority of the time he was in remarkable control of his anger, and he did channel it in a forensic manner for the betterment of his and other peoples' situations. But not always. And that was the crux of it. There was a tipping point in him. An ill-defined line in the sand that, when crossed, brought with it a disproportionate response, a fury that he found difficult to contain. It had its uses, for sure, but then so too did it harbor plenty of downsides.

Rainbird gave Dr. Hobart a small conciliatory nod. A tacit acknowledgement that he did, in fact, agree.

"I think that's enough for today," announced Dr. Hobart, unexpectedly cutting the session short after little more than a few minutes of discourse. With that small nod from Rainbird, Dr. Hobart secured some winnings, and was now stepping away from the table with them still intact.

Rainbird didn't like it that Dr. Hobart had gone straight at him all guns blazing from the start of their session. He didn't like it that she'd contacted his colleagues. He didn't like it that she'd obtained his prison records, or that it was she who decided when proceedings began and came to a halt, but he had to admit it, she'd gotten more out of him in a few minutes than all her predecessors had over multiple weeks, and, for that, he held a certain respect for her as an opponent.

CHAPTER 17

Henry Hunt answered the door to his East Hampton home wearing a gold-buttoned gentleman's sports jacket, complete with patterned silk handkerchief poking from the top pocket, and a crisp pinstripe shirt, above which sat a billowing red cravat adorning his neck area. To Rainbird's eye, Hunt looked like he considered himself as a Victorian country gentleman—a "dandy," in Rainbird's lingo. To Georgina he looked rather appealing, thank you very much.

"Mr. Rainbird, Miss Patterson, please come in," said Henry, with a welcoming smile.

His gaze lingered on Georgina, as did hers on him, their eyes connecting with a mutual interest that held them entranced for a second.

"I work from a home office on the far side of the property, we can talk there."

He led them into a polished marble-floored lobby area, more akin to a luxury hotel than a residential property, the sort of place you could imagine taking a big running slide in your socks. The aroma of freshly cut flowers permeated the air from several vases, filled with what looked like the contents of half a florist's shop, and dangling overhead was a chandelier the size of a small automobile, its countless prisms radiating sunlight from a stately window high above.

Henry walked them through the lobby and into a dining room complete with a long beechwood table with twenty-four chairs—Rainbird counted—where a housemaid worked away in silence, polishing a metal art deco sculpture of a silver airplane. Rainbird smiled to the woman as he strolled through, but her eyes dropped to the floor, as if she'd been given clear instructions that under no circumstances would she fraternize with the guests.

At the far end of the room stood two colossal sliding doors, yawning wide onto a lavish outdoor pool area. Henry led them through, into the blinding sunshine, where loungers and hand-crafted furniture resided next to the shimmering waters, beyond which stood the self-contained office—and what an office. It was bigger than any property Rainbird had ever resided in. Twice as big, in fact.

"Please, do come inside," said Henry, opening up.

Inside was lined, floor to ceiling along almost every wall, with hundreds upon hundreds of books. In the corner of the room was a big antique Chesterfield sofa and at the opposite end was a solid writing desk with green leather inlay and matching green banker's lamp. Off the main office was a smaller room visible through an open door, less business and more casual relaxation, where three large emerald armchairs resided, with a fluffy cat on top of the chair nearest to the window, reclining in the sun with views of the ocean beyond.

"Galloway's favorite spot, he loves the sun," said Henry, leading them over to the desk.

On the wall above, on the only section not covered with books, was a collection of framed photos—pictures of Henry's father with some of the bigger names he'd signed, relaxing with them in this very office, mostly on the Chesterfield sofa. Beneath the pictures was a framed sign that proclaimed in big red letters: "The beatings will continue until morale improves."

Rainbird smiled.

"Quote from the late Stephen Hawking," said Henry, spotting Rainbird's amusement. "Always liked that one."

"It's a mighty fine quote," agreed Rainbird, glancing around. "You know, I thought I had a good collection of books, but this is something else."

"Are they all authors represented by the agency?" asked Georgina.

"The majority, yes," said Henry. "That's not to say there aren't any in here that aren't Hunt Agency books—there are some titles I've simply read and enjoyed myself—but I'd say maybe eighty percent of the names you see on the spines of these books are authors who have worked with the agency, at one stage or another. My father was dedicated to his career and he worked with many prolific writers over the years. There are some modern classics up here."

Henry gazed at an old black and white photo on the wall. "The late great Roger Bucklesby. One of my father's first signings. He, if anyone, established the agency. Such a wonderful writer and a man for whom my father had immense respect. Multiple award-winning novelist. The quality of his work is exemplary, which is why it still endures and he remains such a big name."

"Cathleen Miller, I see," remarked Rainbird, spotting a photo of Hunt Senior with a happy-looking Cathleen, smiling in the manner that only people whose dreams have come true can muster.

"That was the day she signed with the agency. Roger himself recommended her. She wrote well for a while, and sold pretty well too, but she was very much of a certain period in time. Her moment came and departed."

"Does she still write?" asked Georgina.

Georgina knew the answer to this, but she wanted to hear Henry's explanation for everything that had transpired between him and Cathleen.

"Oh, well, yes, I believe she does, but her work is no longer a fit for the agency."

"Who represents her now?" asked Georgina, faking ignorance again.

"My understanding is she represents herself."

"Just one photo of you, I see," noted Rainbird.

"Yes, well, I've only been at the helm for a relatively short period of time," said Henry, looking at a photo of him with Lachlan Denoon. "He's not been my only signing. There've been others, some very promising, but I'd be lying if I didn't acknowledge that Lachlan is by far and away my most important…" He paused, a look of regret on his face. "… was my most important client."

"I'm sorry," said Georgina.

"We had a very close personal friendship, you know. People seem to forget that. I've heard on the grapevine that my main competitor has already begun speculating on the damage Lachlan's tragic death will have on the agency's finances, but it has barely entered my mind. The shock of it all, you know. Lachlan was a friend first and a client second."

Henry walked over to a drink's cabinet filled with expensive liquors.

"Do you partake at this time in the morning?"

"I would not put a thief in my mouth to steal my brains…" said Rainbird, with a smile, "… at least not this time in the morning, you know."

"Shakespeare!" exclaimed Henry, delighted. "From Othello."

"Not with the agency, is he?" asked Rainbird, grinning. "Be quite a back catalog."

"Indeed, but sadly no," smiled Henry. "Someone else must have nabbed him."

"Such is life."

The two of them were bonding, Rainbird was working his charm and it wasn't long before they'd settled in on the sofa and were chatting away like old buddies, while Georgina watched on somewhat amused, somewhat impressed, at the ol' Scottish charmer.

"I have to ask," said Rainbird, tentatively, "do you think that the server, our client Mr. Mitch Owens, is responsible for Lachlan's death?"

"I want justice for Lachlan, and if I believed the server did kill my friend, then I would want the full weight of the justice system brought to bear upon him. The thing is, I just don't know if he did do it. And if he didn't, then I don't want him to be a scapegoat. I want the true perpetrator held accountable. I was there that day, I saw the comings and goings, the arguments and the petty jealousy in that house. Trust me, there was no shortage of animosity running through that place. But do I think he did it?"

Henry took a deep breath.

"Maybe. But then maybe not. I think people, perhaps every one of us, are capable of some horrendous things, but to kill someone, and in the manner that he is accused, seems strange, extreme, or should I say illogical. Yes, that's it, illogical. But then are most of us directed more by emotion than by logic? For many that is undoubtedly the case," said Henry, trailing off. "I'm sorry, I fear that I am not being of much help. You probably want a black and white answer one way or another."

"Not at all," said Rainbird. "We want nuance. We want the subtle and the variable. How else can we build a true picture of events."

"I don't mean to pry, but is the case against your client strong?"

"I'm afraid I can't disclose that sort of thing."

"Of course."

"May I ask you about your own discussions with Lachlan?" asked Georgina.

Henry nodded his approval.

"It was put to us by one of the other attendees of the event that the two of you argued at one stage, is this so?"

"Oh, has Audrey been talking again? She's such a gossip. Listen, Lachlan and I had frank discussions all the time, but really, argued? Hah! The two of us were like brothers. Audrey said it, didn't she?"

"It would be unethical of us to divulge that information," said Rainbird.

"Look, Lachlan was my friend as well as a client, and sometimes that got messy. I had to confront him with some hard truths. Lachlan was getting rather arrogant, starting to believe the public image he'd created of himself, but the fact is, he wasn't as in control as he would've liked. He was mistaking popularity and acclaim with power and influence. Yes, he had some influence, but where it mattered, he was just as controlled by the people pulling the purse strings as anyone else."

Rainbird and Georgina exchanged looks.

"So, who was he controlled by and why is that relevant?" Rainbird probed.

Henry looked flustered.

"Well, I mean, I don't know that it's relevant to his murder. That is to say, um, there are confidentiality agreements and contracts and maybe even NDAs in place. I need to be very careful about what I say. Which is exactly how Lachlan should have behaved. But instead, he'd go shooting his mouth off about things before the paperwork was even signed."

"Are you talking about the television series?" Georgina asked.

Henry hesitated, then nodded.

"The producers, and the owner of the production company, Magnus McLean, were not happy that Lachlan was disclosing his plans for the series before it was confirmed."

"Magnus McLean owns the television rights to Lachlan's work?"

"Just another one of his pies. I don't believe he's very hands-on but, yes, the production company is owned by his media group, as is the video-on-demand streaming service, *MagNet,* which is set to broadcast the series. Most of the filming has been completed, but there is a lot of editing still going on and some scenes to be reshot. Not all publicity is good publicity, especially where contracts are involved. Getting sued is not good for business and Lachlan was in danger of sinking the entire project."

"You must admit that if the television deal fell through, that would be bad for you too," said Georgina.

"Of course, that's why I had words with Lachlan. He was trying to say that we could approach other production companies or a different streaming service for his next book, that he'd do so on his own if I didn't want to do the work, but I reminded him of the details of the contracts he'd signed, both to me and Magnus's companies. He could be quite immature at times, even suggested he could get Magnus to drop him to get out of his contractual arrangements, but it doesn't work like that. He saw sense in the end though and laughed it off, not one to take things too seriously, was Lachlan."

Henry sat back with a sigh.

"Truth is, Lachlan had a very 'easy come, easy go attitude.' He could never quite understand why people would get upset by things that for him were just insignificant, and I suspect that has been his undoing. Take Stamford Williamson, for example. His reputation is important to him, but Lachlan would nettle him about it constantly. Anything Stamford said in return, Lachlan would just shrug and laugh, it drove Stamford mad."

For a moment Henry just sat, reflecting on the past before clearing his thoughts and returning to the present.

"Not that I'm suggesting Stamford had anything to do with Lachlan's murder, of course. The same goes for your client, Mr. Owens, I'm afraid. To Lachlan, having a dig at his old friend's current situation was just a momentary amusement, I fear for Mr. Owens it might have cut deeper." Henry shrugged. "I don't think I can shed any further light on the situation. I hope I have been of some assistance to you."

Rainbird stood and extended a hand to Henry who rose to shake it.

"Thank you for your time, Mr. Hunt. And our condolences for the loss of your friend."

"Thank you, Mr. Rainbird. And Miss Patterson. I hope you find out the truth of the matter. He was flawed, but he was a good friend to me."

He shook Georgina's hand and, as her eyes met his, he smiled, a smile laced with a subtle attraction that hinted at future possibilities.

When back on the road, making their way toward the beach house, Rainbird frowned to himself. "Mr. Hunt is being economical with the truth. For what reason, I'm unsure. If he had anything to do with Lachlan's murder, then wouldn't it be better for him to point the finger at Mitch, not subtly deflect it away, but then perhaps that, in itself, is all part of his subterfuge."

"This is not an open and shut case," said Georgina. "Which means, Mitch has a chance."

Rainbird's cell phone rang.

"Answer this for me, will you?" he said to Georgina, digging into his pocket for the phone.

"Alfie Rainbird's phone," said Georgina, picking up the call.

There was a pause as she listened.

"You're absolutely certain?"

She paused again.

"OK, I'll let him know."

She hung up.

"Anything important?" asked Rainbird.

Georgina took a deep breath.

"I'm afraid so."

"Oh?"

"Prosecution has just named its lead counsel."

"And whom might that be?"

"Jon Veitch."

Rainbird's expression darkened and he kept his eyes on the road ahead.

Silence hung heavy in the vehicle for a long moment, only the dull drone of the tires against the hot asphalt lingered in the cab. Twice Georgina thought Rainbird was about to say something but then stopped himself. He was rarely short for words, but this name, this ghost from his past had left him speechless. Georgina considered outlining the specifics, that Veitch had transferred back to the East Coast from Los Angeles where he'd moved after convicting Rainbird and seeing him incarcerated. But there was little point right now, she didn't try to break the awkward silence. What's more, she didn't want to interrupt Rainbird's thought process. They both knew the gravity of the situation.

"It's a lingering debt from the past," said Rainbird finally. "It's time it was settled."

CHAPTER 18

He hadn't seen him in over twenty years. But that didn't mean he hadn't thought about him—Jon Veitch, the prosecutor who put Rainbird away. The man who'd trashed his already shattered life. Some had argued that Veitch was just doing his job, that as a state prosecutor he had no choice in taking the case, and that there was no animus in what he did to Rainbird. But Rainbird knew better. The sadistic glee in Veitch's eyes when Rainbird was sentenced said it all. Perhaps he could have forgiven him that. Perhaps too for the underhand tricks he played in court. And maybe for the post-conviction comments he'd made to the press. But one thing he could never forgive Veitch for was the character assassination. Not of him but his late wife. When he brought Abigail into it, he crossed a line. Dragging her medical history into court to be aired by the media, dissected and commented on like it was a goddamn sporting event, in which everyone had an opinion, even questioning the validity of her diagnosis and cause of death. He made her sound like a hypochondriac. That all the pain that Rainbird had been witness to was in her head, and maybe it wasn't the chemical company who was to blame after all. He besmirched a woman whose name he wasn't fit to utter, but Rainbird was eternally proud she carried his last one—*Abigail Rainbird*.

"Before you embark on a journey of revenge," read Rainbird aloud from Patricia Parry-Jones's smash hit *Harness the Power of Hate*. "Dig two graves: one for your enemy, and one for his dog too!" He put down the book and turned to Georgina in the café where they'd agreed to meet Veitch. "Just as well that I don't see Veitch as a dog sort of person, hey? That's something I would never do. Perhaps I could dig two and push in his assistant prosecutor instead. Do you think that would be permitted by the great Patricia Parry-Jones?"

Georgina didn't respond. She knew he was trying to lighten the mood. But it was a tense moment so why pretend otherwise. She sipped her coffee and looked out the window at the ocean views. They'd been in the café for fifteen minutes. It was a nice spot, all old timber and fishing memorabilia, a place that billed itself as having the best lobster rolls in Suffolk County. It was a tall claim in these parts and possibly true, but today Rainbird's was left barely picked at on his plate. He'd been dipping into the book all morning, part research into an attendee at the house the night of Lachlan Denoon's murder, and partly to pass the time while they waited for his long-term nemesis to arrive.

"Here's one I agree with," said Rainbird. "The true way to mourn the dead is to attack the living who have wronged them."

Georgina cared for Rainbird but right now she was finding him vexing. "Aren't these just other people's original quotes ripped off and given a nasty makeover a la Parry-Jones?" asked Georgina, taking the bait. "Isn't the original, 'The true way to mourn the dead is to *care* for the living who *belong* to them.'? And 'Before you embark on a journey of revenge dig two graves, one for your enemy, and one for yourself.'? I think I prefer the originals."

Rainbird didn't answer. He was too wrapped up in his own revenge fantasies, considering the man who'd once ruined his life and was about to walk back into it. Veitch had moved West soon after Rainbird's conviction, relocating to L.A. where his wife's family were from, to enjoy the sunshine and the good life, while Rainbird rotted in oblivion in the dungeons of the prison system. Veitch had been state prosecutor in L.A. for many years, he'd had a successful career before switching to the more lucrative side of criminal law, the defense, but following a recent acrimonious divorce, Veitch had moved back east to his old stomping ground, New York, and had decided to go back to what he loved more than anything else—putting people away. He wasn't driven by justice or even punishment for wrongs committed, but by simple power and the pleasure he got in wielding it over others. That he was good at what he did was unquestionable; he was a worthy adversary who was feared by many. With his return to the prosecution, it was obvious that sooner or later he and Rainbird would have a run-in. That it would be during Veitch's first case back, and that the case would be a murder trial defended by Rainbird, was something neither of them could have seen coming.

The clock struck the hour and with ludicrous promptness the door opened and there he stood. His appearance took Rainbird by surprise. Twenty years had passed but, in a sense, he hadn't changed at all. Sure, there were the gray hairs on his head and new wrinkles on his brow, but there was something about Veitch's presence, his mannerisms, the way he carried himself, and how he glanced about the room with those beady-little eyes, devoid of any worthy emotion, that took Rainbird immediately back to that terrible period in his life and the fateful trial that stole his freedom.

He had once confided in Georgina that during the actual moment he was sentenced to life imprisonment he had something akin to a near-death experience. That it had been more like watching a movie of himself than actual reality lived; that he was entirely detached and separate from his being. Even his memory of the event was as if looking down from above the courtroom as a passive observer. Only there was no peaceful all-embracing tunnel of light to accompany Rainbird's near-death experience. After the shock of sentencing, he was thrust into a waking nightmare, a tunnel of darkness that brought not a loving encounter with his savior at the end, but torment with the devil himself and all the hideousness he embodied. There was nothing passive about it, and especially no way out.

By Veitch's side was Rachael Mears, the prosecutor from the bail hearing, carrying a thin light brown attaché case, who'd now taken a step back to be Veitch's second in command. She was a ruthless prosecutor in her own right, who'd won many notable cases. The bail hearing was the first time Rainbird and her paths had crossed, but he and Georgina knew of her work, and a serious allegation made against her—obtaining false evidence. It was said that during a recent trial she'd been instrumental in enticing a prisoner to offer up a favorable and untruthful witness statement against a defendant in exchange for a sweetheart deal, and that she had not disclosed the deal to the court.

It was a serious accusation, but as seemed the case with anything she did, nothing had ever stuck.

She'd slipped through the grasp of the system like a greased piglet.

Rainbird and Georgina saw the two of them walk in but it was several seconds of glancing about before Veitch spotted them. He looked Georgina's way first and then Rainbird's. He didn't smile or nod but instead jutted his chin out slightly with a little backward jerk of the head, as if to say, *Ah, there you are*. To Rainbird he looked pompous, like he was trying to appear superior, like a prince. But in truth there was nothing for Veitch to feel superior about. Sure, he'd got one over on Rainbird by putting him away, but then Rainbird had got one over on Veitch by getting himself out, and with a full exoneration to boot. Veitch's reputation had taken a hit after that, but the two were going into this one with an even tally. And there was everything to play for.

"Thank you for agreeing to meet with us," said Mears, as they approached the table.

"Not at all," replied Georgina.

The women shook hands, exchanged pleasantries and formal introductions, as did the men with them, although not each other. Not yet, anyway. They were waiting for the other to make the first move, to be the first to crack in a standoff that was as much about pride as it was ego.

"Alfred," announced Veitch, being the first one to cave. "We must not let the shadows of our past cloud the future."

He held out his palm. To the casual observer he looked and sounded noble. But it was all a facade. Nobody had ever called Rainbird "Alfred," not even his mother, for Veitch to do so was his subtle little way of patronizing him, as was the nuance of his offered handshake. Rainbird was a master at reading non-verbal gestures and Veitch's palm down handshake offer was a classic signal that betrayed his true feelings of dominance and control. Rainbird knew that in the same way a dog will roll onto its back and expose its throat to demonstrate submissiveness, so too do humans use the palm up gesture to show the same—think a beggar asking for a handout or someone head down, palms out and up, pleading for mercy. Forcing Rainbird's hand into this position by offering him a palm facing the other way would place him in symbolic submission.

Rainbird reached out, his palm up as if accepting the shake at face value, but then the moment he grasped Veitch's hand he rotated it over, forcing Veitch into the submissive position, so that it was his now facing up and Rainbird's was on top.

"*Jonathan,*" replied Rainbird. "He who keeps one eye on the past is blind in one eye. He who keeps no eyes on the past is blind in both."

Silence hung in the air as Rainbird held Veitch's stare, along with his palm, that little bit longer than necessary.

Mears looked uncomfortable.

Rainbird released his grip.

"I believe you wanted to discuss a potential pretrial resolution?" said Georgina.

"Potential," stressed Mears. "The nature of your response will determine the specifics of any offer made. But we have some broad brushstroke suggestions."

Rainbird and Georgina listened.

"As you know," said Mears, "we have a strong case against your client, one which we are confident will result in a conviction should it proceed to trial."

She began counting on her fingers.

"Previous conviction, witnesses to the argument, witnesses to the physical assault, witnesses to his threat to kill, picked out of a lineup, at the scene of the crime, forensics..." she trailed off, making little circles with her hand, as if to say the list went on. "We do, however, recognize your client's possible reluctance to consider a plea bargain, since any offer would still entail serving significant custodial time, perhaps motivating him to pursue an all-or-nothing approach, do or die, or, in his case, freedom or incarceration. With this in mind, we would entertain fifteen years for manslaughter. That's a just settlement, a punishment for the crime but one that after serving he could still rebuild a life, of sorts. Whereas if he gambles and loses, well, I think we all know that would be game over."

Before Rainbird or Georgina could respond a waitress approached the table.

"Good morning,' she said to Veitch and Mears. "Will you be joining us for lunch today or can I fetch you some drinks?"

"Espresso coffee, black, double shot," snapped Veitch, like it was an order that he expected to be met in double quick time.

"Ice tea, please," replied Mears.

"Can I get you guys refills?" asked the waitress, turning to Rainbird and Georgina.

"I'm fine, thank you," replied Georgina.

"Black tea, please, two bags with a wee dab of milk."

"Oh yeah, English style," replied the waitress.

Rainbird pretended to choke.

"Scottish, I think you'll find," he said, with a cheeky smile and a wink.

The waitress smiled back. He was always this way with serving staff, good natured, polite and, when he could be, fun. So too was he always correcting them on this particular point—whether it was English or Scottish to take milk in your tea. Georgina would roll her eyes. She'd heard it all before, along with his normal insistence that English tea was "nay as strong or hearty as a Scottish brew." Rainbird wasn't in need of additional reasons to detest Veitch, but the curt way that Veitch dealt with the server gave him a new one. For Rainbird this was a big reveal of character, how you dealt with people who on the surface could offer you little. Rainbird's character was never situational or based on status. Everyone was due equal respect. That Veitch's was not was all too plain to see.

As the waitress departed, they got down to business.

"So, what do you think?" asked Veitch.

"It's a very interesting offer," said Rainbird. "Yes, very interesting indeed. I can see how a defense lawyer would be awfully tempted by an offer like that."

Mears and Veitch nodded.

"There's just one snag," he said, pausing for effect. "We're not taking it."

Their faces dropped.

Rainbird smiled.

"Your case is nowhere near as strong as you claim it is. Obviously, we're not prepared to divulge specifics of our intended defense, but I would say that we are equally confident in this case resulting in a not guilty verdict," said Rainbird.

Veitch scoffed.

"We'll take this to our client but I have to tell you now," said Rainbird, "I don't think he'll accept. And I might add, our professional advice to him will be to reject the offer. This is a case we can win. And we intend to do so."

"You don't believe that," said Veitch. "Come on, let's drop the posturing. We all know the kid did it. And what's more, we all know he stands next to no chance of beating the rap, not this time. Don't make this into a show trial, this isn't about you and me and our past, this is about first-degree murder. What we're offering is generous. Generous by any measure. His chances are poor, manslaughter is the very best you'll get," said Veitch with the sanctimonious air of a monarch casting off a scrap of food to a subject.

"If his chances are so bad, you wouldn't be offering us anything. Never forget who he has in his corner. Don't underestimate me. Not twice."

"I would acknowledge that he wouldn't be the only guilty person you've helped evade justice. Recurring theme with you that, isn't it?"

"Let's keep this professional," interjected Georgina.

"Goad me all you want, Veitch. It won't work," said Rainbird with a stare, unflinching and uncompromising. "Never make the mistake of thinking I am in any way afraid of you; I am afraid of no man, only God!"

"If that's the way you want it, fine," announced Veitch getting to his feet. "We will win this case, Rainbird, you mark my words, and by the time we're finished, your little fairy tale story will be over too. You may have beaten the system once but not this time, we will bury you in court and I look forward to dancing on your grave."

"A hyena can dance on the grave of a lion, but he can never be a lion. Not that you'll be putting anyone six feet under, Veitch. Habeas corpus—there'll be a body in court all right, the corpse of your career. You want to go toe to toe with me? You want to banter words with me in the courtroom? Come and have a go if you think you're hard enough, wee man."

"By the time this is over, you'll wish to God you'd taken our offer, Rainbird. I want you to remember this moment, the moment you had your chance, had it in your grasp and you blew it like an amateur," said Veitch.

"Don't you swan in here like a prince telling us what's what," said Rainbird, glaring at Veitch. "You're nothing but a drink-soaked wife beater, Veitch. Oh, don't look so surprised, I know all about you, word travels fast in legal circles, you should know that. You may have kept that little detail out of the public domain, what with that hefty divorce settlement you had to swallow, but I know, people know, and I've got you marked for what you are. Never trust a man who hits a woman."

"This meeting is over," announced Veitch. "Consider our offer retracted."

Mears got to her feet too.

"As a final thought," said Rainbird as they were about to leave. "I would refer you to the statement by defending lawyers in the case of Arkell versus Pressdram."

Veitch and Mears both looked confused.

"Look it up, why don't you."

A dismissive tut from Veitch and they turned and left.

Rainbird called after them. "That's Arkell versus Pressdram."

Only when the door had closed behind them did Georgina turn to Rainbird.

"OK, just what exactly was their statement?" she asked with a smile,

"Two words," said Rainbird. "The first rhymes with 'yuck' and the second one is 'off'."

"I do hope they'll look that up," said Georgina. "Nice to have the last laugh."

"Oh, they will, don't worry about that," said Rainbird. "They won't be able to resist."

At this moment the waitress waltzed in and placed three drinks on the table then waltzed out again.

"Looks like the last laugh is on us," said Rainbird. "We'll have to pick up their bill."

CHAPTER 19

The shiny blue hull glistened in the sunshine as it sliced through a placid sea, throwing up a bright white V-shaped jet in its wake, gushing like a hydrant down the opposing sides of the motor yacht's bow, as it powered toward its destination in the distance—*Eleni*, Magnus McLean's colossal superyacht. Rainbird stood on the deck of the taxi boat, ignoring the superyacht but admiring the water's beauty and motion as it erupted from the sleepy ocean, while cool salty air danced on his face, where a smile rested. He looked utterly content, gazing out at the enormity and timelessness of the ocean, as he listened to the lonely cry of gulls drifting overhead. It was at times like this that he felt an overwhelming privilege to be alive and to own that most precious of all possessions—his freedom.

Soon the smaller boat had docked with the magnificent *Eleni*. A beautiful blonde woman dressed in a uniform of pressed and starched whites waited at the bottom of an external flight of stairs leading to *Eleni's* main deck.

"Welcome aboard, Mr. Rainbird," she said with a smile. "Please follow me. Mr. McLean is looking forward to meeting you."

Up the stairs and across *Eleni's* vast immaculate wooden deck they strode, past reflective metal adornments dotted here and there, that spoke of hours of polishing and maintenance to keep the corrosive sea air at bay, as well as the even more corrosive eye of the superyacht's owner, should he spot any metallic surface he couldn't see his face in. Rainbird had attended some meetings in his time but none in quite so opulent a setting. Magnus had agreed to meet with him and had chosen the location. It was all a show of status and bravado, and Rainbird knew it, but he wasn't about to let that stand in the way of a pleasant outing. "Super" the yacht most certainly was, and the extravagance increased as they made their way inside. Deep plush carpets compressed underfoot as they entered an open plan area with high ceilings and a profusion of indoor plants, more akin to an old colonial hotel in the orient than a vessel out at sea. They headed toward a spiral stairway at the far end of the room that corkscrewed its way to a lower level. As they reached the bottom rung of the stairs a room of luxury and abundance stretched before them. Bathed in pools of natural light and decorated with cobalt blue sofas and matching patterned carpet, it was a sight to behold. In the center of the room was an indoor water feature, a three-tiered fountain where water dyed the same cobalt blue as the furnishings cascaded across the levels. The whole feature was gimbaled, so that it swung on a pivot with the motion of the boat, remaining upright at all times to prevent spillage. And beyond was a grand marble table with several ornate chairs, one bigger than all the rest, a suitable throne to hold court and issue directions to subordinates maintaining your empire. Here, leaning up against the corner of the table, was Magnus, a wry smile on his face and a crystal cut tumbler of spirits in his hand.

"Welcome, Mr. Rainbird. Can I tempt you with a dram of your homeland's finest?"

"Single malt?"

"Naturally."

"A man after my own heart."

A quick glance from Magnus to a subordinate, and Rainbird's drink was prepared from a mock art deco style bar on the other side of the room, then promptly handed his way.

Rainbird took a sip.

"Mmm," he said, impressed. "Sherry oak casks I'd say; rich, smokey, hints of green apple and vanilla. A Macallan?"

"You know your Scotch, alright. A *Macallan M*," said Magnus, a broad smile stretching across his face.

He looked at Rainbird with a touch of endearment. "If someone had told me three years ago that I would be sharing a 30-year-old bottle of single malt with the man who defeated me in the most public and uncompromising realm, the law courts, dragging my name through the gutter and costing me no small fortune in the process, I would have laughed in their face."

"And possibly punched them in it too," ventured Rainbird.

"Quite possibly," said Magnus with a chuckle. "So let us laugh together instead, Mr. Rainbird. Your health, sir."

He raised his glass.

Rainbird reciprocated.

"When I first laid eyes on you in court, sitting patiently for proceedings to begin, I had no idea what I had in store for me," said Magnus. "I imagined you to be a timid legal academic with a big pile of papers and a box of paperclips. Someone with the personality of an accountant, who'd peruse his case in a softly-softly manner, not so much arguing a case as gently raising technicalities from time to time with polite regard for the sensitivities of the court."

"That's me," said Rainbird.

"If only, then I might have won. You're the most ruthless street fighter of a litigator I've ever seen, the sort of person who'd sooner slit my throat than smile at me. And that's what I admire about you, Rainbird." Magnus took another sip. "I always hoped you might represent me in the future, if the need ever arose, of course. What I didn't bargain for was you taking my daughter on as a client."

"Mitch Owens is the client."

"But we both know who's footing the bill. Without Stephanie there is no client."

Rainbird didn't respond.

"I know you fight to win, Rainbird. So do I, but there are times when you simply cannot win. Sometimes the cards are so stacked against you that to commence battle is a poor strategic decision. And life is all about strategy. From where I'm standing, my assessment of the battle you're about to engage in is not favorable to your side."

"Oh, how so?"

"The evidence against the kid is strong. Even you must admit that. All that talk of the animosity between him and Denoon. He threatened to kill him for God's sake. And kill him I'm certain he did. But guilt or innocence, these are mere incidentals to the likes of us, what matters, of course, is the end result. The end always justifies the means, but no matter what means you employ in this case, the end result is a guilty verdict. The writing's on the wall for that kid. Sometimes it's better to cut loose a dead weight before it drags you under too. Think of the damage to your reputation."

"Touching," said Rainbird. "Concern for my reputation. Isn't that really concern for yours?" Magnus didn't respond. "I can see why you might very well like to see me drop Mitch as a client, as you, perhaps more than anyone, knows that no matter how bad things look, while Mitch still has me in his corner he has hope. Whereas if I palmed him off on some incompetent, well, a guilty verdict would get him out of the way, wouldn't it?"

"I'm not going to lie to you, Rainbird. I don't like the kid. He was an employee of mine for a while, but someone like that has no business with my daughter."

"She disagrees."

"She doesn't know what's best for her!" snapped Magnus, before calming himself. "Sometimes parents have to make decisions that our children disagree with, but they are the right decisions for them in the long run. Experience and wisdom are on our side, not theirs."

"How long have you known Mitch and Stephanie were together? Did you know about their relationship before Mitch's bail hearing? Maybe even before his arrest? Back when the two of you were at the Bucklesby mansion together, perhaps?"

"There are many things I know or am informed of, you know that. I imagine you also know that I don't answer questions like those, be they from cops or lawyers, other than the ones in my employ."

"Lawyers in your employ or cops?"

Magnus smiled, a tiny smile, self-satisfied and smug. "Both."

"You should know that as a lawyer, I have to consider everyone a potential suspect until proven otherwise. You were in the house, after all. If you knew about Mitch's relationship with Stephanie back then, well, that's quite the motivation to point the finger."

Rainbird watched Magnus carefully, looking for any sign that he'd struck a nerve, but true to form, Magnus revealed nothing, not even deigning to reply. It was time for a change of tack.

"I understand you own the production rights to Lachlan Denoon's work, as well as the streaming rights to his and Stamford Williamson's television programs. You must know them quite well. Is it true there was no love lost between Stamford and Lachlan?"

Magnus paused before answering, considering the topic and whether it was detrimental to his position to enter into conversation on it. He shrugged before he spoke.

"Williamson was wary of the young whippersnappers biting at his heels. Lachlan was a star on the rise, with many options in front of him. Stamford is almost certainly on his way down."

"That's an interesting way to speak about your own client."

"I'm a pragmatic man, Mr. Rainbird. I don't hold with sentimentality. Stamford has been pushing the limits of late, desperate to stay on top, but it's not working and I don't mind telling you that as soon as I can find a suitable replacement for his line of programming, then I will take it."

"Could Lachlan Denoon have been that replacement?"

"Lachlan could very well have fit the bill. But he wasn't interested. He was only interested in being respected as a serious creative—for the time being."

"I was told that Lachlan was getting too big for his boots, that he was trying to call the shots with those who really held the power. That true?"

"Lachlan was an opportunist, but a small-time player, even told me to drop Stamford Williamson. I laughed in his face."

"Did Stamford know this?"

Magnus snorted. "Are you suggesting Stamford killed Lachlan?" He laughed with bemusement. "Well, I suppose it's a possibility. Although Stamford doesn't like to get his hands dirty, but desperate times, as they say. If he could get the right publicity out of it, I suspect Stamford would do anything."

"And you, Mr. McLean, what would you do for the right publicity?"

Magnus took a slow methodical sip of his single malt.

"I know your history, your background, and I admire that too, Rainbird. We're both self-made men, you and me, we both came from nothing and have fought against adversity to rise as rulers and conquerors of our respective fields, and we've never asked help from anyone. It's my understanding that there's been a degree of friction between you and your current employers. That being the case, it seems obvious to me that a man of your abilities deserves a position where he is not only fully appreciated, but is handsomely remunerated for those abilities."

"Working for you?"

"Naturally. Take a look around you, Rainbird, this could be your office, this could be your world moving forward. Why answer to the faceless nobodies of a corporate board. Why not jump ship to this literal one? Drop the case and join my legal team. My last head of legal earned over two million dollars a year."

Rainbird took a final sip of his own single malt, savoring the flavor of wood spices and smoke that culminated in a lingering finish with notes of dried fruit.

"The measure of a man is not how much money he has in the bank. Not everything has a dollar sign hanging from it, not everyone can be lured with golden trinkets and sparkling jewels. I'm my own man and I like it that way, there's a value in that which supersedes any monetary price. Oscar Wilde said it best, 'A fool is he who knows the price of everything but the value of nothing.' Thanks for the drink, Magnus," said Rainbird, putting down his glass. "But I'm not for sale. Mitch Owens is my client and I intend to see him as free a man as I."

CHAPTER 20

For Georgina, awareness was an inborn instinct that she could activate through conscious choice. When she was doing her private investigator training, one of her instructors had been at pains to stress as much. "Awareness is a choice," he'd bellowed to the class in the manner of a grumpy drill instructor. "If I were to tie a pork chop necklace around you, and leave you out in the woods at night near a dump where a pack of wild dogs roam, then every last one of you would become hyper aware in an instant, your senses reaching out to detect those hungry animals. You'd notice every rustle of leaf, every creak of tree, every snap of twig. Vague images would jump out of the dark with clarity and you'd notice minute changes in the scent of the air. It's a choice people—choose to be aware."

Sadly, her instructor died soon after saying this—hit by a bus he didn't see coming, or so Georgina liked to tell people.

As surveillance targets went, Stamford Williamson was proving more aware than your average Joe. He had a greater number of fleeting moments of awareness than most, although he was still blinded by his own ruts of routine. Georgina had been tailing him for most of the morning, observing his character as he went about his normal business, unaware he was being watched. She paid special attention to remain at a distance great enough for Stamford to miss her presence but close enough for her to observe. That was the key. She knew through experience that people found it difficult to extend their awareness to things far away or on the periphery of their vision, and so it was here she would dwell, especially on the move. When walking she made sure random people were between her and Stamford; when in her sporty VW Eos she maintained a buffer zone of several vehicles in the space between her and him. And she never focused on her target to the detriment of everything else around her. She needed to be sure there was no third party monitoring her. Occasionally, when the target proved tricky, Georgina would call on the help of other investigators to back her up, so they could switch roles and the target didn't encounter the same faces or vehicles everywhere they went. But today she was working alone.

Over the course of the morning, what she witnessed of Stamford Williamson didn't enamor her to the man. He'd been to the gym, to a café, got gas and bought a paper, but somehow he'd managed to have two separate altercations with strangers. Stamford's first reveal of character was at the gas station as he sat in his green Land Rover with personalized plate *O.B.E. 1,* waiting in a line of cars. His irritated tapping of the steering wheel increased in tempo the longer he waited, his face contorting into a glare. When the car ahead crawled forward, Stamford seized his opportunity and cut in front, his lips curling into a smug grin. The mild-looking office worker type he cut in on gave a gentle *beep beep* of his horn in response, nothing aggressive, a sort of "hey, hold up buddy," but Stamford went nuts. He jumped out of his vehicle and with rage in his eyes paced toward the man. The guy's window was down and Stamford took full advantage, thrusting a finger into the guy's face, as he cussed and shouted.

"You got a problem with me, loser?" yelled Stamford.

The guy turned white and backed down quicker than the French Army.

It was touch and go as to whether Stamford was going to punch the guy, but, perhaps mindful of CCTV or maybe the bystander nearby who looked like he might recognize him, Stamford turned about foot and strolled back to his Land Rover, filling up as if nothing out of the ordinary had occurred.

An hour later when at the gym, Stamford's true character leaked out again. Georgina followed him inside but without her own sportswear she pretended to be interested in joining up instead, making inquiries about membership with a buff-looking guy at the front desk. As she strolled around the facilities with personal trainer "Brad," she spotted Stamford on the punchbag, hitting it Queensbury Rules style, "dukes" held high with an upright posture like an eighteenth-century prize fighter. After prancing around the bag for a couple of minutes, Stamford moved on to the free weights. Picking up a dumbbell, he pretended to film himself on his phone doing curls, but the actual target of his little clandestine movie was something else—the rear end of a young trim woman doing squats. Stamford almost licked his lips at that one, his ravenous eyes gorging upon the woman in her yoga pants.

The second proper altercation came at a coffee shop. When asked by the young female server for his name to scribble on his cup, Stamford responded, "I know you know who I am, and you're just trying to play it cool."

But she didn't and she wasn't. She had no idea who the strange middle-aged Englishman in dire need of dental care was in front of her. Nor did she care. She just wanted to scribble a name on a paper cup and move on to the next customer.

"I'm sorry, sir. I don't believe we've met before. May I please take your name?" was her polite response.

"My name? It's..." he paused for effect, raising an eyebrow expectantly in a manner that implied: *I believe you'll recognize this.* "... Stamford Williamson, O.B.E."

It was tumbleweed and a lonely church bell time.

She looked at him with a blank expression, no idea who he was.

A quick scribble on the cup and she turned to prepare his beverage.

Taking the drink, cup emblazoned in thick black pen with "Strampfred," he found a seat and sat, stewing on the encounter. With a look of obvious aggravation, he raised the beverage to his lips. His face screwed up as if his taste buds flinched in foul objection. Up he jumped and demanded to speak to the manager, and didn't he make a scene out of it. Painting the young server the color of the darkest coal, Stamford said her manner had been "curt to the point of rude" and that the beverage she'd produced was "practically undrinkable." Not that he left it there, suggesting she go through retraining and be watched in future whenever on front of house duties dealing with customers.

"Her attitude was as unpalatable as the coffee," Stamford finished up to the manager.

By the time he left the girl was in tears.

Georgina had reached out to Stamford Williamson for an interview the day before through his publicist, explaining that she worked for the legal firm representing Mitch Owens. And so, having followed him all day, by late afternoon she drove to meet him at his property.

Perched on a small hill overlooking the water, it was a prime piece of real estate, but the house itself was rather rustic and humble, charming even, being wooden clapboard painted a jaunty pastel yellow, with a large veranda out the front to observe the land down below and sparkling ocean beyond. It was a far cry from some of the in-your-face grandeur she'd encountered from other attendees of the writers retreat. Georgina pulled in and parked next to the Land Rover she was, by now, thoroughly acquainted with, right down to the small sticker of a British flag on the driver's side door.

She stepped from her car, and there he was in all his glory—Stamford Williamson O.B.E., sitting on the veranda in a linen safari suit, having dressed up for her arrival, holding a saucer and cup, his pinky finger protruding like it was an essential counterweight required to get cup to mouth without unsightly spillage.

"Welcome to my HQ," he said, taking a considered sip that barely moistened his lips, as Georgina made her way up to join him. "Can I tempt you with a cup?"

He gestured to a teapot on a cane table. "It's pine needle tea, one of my favorites, *Pinus strobus*, from that very tree," he said, pointing to a gnarled old pine in the grounds. "Do you know there's more vitamin C in pine needle tea than freshly squeezed orange juice?"

"I didn't know that," said Georgina with polite interest. "But does it taste any good?"

"It's an earthy taste, which I've come to appreciate."

"Not for me, thanks."

"Snack?" asked Stamford, reaching for a bowl with some unidentifiable dark-colored contents, which, on closer inspection, appeared to be some sort of dried dead insects.

"I'll pass."

Stamford smiled with a hint of condescension.

"In the world of survival, palatability and edibility, or, more accurately, sustenance, don't always go hand in hand. But these little suckers..." he popped a couple of insects into his mouth, "mmm, delicious. Got a taste for them from my time in Borneo, but they're the exception. Most of the time when you're out in the wild, you have to separate your wants from your needs. The body needs sustenance, whereas the palate wants taste. If necessary, that can be overcome. There is a saying from the deserts of Arabia, 'What a piece of bread looks like depends on whether you are hungry or not.' From my experience, the same can be said for raw witchetty grubs or even the decomposing carcass of a dead badger."

"You haven't?" asked Georgina with a combination of revulsion and intrigue.

"Sure have," replied Stamford with a touch of manly pride. "Along with elephant dung, snake's innards, lizard's tongues, you name it. I recently came back from the Siberian far north, where I dined, and dined well, on the undigested moss from the intestines of reindeer, surprisingly good actually, if a little chewy. Most of the time though, when I'm in survival mode in the bush I'm very much a scavenger. Trying to hunt down fresh palatable meat is energy consuming and, to be frank, downright dangerous, whereas if you can scavenge a carcass, it becomes a much more hand to mouth existence—that's true energy efficiency and the key to survival living. But I'm sure a 'suit' like yourself hasn't come all this way to get tips from me on what to do if your plane goes down in the jungle."

"Not exactly."

Stamford smiled, a big, nasty, gap-ridden toothy grin that would have made the most hard-nosed dentist wince.

"Well, it's a pleasure to meet you, Miss Georgina," he said, reaching out a hand. "Stamford Williamson."

"*O.B.E.*," added Georgina, glancing at his personalized plate in the drive.

"Oh, just a small acknowledgement from the palace for some of my less publicized charitable works, but you *may* call me Stamford. Please, follow me inside, we can talk there."

The smell of aged books and dusty artifacts filled the air as they stepped into a house that was as much natural history museum as residential property. Adorning the walls were numerous framed specimens in glass-fronted boxes—a collection of exotic butterflies, some iridescent beetles with big powerful-looking claw-like jaws, scorpions ranging from the minute to the massive with every size in between, and numerous other displays. From the ceiling hung several Amazonian blow pipes of colossal proportion, as did a ceremonial headdress from some far-flung corner of the globe. Carvings, fossils, wooden bowls, antique maps and other intriguing curiosities were everywhere.

"You've such an interesting place," exclaimed Georgina.

"I try to pick something up from everywhere I'm on expedition. Each object tells a story, a tale of adventure and discovery that transports me straight back to the place I acquired it."

Nearby, a round table caught Georgina's eye, decorated with every conceivable design of machete, placed so their blades fanned out from the center like rays of a cartoon sun.

"What's with the gap?" asked Georgina, pointing to an obvious space where one was missing.

It was fleeting, but Georgina thought she saw a micro-expression of panic in Stamford's eyes.

"Oh nothing, just changing the display around a bit, damaged one recently and am having it resharpened" he said.

"What did you damage it on?"

Stamford flexed his jaw. "Just chopping wood," he replied, unnaturally holding eye contact the entire time.

Georgina picked up one of the machetes.

"Be careful with that, it's razor sharp," said Stamford. "There's an old saying in the survival world, that 'a woodsman is only as sharp as his knife.' It's a philosophy I live by."

Stamford took the machete from Georgina's hands and, after caressing the blade, started to shave the hairs off his forearm with it. He gazed with affection at the blade for a final moment, then placed it down and picked up a nearby wooden flute.

"Made this myself in the traditional manner of the Makamazza, some of the most feared head hunters of the Andaman Islands. People call them savages, but in my experience savage people usually live in cities. They initiated me into the tribe as an honorary member," he said, before quickly adding, "—a senior member, with full tribal perks, in recognition of my status among the men."

He began to play a little ditty for her on the flute, not so much snake charmer as Georgina charmer, doing his best to throw seductive eyes her way as he played the sort of tune a grade schooler would learn on the recorder.

"I composed this piece myself, combining the Makamazza's traditional knowledge with my own innate understanding of musicology."

Georgina squirmed under Stamford's gaze. "Right... um, what's that?" she asked, quickly pointing to the first thing that caught her eye on the wall, a dried pressed leaf in a frame.

"Plant genus I discovered and therefore got to name from the rainforests of central Africa."

"What did you call it?"

"*Williamsonia stamfordensis*. There's a sample in the tropical house at the Royal Botanical Gardens in England. Do take a seat," said Stamford as they reached a thick wooden table.

"Stamford, I'd like to ask you about the night of Lachlan Denoon's murder at the Bucklesby retreat," said Georgina, steering things away from Stamford's exploits and ego. "I believe it was your second year in attendance?"

"It was, I visited the previous year as well. Such a lovely event, which I'm delighted to be a part of, wonderful people."

"One of your fellow attendees was the sponsor of the event, Magnus McLean. He owns the streaming rights to your next series, is that correct?"

"Yes, my production company *Stampede Films* produces *Williamson's Will To Survive,* the exclusive streaming rights to which Magnus owns through *MagNet*. The first series was a runaway success, after which Magnus approached me with a deal I couldn't refuse. Have you watched it?"

"I have," said Georgina. "Compelling viewing."

Stamford gave a shrug of fake modesty.

"Are you working on anything new?"

"*Stamford's Stamp of Approval*."

"What's that about?"

"I assess the survival skills of a group of hopefuls, who have to take on different survival challenges every week. Pushing themselves harder, faster and for longer than they've ever done before, until there's only one left at the end, the winner, who officially gets my stamp of approval."

"What's the prize?"

"A handshake."

"A *ham shank*?"

"Hand *shake*, it's symbolic of my approval. We wanted to get away from monetary gain being the motivation for participation and move instead to accolade alone as the prize," said Stamford, before adding, almost to himself, "—which does keep production costs down too."

"Could we talk about your relationship with Lachlan Denoon," asked Georgina. "One of the attendees of the retreat said the two of you argued at the event and that there was intense competition between the two of you. That Lachlan tried to pull the same trick he is said to have done with Henry Hunt when he allegedly got him to drop Cathleen Miller as a client, but that this time he wanted Magnus McLean to drop you."

"Did Audrey tell you that? God, she's such a nosy old cow that woman, not at all as she'd have the public believe. She's a nasty piece of work who makes up rumors to liven up her boring old life," said Stamford, revealing a flash of the aggression he'd displayed at the gas station.

"So there's no truth in it?"

Stamford clenched his jaw momentarily and scratched his neck as he spoke. "It's an inversion of the truth. Lachlan and I got on very well. In fact, I think it's fair to say that Lachlan saw me as something of a mentor. You see, I've been there and done it all in the writing world over many years, whereas he was the new kid on the block. He listened to my advice and, I like to think, took heed of some of it. His passing was a great personal pain to me, a great pain. Even if what Audrey told you is true—which it's not—Magnus McLean would never drop a big name like me. So, I say to hell with Audrey Adams and her own unique deceitful brand of knavery."

CHAPTER 21

Rainbird glanced toward the prosecution bench and locked eyes with Veitch, a sense of impending collision hanging in the air between them.

Both men had a lot on the line. The media was in a frenzy about the case: about Lachlan Denoon, the forthcoming TV series based on his book, and Mitch and his relationship with the daughter of a well-known business figure. But there was also the underlying story of two titans of the legal world: the former vanquished and the conqueror who would now face each other in the ultimate grudge match in the most unforgiving arena of them all—the courts.

The place was packed: court officials, lawyers, members of the public, journalists and a whole bank of photographers—the latter permitted for this pretrial hearing, although not the actual televised trial to come. To draw so big a crowd for such a hearing was highly unusual, only the biggest cases could fill out a court before the main event, especially one where the defendant himself wasn't even present, but then the clash between Rainbird and Veitch had people talking. They were expecting fireworks, and they were not to be disappointed.

"All rise. Court is now in session. The Honorable Judge Jenkins presiding," announced the Court Clerk.

The court rose, as in strode Judge Jimmy Jenkins with a presence of absolute command, his piercing gaze scanning the assembled onlookers. With a different judge from the one at the bail hearing, both teams were starting again from scratch. Uncompromising and belligerent, Jenkins was a formidable hard-headed judge with a reputation for severe sentencing—a punishment to really fit the crime, if he could find one. If a jury returned a guilty verdict to Jenkins, then you might as well forget about leniency, you were going to get punished to the full extent of the law. If it could go either way, he'd lock 'em away. The joke in legal circles was that if thumb screws and medieval torture devices had been available as sentencing options to Jenkins, then he wouldn't just have administered them, but would have done so with glee for non-violent first offenses, including routine traffic violations. He smiled to himself as he sat down, but that didn't mean anything, he'd been known to let a smile slip during sentencing too.

"Be seated everyone," said Jenkins, in a voice that even for this routine instruction resonated like thunder.

Everybody sat, but then Veitch shot up to his feet again.

"Your Honor, may it please the court, the motions for consideration today are references 125.26, and 155.25, being the murder charge, and possession of stolen goods, against Mitch Owens for the murder of Lachlan Denoon and possession of items belonging to the deceased. If we could address the state's motion to enact a protective order."

"Objection, Your Honor," said Rainbird, rising to his feet with fire in his eyes. "That is *not* the purpose of our being here today, it is for the defense's motion to compel! The state has no right to try and hijack this proceeding by adding new matters to the court list without notice. We are here for the defense motion, which was filed and served two weeks ago, long before their half-cooked request for a protective order that dropped but moments ago. It is only right and proper that we proceed, with our motion to compel, without this wholly intentional distraction."

Veitch was straight back at him.

"Your Honor, the two motions should be heard today, primarily because our motion for a protective order cancels out the defense's motion to compel. This is self-evident. The state has been willing and ready to provide discovery to the defense, however, since there is commercially valuable material within the discovery, material which is under strict copyright and the property of publishing house, McLean Press, who has yet to release it in book form, it is only right to establish a protective order first, so it doesn't fall into the wrong hands. With a protective order in place there will be no need for the motion to compel."

It was typical maneuvering from Veitch. The state was required to provide the defense with the evidence they intended to present in this case—*the discovery*—something they should have done weeks ago and were legally obliged to do. But the prosecution hadn't done this despite the clear legal requirement to hand it over. Rainbird's Motion to Compel was to compel Veitch to provide this evidence in a timely manner, otherwise the case would be thrown out. Veitch was purposefully stalling as long as possible, tying up Rainbird's time and frustrating his efforts to adequately prepare a defense by filing his own Motion for a Protective Order. His reason being concern over sensitive and valuable commercial material—the unpublished writings of Lachlan Denoon—from entering the public domain through it being leaked. At least this is what he wanted the court to believe the Protective Order was about, but strategically Veitch sought an advantage. By dragging his feet and filing his motion, Veitch was throwing up another roadblock in Rainbird's way.

"Your Honor, our motion was filed weeks ago because the state failed to provide discovery to us," stated Rainbird, precise and deliberate. "This is in clear contravention of Rule Five and Brady. By casting established legal principles to the wind, the state makes a mockery of not only this court, but the entire justice system. That they should conceal evidence from us is—"

"—That is not so," interjected Veitch, rising to his feet again before Rainbird had finished. "The purpose—"

"—Your Honor, I have not finished," boomed Rainbird, his voice slicing through the air like a guillotine's blade, cutting Veitch short. "It would be nice if the state could show the court due respect by not interrupting the defense until it has concluded and by not attempting to hijack proceedings in the first place by hampering our discovery of vital evidence. But I'm afraid this is indicative of our entire dealings with them thus far. These constant delaying tactics, this concealing of evidence will not stand!"

"Your Honor, no one is hiding evidence, the protective order must precede any motion to compel. Once in place appropriate evidential discovery will be provided," said Veitch in rebuttal.

Their argument set the atmosphere of the court ablaze. The room's collective heartbeat seemed to synchronize as one and its four walls shrink in size as the battle between these adversaries escalated further.

"This is as clear a contravention of Rule Five and Brady as there could be," said Rainbird in a voice that demanded attention. "The grounds for a protective order are a spurious attempt to thwart our abilities to prepare a defense. My learned colleague has an eminent position, we all know he's a respected and important man, but that in no way trumps my client's absolute inalienable right to a fair trial. That can only be provided by the discovery of evidence. We need to know whether they interviewed any other suspects, why they suspected them and what their reasons were for excluding them from the investigation. This and much more should already be on our desk and yet we are still waiting, and now the defense is obfuscating behind an unnecessary protective order, the notification of which we received late Friday afternoon, and here we are on Monday morning, having scrambled over the weekend to file a response. They could have raised this a long time ago but chose to do so at the final hour in the most calculated manner."

As Rainbird sat down, Judge Jenkins cast a stare toward him and then Veitch, his eyes blazing with authority. "Your argument is to the court, not between each other. There will be no interrupting from this moment forth. Is that understood?"

"It is, Your Honor."

"Yes, Your Honor."

"Mr. Veitch, what is your response to the defense's last statement?" demanded Judge Jenkins.

Veitch rose respectfully to his feet.

"I would like to make it as lucid as possible for the court, that the state more than anyone desires a fair trial in this case. It serves no one to have this case come to trial a second time. That the defense will receive discovery is not in question, but we need to establish the rules for this first," said Veitch.

Rainbird stood. "The rules are already there and enshrined in law, Rule Five and Brady. But who will it be that decides what we get from the state? Let me speak lucidly, as well. I have no faith in the state playing by the rules. Their conduct up until this point shows a wanton disregard for the rules, and so I would ask the court to appoint a special master to oversee the discovery process, to make sure that we receive everything we are entitled to."

Rainbird sat down.

Time seemed to freeze, a minute stretched out to eternity as Judge Jenkins considered his decision and a palpable silence filled the room. Rainbird and Veitch both tried to decipher the judge's decision before he gave it, to infer the inner workings of his mind through facial expression alone. The gravity of the moment held the room in its grip. And then, Jenkins lifted his chin and broke the silence.

"Rule Five does indeed establish that discovery should be granted to the defense. Let this occur with no further unnecessary delay. However, counsel for the state raises a valid point with regards to sensitive commercial material and, as such, it is necessary for this to be withheld from anyone other than the defense counsel and for the material itself to be carefully assessed by an outside party. For this reason, I shall appoint a special master, a retired judge I imagine. I think I know the man to assist in this process."

With that Judge Jenkins raised his wooden gavel, paused momentarily as he peered out across the court—his court, and let no one forget it—then slammed it down hard onto the bench, echoes reverberating throughout the room as he rendered judgment.

CHAPTER 22

Georgina entered the kitchen to find Rainbird with a look of concentration on his face, pouring a thin trail of milk from a carton into his trademark Taylor's Scottish Breakfast Tea—his third of the morning already—while softly stirring the beverage with a spoon in the other hand. It looked like a very delicate operation, as if some precise chemistry was taking place, not merely the sloshing together of the liquid components of a hot drink. But to Rainbird this went beyond chemistry, to him it was art. Scottish Breakfast Tea was serious business, very serious business indeed.

"You've got to let the water breathe first," he would say to Georgina when running the tap for several seconds to aerate it before boiling. "And only boil it once to keep the oxygen level up."

Next, he'd reach for his battered old tea tin, or "caddy" as Rainbird referred to it, decorated in the blue and white flag of Scotland. From here he'd take not one, but two tea bags and, with an attention to detail more akin to a brain surgeon making the first incision, place them into his mug on top of each other so that their largest surface area was facing up. With a direct hit right in their center he'd pour the boiling water, so the liquid gushed through the tea bags for a fuller release of flavor. With a spoon he'd gently, ever so gently, stir the bags in a circular motion and then he'd take a respectful step back and wait. Only when it had "brewed" for a good five minutes and its color was as dark as night would the flavor be unlocked and he would add the milk—always whole milk, and no compromise.

"What we're looking for here, in culmination, is a golden-brown hue," said Rainbird to Georgina, giving a running commentary on the process. "This cannot be rushed. Always take your time, George. Too much milk and it's ruined. Remember, you can always add more, but you cannae take it out once in. And I will nae drink a brew the color of dishwater."

A knock on the door brought today's little tea ceremony to a close. Rainbird headed to the door, cup in hand. Standing there was a motorcycle courier carrying a package that was long overdue—the prosecution brief that Veitch had been dragging his feet to disclose. Rainbird signed for the sealed document and brought it back into the kitchen, opening it up on the table. Inside among a collection of legal inventories and procedural documents was an interesting admission: that the police had interviewed a female dog walker who claimed to have seen someone running over the sand dunes at the rear of the Bucklesby mansion around the time of Lachlan Denoon's murder. The dog walker had participated in a police lineup, but had failed to pick Mitch out. In fact, their description of the person they claimed to have seen bore little resemblance to Mitch.

"This is good," said Rainbird, showing Georgina the document. "We need to get her on the stand when making our defense."

"Definitely."

It was an encouraging development. They'd have to wait until the prosecution had finished making their case to call her, but when they did Rainbird could use her to blow a significant hole in the prosecution's version of events. Also contained within the parcel was a three-hundred-page bundle of papers—the as yet unpublished second book by Lachlan Denoon: *The Audacity of Triumph*.

"Looks like we've some reading ahead of us," said Rainbird.

"Do you really think it will reveal anything relevant?"

"Probably not, but it's worth a look. Why don't you get started on it while I'm out ticking boxes with Dr. Hobart in…" Rainbird glanced at his watch, "Urgh, an hour from now."

*****

Rainbird entered Dr. Anna Hobart's office with a mixture of resignation and rebelliousness. Although he had no intention of taking these therapy sessions seriously, he realized there was no way to get out of them, and if he wanted to be able to get on with his life, then he would somehow have to pass this test. With that in mind, he planted himself in the comfortable armchair and took a subtle deep breath, releasing the air with a slow countdown from ten as he waited for Dr. Hobart to begin the session, who sat at her desk absorbed in some paperwork. She wore smart gray slacks and an oversized light blue mohair cardigan, leaving Rainbird feeling underdressed in his beach attire of an old pair of shorts and a faded t-shirt.

After several minutes, Dr. Hobart looked up from her desk. Rainbird had watched her working, trying to decide if this was a ploy to unsettle him or not. She'd barely acknowledged his presence when he walked through the door, the merest gesture toward the chair being all the greeting he received, before she returned to the paperwork in front of her. With a final glance at her open laptop to clarify some detail in the paperwork, she came over and stood opposite him.

"My apologies for keeping you waiting, Mr. Rainbird. We shall get started in just a moment, but I'm afraid I need to take this form down to Nicola as it needs to be dealt with immediately."

With that, Dr. Hobart walked out of the room.

For a moment, Rainbird stared at the closed door in bewilderment, before chuckling to himself and taking another breath to refocus his thoughts. If Dr. Hobart's plan was to put him off guard, she would be disappointed. Rainbird was used to dealing with all sorts of mind games; he could handle this with ease. Although, he had to admit to himself, he didn't think the good doctor was messing with him, she seemed surprised when her secretary had shown him into her office, annoyed even, as if she'd forgotten the appointment or at least lost track of time. Not that it bothered Rainbird, he'd come today resolved to see out the full appointment time. He was determined to show his commitment, even if Dr. Hobart tried to send him on his way early again, but if she spent the first fifteen minutes dealing with other business, so be it.

Dr. Hobart re-entered the room.

Rainbird sat up a little straighter in his seat.

"Doc, you already know all about me, you've done your research. How about you just tell me what I need to do to satisfy your remit?"

Dr. Hobart sat down and considered Rainbird for a moment.

"Mr. Rainbird," she began.

"Call me Alfie."

"Alfie, these sessions may simply be an inconvenience to you, or a diversion to take a break from what you consider more important matters, but let me assure you, I take my job seriously. And I can tell you, working through the manifold issues of the human mind is no laughing matter. Were it possible to regale you with the conversations I have already had today, without breaking patient confidentiality, I sincerely doubt you would find anything amusing and would certainly think twice before making light of what goes on inside this room. I consider myself privileged to be granted insight to my clients' deepest fears, concerns, and losses, and to help them to move through their grief and anger to a place where they can once again live their lives, not entirely free of the trauma, but incorporating it in a way that doesn't hinder their ongoing existence."

Rainbird was silent for a moment, before challenging Dr. Hobart.

"What do you know of loss?"

"Alfie, you are an intelligent man, although grief makes fools of us all at times. We have all suffered loss, in varying degrees. Whether it is as mild as the loss of a friend who has moved away, or the death of an elderly relative who has lived a long life, or the unforgettable bittersweet feeling when an only child is introduced to a sibling and must now share a parents' love. I have, of course, been through many losses."

Dr. Hobart trailed off momentarily.

"My most recent and deepest loss was that of my sister. It was almost ten years ago now, but there are still times I don't really believe it happened. It's almost as if, the harder I think about it, the more I feel she is just traveling again, somewhere on the other side of the world, too busy to keep in touch regularly. And one day soon, I will get an email or a text message saying she has booked flights home for Christmas, and it will be just like it used to be. Obviously, that won't happen. Instead, I too must face the fact that she is gone and deal with the associated feelings. My profession doesn't make me immune to the grieving process and I sought professional help to find my way through. To understand the anger I felt, still feel sometimes. Although it was an accident, I get angry that Lorna was driving in icy conditions, despite the fact that it was no worse than any other early winter morning. I get angry at myself, for not having made more effort to keep in touch with her, that we let our busy lives get in the way of our relationship. That I always thought there would be more time. How could I be so stupid?"

Dr. Hobart looked sympathetically at Rainbird.

"This is all natural and normal, as infuriating as that is. It is a process we have to work through, as human beings, dealing with the inevitable losses in our lives. It is not a linear journey but it does follow a predictable course, though it is also unique for every individual. The only way to heal is through. You cannot avoid it, you can try to deflect and delay, but it will come to the surface one way or another. I can help you with that process if you're willing to try."

For a moment Rainbird stared at the frosted window, an involuntary reflex trying to find a view to distract his mind, but as there was nothing to see it had the opposite effect and he found himself reflecting on his life with Abigail.

"She was a breath of fresh air, and so different from the people I usually found myself associating with. I was just a cheeky chancer, I never thought she'd look twice in my direction, but we got along so well. She always had a delicate constitution, I guess we know why now, but she was fun. And even on her bad days, when she was too tired to get off the couch, we could still make each other laugh."

Rainbird sighed and rubbed his forehead, "For a long time, I thought no one would ever be able to make me laugh again. It was as though all the color had drained out of the world, and I was left behind in a monochrome existence."

Dr. Hobart nodded. "But eventually, no matter how hard we resist—and resist we do—the pigments start to creep back in."

"It was barely perceptible at first," Rainbird agreed. "I noticed a daffodil in spring, I ate something tasty and considered going back for more. Then I would get angry. I was furious at myself for enjoying things that Abigail would never have again."

For a moment, silence hung in the room as they each processed these words, before Dr. Hobart broke the quiet.

"Thank you, Alfie. I know how hard it was for you to share that. I'm afraid the session is up for today, but I hope you feel our time was not wasted. I do look forward to seeing you again. Please make an appointment with Nicola on your way out. Within the next two weeks if your schedule will allow. It is important we don't leave it too long, and not just because your boss insists upon it."

With that, Dr. Hobart stood up and stretched out a hand for Rainbird to shake.

"Thank you, Alfie."

"Thank you, Doctor Hobart," he replied.

"Please, call me Anna."

CHAPTER 23

It happened in a blur and at point blank range. There was an abusive shout. A flurry of motion. Then an almighty explosion in the middle of the victim's face. The impact propelled him backward down three stone steps, where he landed at the bottom in a pathetic heap on the cold pavement, crimson covering his face and crisp white shirt. A collective gasp rippled through a group of bystanders. Several stood in shock, splattered with their own new adornment of red, a trail that marked them in the manner of a flamboyant final flick from an artist's brush.

It was all caught on camera, the moment crazed fan girl of Lachlan Denoon, Rosina Pavlova, launched a plastic bottle of bright red dye into Mitch's face as he made his way toward the entrance of the Riverhead courthouse.

"Murderer!" she yelled in a blood curdling cry as Mitch struggled to get to his feet in shock, his hands covered in theatrical blood. "Lachlan was a once in a generation genius! You stole a genius from the world!"

An artillery barrage of paparazzi cameras erupted nearby, while film crews pushed their way to the front to secure their raw footage for the evening news. A "blood bath" was ratings gold and the media was consumed by its own blood lust for the sacrificial lamb of Mitch Owens.

"Did you kill him, Mitch?" asked a brain-dead paparazzo.

"Of course, he killed him!" yelled Rosina Pavlova.

Chaos broke out as Rainbird lunged his way to the fore, protecting his client, as security guards rushed in from nearby, shoving people out of the way like a relentless current to apprehend Pavlova.

"Get back!" yelled Rainbird as he dragged a dazed and vulnerable Mitch through the crowd and into the safety of the courthouse. Only was it safety? Didn't the greatest danger of all reside within its four walls? Here your liberty could be snuffed out with clean, respectable, bureaucratic efficiency. The legal system might not scream, shout or throw things in your face, but it could destroy your life nonetheless, and in a terrifyingly respectable manner. And after a life sentence, your only remaining hope was for death to free you at the other end.

"You hurt, Mitch?" asked Rainbird, as they stepped inside the expansive lobby of the courthouse.

Mitch took a deep breath. "I don't think so," he said, visibly shaken, as red dye dripped onto his new shoes and spread into a puddle on the polished marble beneath his feet.

Security guards and court officials swarmed around Mitch, offering hollow sympathies and reassurances that proceedings would be adjourned until he acquired a change of clothes. Mitch stood with a look of quiet bewilderment as Georgina tried to soothe his nerves and Rainbird went off to speak to the judge's clerk. A hunched janitor arrived, mop in hand, and began swiping at the bright red puddle, his eyes filled with anxiety.

An officer of the court escorted Mitch to a side room where he could wait until spare clothing arrived. There was something humiliating and unsettling about the process, like an elementary school kid waiting in a staffroom for a clean set of clothes after having had an accident. He felt helpless, like he was being nannied and it threw his mental preparation off kilter.

Two hours and a new suit and shirt later—hastily delivered by Georgina—and proceedings were ready to begin.

"Deep breath, Mitch," said Rainbird to his client as they strode together toward the courtroom door.

Nothing could have prepared him for the moment he stepped inside the packed court. There was a collective intake of breath as Mitch entered the room, tension crackling like an electric storm about to unleash its fury after the elongated wait to begin. The courtroom was twice the size of the one used for the bail hearing and infinitely more intimidating. Mitch had imagined walking in with quiet confidence, of taking his seat and looking straight ahead, but when the moment came, it all fell apart. As Rainbird led him down a central aisle, lined on both sides with multiple benches, Mitch could feel the collective weight of the room's stares directed toward him and made the mistake of looking around. The place was packed, abuzz with anticipation, and all eyes were upon him. His throat tightened with a fearful knot, while a wild chaos of nerves swirled inside him. Friends and supporters were visible in the public gallery. So too were those of the deceased, whose stares were imbued with a tangible ill will, heightening Mitch's already frayed nerves and sense of foreboding.

"Sit here, Mitch," instructed Rainbird as he showed Mitch to the defense table.

Beyond was "the bench," the raised area where a large solid wooden table was perched, the location the judge would sit, peering down on all below. It reminded Mitch of church. Growing up with Catholic parents, Mitch had been forced to become an altar boy, and to him the bench appeared much like an altar, a place where a high priest would sit, wielding power and judgment, and administering penance. There were other ecclesiastical overtones: the central aisle, the ritualistic nature of procedure, the high-raftered ceiling and windows above the bench, which, although not stained glass, filtered light down from on high in much the same manner. He hoped to find salvation between the court's four walls, but if found guilty it wouldn't be two Hail Marys and three Lord's Prayer for wrongs committed.

Mitch glanced to his right, catching the eye of the two seasoned veterans waiting up front whose job it was to destroy him—prosecutors Veitch and Mears. Their meticulous legal and tactical preparations were complete and the battle was about to commence. Mitch felt relieved that Rainbird was in his corner, but to have Veitch and Mears opposing him, knowing they were collectively plotting his downfall, was a terrifying thought nonetheless. All their collective years of experience and tactical knowhow, as well as their intellect, savvy, underhanded chicanery and natural animal cunning were directed toward one objective—finding him guilty, and locking him away for the rest of his life.

The best view belonged to the twelve men and women on whom everything depended. These supposed peers of Mitch who would be the ultimate deciders of his fate. Mitch's gaze sailed across them one at a time, as a fusion of unease and promise spread throughout his being. Each face seemed to recount a different tale, a unique testimony to their own individual life experience and background. He gravitated toward a motherly type in the front row with a supportive smile, but couldn't help notice the stern-looking retiree behind her who seemed to eye him with suspicion. They were a varied group, in whose hands lay both salvation and destruction. Could they deliver a verdict based on the evidence and it alone, or would they let their prejudices and biases get the better of them? The jury selection process had been a battle in itself. Rainbird had fought hard, he'd won a few, lost a few, and in the end the deck was, he hoped, an even stack.

"All rise. Court is now in session. The Honorable Judge Jenkins presiding," announced the Court Clerk.

The court rose in unison, as in walked Judge Jenkins.

"Be seated please, everyone," he said, once settled in. "A very good morning, ladies and gentlemen of the jury, we will start with the opening statements from the lawyers in the case. These, as I explained to you when we all met yesterday, are not to be considered evidence. They are statements that should be thought of as a sort of roadmap of the type of evidence the attorneys plan to present to you during the case."

He looked toward Veitch and Mears, then over to Rainbird.

"Everybody ready to proceed?"

"We are, Your Honor."

"Yes, Your Honor."

"Then let's get things started."

Veitch rose to his feet and with a self-assured smile strode out to the front of the court.

"Your Honor, Judge Jenkins, my legal colleague representing the defense, Mr. Rainbird, to those most invested in the verdict of this case, the Denoon family and the Owens family, and, of course, to you, ladies and gentlemen of the jury, a very good morning."

He stood in the middle of the room motionless for a moment, his presence filling the space, then turned to the jury, looking them over, one by one.

"My name is Jon Veitch, I'm the state attorney for this case and I'd like to begin this morning by reminding you of the supreme importance of the task ahead of each and every one of you. At the culmination of these proceedings, you will be asked to reach a verdict on the most serious of all charges—whether the accused is guilty of killing another human being. 'Human being.' I say it that way intentionally, for language is important. Sometimes it's too easy to view others in an abstract manner, especially when they're not known to us personally—the accused, the deceased, the perpetrator, the victim. It can trivialize what we are really discussing—the intentional killing of another human. I guess we all trivialize to a degree, we hear about murders on the evening news, we read about them in newspapers, this statistic, that statistic. We become immune, calloused from it all even. We normalize the unthinkable, in part as a coping mechanism to deal with all the barbarity in the world. I implore you not to let that happen during this trial. Before his murder, Lachlan Denoon was a person so full of life and joy, a real, living, breathing, loving man with a family and friends who loved him dearly. He was loved in the manner that we all love those closest to us. I want you to remember that. His family and friends are seated here today. They, more than anyone, are relying on you for justice. And only you can give that to them."

He gazed up toward the public gallery, encouraging the jury to look into the faces of the bereaved, letting the gravity of his remarks sink in.

"What is life without love?" He let the question hang in the air, looking at each juror in turn. "It is hollow. To snuff out a life is to snuff out love and destroy the most precious thing any of us possess. It is the most heinous of crimes. I've been prosecuting murderers for over thirty years now, and I can tell you from my long experience, that for the family of those killed, the pain never ends. It might fade. Sometimes it does; not always, but it can. However, it never goes away. It is always there. If you steal from another person, oftentimes what was stolen can be replaced, in one way or another, but no one can give a life back. It is irreplaceable. Lachlan Denoon was irreplaceable. You have a responsibility to his memory too, to give justice to Lachlan. And to do that, you need to answer a simple question—did Mitch Owens kill Lachlan Denoon?"

Veitch looked straight at Mitch as he said this.

Mitch's eyes widened as a jolt of adrenaline raced through his body.

"My job is to assist you in answering that question through the use of clear, unambiguous evidence, of which there's an overwhelming amount in this case. An overwhelming amount. By the end of this trial, you'll have heard many credible witness testimonies, you'll have watched damning CCTV footage from the night of the murder, you'll have learned about clearcut forensic evidence and DNA analysis, and much more besides, all of which will leave you in no doubt, no doubt whatsoever, as to whether Mitch Owens killed Lachlan Denoon. In the end it will actually be remarkably easy to answer."

He strolled a couple of paces to his right, until he was in front of the head juror, a man in his fifties with a bald head and bushy beard that made him look like he had his hair on upside down.

"Did Mitch Owens murder Lachlan Denoon?" He looked at the head juror and waited. And waited still, uncomfortably long, like he was anticipating an actual verbal answer, right there and then in the packed courtroom, from the man.

For a moment the head juror looked concerned and confused. Panicked, even.

Veitch waited a split second longer then broke the tension.

"Yes, he did!" he answered in a resounding manner, like it was a clear instruction, which it was. "Yes, he did," he repeated again.

Although part theater, it was also clever subliminal psychology. Veitch knew that people are more subconsciously suggestible when they're confused or put in an awkward position, at which point if you offer them direction, they're much more likely to take that direction as a means of ending their confusion. It was an old hypnotist's trick. At the precise moment a flash of confusion and concern registered on the head juror's face, Veitch hit him with his direction. And just like first impressions, first directions last, and Veitch wanted to embed a strong subconscious one from the offset in the most important person.

It was typical Veitch. He was a wily old operator, and seriously adept at the subtle art of manipulation, both conscious and subconscious. One way or another he was always playing to the jury, even when he was speaking to the judge, arguing the specifics of a legal point, he still retained an acute awareness of how this interaction was coming across to the jury, his "malleable dozen" as he liked to refer to them—the most important people in the room. Sure, the judge liked to think it was him or her, but Veitch knew where the real power lay. To him the jury were passengers on board a boat and he was their mariner at the helm, ferrying them to a predetermined destination of his choosing. The judge and the legal process were the waters to be navigated through en route to this terminal stop, which, if he got his way, the jury would arrive at come hell or high water—Port Guilty Verdict.

Veitch continued for the best part of ten minutes, dipping the jurors' toes into the specifics of this piece of evidence or that, but generally painting broad brushstrokes about the case: Mitch Owen's unquestionable guilt, and the evidential journey the jury would be going on to realize this self-evident truth.

He closed by thanking the jury once more for their service, and reminding them of the importance of their task. Then he smiled. It was a smile that implied the utmost respect, as if he held them in high regard and that not only was their role important, but so too, actually, were each of them as individuals. It was nonsense, of course, but he was a good actor. To his mind, if they had been important, they'd have managed to get out of jury service in the first place. He looked upon a jury in the same way a corrupt politician looked upon the voting public—with utter contempt. But he wanted what only they could give him, and he would do everything in his power to acquire it, either by consent or outright steal it from them.

Veitch walked back to his chair and sat down.

It was an impressive first performance.

Rainbird adjusted one of his trademark thistle-embossed cufflinks, rose to his feet, and entered center stage.

"Your Honor, Judge Jenkins, my colleagues on the prosecuting counsel, Mr. Veitch and Ms. Mears, and to you ladies and gentlemen of the jury, good morning."

Rainbird looked toward the jury.

"Back in the eighteen-hundreds, a prominent American statesman named Daniel Webster remarked that 'Justice is the great interest of mankind on this earth.' History has long demonstrated the vital importance of jury service in attaining true justice. All the way back in 1468, the Chief Justice of England, a man called John Fortescue, observed that 'trial by jury is the most rational and effective method for discovering the truth.' That statement is as true today as it was then. But why? What is it about a trial by jury that is so important in discovering the truth? Why not just leave it up to the police and a judge?"

Rainbird paused, letting the jury ponder the self-evident for a moment.

"Because, ladies and gentlemen, you have no dog in this fight, you have no conflicts of interest or personal animosity toward the accused. You have no pressures of career relating to this case. You have no pressures of reputation relating to this case. You have no pressures of time and budget relating to this case. Others do. Be they arresting officers, prosecuting counsel or other organs of the state and the criminal justice system. Because sadly, and we all know this to be true, the state cannot always be trusted to act impartially. That's not a remotely controversial statement. The founding fathers of America knew this to be true, which is why they included the right of a trial by jury in the Constitution. Were it not true, we would just defer to the say-so of the police department and a state-appointed official, and then leave it at that. It sure would make things quicker and a lot more convenient. Although there would, of course, be a monumental number of miscarriages of justice. Our founding fathers knew better and insisted on trial by jury. To prevent the absolute power of the state from riding roughshod over the individual. In other words, to prevent tyranny—their words—to prevent power being vested in a singular person or organ of the state. Trial by jury is the antithesis of this. You, members of the jury, are together entrusted with this absolute power, and in your hands it resides. Use it wisely."

Rainbird paused and took several steps, letting them mull this over.

"I've been a defense counsel attorney for many a year, and I know the system well. I know from my long experience that one of the greatest pressures of all for those bringing a person to trial, especially the police force, is the pressure to get a result no matter what, and to tie things up quickly and neatly in a simple way before moving on to the next case. But just like the old maxim goes: for every problem there is a solution that is simple, neat—and wrong. All too often this pressure to be quick, leads to a fatal tunnel vision that sees an individual identified as a suspect based on little more than assumption—with a dash of prejudice. When this occurs, there's a frantic search for evidence, not to uncover the truth but to back up the original assumption. Evidence that doesn't fit or even downright contradicts the assumption is simply discarded, or even suppressed. During the course of this trial, I'll be showing you plenty of evidence of this sort, credible evidence that doesn't fit the police's nice simple theory but exonerates my client. Anyone can point a finger and accuse someone of a crime, but does the evidence back up that accusation? That's what matters. Over the course of this trial, you'll see time and time again how the evidence points to the innocence of Mitch Owens, not his guilt. The DNA and forensic analysis which Mr. Veitch was so enthused to extol the virtue of, actually shows, when analyzed in the cold light of day by independent experts with no ax to grind, something quite different. It shows that not only did Mitch Owens not kill Lachlan Denoon, but there's no way he could have done so. Mr. Veltch told you much about the facts he intends to present to you, but there are several things he, crucially, left out, such as the open gate at the rear of the property, a gate that gave access to anyone whatsoever, whether invited to the event or not, onto the property from the beach. And there are sightings from a woman walking a dog along the beach of an individual whose description bears no resemblance to Mitch Owens, none whatsoever, entering the property in this way at a time that ties in perfectly with the estimated hour of Lachlan's murder. The woman on the beach was close by, got a good look at the person entering the property, and yet failed to pick Mitch Owens out of a lineup. Perhaps the prosecution would like to sweep her testimony beneath the carpet, but they can't. We'll have to reach our own conclusion as to why Mr. Veitch failed to mention her during his flamboyant address, but by the end of this trial that should be pretty clear. There are several attendees of the event whom you'll hear from too, people who will cast significant doubt on the prosecution's version of events. Some will even identify others with significant motive and opportunity to kill Lachlan Denoon."

Rainbird cast his gaze toward the public gallery.

"Mr. Veitch stressed giving justice to the family of Lachlan Denoon and to the memory of the man. On that I agree wholeheartedly, and I implore you to do just that. But justice is not served through the incarceration of an innocent man for a crime he didn't commit. Justice is not only denied but compounded by further injustice. And the pain of that also never fades."

For a moment Rainbird locked eyes with Veitch.

"Ladies and gentlemen, it is an immensely important task you have ahead of you, maybe the most important of your lives. People all across the world are watching this trial and a man's life hangs in the balance. The prosecution's case is a flimsy circumstantial house of cards built on an ill-thought-out charge forward to convict. But justice is only ever found with a level head and requires a finding beyond reasonable doubt. A burden the prosecution cannot satisfy. That you will deliver a verdict that represents true justice by exonerating Mitch Owen, I am supremely confident."

With that Rainbird sat down.

The opening round had played out. Punches had been thrown on both sides and the fighters were warmed up, ready for the epic battle ahead. The stakes were high and both men were itching to get back in there and land the fatal blow.

CHAPTER 24

"The state calls Dr Susan Zhang," announced Veitch.

With confident, measured steps a small Asian American woman made her way toward the witness stand. She'd been through this process many times before, revealing unsettling truths hidden within corpses, and exuded the competent air of the eminent physician that she was.

"Please raise your right hand to be sworn in," said the Court Clerk. "Do you swear or affirm that the testimony you are about to give in this matter will be the truth, the whole truth and nothing but the truth, so help you God?"

"Yes, sir, I do."

"Have a seat. Please state for the record your true and correct name."

"My name is Dr Susan Zhang."

As the Court Clerk sat down, Veitch stood up and approached the lectern.

"Thank you, Dr Zhang, and good morning. Would you please tell the jury where you work?"

"I work in the office of the chief medical officer for Suffolk County," she said with precision, each syllable delivered with clinical accuractely.

"And what is the title that you hold there?"

"Director of Forensic Pathology."

"Could you sketch out in broad terms for the jury what it is that you do as a forensic pathologist and could you also include a little about your background?"

"Forensic pathologists investigate deaths. We examine the body of a deceased person to define how that person's death was caused. We also examine factors that may have contributed to their death and help reconstruct the circumstances of their death. My own work deals with death of an unexpected nature. So instead of old age or disease, I specialize in trauma injuries, shootings, drug overdoses, stabbings, road traffic accidents, that sort of thing. Regarding my educational background, in 1982 I received a degree from Harvard University, and subsequently practiced pathology for ten years at Clifton Medical Center in Los Angeles, after which I practiced forensic pathology for the state of New York for a further ten years. I then earned a second degree from Stanford University and took up a teaching position there for seven years, before becoming the Director of Pathology for Suffolk County, a position I have held since. I hold qualifications in anatomic, clinical, chemical and forensic pathology and am currently also the Deputy Chief Medical Examiner for the entire state."

"Please give an estimate as to the number of bodies you have examined over the course of your professional career?"

"I have performed thousands of autopsies."

"You mentioned earlier that your role involves determining the manner in which a person has died."

"Yes, it is a large part of what I do."

"Dr Zhang, I would like to take you back to the evening of Friday, May the twelfth of this year. What were your professional duties that day?"

"I was called to a private residence, a large property in North Haven, where a literary event had been hosted until the discovery of a body in a separate building off the main house. My arrival occurred at 9:55PM, at which time I made my initial assessment of the deceased as well as the surrounding environment."

"Please tell the court what you found at the scene."

"I found the body of a male whom I estimated to be in his early to mid-thirties, face up on the carpet, having been moved by those first on the scene in a failed attempt at resuscitation. Blood covered much of the immediate surroundings, emanating from a puncture wound to the carotid artery on the neck, caused by a sharp or pointed object. Blunt force trauma damage was also present to the back of the head and face. It was the neck wound that proved fatal, the result of the victim losing a significant amount of blood."

"Could you give an opinion as to the sequence of these wounds and any details as to how they might have occurred?"

"It is my professional opinion that the deceased was struck more than once from behind with a blunt object to the rear left-hand side of the skull, with the blows being delivered in a looping or circular manner." The pathologist demonstrated the action, doing so with her left hand. "The fatal blow came next and occurred not with a circular motion but with a thrusting action, sufficient to puncture the neck itself. This likely occurred when the victim was recoiling from the previous blows, and it too was delivered to the left-hand side. Then, when the victim was bleeding to death face up on the ground, he was struck again, probably twice. Damage was present to the nose and to the center and left of the mouth where two front teeth had been dislodged."

"Is there any significance to the injuries having occurred on the left-hand side of the skull and neck, and to the left-hand side of the mouth?"

"There is, and I would like to clarify, when I say the left-hand side of the skull and neck, that is when we are looking at the deceased from the rear. The damage here strongly indicates the blows were delivered from this direction by a left-handed person. As does the damage to the face that was likely struck from the front by a left-handed person."

"A left-handed person?" repeated Veitch, emphasizing the point for the jury's benefit, but also encouraging Dr Zhang to do so too.

"Yes, a left-handed person."

"And this *left-handed person*, would they have got blood on themselves?"

"Almost certainly."

Veitch continued to question the pathologist for another ten minutes, during which he got her to identify the likely murder weapon as Lachlan Denoon's own McIntyre Award for best fiction—the base for the bludgeoning blows to the head and face, and the pointed section for the thrust into the neck—although she did acknowledge a different weapon might have been used. Veitch circled back no less than three times to the point he wanted embedded in the jury's minds—that it was a left-handed person who struck Lachlan Denoon. As he was doing this, Mitch took a sip of water from the glass in front of him with his dominant left hand. With perfect timing, Veitch cast a casual glance his way, as did the jury and then the court at large. All eyes fell upon him. Mitch looked flustered, unsure what to do with the cool glass in his hand. Veitch said nothing, it was more powerful that way right now, but the implication was clear, and he would savor this juicy piece of evidence again later on during the trial to full effect. As Mitch's glass went down in a left hand displaying noticeable tremors, Veitch locked in his winnings.

"No further questions, Your Honor."

"Your witness, Mr. Rainbird," announced Judge Jenkins.

Rainbird rose and entered the arena.

"Good morning, Dr Zhang, and thank you for your time. I'd like to take you back to a comment you made a moment ago, where you discussed the nature of the injuries sustained by Mitch Owens. You said, and I quote: 'The damage here strongly indicates the blows were delivered from this direction by a left-handed person.' By 'strongly indicates' you obviously don't mean it is an absolute certainty that they were the result of a left-handed person, do you?"

"No, I do not."

"So, they could, in fact, have been delivered by a right-handed person?"

"Yes, they could."

"Or an ambidextrous person?"

"Yes, they could."

"Only, you think it's more likely they were delivered by a left-handed person."

"Yes."

"Would you please give the court an example as to how these injuries could have been inflicted by a right-handed person?"

"If the person was already carrying something in their dominant right hand, then they might instinctively use their free non-dominant left hand to attack the person. Or if the object used was picked up from a location nearer to the left hand."

"So, let's break this down: someone walks in carrying, say, their phone, in their right hand, gets into an argument with Lachlan Denoon and attacks him, under those circumstances it would be perfectly normal, in fact, likely, that they'd use their left hand. Isn't that the case?"

"Under those exact circumstances, yes."

"What about someone who, despite being right-handed, had been trained to predominantly use their left hand to attack someone?"

"Err, well, if that were the case then it might happen, but I don't understand why that would be the case?"

"I used to box in my youth, you know the ol' 'sweet science,' amateur stuff, never made it to the pros, alas. But as all good boxing coaches tell their right-handed fighters, it's left hand forward and right hand back, with the left hand leading nearly all attacks and the left jab alone making up somewhere in the region of seventy percent of punches thrown."

Rainbird took up an orthodox boxing stance and began to demonstrate for the court, doing so with no small quantity of theatrical flair, which, going by the looks on the faces of several members of the jury was well received, if slightly less so by Judge Jenkins, who peered at him over the top of his spectacles.

"Probing, moving, monitoring distance, setting up for the less frequently thrown power shots—the right cross or the big left hook... Boom!"

Rainbird threw a looping left hook then stood naturally.

"As I said, a right-handed boxer will, paradoxically, still throw up to seventy percent of their shots with the left jab alone; add in the left hook and left uppercut and it can be closer to eighty percent of attacks thrown with the left hand. It would be perfectly reasonable for such a right-handed person to attack from the left side, wouldn't it?"

"Yes, under those circumstances."

"So, if such a right-handed person had been present in the house when Lachlan Denoon was attacked, then this right-handed person could well have attacked him in this way?" Rainbird looked across to the jury as he spoke. Their interest piqued: *who might that be?*

"It's a possibility, yes."

"So, to clarify: it could have been a right-handed person already holding something in their right hand?"

"Yes."

"It could also have been a right-handed person trained to frequently use their left hand?"

"Yes."

"It could also have been someone who is ambidextrous, correct?"

"Yes."

"Or it could have been a right-handed person who, for whatever reason, picked up the McIntyre Award with their left hand, perhaps because it was nearest to this hand?"

"Yes."

"Dr Zhang, do you know what the percentage of people who are left-handed is?"

"I believe it is around ten percent of the population, but I would have to check the official statistics."

"It is slightly over thirteen percent of the population of the United States. Statistically speaking, given the number of attendees and staff present at the Bucklesby writers retreat, there should have been three lefties present, maybe more. In fact, there should even be at least one sitting among the jury, shouldn't there?"

"Yes."

Rainbird cast his eye over toward the jury. He knew for a fact there were three lefties among them, not one, having favored left-handed jurors during the selection process, closely watching their movements to stack the deck with a much higher percentage than the average population. That way, during deliberations the jury would see how many left handers there were in such a small group and so would give less significance to the fact Mitch was left-handed than they otherwise might.

"No further questions, Your Honor."

CHAPTER 25

"The prosecution calls Detective Vernon Bruce."

Detective Bruce jumped to his feet from the bench in the corridor outside the court, raring to get sworn in and take the stand. He always loved this bit. The attention and the power. Sitting up there, center stage, being asked questions about himself, his job and what he did, while playing up his importance, and doing his best to twist the knife into whoever it was that had been arrested, especially if their guilt was in question. In that sense he was just like Veitch, but unlike Veitch, Detective Bruce was a fool with none of Veitch's cunning, intellect or shrewdness.

After swearing in, Veitch got Detective Bruce to give a brief rundown of his job, which, predictably, he exaggerated the significance of—like he was practically the Chief of Police—before turning to the arrest of Mitch.

"What time did you arrive at the property of Mitch Owens?"

"Approximately 9:00PM."

"Was he at the property?"

"No."

"Was anyone else there?"

"Yes, we were met at the door by his roommate, Mr. Michael Haines, who, upon questioning, volunteered Mitch's movements, where he was heading and when he was planning on arriving there."

"Which was where?"

"A hideout. In a boatyard."

"Where was this boatyard?"

"On the waterfront," said Detective Bruce. "Right on the waterfront, in fact," he added, in a manner that implied he'd deduced something unique and significant.

"Err, yes, indeed," replied Veitch, rapidly coming to the conclusion that Detective Bruce was thicker than two short planks. "But in which locality was this boatyard?"

"Sag Harbor."

"Could you please describe how you apprehended Mitch Owens."

"Well, we was waiting there for him, four of us, in an unmarked car, just up from the boatyard, looking out for him, like, when one of my officers said he thought he might have seen someone down the street. There was a discussion as to whether he was right, and after some further back and forth it was decided we'd go take a look."

"Describe what happened next."

"I led my officers down to the boatyard, we entered the premises and there he was inside a boat house, hiding up in a spider hole. First thing we did was clearly identify ourselves as police officers and that we wanted to question him. But the moment he hears this he bolts, makes a run for it and tries to escape. He then attempts to kick down a door, he was that determined to avoid arrest."

"Hardly the actions of an innocent man."

"You betcha!"

"Objection, Your Honor, speculative," said Rainbird, rising to his feet.

"Sustained. The jury will disregard that last statement from counsel for the prosecution."

"And what happened when you caught up with him?" asked Veitch.

"He was kicking and fighting. We could barely caution him. Lashed out at us too, assaulted us, assaulted one of my officers pretty bad, had to make a claim for medical expenses."

"Objection, Your Honor," said Rainbird, getting to his feet again. "Mitch Owens has not been charged with assaulting a police offer, if this was the case then his charge sheet would reflect it. And yet it does not."

Judge Jenkins turned to Veitch. "Does the state intend to add charges of assaulting a police officer to those the defendant already faces?"

"We do not, Your Honor."

"Then sustained," said the judge. "The jury shall also disregard the assertion that Mitch Owens assaulted a police officer. Proceed, Mr. Veitch."

"Detective, I'd like to take you back to your arrival at the residence of Mitch Owens. Did you enter the property at any stage?"

"Yeah."

"And did you discover anything of evidentiary significance?"

Detective Bruce looked at him confused.

"Did you find any evidence there, Detective?"

"Blood-stained shirt," said Detective Bruce, nodding to himself enthusiastically, his five chins wobbling in the process.

"A blood-stained shirt, you say?"

"Yeah, a blood-stained shirt, soaking in a bucket, trying to remove the stain and wash away all the evidence. Not that it worked."

"And when this shirt was sent away for forensic analysis, what did it show?"

"That it was the blood of Lachlan Denoon."

"Did you discover anything else of significance at the property?"

"Stolen goods—a fountain pen belonging to Lachlan Denoon."

"A pen? Stolen from the scene of the murder?"

"Yeah, pretty worthless as it turns out, probably taken in a panic to make it look like a botched robbery."

"Thank you, officer. No further questions."

Rainbird got up and approached the lectern, fixing Detective Bruce with a penetrating stare.

"Detective Bruce, you and Mitch Owens have history, don't you?"

"Objection," said Veitch, rising from his seat. "Misleading, *have history* implies some previous grudge or some such, not merely a previous arrest in the execution of the officer's duties."

"Yes, it does," said Rainbird. "And that's what I intend to show, a grudge."

"Overruled. But tread carefully Counsel."

"I arrested him," stated Detective Bruce. "When he smashed up a fence at a family home about five years ago."

"Whose family was it?"

"Objection. This has no relevance to the case at hand," said Veitch.

"It has every relevance, Your Honor, which I shall demonstrate, if the prosecution would stop needlessly interrupting."

"Overruled. Mr. Veitch, this is a line of questioning that I am prepared to hear. Detective, please answer the question."

"It was the Hawthorne family."

"That would be Mr. Matthew and Mrs. Roberta Hawthorne?"

"Yeah."

"Had you met them prior to the arrest of Mitch Owens?"

"Erm, well, yes. But I meet a lot of people."

"How, exactly, did you meet?"

Detective Bruce shifted in his seat. "Matthew Hawthorne is on the same bowling team as me."

"That would be the *East Hampton Hurricanes* bowling team, would it not?"

"Yes."

"So, you knew him socially before arresting Mitch Owens for dismantling his fence?"

"Er, yeah, I guess. But not very well."

"Sounds like you're *fencing* around yourself, Detective. How often do the East Hampton Hurricanes meet?"

"Weekly."

"And how long have you been on the East Hampton Hurricanes bowling team?"

Detective Bruce squirmed again. "Ten years."

"So presumably, Mr. Hawthorne must be a new arrival to the team for you to not know him '*very well*'?"

Detective Bruce looked at Veitch but there was nothing he could do.

"Let me be specific, Detective Bruce," said Rainbird. "During your ten years on the bowling team, how long has Matthew Hawthorne also been on the team? A month? Two months? Six months? A year?"

Detective Bruce mumbled. "The whole time."

"I'm sorry Detective, I didn't catch that?"

"The whole time," stated Detective Bruce.

"Let's do some quick mathematics. Fifty-two days a year, multiplied by ten years is five hundred and twenty days. So you would like the court to believe that over the course of a whopping five hundred and twenty social meet ups, you and Matthew Hawthorne never got to know each other very well?"

"Well, I, erm…"

"I put it to you, that you did know him well. In fact, that the two of you are friends."

"I wouldn't say that."

"Your Honor, may I approach the witness?"

"Granted," nodded Judge Jenkins.

Rainbird walked over to Detective Bruce and handed him a photograph. "Detective, do you recognize this photograph?"

"Err, yeah."

"Let the record reflect that Detective Bruce is being shown defense exhibit five, a photograph taken from a social media account dated before the incident with the fence. Detective, would you please describe for the court what the photograph depicts?"

"It's a photo from a fishing trip."

"It is a photo on board a boat during a fishing trip, isn't it?"

"Yes."

"Specifically, it is of two people grinning together, holding a different end of a substantial fish—a striped sea bass, I believe—grasping a beer each in their free hand. Do you recognize these people sharing a cold beer and enjoying a bit of fishing together?"

"Yes."

"Who are they?"

"Matthew Hawthorne and me," mumbled Detective Bruce.

"Louder please, Detective?"

"Matthew Hawthorne and me."

"You both look pretty friendly. Are you seriously suggesting that the two of you weren't friends?"

"We knew each other."

"We know each other too, Detective. How come we've never been fishing together?"

"Objection, Your Honor," interrupted Veitch.

"Sustained."

"Detective, I think your friendship clouded your approach to Mitch Owens during your first arrest of him and it is doing so now. Isn't that true?"

"Nah, that's not true."

"You took an oath to act without fear or favor. You may well deny there was any element of favor involved in your dealings with your social acquaintance Matthew Hawthorne when he accused Mitch Owens of unlawfully dismantling his fence. But at the very least, it doesn't look good. During that investigation, shouldn't you have recused yourself?"

Detective Bruce looked at him with a blank expression.

"*Recused*, stepped aside because of a conflict of interest. But you didn't; you personally took on the case and pursued it regardless, correct?"

"I acted professionally from start to finish."

"During this period, did Mitch Owens make a complaint against you?"

"Objection, Your Honor," stated Veitch. "Detective Bruce has an exemplary record of service. Unsubstantiated complaints are made against public servants all the time, even against judges. But are they upheld? That's what counts and Detective Bruce's record is as clean as the day is long."

"Your Honor, my intention is not to substantiate any previous complaints leveled against Detective Bruce, but rather to show that he and my client have history. Whether upheld or not, a complaint against someone could well prejudice their future dealings with the person who made the complaint."

Judge Jenkins mulled this over.

"Overruled. Please answer the question, Detective."

"Yeah, he said I hit him, but I never did. He made it up, CCRB dismissed it."

"That must have angered you to hear a complaint had been lodged against you by Mitch Owens?'

"Nah, not at all."

"How did you feel?"

"To be honest, I was shocked because I'd never do a thing like that."

"Has anyone else ever made a complaint against you?"

"Objection, Your Honor," said Veitch. "Defense counsel was given leeway in regards to this false accusation as it relates to Mitch Owens and Mitch Owens alone. To ask opened-ended questions in this way is clearly an attempt by defense counsel to try and besmirch the good character of a fine and upstanding officer whose record really does speak for itself."

"Sustained," agreed Judge Jenkins. "Detective Bruce, please disregard the question. Mr. Rainbird, this is an unacceptable line to follow."

Rainbird gave Jenkins a small conciliatory nod, then focused back on Detective Bruce unperturbed.

"I put it to you, Detective Bruce, that you did have a historic animus with Mitch Owens, due in part to the charge against him relating to your friend's property, and in part due to his complaint against you. I put it to you that this ongoing animosity, this bad blood between the two of you, means that you are hardly impartial in this case too. It looked personal then and it's personal now. Isn't that so?"

Detective Bruce shook his head. "Nah."

Rainbird decided to let the jury ponder this one and changed tack.

"Have you ever been accused of planting evidence, Detective?"

"Objection, Your Honor," exclaimed Veitch. "Counsel for the defense is on his own *fishing expedition* with this line of questioning, based on zero evidence and a big helping of wishful thinking. Detective Bruce is an officer of the law and, as stated a moment ago, he has never had a complaint substantiated against him."

"Sustained," announced Judge Jenkins. "The jury will disregard the inference that Detective Bruce has ever planted evidence. Really, Mr. Rainbird, this is wholly unacceptable. Move on and move on now."

"Detective," continued Rainbird, "you stated that Mitch Owens was arrested in, and I quote, a 'hideout,' something you later embellished further to describe as a 'spider hole.' How do you reconcile such misleading rhetoric with the written statement from Stephanie McLean that states clearly that Mitch was there to meet her?"

"Then how come she wasn't there when we arrived?"

"In any meeting, unless all participants get there at the exact same time, then someone has to arrive first and someone last, don't they?"

"I suppose."

"And the fact that Mitch's roommate provided you with a location and expected arrival time, shows that he was neither hiding nor holed up, doesn't it?"

"No."

"People don't have a schedule to go into hiding, they just go into hiding. Given that you were there waiting for him, knowing that he was due, proves that his arrival at the boatyard was something other than hiding, doesn't it?"

"I don't accept that."

"I think you were embellishing when you described it as a hideout, Detective. And for a clear and quite obvious reason, your past history with Mitch Owens, isn't that so?"

"No.'

"And if you're embellishing with this, then we have to ask ourselves, what else? I put it to you, Detective Bruce, that Mitch Owens was not hiding, that soon after his arrival at the boat house he was attacked in the dark by your officers, and that your officers failed to identify themselves. That he was then manhandled and viscously assaulted by you and your men, and that once Mitch Owens knew he was being arrested, he fully complied with the police."

"Nah. That ain't right," said Detective Bruce, shaking his big round bowling ball of a head.

Rainbird gazed over at the jury then turned to Judge Jenkins.

"No further questions, Your Honor."

CHAPTER 26

Georgina stepped into the dim basement of *The Cliffs* and wrinkled her nose with distaste. As the door closed behind her, the rays of sunlight that had streamed inside perished into darkness. Why was it Rainbird always suggested the most god-awful bars imaginable to have a meeting? Outside, the sun shone, trees rustled in the breeze and the world seemed imbued with a boundless optimism, and yet here she was, entering what felt like a group therapy session in a cave for lost and lonely souls. Spread throughout the establishment at little booths or lining the scratched and dented bar, were the patrons, heads down, escaping their lives, if but for a moment, under the allure of booze and fatty food. The décor matched their tired and worn appearance. It too had seen better days and by the looks of it had last been updated around the same time as their wardrobes—the eighties. There was no natural light whatsoever. The carpet was sticky underfoot. The glass on two framed pictures was cracked. On the specials board were two words "big steak." And the place was permeated with the smell of fried food and cheap beer. On the upside, it did look like it was regularly cleaned. Unfortunately, this appeared to be annually.

Lewis Capaldi was belting out a number on the jukebox, so Georgina knew that Rainbird must already be inside. She found him nestled in a booth, swaying to the music, eating a plate of ribs, with the table manners of the famished.

"Why?" asked Georgina.

Rainbird glanced up and smiled. "Why what?" he replied, through a mouthful of greasy meat.

"Why this?" said Georgina, gesturing to the surroundings. "Why that?" said Georgina, gesturing to the food. "Just why, Rainbird? Why?"

He laughed. "Tell me you're kidding, George. The ribs are superb. Shall I get you a plate?"

"I would sooner choke on my own vomit."

"Well, if you put it like that."

"I do."

"Oh, come on. Don't tell me you'd prefer we had our lunch meetings in some trendy bistro or café, where you could grab a latte and an avocado wrap from some handsome hipster with chiseled cheekbones and skinny jeans."

"Now that you mention it."

"What's wrong with Anton?" said Rainbird, gesturing to the barman.

Over at the bar was Anton, sweating in a string undershirt, while coughing hard into his hand, like he was trying to remove something stuck on his lungs.

"Oh, Anton's a catch, alright."

"I could put a word in for you if you like, it's nae bother."

"Perhaps later."

Georgina settled in opposite him. "So what's our next move, boss? Who and what is our priority?"

"We've had a good start to the case but it could definitely go either way. We need to consider who's in the frame, build a picture around every suspect so we can convey this to the jury. We don't need to solve a murder—although, let's face it, that would be mighty helpful—what we've gotta do is cast enough doubt in the jury's mind that they can't convict. And the best way to do that..." Rainbird smiled suggestively.

Georgina smiled back, she knew the drill. "...Is to present them with other suspects."

"Exactly. So let's consider motive. This is our prime concern as all the attendees of the event had opportunity. We're not looking for a dislike of the guy or an annoyance at him, but a clear and present reason to kill him, and in a nasty manner too. Pathologist was quite clear about the way he was dispatched, not one blow but multiple, and the final one to the mouth after he'd been stabbed in the neck—as a malicious goodbye. That brings a whole new level of menace to it."

"Sure does. But who fits the bill?"

"The way I see it, Stamford Williamson, Cathleen Miller and Henry Hunt all have motive."

Rainbird licked the grease off his fingers.

Georgina gave a small grimace as she responded. "For sure."

"By the sounds of it, there was more going on behind the scenes between Lachlan and Stamford than we're currently aware of. We need to keep digging, get more ammunition, but Lachlan suggesting that Magnus drop Stamford, surely that alone hints at something bigger between them."

"Agreed. I don't buy Stamford's claim that the two of them were friends. If he found out Lachlan had spoken to Magnus behind his back and suggested he drop him, Stamford would have seen red. The guy's got a temper all right, I saw it first hand when tailing him. I wouldn't put it past him to attack Lachlan."

"And let's not forget we're talking big money here," said Rainbird. "Although Magnus says he laughed in Lachlan's face—which, I have to say, I'm inclined to believe—had Magnus run with Lachlan's suggestion and dropped Stamford, then Stamford would have lost out big time. We're talking eight figures."

"Which brings us to Cathleen Miller," said Georgina. "It's well known the two couldn't stand each other, and word is that what Lachlan tried to do to Stamford Williamson, he succeeded in doing to Cathleen, albeit with Henry Hunt, not Magnus McLean. That's a pretty serious motive right there."

"Could be," agreed Rainbird, pushing his empty plate away and leaning back with a satisfied smile. "If anyone's got reason for hating Lachlan it's her. Can you imagine it, not only seeing Lachlan's success splashed all over the media, but having to stomach his jibes on TV and in the press about her work too?"

"Then seeing him at social events where she used to be the top dog but is now forgotten."

"It's enough to drive most people crazy. Is she capable of it? I'm not sure, but we need to lay the suggestion with the jury that after Henry Hunt dropped her, she definitely was."

"What about Henry himself?" asked Georgina.

"More complex. All this talk of Lachlan and him disagreeing over contracts is intriguing. The devil will be in the details. There could be a lot more going on, but with NDA's and confidentiality clauses in place, it will be difficult to ascertain what's what. Still, we need to keep digging, and by the sound of it Lachlan did take it upon himself to approach Magnus directly, so it's undeniable he was stepping on Henry's toes."

"Or stamping on them," added Georgina. "What are your thoughts on Magnus?"

"Difficult. Magnus, more than anyone, is capable of such a thing. There've been rumors swirling around for years of business adversaries disappearing, others have been found dead in very questionable circumstances. Strange deaths ruled suicides that seem impossible to carry out alone—tied to a tree and shot in the back of the head, twice. That sort of thing. Nothing has ever stuck, mind you, but I don't doubt he's had people killed before. Magnus is a shrewd man, alright. He's not the sort to do it himself, not out of squeamishness, but savviness. He'd outsource the job. Unless something in the heat of the moment made him snap."

"He could be our man," said Georgina. "The contracts with Lachlan were worth a lot of money. If Lachlan was somehow putting these in jeopardy, well, that's motive. And if he could arrange for the finger to be pointed at Mitch, it'd be sort of an added bonus."

Rainbird nodded, thoughtfully.

"Time is against us. We don't have long. There are some strong witnesses and evidence coming up. We need to know what's going to be said and what their weak points are. We need to speak to someone who isn't afraid to unburden themselves of information and who'll speculate. The person who best matches that description is a gossip and, by all accounts, we know the perfect one."

CHAPTER 27

An abundance of natural light streamed through the skylight, illuminating the interior of the art studio, almost to the point where the stark white plaster walls glowed. A sterile, clinical smell of fresh paint permeated the room, around which hung various works of art. Some were from her renowned bestselling children's books. Others had been created for her own pleasure: landscapes, portraits, a couple of still life. It was obvious to Rainbird and Georgina why she was so popular; why she'd sold so many books and why her success seemed to roll on and on. Her work was exquisite. Together they sauntered around the gallery in the respectful manner you would a church, almost transfixed, as Audrey Adams followed behind in her electric wheelchair.

"Your characters are so timeless," ventured Georgina. "I can see why children, parents and grandparents alike love your work so much. There's such a beautiful childlike quality to them."

"I hope not!" snapped Audrey Adams. "I so dislike that expression 'childlike.' Picasso may have said, 'Every child is an artist. The problem is how to remain an artist once we grow up.' I, on the other hand, say, some of the worst art I've seen has been by children and the sooner they grow up and pursue something they actually have talent for, the better. Just because they enjoy the process of sloshing paint around doesn't mean they're any good at it. Big daubs here, there and everywhere. No understanding of light and shade. Nor any semblance of motor control over what they're doing. And I'm not one to sugar coat it to them either. Try painting, by all means, but don't call it art. Leave that to the trained professionals, that's what I say."

"Well, yes, quite," replied Rainbird, as shocked as Georgina that the fluffy image Audrey Adams portrayed in the media of a grandmotherly author and illustrator who read to children and patiently painted with them bore little resemblance to reality. The PR company that represented her had done an admirable job.

"As you know, we are here as representatives for the defense of Mitch Owens, who is standing trial for the murder of Lachlan Denoon."

"Good luck with that," interrupted Audrey with a snort. "I saw the way Mitch attacked Lachlan at the party. Not that it wasn't justified, mind you. Lachlan was due a punch on the nose to take that overinflated ego down a notch. But Mitch obviously holds more than the average amount of resentment toward Lachlan and had the ability to see it through. Lachlan didn't stand a chance against him."

"I see," Georgina replied.

Audrey smirked, "I'm sorry my observations disappoint you."

"Not at all," Rainbird put in. "We need the hard honest facts if we are to defend our client to the best of our abilities, even if it's not what we'd like to hear."

Audrey nodded, with a hint of disappointment.

"We'd like to ask you about some of the other attendees at the Bucklesby writers retreat, if you don't mind?" Rainbird continued.

Georgina flicked open a notebook, ready to record any details that might be useful.

"Did you have much to do with Henry Hunt, Lachlan Denoon's agent?"

"I did not," Audrey replied haughtily. "His father could be relied upon for some stimulating conversation. He'd been around long enough to have some entertaining stories and opinions. Hunt Junior, though…" Audrey gave a look of distaste. "I have no time for people who've only gotten where they are because of who their parents are. How fortunate for him to have inherited such a well-respected business, but he'll have to prove himself worthy before I will risk wasting my precious time conversing with him."

Georgina hid a smile as she consulted her notebook.

"I see, and what was your impression of Patricia Parry-Jones?" asked Rainbird.

"Ghastly woman. No ability as a writer, just came up with a controversial title and clobbered together a bunch of nasty quotes and anecdotes to support it. Do you know where her inspiration for *Harness the Power of Hate* came from?"

"No," replied Rainbird, intrigued.

"Smash bestseller *Chicken Soup for the Soul.* Told me she found all the fluffy, positive affirmations so nauseating she felt compelled to produce the antidote to it. Give Parry-Jones her due though, she's a shrewd and cunning woman, and no mistake. Cross her at your peril. You should hear the things she claimed to have done to her ex-husband. It made my blood run cold. She doesn't believe in an eye for an eye, she believes in two eyes for an eye, and that's just to get warmed up."

"Do you know if there was any reason her and Lachlan might have fallen out?"

"Can't say I do? But if they did, I wouldn't have wanted to be in his shoes."

"What about the host, Mavis Bucklesby, did you interact much with her?"

"As little as possible. She's a simpleton living off her dead husband's estate. Rustles up a good spread, mind you. Can't fault her there, the woman can cook."

"And Professor Aris, did you speak to him?"

"From time to time, not for any protracted period, mercifully. He's an overrated deluded old fool. It's well known in literary circles that he gets his PhD students to do most of the actual writing and research for him. To say he's got a high opinion of himself is a gross understatement. But compared to Cathleen Miller..." She rolled her eyes. "She wrote two books a lifetime ago and thinks she's Shakespeare—nothing but a sad little blogger woman."

"Is that a picture of Lachlan Denoon?" asked Rainbird, spotting a half-finished canvas in the corner and strolling over for a closer look.

"It was going to be," said Audrey, driving over to join him. "Sadly, I've only ever heard of the value of a painting going up when the actual artist dies, not their subject." She paused for a moment pondering this, then added with an optimistic air. "Still, perhaps it could work the other way around. Do you think it might?"

"Err, well, I mean, sure. Supply and demand do dictate price, after all. And the supply has just ceased—sadly," said Rainbird.

"Yes, I think you're right," said Audrey with a twinkle in her eye. "Might be worth looking into. I could finish it without him, I suppose. I imagine someone would buy it now Handsome's become worm food."

Georgina and Rainbird shared a look. This woman did not mince her words.

"How was it that the two of you worked together?" asked Georgina.

"*Worked* together? I think you'll find only one of us put any actual work in," replied Audrey, throwing Georgina a little scowl. "Maybe sitting down with a vacant expression on your face constitutes work for you, young lady, but it doesn't in my book. I was the one, and the only one, who put work in on that project."

Audrey turned back to Lachlan's portrait, considering his face as though weighing up his worthiness. "To be brutally honest, I don't know how he managed to sit still for long enough to write that book of his. He didn't strike me as the writing type."

Georgina jotted a quick note in her book. "Are you suggesting it was ghost written?"

"No," laughed Audrey, noting with satisfaction the looks of surprised interest on Rainbird and Georgina's faces. "Only that Lachlan was not obviously in possession of the normal characteristics associated with writing a book, patience being the main one."

Audrey gave the painting one last contemptuous glance before turning away.

Rainbird and Georgina exchanged bemused looks.

"So, how did it come about that you painted a portrait of Lachlan Denoon?"

"Urgh, look," she said with a dismissive air, as if the question itself was tedious. "We share the same television production and streaming company. They make the adaptations of my books into kid shows, and their adult division had purchased the rights to Denoon's book. Someone there suggested I paint his picture, as well as a couple of their other big names, to hang on the wall at some banal exhibition for a couple of weeks to promote the company's work. I wasn't too keen and wouldn't have done it but for the fact they offered to remunerate me handsomely for my time, so I thought, *why not?*"

"Magnus McLean owns the television rights to your work as well?" asked Georgina.

"Sure does, they don't call him *The Pie Man* for nothing," replied Audrey. "I've got a lot of time for Magnus. It's been a mutually beneficial relationship over the years. He recognized the commercial potential of my product a long time ago, and I recognized his ability to move it through his streaming service. He does what he's best at, and I do what I'm best at. And he doesn't waste my time on the details."

"Was Lachlan a good subject?" asked Rainbird.

"Too fidgety. Always seemed to have somewhere else he needed to be. Not as good as Stamford. He sat still, although he bored me senseless."

"Stamford Williamson? You've painted him too?" asked Rainbird.

"Follow me," instructed Audrey, hitting the spin control on her joystick, rotating her wheelchair 180 degrees and banging hard into Georgina's shin in the process, shoving her out of the way. She powered forward without apology, making her way to the opposite end of the gallery where a canvas of Stamford Williamson's ugly mug, complete with trademark crooked teeth, was propped up against the wall. "Williamson has his own production company but *MagNet* streams his show too—*Williamson's Will to Survive*. I practically gave up the will to live spending half a day with him," said Audrey, blowing out hard.

"Maybe an idea for a new program," suggested Rainbird. "Win a prize if you manage to stomach an entire day with him."

Audrey smiled, faintly, then gazed at a clock on the wall. "I'm a busy woman," she said, with a smile, pained and patronizing. "So, if you wouldn't mind."

She gestured to the door with a sideways double nod of her head. And with that Rainbird and Georgina took their cue.

CHAPTER 28

- "Please state your full name for the record," announced the Court Clerk to the morning's first witness amidst another packed session.
- "Professor Benjamin Aris."
- As Aris sat down, Veitch approached the lectern.
- "Thank you, Professor Aris. I believe you took part in a police lineup recently in which you were asked to pick out a person you saw running over the sand dunes at the rear of the Bucklesby property, is that correct?"
- "Yes, that's correct."
- "According to the official record of that police lineup, you successfully picked out the accused, Mr. Mitch Owens. How sure are you that it was him you witnessed?"
- "I'm certain."
- "Do you see him here in the courtroom today?"
- "Yes."
- "Please point him out to members of the jury."
- "Your Honor, please let the record reflect that Professor Aris has identified the defendant, Mitch Owens. Professor, in which direction did you see him running, to or from the property?"
- "From the property, toward the beach."
- "What were you doing on the dunes?"
- "Watching the sunset with fellow attendee, Stamford Williamson."
- "Was Mitch Owens aware of your presence? Did he see the two of you on the dunes?"
- "No, definitely not. He was some distance away and running straight ahead, we were off to one side and he didn't look our way, what's more the dune grasses partially concealed our location."
- "Was there anything unusual about the appearance of Mitch Owens?"
- "His shirt had what looked like a blood stain on it."

- "Thank you, Professor Aris. I shall revisit this topic later. For now, no further questions."
- Rainbird stood and made his way to the lectern.
- "Professor Aris, you're quite sure you saw my client, Mitch Owens, running over the sand dunes at the rear of the Bucklesby property?"
- "Yes, quite sure."
- "Isn't it also true, that at the time you claim to have seen him, you were under the influence of alcohol?"
- "Well, I had a brandy."
- "Just one brandy?"
- "No, I'd *had* a couple. I had one brandy in my hand when I saw him."
- "I see. Anything else, a drink over lunch perhaps?'
- "Wine."
- "Single glass?"
- "Two, but—"
- "—Two wines. Two glasses of brandy. Sounds like you'd been drinking rather heavily."
- "Well, heavily for one person is not heavily for another."
- "Do you have a history of alcohol abuse?"
- "I appreciate a brandy and I appreciate a good glass of wine. I hardly think that's abuse."
- "But you would agree that your perception may have been affected by the alcohol you consumed?"
- "It's possible."
- "Your glasses, are they prescription?"
- "Yes."
- "Short or longsightedness?"
- "Short."
- "Shortsightedness being the *inability* to see things clearly unless they are close by?"
- "Yes, that's correct."
- "Were you wearing your glasses on the afternoon in question?"
- "I'd been swimming earlier so—."
- "—A simple yes or no, please."
- "No."

- "So let me get this straight, you can't see things unless they are close, in fact, in order to see things that are *not close* you need to look through clinically calibrated lenses, and yet on the day in question, you weren't looking through your glasses at all but were observing with the naked eye?"
- "Yes."
- "Describe the difference between looking through your glasses and viewing things without them."
- "There is an added clarity with my glasses."
- "So without them things are blurry?"
- "To a degree, but I assure you I can function quite well enough without them."
- "So on the day in question, when you'd had four glasses of alcohol—which you yourself acknowledge could have affected your perception—it stands to reason that your normally blurry vision was even more so, and yet somehow you managed to identify the person running over the dunes with his back turned to you, when they weren't obscured by the grasses. Do I have this correct?"
- "Yes."
- "Presumably whoever that was must have been very nearby?"
- "Nearish."
- "—*ish*? How far?"
- "Hard to say."
- "Let *me* say, that earlier on *you said*, that the person running across the dunes was 'some distance away.' So which is it? Nearish or some distance?"
- "Well, nearish and some distance are both relative terms, but close enough to see."
- "Estimate, how close?"
- "I couldn't say with certainty."
- "Then I shall, for I have measured it. If you were, where your earlier written statement says you were, then the closest you could have been is just under one hundred feet away. Does that sound nearby or even *nearish* to you?"
- The professor hesitated.
- "No."
- "So how on earth can you be certain about the person you saw?'

- "Well, I mean, when Stamford pointed out who it was, I agreed it must have been that man seated over there."
- "No further questions, you honor."

CHAPTER 29

"You've already admitted that you wanted to hurt him," he bellowed, his eyes boring a hole in Mitch. "You've already admitted to a long-standing feud between the two of you, and that you felt deeply aggrieved by his attitude toward you. You've already admitted that you physically assaulted him, and that you found it gratifying. These things you admit as true. Isn't it also true that once you'd left the property, you turned your car around, went back to the house and murdered your former friend? Murdered in cold blood someone you'd known since childhood?"

He'd been grilling him for over thirty minutes. By now Mitch's nerves were frayed and he was struggling to hold it together. His palms were sweaty as was his brow, his heart was thumping in his chest and the color drained from his face. Mitch took a sip of water before answering and tried to compose himself during the brief few seconds this afforded him. It wasn't easy. He was center stage in the middle of the room and everyone present was staring his way. He knew that every word was being filmed, recorded for posterity.

"No, that's not what happened," said Mitch, a quiver detectable in his voice.

"You returned to his room, didn't you?"

"No."

"The forensics are quite clear, your prints were on the door handle. How did they get there if not from you returning to the room?"

"I delivered some fresh towels to the room earlier in the day."

"And yet, there were no fresh towels in the room. Forensics was clear on that too."

"He must have showered."

"With both towels? In the middle of the day? During a professional conference, when he was engaged in other activities. He just thought to himself: *You know what, I'm going to leave what I'm supposed to be doing and go shower, and while I'm at it, I'll make sure I use both new towels?*"

"No. Look, I don't know. Maybe."

"Maybe, hmm, well maybe that's a bald-faced lie. I think you returned to his room with murderous intent. Isn't that so?"

"No, I didn't."

"And when he answered the door, you barged your way in and stabbed poor Lachlan in the neck with the long metallic point at the end of his award. Did he scream when you did it?"

"No."

"He didn't scream?"

"No, I mean, no I didn't do it. No, I didn't stab him. Why are you twisting everything? This is unfair, this isn't what happened!"

Rainbird hit the pause button on the camera. "OK, kid, let's take a break."

Mitch let out a deep exhalation and visibly sagged, resting his head in his hands.

Rainbird had wanted him to crash the car first time around in their mock cross examination in his kitchen. For Mitch to have zero preparation or advice from him before the role play, to see how he'd do under the pressure of Rainbird bullying him. Just like a bootcamp, Rainbird wanted to break him down and then build him up again from the bottom. Georgina was there too, watching the process, and it hadn't been going well. Mitch was easy to get a rise out of, easily flustered and needed some solid coaching to bring him up to par. Luckily, he had two of the very finest to take him through the process.

"Proper preparation prevents poor performance. We're going to drill this until you can answer every question in your sleep, and in a calm and concise manner. Familiarity with this process will breed confidence, and confidence will breed calm in you. When you're calm, you'll be able to perform at your best," said Rainbird.

It was an important job, getting Mitch immersed in the reality of facing hostile questions, so he didn't encounter any surprises on the day itself. Rainbird was a firm believer in the old Samurai philosophy of *cry in training in order to laugh on the battlefield*. And so, he wanted to make the preparation harder than the real thing. Rainbird knew Veitch's normal manner of operating, if he was true to form then he was going to attack Mitch relentlessly, determined to make him angry, so as to undermine and destroy his credibility, to leave him exposed and vulnerable on the stand, and then twist anything Mitch said so as to make him appear guiltier than the devil.

"First thing you've got to remember, Mitch," said Rainbird, taking a slug of his now lukewarm tea. "Is to really listen carefully to the question being asked, and, once it's understood, give a concise answer to that exact question. Never volunteer any information. Don't give the prosecution even a sliver more than you have to. Answer questions with as few words as possible and then stop talking. Don't try to be your own advocate, leave that to me. Obviously, I don't want you to appear stiff or wooden, but the more you talk, the more opportunity you give the prosecution to manipulate what you've said. If you can answer 'yes' or 'no' then do so, and never look my way when answering, it appears untrustworthy."

"Got it, I think," said Mitch, raising his head.

"The lead prosecutor, Mr. Veitch, will try to encourage you to keep talking through the use of uncomfortable silences after you've given your answer. Silences he wants you to fill with words you didn't plan on saying. Don't fall for it. Once you've answered in a clear voice, loud enough for the judge and jury to hear, zip it, and wait respectfully for his next question, even if it seems rude," said Rainbird.

"And admit when you don't know something," added Georgina. "Never guess. Some witnesses think they should have an answer for every question posed by the prosecution. This is nonsense. How can you possibly know each and every fact relating to the case? And so, if you don't know the answer to a question, admit it."

"You'll come across much more honest and trustworthy if you do," said Rainbird. "Making a trustworthy impression on the jury is of supreme importance. If they think you're an honest, fair and decent person, you've taken a great stride in convincing them of your innocence."

"And avoid giving opinions," said Georgina. "Why something may have happened, how long something might have taken, if something could have occurred. We want to deal in facts, not estimates or hearsay."

"On the day, I'll be there to jump in and object to questions during your cross examination," said Rainbird. "When I do, the moment I stand up, you need to stop talking, even if you're mid-sentence. Not a word more out of your mouth, understood?"

Mitch nodded, trying to take it all in.

"At that moment you need to listen carefully to what I say. If, on the other hand, when I am questioning you, the opposing counsel stands up, you must continue answering my question until the judge tells you to stop."

Mitch looked daunted by the task ahead, but that was to be expected. On the stand his credibility was going to be questioned at every turn in the path. It wasn't a friendly chat that lay before him, but a hostile interrogation in the middle of a room filled with no shortage of hostiles baying for his blood, and the consequences couldn't be higher.

Rainbird and Georgina had a lot of work ahead of them. But they'd been through this many times and knew the territory well. Georgina had conducted a thorough review of Mitch's witness "brand" on social media, that potential minefield where Mitch presented himself to the world, and any information or images that could be used by the state to support their case would be ruthlessly exploited or misrepresented. It was an essential step, the last thing Rainbird wanted was to be surprised by any information that Mitch hadn't already volunteered. Luckily, Mitch had come up clean. He didn't post very often and what he did was pretty banal, some sailing photos, pictures of him playing the guitar or sharing a drink with friends.

Georgina had already gone over with Mitch the likely evidence he'd be shown. She'd also brought him up to speed on procedural rules of the court, and Rainbird had been through the overall strategy for the case. Today was about how to answer, what to answer, and how to interact with opposing counsel when on the stand. Every defense counsel did this, to one extent or another, but Rainbird took it a step further, with his own twist on proceedings. When Rainbird was growing up, his uncle not only taught him to sell goods at their market stall, but also how to box. He taught him that one of the best ways to defend against a given attack was to become adept at that very attack, to have an intimate knowledge of the processes involved in employing it. And so, what Rainbird did with his clients was not only get them to role play being on the stand, but to switch sides and play the prosecution lawyer too, with Georgina as defendant on a fictitious charge. He would teach them the tricks of using leading questions to plant the suggestion that the witness was mistaken, unreliable, forgetful, or, best of all, had a malicious motivation behind their testimony: *While the altercation occurred, you were on the other side of the room with many people in between you, weren't you? It was very noisy at the time of the discussion, wasn't it? You'd been drinking on the night in question, hadn't you? You're still angry that your former partner left you, aren't you?* Such leading questions put doubt in the jury's mind as to the witness's credibility, even if they didn't believe they were outright lying.

To some, it sounded strange that Rainbird got his client to swap roles, but the results were undeniable. It put them at ease and took the pressure off. And the more they did it, the more they were able to recognize the tactics of the opposing side and counter them. The military did it all the time, running war game exercises playing the part of their enemy, not only to test their own defenses but to get to know their enemy better.

Mitch could only be called as a witness after the prosecution had concluded their case against him, and Rainbird got his turn to call witnesses favorable to his case. There was no room for error and they needed to drill it multiple times. If Mitch stumbled on the day, it could mean the difference between life in a cage and freedom with the girl he loved.

"Go get yourself some fresh air, Mitch. We'll get back to it in a bit," said Rainbird.

Mitch needed no further encouragement and went outside to fill his lungs with salty sea breeze.

Georgina turned to Rainbird. "How do you think he's doing?"

"Average, but he'll need to be good—better than good. Veitch is a savage cross examiner, sadistic even, and will delight in taking Mitch apart, holding his feet to the flames until he squeals."

Georgina nodded.

It was going to be a long day. They both wished they could spend all weekend prepping Mitch but there were other things to do.

CHAPTER 30

The majority of the students sat listening with rapt attention to the woman in the knitted sweater at the front of the classroom, doling out advice to the eager hopefuls in the manner of a venerable and insightful oracle, while a couple of others gazed out the window, mentally doing their grocery shopping or meeting up with their next hot date.

Cathleen Miller had been a creative writing teacher running evening classes after her own writing career headed south and she had to make ends meet, by teaching instead of doing. If she seemed bitter about it, she was.

"So remember: *Keep my attention*. And *make me care*. For me, those are the two biggest rules of creative writing, and I implore you to abide by them in your own work. All too often, people forget to do these two simple things. Writing is a simple process complicated by fools. The other day I started reading a new book, popular young author—I won't mention his name—but I'm afraid to say that after little more than a chapter I had to give up. Why? Because I simply didn't care. So make me care. Your submissions are due Tuesday next week. Good writing is hard to define, although easy to recognize. Please do delight me."

The clock struck the hour and that was the end of the class.

As the students began packing up notepads and laptops into their bags, Rainbird and Georgina headed to the front of the room.

"Thank you for letting us sit in on your lesson," said Rainbird.

"You're most welcome," replied Cathleen. "I hope you enjoyed it."

"Very much so," said Rainbird. "It was very insightful."

"I'm pleased you thought so," said Cathleen. "Ever penned anything yourself?"

"*Some books are lies frae end to end. And some great lies were never penn'd.*"

"The great Robbie Burns!"

"I was practically raised on his work—my mother's doing, you know."

"She was clearly a woman of fine taste."

"That she was. She loved poetry, even wrote a bit. Although she was always reluctant to share her work with anyone."

"A lot of people are, and that's fine, not everyone has the desire to see their writing regurgitated by the cold, standardized mass production of a printing press, or even to have it read by anyone at all. Some of the finest work I've ever read has barely been seen. And some of the worst has been consumed by countless millions. It's a great shame, but sadly there really is no accounting for taste, and going by the current crop of bestsellers, a lot of people don't have any. Not that I pay attention to that sort of thing, of course."

"Of course," concurred Rainbird.

"Don't get me wrong, there's still some fine work out there, but others have floated to the top, much like the scum they resemble. But it won't endure, that's the true test, will their work be remembered twenty years from now or is it just a flavor of the month? Although I imagine you didn't reach out to me to discuss literature."

"Not entirely, but given the nature of the event that both you and my client attended, albeit in very different capacities, literature does come into it."

Cathleen pursed her lips and gave a little nod.

"I'd like to ask you about your time at the Bucklesby writers retreat, whether you saw or heard anything to indicate that Mitch Owens had anything to do with the death of Lachlan Denoon," said Rainbird.

"Well, he did threaten to kill him, no doubt about that. Although whether that was empty rhetoric or not, I don't know. I saw the two of them argue, and then there was the physical assault, when the waiter, your client, hit Lachlan in the face, but my understanding is that your man was thoroughly provoked. And Lachlan was quite detestable. If he hadn't been hit by your client, I imagine it was only a matter of time before someone physically took him to task. As for the murder itself, I'm afraid I wasn't in the vicinity when the police say it occurred, although I did witness its aftermath: everyone running around in panic, Mavis screaming the house down and Stamford nearly passing out."

"How would you describe your relationship with the deceased?" asked Georgina.

"I had the same respect for him as a dog does for a fire hydrant."

"Have you read Lachlan's debut work?" asked Rainbird.

"I haven't, and I've no intention either. If his personality is indicative of the quality of his writing, and I can't believe it's not, then frankly, I'd be wasting my time."

"But it did receive many favorable reviews," said Rainbird. "I read one the other day, quite poetic I thought, it said, 'His words swim on the page through an ocean of mystery.'"

Cathleen scoffed. "You can buy any review you want these days, the honor has long since gone out of the system. That his book received glowing reviews is a sad reflection of the sorry state of literary criticism today. I doubt very much that it lives up to the hype."

"Had the two of you met before the Bucklesby event?" asked Georgina.

"Our paths had crossed."

"How?"

Cathleen bit her nail. "Look, it's no secret, we used to share the same representation, the Henry G. Hunt Literary Agency. Only Lachlan was instrumental in having me dropped from their ranks, along with my entire back catalog—leaving me with no representation to get my previous work republished in the lucrative new audio or e-book markets. Not that I'm bitter so much about that, I'm a big believer in the charm and character of an actual physical book, and more so again in handwritten work—poems, notes and such—but the way in which it all went down was quite reprehensible."

"What did Lachlan do to have you dropped from the agency?" asked Rainbird.

"He refused to sign unless they got rid of me first."

"Why?"

"This sounds ridiculous, and I feel ridiculous even saying it, but apparently, and I have this on good authority, Lachlan read about some rock band or other from the mid-nineties who refused to sign a record deal unless the record company first dropped several acts from their roster that the band didn't like. Lachlan being the prima donna that he was, thought this was very rock and roll, and so insisted on the same at the Hunt agency. Henry bowed to this pressure, showed no character whatsoever and cast me aside, one of his father's founding authors, someone who made the agency what it is today."

"He just thought it would be fun to emulate the cocksure actions of a rock band?"

"Yes. He never admitted this was his inspiration, but it was, and he was cunning enough to realize the story of him insisting the agency get rid of me would produce lots of publicity for him."

"Was there no previous animosity between the two of you before this?"

"None. I wasn't even aware of him. Then all of a sudden, he burst onto the scene, got me dropped from my own agency, then used every opportunity to publicly criticize me. It was all contrived. Lachlan knew a rivalry was publicity gold, just like it had been during his reality TV days, where he did exactly the same thing—singled out a suitable candidate to feud with, then relentlessly attacked them to manufacture a conflict. And conflict is drama, after all—something I'm always telling my students. It guaranteed him media coverage off my credibility. Although a tactical stunt, I suspect it was fueled by petty jealousy too. I might not chase the big bucks like others, but my name is very much respected in the literary world—after all, you don't get a glowing endorsement from the likes of Roger Bucklesby for nothing. I imagine he wanted a bit of that for himself through association, but I wanted no part of his manufactured rivalry. It was all one way, him attacking me."

"Did the publicity help you?"

"Not a bit. In fact, quite the opposite. I became a laughingstock. Many of Lachlan's followers parroted his offensive remarks about me being a 'has been' and amplified them on social media, producing some very hateful memes at my expense."

Cathleen paused with hurt in her eyes, the wounds still raw.

"Why don't you ask me what you must be wondering?" she said. "Am I pleased he's dead? Yes, actually I am. I never used to hate anyone, but after what he did to me, I am now comfortable in saying that, yes, I did hate Lachlan Denoon. It's taken me a while to accept that realization, but there it is. That being the case, you must also be wondering whether I had something to do with his death."

Rainbird raised an inquisitive eyebrow.

"The answer is, I had nothing to do with his death. But that he's dead, I'm pleased."

"I appreciate your candor," said Rainbird.

"There's no point in me pretending otherwise, if I did, I imagine you wouldn't believe me anyway. I've had counseling, of sorts, regarding all this, and am finally comfortable admitting my feelings."

"Do you feel the same animosity toward Henry Hunt as you did toward Lachlan?" asked Georgina.

Cathleen took a deep breath. "I used to, although it is now replaced by a certain feeling of satisfaction. Sun Tzu once said, 'If you wait by the river long enough, the bodies of your enemies will float by.' Lachlan is no more and, at a stroke, Henry has lost his biggest client. Although to be fair, that was probably going to happen even if Lachlan hadn't been murdered."

"What do you mean?" asked Georgina.

"After everything Henry did to me at Lachlan's behest, it seems Lachlan was about to do much the same to Henry himself—drop him and sign with a different agency."

"Really? Why?"

"Oh, I'm not sure of the specifics, you'd have to ask Henry."

"Could you tell us where you heard this?"

"I wouldn't feel comfortable betraying a confidence."

Cathleen began shuffling her papers together on the desk and putting them into a folder. She glanced at her watch.

"I have to meet a friend in a moment, I'm afraid."

"Of course," said Rainbird. "Thank you for your time."

As Rainbird and Georgina left the adult learning center and stepped into the darkness of the late evening, the passenger door of a car parked across the street swung open and a woman got out. She closed the door behind her and, as she began to cross the street, stepped into the glow of a light pole and her face became apparent—Patricia Parry-Jones. The car that had dropped her off pulled away. A moment later another car—a blue Ford station wagon—parked further down the street turned its lights on and pulled off after the first, at speed. Patricia didn't notice a thing, but Georgina and Rainbird spotted it. Georgina scrambled to get the license, but in the darkness she only got the last three numbers, punching them into her phone. Patricia walked straight past them both, right into Cathleen's classroom, just as Rainbird's cell phone rang.

He didn't recognize the number.

"Alfie Rainbird," he said, picking up the call.

There was a protracted pause as Rainbird listened intently.

"Is that right?" he finally said. "And when did this occur?"

Georgina could recognize concern in Rainbird's voice.

"OK," he said. "I'll file an appeal in the morning."

He hung up.

"Problem?" asked Georgina.

"I'm afraid so, and a serious one. Mitch's bail has been revoked; he's back in prison."

"What? How? What did he do?"

"Broke the terms of his bail agreement by meeting up with Magnus, apparently."

"Or Magnus met up with him."

"Exactly," said Rainbird. "Sounds like a classic Magnus stitch up to me. I've got to deal with this and see what, if anything, can be done. Please meet Henry Hunt in the morning solo, see what truth there is to the rumor Lachlan and Henry were about to go through a very public and messy divorce. We'll reconvene afterward."

As the two of them headed to Rainbird's Avanti, an uneasy feeling came over him. He knew how Mitch must be feeling right now, the aloneness, the despair, but mostly the fear. It was justifiable. The dangers that lay ahead for Mitch were real. Prison is never safe. It is a dangerous world filled with dangerous people and Mitch had made an enemy of a man connected with the worst of them. Was this all part of Magnus's plan? To have Mitch placed in harm's way where he could pull the trigger with plausible deniability. The stakes were high and Rainbird had to act fast.

CHAPTER 31

A clenched fist dug deep into his cheekbone, shaking his brain and sending him across the shower room in a semi-conscious stagger, before he slipped on the wet surface and hit the floor, hard. A swarm of thugs were on him, attacking like a pack of wolves, practically panting with excitement as they rained in punches and kicks from all angles. He curled up into a ball in a desperate bid to avoid the onslaught, transferring the blows from his face to his kidneys and skull.

In desperation he cried for help, his voice drowned out by the excited frenzy of laughs, whoops and jeers from his attackers.

For them it was sadistic gratification, sport even; for Mitch it was life and death.

"That's enough! Back off!" yelled a new voice, authoritative and uncompromising, cutting through Mitch's torment.

The blows ceased and the pack scattered. Mitch lay bleeding and delirious, a world of pain raging in his bruised and battered head, as a prison guard leaned in and reached a hand out toward him. Mitch looked up at the man with relief and gratitude in his eyes, but then the guard's face hardened and his hand secured a grip around Mitch's throat. He began to squeeze. Tighter and tighter. Compressing Mitch's windpipe and lifting him off the ground as Mitch's eyes widened in fear.

"Keep your mouth shut about the boats," whispered the guard, inches from Mitch's face. "And that includes ratting to your lady friend—you tell her nothing, got it?"

An obedient nod from Mitch and the guard released his grip.

CHAPTER 32

Rainbird's Avanti eased into a parking space. As he stepped from the warm plush comfort of his car onto the cold concrete, it all came flooding back. The tall metal fencing topped with coils of razor wire. The abrupt barking of nearby guard dogs. The watch towers with their sentries poised ready to pump a round into would-be escapees. The preponderance of concrete and the near total eradication of anything natural, even grass. The dark walls of the prison edifice, where anguish seemed built into the very brickwork. Even the air seemed heavy, as if imbued with the combined burden of ruptured dreams and wasted lives.

Rainbird had been in and out of detention facilities like this over the years during his own journey from captivity to freedom, as an inmate, but also after winning his liberty when acting as a lifeline to those he represented, a beacon of hope during their darkest hours. Still, this familiarity did nothing to alter the surge of gut-clenching nausea he got every time he stood outside such a place.

Rainbird hid it well, but all those years of incarceration had left their mark on him. To the casual observer he seemed unaffected as he approached the prison gates, and for the most part, he managed to suppress his emotions. But scars run deep. He used his experience of imprisonment as a driving force, to utilize his talent to win for his clients the freedom he once so desperately needed for himself.

Rainbird strolled toward the entry door and by the time his finger pressed the buzzer, and buzzer permitted entry, he was ready for battle. The heavy metal door clicked open. He pushed through and entered a room thick with the scent of stale body odor and men's feet. A stick-thin guard in a regulation blue uniform, wearing a look of unmitigated contempt, stood by an airport-style security scanner.

"Identify yourself." He spat the words through teeth that barely opened as they worked away at an unseen piece of gum in his mouth, letting out unpleasant squelching noises as his jaw flexed with every exaggerated chew.

"Alfie Rainbird. Attorney for Mitch Owens."

"All personal effects in the box," the man barked.

Rainbird raised an eyebrow with restrained disquiet. He had a lax respect for authority at the best of times and took an instant dislike to the little cretin in front of him, but he was here for Mitch, not an argument with an underling, and so bit his tongue.

"Arms up," announced the guard as he ushered Rainbird toward the scanner.

He stepped to the other side without incident.

"Pick up your effects and put everything in the locker except for writing material and legal documents," ordered the guard with a pointed finger at a bank of dented lockers.

Rainbird did as instructed.

Another guard approached him now, a big man, strong and muscular.

"Follow me," said the guard, in a professional authoritative tone, as he led Rainbird deeper inside the bowels of the prison. A bewildering series of security barriers came and went until Rainbird found himself standing at an official check-in area where an array of documentation had to be signed. From here he was escorted down a long, cold corridor permeated with a chilling stillness, his footsteps echoing like a mournful lament for the condemned who'd trodden this path before him, until, finally, he was led to a gray waiting room with a cheap laminate table and two black scuff-marked plastic chairs.

It was a place where hope came to die.

Only not today.

Not if Rainbird had anything to do with it.

"Your client will join you in a moment," announced the guard, turning and leaving Rainbird alone with his thoughts in the windowless room.

Rainbird took a seat and looked around. Nothing of visual interest presented itself in the sterile room, so he turned his mind inward, deep into his inner recess of being, not cognitive thought or even memory, but feeling, and Rainbird never tried to think a feeling. The feeling this place invoked was nausea. For a moment he sat there and just marinated in it, acquainting himself with the sensation. It wasn't that he wanted to relish something negative, quite the opposite; he wanted to ground himself in the reality of whatever he felt, accepting it in its current form, then with conscious effort employ the power of his mind to shape and transform it into something else—something positive. Rainbird had done this all his life and had seen the results of the power of his mind and its ability to shape not only his current feelings but also future events. He knew through painful lived experience, that although we do not control all of the events in our lives, we do control the way we react to them. Through directed thought, Rainbird had learned to train his brain in the way it responded. Without this basic discipline he had seen many others fall apart.

On the very first day of Rainbird's incarceration, he was thrown into a 6'x10' cell with a concrete bed and toilet, to share with a seemingly pleasant, although entirely silent, Triad hitman. For the best part of two years, the two of them were locked in that cramped little cell for 23 hours a day, with one hour permitted to shower and make a phone call. Eventually, Rainbird's world broadened to include an additional hour of outside time and the notorious "day room," a depressing little area with cold steel seating and tables, all bolted to the floor. On his first visit, he saw a man beaten nearly to death with a padlock in a sock.

"You're not in Kansas anymore," he thought to himself as the man was carried away, limp and unconscious, to the infirmary.

Two years into his sentence, Rainbird was transferred from Allenwood in Pennsylvania out to the notorious Attica Correctional Facility in New York, a popular dumping ground for inmates, like Rainbird, displaying disciplinary problems at other facilities. It was a place that had hit the headlines in the seventies following the infamous Attica Uprising when 43 men were killed in a botched raid to end the siege.

Even after several years inside Attica, Rainbird could still not quite believe that this was his reality and that it was actually happening to him. Regularly he would have lucid moments where he would sort of awaken to realize that he was, in actual fact, living in a box. *How strange life is*, he would think to himself. But Rainbird's world really opened up when he got access to Attica's prison library and started his long and arduous study of the law. If there was one thing he had on his hands, it was time, and he directed this to his study. In the law he found hope, and soon he would pass this hope to others through his ever-increasing knowledge of the legal world.

The door burst open and in came a guard with a shackled Mitch.

"You got ten minutes," announced the guard, who turned and left.

Mitch was in a terrible state, with a swollen bottom lip and two nasty protrusions that stuck out from his forehead like hard boiled eggs. On the back of his head was a gash where thick black stitches had been sewn, not neat and precise cosmetic stitches to prevent a scar, but the sort of haphazard needle work rendered solely to close an opening, and appearances be damned.

"Mr. Rainbird, thank God you came. Please, I beg you, you've gotta get me outta here."

"Come, take a seat," said Rainbird, ushering Mitch to a chair. "OK, Mitch, let's start at the beginning. What happened with Magnus? And then tell me what happened in here."

Mitch sat down and recalled the incident for Rainbird, how he'd received a text from Stephanie's phone asking him to meet her urgently at *Clam Palace,* a restaurant owned by her father at the marina. Only when he arrived, she was nowhere to be seen, but there was Magnus waiting to greet him with a smile. And wouldn't you know it, one of Detective Bruce's minions just happened to be dining in the vicinity, tucking into a lobster thermidor that was way beyond the proviso of his salary. Mitch was arrested for breaching his bail conditions and back behind bars he went. He'd tried to call Stephanie after his arrest from the prison payphone, but her cell phone was no longer working, presumably ditched after Magnus had set him up with it, and Mitch's own cell had somehow "gone missing" during the arrest. When it came to the attack, Mitch was less forthcoming, he told Rainbird how it went down but left out the bit about the warning from the guard at the end. The way Mitch described it, the attack had been random, not targeted, and there was no mention of who was behind it.

"Please, Mr. Rainbird," said Mitch, his voice fear-laced and breaking. "You've got to help me, there's no way I'm gonna survive on the inside."

There was desperation in his voice, but there was no point Rainbird trying to sugar coat it by downplaying the all-too-obvious predicament he faced. Truth is, nowhere in prison is entirely safe, not even solitary. Sure, Rainbird might be able to get Mitch put into isolation for his own safety, but when you're locked up alone twenty-four hours a day, your mind and spirit deteriorate quicker than the Road Runner driving a dragster. Rainbird had seen it himself. He'd already run a bail appeal but it had been rejected. Mitch would be remanded in custody until the end of the trial.

"I'll do everything in my power to win your case, Mitch," said Rainbird. "But you have to understand, the judge has made clear he will not entertain you being let out during the trial. Our only hope is being found not guilty."

Mitch looked crestfallen.

"How am I going to get through this until then? I'm in hell here, it's driving me crazy. It's not just the attack, it's everything about this place."

Rainbird paused before speaking, he wasn't sure Mitch was ready for the hard truths of incarceration, but felt he had little choice but to tell him.

"Life is about choices, Mitch; you have to *choose* to be strong, to suck it up and cope. I need you to do that, both for me, as your attorney, for Stephanie, as the love of your life, and for yourself, as the person we're both fighting for. You need to be focused on a daily basis despite the terrible, depressing gloom of your present circumstances, and that can only come through disciplined choice. The key is to stick to a tightly defined daily routine and rhythm. Mine encompassed exercise, reading, writing, planning, meditation, brain training, sleeping and posture work— to overcome being bent over in bed for twenty plus hours a day as the only place to sit. It becomes your day, every day, and although life that way is terribly monotonous, it is bearable. I used to do three hours of exercise a day, an hour and a half of meditation and brain training, I would sit bolt upright for no less than 90 minutes to stop my back bending, wrote letters and read over 150 books every year. Had I not done this, had I given in, I wouldn't be here today. You can get through this, Mitch, but you have to choose to. I'm in your corner, as is Stephanie. Don't let her down. She needs you to toughen up, to be positive, both in court and in here."

It was the sort of pep talk Mitch needed.

Rainbird could see Mitch's own posture morph in front of him from slumped to upright, changing in unison with his mindset from defeatist to determined.

"I won't let you or Steph down," he said with conviction.

"That's the spirit, Mitch. We can win this case, and I intend to do so."

"What if we lose?"

"Even in cases that are lost, there are appeals. Hope is never extinguished until we give up the fight. And I never give up."

It wasn't a false promise. Rainbird did intend to win, but could he really do it?

The assault spelled bad news for Mitch's comfort and wellbeing, but it provided an unexpected advantage to Rainbird. With Mitch's injuries, Rainbird would now be able to get the trial adjourned until Mitch made a full recovery. Gifting Rainbird and Georgina a brief window to dig deeper behind the scenes of what actually occurred that fateful night at the Bucklesby mansion. But they'd have to act fast, the window was closing with every second spent. Now, more than ever, they needed to discover who really murdered Lachlan Denoon and why.

CHAPTER 33

It was hard to make out the specifics of the muffled conversation on the other side of the door, but it was clear that a heated discussion was taking place. Georgina had arrived ten minutes early at Henry Hunt's place and was shown by his housekeeper through to the office, where she waited while Henry conducted a meeting out of sight in the smaller room adjacent. Georgina was on her fourth cup of water from the office cooler, served in those annoying paper cones that hold little more than a mouthful of refreshment. Still, it was ice cold, merciful given the soaring temperature today, which had people seeking shade or air-conditioning. There was no aircon in Henry's office. The only respite came from a solitary antique fan, oscillating on top of a metal filing cabinet next to Henry's desk. She took another sip from the tiny cone in her hand and pondered the filing cabinet. It was a tempting proposition. There it stood, not fifteen feet away. Maybe it was unlocked and contained important information. She could feel its draw, tempting her to take a furtive glance inside at the specifics of the contract between Lachlan Denoon and Henry Hunt. Maybe something else was hidden within, information that might shed light on the true nature of the relationship between the two of them, or could confirm Cathleen Miller's assertion that Henry and Lachlan were about to split.

Georgina slowly moved toward it, a measured step at a time, followed by a pause between steps as she glanced over at the side room door. Her heart pounded as she inched closer. A final step and she reached the cabinet. She took a deep breath and reached out, grasping the cool metal handle in her clammy palm.

The side room door burst open.

Out strode Henry Hunt followed by none other than Patricia Parry-Jones, a smug and satisfied look plastered across her face.

Henry whipped his neck around, spotting Georgina out the corner of his eye, as a concerned look spread across his face at seeing her beside his desk.

"It's sooo hot," said Georgina, breathing hard through pursed lips as she bathed her face in the breeze of the fan.

Henry's concern melted.

He smiled.

She'd got away with it.

"If you're considering signing with him, don't," said Patricia to Georgina. "His agency is a sinking ship. And the sooner it goes under the better. He had one good client and look what happened to him."

Patricia trotted out of the office.

"Sorry about that," said Henry.

"Not at all," said Georgina, her heart still racing. "Is Patricia Parry-Jones a client?"

"No, it seems I was just her latest project in hate, supposedly out of respect for her new best friend Cathleen Miller. She's been stringing me along for the last few weeks, pretending she was going to sign with the agency for her new self-help book: *Hate and Grow Rich*. We were supposed to sign the contract today, she even got her fancy fountain pen out and then, just at the last minute, turned to me and announced in that sanctimonious voice of hers, that she would rather sign away her first-born child than ever put pen to paper on a contract with me. It was all very contrived; I dare say it will end up as an embellished revenge anecdote in the book. She's a bitch."

Henry scrunched up the contract in his hand and threw it into a waste paper basket, landing on top of a thick dog-eared manuscript.

"What was it you wanted to discuss with me?"

"I spoke with someone who said Lachlan Denoon was planning to drop you as an agent. Is there any truth in that? Were you about to go your separate ways?"

"Total nonsense. Whoever said that is spreading a malicious falsehood. Lachlan and I were good friends," said Henry, looking flustered, a crack appearing in his normally composed demeanor. "Look, who else, other than me, could be relied on to deal with all his obsessive fans, infatuated crazies like Rosina Pavlova. You see, it's not just books and contracts with me. There's plenty that goes on behind the scenes too. No other agent would have done that sort of thing for him."

"Rosina Pavlova? The woman who threw the red dye on Mitch? What were your dealings with her?"

"I assumed you already knew," said Henry with a look of surprise. "I did mention her presence to the police officer in charge of the case—Detective Bruce, I believe—but he assured me it was unimportant. I suppose they don't have to disclose everything to the defense. Is that how it works?"

"I'm sorry," said Georgina, taken aback. "Are you saying there was someone else present at the Bucklesby residence on the day of the murder, someone unaccounted for by the official list of attendees or staff members?"

"Well, yes. Although not for long. She departed long before this whole foul business occurred. She couldn't have had anything to do with it, and I know as much because I was the one who personally escorted her off the premises"

"What was she doing there?"

"How can I put this," said Henry, choosing his words carefully. "She attempted to have a *liaison* with Lachlan."

"You're telling me, that a person who was obsessed with the deceased sexually propositioned him at the scene of the crime on the day he was murdered?"

"Look, it's a delicate situation all round, and I did warn Lachlan about this, tried to guide him to act in accordance with what was clearly his best commercial interest, you know. But he was an impulsive character, and, I'm afraid to say that just recently, he'd indulged in, shall we say, a brief dalliance with Miss Pavlova. A single encounter, mind you, it wasn't a relationship. She caught him at a low ebb and I'm afraid he let himself down. But there was nothing that occurred on the night of his murder."

"This single encounter, when and how did it occur?"

"I don't know the exact ins and outs of the situation. But Lachlan had a motor yacht, *Billy Doo*—nothing flashy, quite understated, an old wooden vessel originally from Sierra Leone—that he'd been renovating as a hobby down at the marina. *Billy Doo* served as his writing office, he'd go down there and putter about, a bit of sanding, a lick of paint, tinkering with the engine, that sort of thing, but mostly he'd get his head down and put pen to paper. He was very productive there, it's a good secluded spot, a nice grounded place with good ordinary people, very different from the more glamourous side of life in these parts."

Henry paused, contemplating how best to impart the next bit.

"Anyway, one day when down at the marina, he climbed on board, and there she was, waiting for him in one of the cabins, sprawled across the bed using nothing but a signed copy of Lachlan's debut bestseller to preserve her modesty."

"Classy lady," smiled Georgina.

"As I say, I don't know all the details, but Lachlan did confide in me that, well, one thing led to another and, I think you get the picture."

Georgina nodded.

"She's a fair-looking woman, Rosina Pavlova," said Henry. "I'm afraid Lachlan was seduced that day."

"And presumably this only served to exacerbate an already tricky situation. I mean, if she was infatuated before…"

"It made things a hundred-fold worse."

"And with regards to the party. This was a strict invitation-only event. How did she manage to get in?"

"I believe she accessed the property from the beachfront, snuck in with, well, the idea of propositioning Lachlan again, this time in his room."

"And the police thought this wasn't important?" asked Georgina, incredulous.

"I did follow up with Detective Bruce, called him after the event, and he assured me that they'd looked into it and had eliminated Miss Pavlova from their inquiries. I have to say, I did question that at first, I mean, she was obsessed with him, no question about that, sent photos to the agency to pass onto Lachlan, all X-rated stuff, even sent items of clothing, undergarments, of the worn variety."

"Did you retain any of them?" asked Georgina.

"Certainly not!" exclaimed Henry, looking flustered again.

"I meant for evidential purposes?"

"Oh, I see," he said. "Tossed them all, didn't show or mention them to Lachlan either. He worked best with a clear head. The demon of distraction is an author's worst enemy, you know."

"Talk me through your encounter with Rosina Pavlova at the writers retreat," said Georgina.

"She arrived around midday, about an hour before Lachlan was assaulted by the server, by your client, this Mitch Owens man, at least that's when Lachlan and I discovered her. We walked in on her, lying in the middle of his bed in a state of undress, no book to cover her up this time, I'm afraid. I shooed Lachlan straight out of the room, instructed her to get dressed immediately and personally escorted her outside, back onto the dunes from whence she came."

"Did anyone witness this or her presence in the house other than you and Lachlan?"

"Hard to say for sure. Nobody saw me escort her out, I know that as they were all on the other side of the house at the time, participating in this year's preordained meaningless group discussion: *Metaphysical ethics vs political aesthetics in the collective works of Barbara Cartland*, or something like that, I can't quite remember, but regardless, it was tedious," said Henry, rolling his eyes. "Lachlan made his excuses and left. I did the same moments later and caught up with him on his way to his accommodation."

"So, it is *possible* someone saw her come in earlier?" said Georgina.

"Possible," conceded Henry. "Although not probable. If they had, I would have expected them to question her presence in the house or at least bring it to the attention of the group or Mavis Bucklesby. But since no one did..." he trailed off and shrugged his shoulders.

Henry reached for a bound manuscript on his desk.

"First draft of *Hate and Grow Rich*," he said, tossing the manuscript onto a huge pile of other manuscripts in a big recycling bin. "Don't suppose I'll be needing it now."

"What are all the others?" asked Georgina.

"Submissions to the agency. On average I receive thirty a day and only take on two new clients a year."

"Tough gig for a budding writer."

"And for the reader. It's a big part of my job and it's not easy. If they don't hook me in the first five pages then onto the pile it goes. And I won't even look beyond the title page if it's not in the correct industry-standard font or if it's not double-spaced. As a reader at a literary agency, you're always looking for reasons to reject a submission. I simply don't have the time to waste on average or below average work."

Georgina picked up a random manuscript from the pile.

"*Tales of the Clumsy Beekeeper* by NT Gallagher," read Georgina from the cover. "What's this one about?"

"French Revolution, apparently. Very weak submission, didn't get past the cover letter."

Georgina put it down and picked up another. "*The Long Hitch Home* by Jamie Maslin, any good?"

"Travel writing. Utterly soporific. Worth donating to insomnia clinics. Some Stamford wannabe ripping off his ideas. If I were stranded on a desert island and this was my only book, I would sooner use it for kindling or bathroom tissue than read it."

She hastily dropped the manuscript and reached for a third.

"*The Audacity of Triumph* by Lachlan Denoon. Hold on, what's this doing in here?"

"Oh, it's irrelevant now, it's all been rewritten. Much of it has been superseded by the latest version, which luckily Lachlan finished just before his sad passing."

"Goodness, I feel lucky just holding it," said Georgina, flicking through the work that was embellished with random notes and scribbles in the margins.

A name jumped out at her—Mitch. Mentioned frequently, it replaced an existing character's name that was crossed out.

Georgina disguised her intrigue and played it cool. "I'd love a look at his raw work, I'm a big fan of his first book."

"Oh, I'm afraid I couldn't permit it. I wouldn't be comfortable with that. Many writers are fiercely guarded about their work until it's absolutely finished, polished, edited and ready to go. It would feel like a betrayal of Lachlan."

"Of course," said Georgina, dropping the manuscript back onto the recycling pile.

A sudden interruption cut through the air as Henry's phone rang, severing the connection between them. He glanced at the screen, and snapped into business mode.

"I'm sorry, I'm going to have to take this, can you see yourself out?"

"Yes, of course. Thanks for your time."

Henry nodded and picked up his call. "Magnus, what's the latest?" he said, turning and heading back into the side room, closing the door behind him.

Georgina stood motionless for a second, her eyes going from the side room door to the recycling pile.

Would Henry notice? Maybe, but then maybe not.

She didn't like the idea of swiping the manuscript; it wasn't how she normally worked, but on occasion part of her work was dumpster diving, going through people's trash to gather information on them. It was perfectly legal, so long as the trash was at the curbside or not on private property, although it was mighty smelly work.

Was this really that different? she wondered.

Afterall, the manuscript was destined to be thrown out, so it wasn't like it would be missed. She hesitated, from a technical point of view it was unethical, but then there were bigger things at stake than ethics—there was a life on the line. Mitch Owens was facing the rest of his days behind bars and if there was anything in the manuscript that might, just might, help answer the big question of who killed Lachlan Denoon and why, then surely she had to take this opportunity while it was here? With a deft swipe she reached down and picked up the manuscript of Lachlan's book, and made a hasty exit.

CHAPTER 34

The heat hit Georgina as she stepped from Henry Hunt's office into the glaring sunlight of the day. She put her sunglasses on and quickly headed for her car where, to her surprise, Patricia Parry-Jones was waiting nearby, taping away impatiently at her phone.

"Hello, again," said Georgina.

Patricia smiled weakly.

"Didn't take it on, huh?" said Patricia, looking at the manuscript in Georgina's hands. "Trust me, you dodged a bullet."

She looked at her phone again. "My Uber hasn't turned up. Someone will pay for this."

"I could give you a lift if you like, where you heading?"

"Southampton, Main Street, thank you."

They climbed in and, after Georgina stuffed the manuscript in the door panel, got the hell out of there. Thirty seconds down the road Georgina spotted it again, pulling out behind them—the same blue Ford station wagon that had followed whoever dropped Patricia off to meet Cathleen.

Someone was tailing Patricia, and, by the looks of it, she hadn't noticed yet. Georgina kept her observation to herself, making small talk, while subtly monitoring the vehicle behind, glancing from road to rear-view mirror with veiled curiosity. They pulled onto Main Street and Patricia pointed out where she wanted to be dropped—an upmarket restaurant, *75 Main*, where patrons were sheltering in the shade beneath a large yellow awning, sipping icy drinks adorned with fresh leaves of mint at tables attired in snowy white tablecloths. Georgina pulled over and the Ford drove past, but then, right on cue, hit its turn signal and pulled over as well.

"Thank you," said Patricia, striding toward the restaurant.

Georgina glanced ahead at the blue Ford and drove off in its direction. As she drew parallel, she stole a subtle glimpse at the driver—a middle-aged white male with dark sunglasses and a Panama hat. She continued up the street and glanced into her rear-view mirror, but the car stayed put. Whoever the driver was, he didn't want to lose sight of his original target. When out of sight, Georgina hit a left, then another three after that, until she'd gone around the block and was back on the main road, only this time parked behind the blue Ford.

The hunter had become the hunted.

A low rhythmic hum emanated from the heart of Georgina's vehicle as the engine ran, not so much to be ready to give chase, more to keep the air conditioning circulating. She wondered if the man in the hat was doing likewise, or if he had air conditioning at all. She hoped not. If so, then he'd be solar-cooking inside a metal box.

After about fifteen minutes, he pulled out into the traffic. Maybe the heat got to him, maybe he needed to be elsewhere, maybe he'd gotten whatever information he was looking for. In any case, he was on the move again and now Georgina was in pursuit. She tailed him for twenty minutes, leaving other vehicles between her and him, but when they left the main drag and were heading up a deserted backroad near a secluded bay, it must have become obvious. He took a couple of random turns as if to test the hypothesis, then suddenly hit the gas. There was no point in pretending she wasn't in pursuit now. Georgina thrust her right foot to the floor. A split-second delay hung in the air, then the fuel injection kicked in and she was thrust back into her seat. Her pulse accelerated in tandem with the car, engine wailing like a contorted beast beneath the hood, as her heart felt like it might explode in her chest.

Greenery blurred in the periphery of her vision. Georgina's face was etched with determination as her eyes locked on to the blue Ford like a heat seeking missile. She pushed the car further into the red zone. The road snaked from side to side, forcing her to shift through the gears, rapidly slowing then speeding up to keep a visual on the Ford, which disappeared in fleeting bursts behind bushes and trees as they engaged in a lethal battle of flight and pursuit.

She lost sight of it altogether.

Ahead lay straight, empty road.

She jumped on the brakes, glancing into her rear-view mirror. Barely visible on the lefthand side of the road about five hundred yards away was the beginning of a small dirt track. She slammed the car into reverse and accelerated fast, gaining momentum and yanking the wheel to one side, tires screeching in protest as she threw the vehicle into an arcing curve, back in the right direction. She turned down the sandy track, bumping over its uneven surface as she remained on high alert for the Ford. The track curved from side to side, limiting visibility, as limbs of overhanging trees and bushes closed in, scratching against the car.

A couple of minutes passed—nothing.

Georgina began to think she might have missed another track elsewhere, that she'd made a critical error. But then she rounded a final bend and there it was ahead—parked at the end of the track, where a thin path led between bushes toward the ocean.

She approached with caution, crawling to the Ford and positioning her car to block its exit. As her door creaked open, the call of a lone crow rang out and the faint smell of cigarette smoke drifted her way from the beach. She moved toward it, pushing overhanging foliage from her face as she stepped along the path. Ten steps and there he was—the man with the Panama hat, standing at the beginning of the beach, smoking a cigarette in his left hand, holding a hefty-looking piece of driftwood like a club in his right.

He was deep set, unshaven and sweating, two nasty wet patches visible around the underarm area of his shirt. He caught sight of Georgina and smirked—an unarmed woman was no threat to him. Or so he thought. But then not every woman was a former nationally ranked judo competitor.

With a nonchalant toss, he ditched his club into the nearby grasses of the dunes.

"For a moment you had me worried there," he said.

"Oh, you should be worried," said Georgina. "Are you going to tell me why you followed my car this morning? Or am I going to have to beat it out of you?"

The man scoffed and took a deep drag on his cigarette.

"Oh, you're going to have to beat it out of me, little lady," he said with a grin, flicking his cigarette into the bushes, annoying Georgina with his littering in the process.

He took a step toward her, back in the direction of his car.

When he got within touching range, he stuck out an arm to brush her aside, to swat her like an irrelevant little insect. To him she was an insignificant mound of earth, but underneath her lay a land mine. Georgina took the gift, an opponent's arm or hand was the means by which she was about to smash them into the ground.

She grabbed him by the wrist with one hand, thrust a second hand around his nasty sweaty back, while simultaneously making a super-fast two-step entry, so her back was facing him.

Gotcha! she thought to herself, as the man began to lose his balance.

The rest was a formality: she thrust out a hip and pulled on that gift of an arm in a circular manner, corkscrewing him up and over, head over feet in mid-air, before offloading him hard onto the sandy ground at her feet—a classic judo "seoi nage" hip throw.

"Urgh!" he groaned as his back impacted the ground, the fat around his waist reverberating in an aftershock like a beached whale.

"Going to tell me what you were up to now?" said Georgina, looking down on the man lying helpless at her feet, sucking at the air with a look of shock on his face, brain in full spin. She maintained a grip on his wrist in a controlling manner and gave it a little tweak, cranking it to one side.

"Ah," he protested, "alright."

"Well?"

"I'm a P.I. on assignment, the woman I was following is having an affair with my client's husband. I'm collecting proof for her before she files for divorce."

"Who's your client?"

"Mary Aris, wife of the author Professor Aris."

Georgina let go of the man's wrist.

"Patricia Parry-Jones is having an affair with Professor Aris?" she asked, incredulous.

"Yeah. Wild, ain't it?"

Georgina helped the PI to his feet and held out her hand to shake.

The man looked at it warily, concerned there was another judo throw at the end. He tentatively reached out.

They shook.

"Georgina Patterson, legal investigator."

"Hell!" exclaimed the man. "You're an investigator too?"

"Sure am," replied Georgina with a smile.

The man laughed.

"Dwayne Gospel. Nice to meet you, I guess," he said, rubbing his back. "What's your case?"

"Murder of Lachlan Denoon. Working for the defense."

"Well, I'll be! I met him, you know. He thought I was a paparazzi taking photos."

"Huh? Where was that?"

"On the dunes at night out the back of the house near where he was killed. I was collecting evidence on Patricia Parry-Jones and Professor Aris, when he happened upon me with my big telephoto lens. He threatened to have security remove me and call the cops, so I came clean, told him I was a PI investigating an extra-marital affair, basic stuff, you know, keeping names out of it, when he blurts out, 'PPJ and the Professor, right?' and I'm like 'Yeah. How the hell you know that?' Told me he walked in on them in the sauna earlier on, found it hilarious that the professor could still womanize at his age, even showed me a text he sent his agent telling him all about it. Was real funny too."

"Did he give you a copy?"

Dwayne Gospel reached for his phone, found the message and handed it to Georgina with a chuckle.

Bro, you're not going to believe this, went for an evening run on the beach and decided to go for a sauna afterward in the pool room, I open the door and there, right in front of me, bobbing up and down like a big wrinkly pudding, was Professor Aris's fat white ass, going at it, on top of none other than... Patricia Parry-Jones! Talk about caught in the act, you should have seen them both. He was begging me not to tell his wife, while she was just laughing at him. She's such a bitch, just like the whore my father cheated on my mother with.

Without asking, Georgina hit "forward," punched in some numbers and sent the text to her own phone. She was half expecting Gospel to try and stop her mid-typing, but by the looks of it he didn't feel like a second round on the "mat."

"Do the police know about this?" asked Georgina.

"Only Mary Aris and me, and Lachlan's agent, I guess. As well as you now. Mrs. Aris didn't want that sort of thing in the public domain. Felt she'd become a laughing stock. But, like I told her, it's all gonna come out when she files."

"Is it enough for her to get what she wants?"

"Lachlan asked the same question. Thing is, it's hearsay, as I'm sure you're aware. Would be nice to have corroborating photos and video, and Lachlan offered to get them for me. He seemed like a nice guy, you know. I think he relished the idea of doing something a bit undercover, like James Bond; said he was bored of all the authors in the big house. Not that he ever managed to get any photos or video for me, poor guy died the next day."

CHAPTER 35

To watch someone's final breath is both a horror and a privilege. He held her hand as she softly slipped through his fingers forever, her spirit, that once shone so strong in those beautiful blue eyes, finally disappearing in its entirety. Rainbird remembered the moment all too well. One second she was gazing at him, her eyes registering an indefinable charge; the next they were empty and he was all by himself in the world, struggling to make sense of it. Abigail was the sun that rose and set on Rainbird's day, filling his world with light and joy, and a sense of optimism and contentment that he barely knew existed before their meeting. With Abigail he felt real and authentic, the very best version of himself. With her gone he was a castaway stranded on a tiny island, surrounded on all sides by an ocean of grief, with no way to navigate back to the life he once knew.

It wasn't long after meeting that they first talked of the children they would one day have together. Rainbird suggested five—three girls and two boys. Abigail three—two boys and a girl. Now they would have none. It was as if Rainbird had lost a whole family, not just a wife. And for them he also grieved. In the months before Abigail got ill, they'd planned to explore and take a road trip to the magnificent scenery of the southwest. Before they could depart, Abigail's health deteriorated and it was put on hold, but the dream remained. When the end was close and Abigail was very ill in the hospital, they'd still talk of that road trip, discussing it in the manner of an adventure just around the corner that they'd both soon take together. They knew it was impossible, but there was solace in holding onto their dream. Rainbird would tell her of all the places he'd learned about that they'd visit, hidden attractions far off the beaten path—the swirling orange rock formations of Arizona's Vermillion Cliffs, where a maximum of twenty people were permitted a day; the towering red monoliths of Cathedral Valley in Utah's Capital Reef National Park, a place they'd camp together beneath the stars; and the majestic Shiprock in New Mexico, where they'd hike across a flat desert plain to the foot of a 27-million-year-old remnant of a volcano, towering 1,500 feet above. Maybe they felt by discussing it, a little part of their spirits left the hospital room and made it there after all.

When Rainbird looked back on the person he was before Abigail's death, he saw a better man than he was today. A kinder, more tolerant person. Her death had left him a wounded lion, and his faith had taken a serious dent. He'd never been an overly religious man, but with his mother he attended mass every week. He had long since abandoned that routine, but before Abigail's death he'd firmly believed. Now he was uncertain, but from time to time, when he was alone and the world around him was quiet, he felt the stirring of something inside him. A faith that he found hard to define. A sense that there was much more to life. He wanted to believe so that he would one day see Abigail again. But whenever that tantalizing thought arose, he would deliberately trample upon it. He didn't want false hope. He didn't want to dream. He wanted justice.

The anniversary of her death was always a difficult day for Rainbird. He'd arrived at the church with mixed feelings, a contradiction of beliefs. His Christian upbringing had taught him to forgive, but he couldn't claim he intended to honor that. The way he saw it, that was all very well when the wrong committed was against yourself, but he could never extend that courtesy to those who'd wronged Abigail. For her, he'd resigned himself to fight, to get justice and avenge her death one way or another. Only when everyone at PrimaChem who'd played a part in her death, or tried to whitewash it, had felt his wrath, could he even consider finding peace.

He sat on the pew in the cool interior of the old stone church and looked toward the alter, his vision softening as the stillness of the place seeped into him, the thrashings of his logical mind evaporating like the mists of dawn, if but for a moment. There was no one else around and, after a while, thoughts of prison drifted into his consciousness. How he'd tried to grieve inside that hellhole, and that by being inside he'd been forced to leave Abigail's grave untended. The tears came from deep within him and he began to sob. He was not a man to normally cry, only when alone and his guard was down did it ever happen. But the thought of her grave left abandoned during his years incarcerated was too much to bear. Despite everything, he would gladly spend the rest of his days in that little box if it could bring Abigail back to life, even if he himself could never see her again. Just to know that she was OK and happy would be enough.

He began to whisper to her, at first sweet words of love but then resolve, of his commitment to continue the crusade against those who robbed them of the life they should have led and of the family they would now never have. He sat in that church for over two hours, and by the time Rainbird got up to leave he felt a certain relief, like he'd unburdened himself and the load carried was now a little bit lighter.

He stepped from the church's cool dark interior, blinking into the light from another perfect day. Only after his eyes adjusted to the sunshine did he became aware of another presence in the churchyard. Nearby, standing before a small gravestone, was Mavis Bucklesby, a fresh and colorful bouquet of flowers in her hand. For a moment he watched as Mavis lowered her head and whispered her own tender words to her dearly departed. The inscription on the grave of her late husband, Roger, was just visible from where he stood. Rainbird considered going over, but he didn't want to disturb her, so headed toward a small wooden gate at the churchyard's entrance. Before he reached it, Mavis turned and spotted him.

"Alfie," she said, surprised. "What are you doing here?"

"Oh, I'm just, you know, I'm, err, well." Rainbird paused, and took a deep breath.

"Are you OK?" asked Mavis, spotting the absence of Rainbird's normal composure.

"It's the anniversary of my wife's passing. I thought some time alone in contemplation might be a good idea."

Mavis moved closer and grasped his hand. "I'm so sorry for your loss. I too know what it means to have a loved one taken away. When all else is gone, it is our love that remains. We must always cultivate their memory in our heart. When your memory fades, you need to find other ways to keep them alive. We owe them that much."

"We do," said Rainbird. "Thank you."

"Come. This might cheer you up," said Mavis, leading Rainbird over to the grave.

On it was an engraving:

Roger Bucklesby
Best If Used By:
12 Jan 2020

"He was always such a joker," said Mavis. "Insisted on it long ago."

Rainbird smiled. "He sounds a lot of fun."

"Oh, he could be," said Mavis. "He did enjoy making people laugh."

"How long were you together?"

"A lifetime really, that's how it feels. And you? How long were you with your wife?"

For a moment Rainbird hesitated before speaking, tears welling in his eyes.

"She died the day after our wedding. We married before her time was up. If only she hadn't been taken from me. We had such plans together; I might even be a father by now."

"My dear Alfie," said Mavis. "I do share your pain."

Mavis gestured to a much smaller grave to the side of her late husband's, where she had placed the flowers. On it read:

Charlie. Here but for a moment, loved forevermore.

"My beloved Charlie," said Mavis. "Died in childbirth. We never had another child."

"I'm so sorry," said Rainbird, reaching for Mavis's hand.

"The ache of loss remains within me but I embrace its pain, for it reminds me that Charlie existed."

Rainbird gripped Mavis's hand tighter, he knew what she meant. Time stood still, as did they together in reverence to the sacred memories they both carried within, creating a bond forged in grief.

CHAPTER 36

Stephanie didn't like the idea of snooping on her father; it wasn't in her nature to live in the shadows, but she felt she had little option anymore. During moments of self-doubt, she would reassure herself that Magnus had brought it upon himself, not only in the violation of trust by having her followed, but by instigating the breach of Mitch's bail conditions that had seen the man she loved thrown inside a hellhole. And so, she set her mind to finding out what, if anything, there was beyond her relationship with Mitch that drove her father's vendetta against him. Gaining Magnus's trust again proved easy. After all, she'd done as he himself suggested and moved back to the family home, doing so under the pretext of a foolish wayward child returning to the fold. Magnus had been only too happy to welcome the prodigal daughter back, and took delight in offering her his own particular brand of patronizing counsel in the process. It was hard to swallow, but Stephanie resolved herself to playing the long game. However, the opportunity she'd been waiting for occurred on her second evening back.

Magnus had retired to bed after his normal scotch and cigar, leaving his keys, wallet and phone on the kitchen table. Stephanie took a seat at the table and tentatively picked up the phone, swiping it on with a shaking finger. The passcode screen appeared—six digits. She had an inkling what it would be. She panicked, hit the wrong numbers and access was denied. Stephanie took a deep breath and composed herself, entering: 101598. Her birthday.

The phone sprang to life.

She was in and scrolling through his private messages.

Most of it was mundane, this deal that deal, this contract that contract, but in among the business chit chat and the legal maneuvering was a collection of ambiguous messages between Magnus and someone listed in his phone as *The Commodore* that spoke of something altogether shadier.

One message in particular grabbed her attention:

Successful meeting with Swineherd 1. Romeo has fallen into our lap like a rotten apple. No more reason for concern. In other news, shipping forecasts favorable for the beginning of the month. We shall put into deep water and lower our nets for a catch... of biblical proportion.

Could Romeo be Mitch? she wondered. And what was this catch they spoke of? How could they know in advance as to its size?

Stephanie took a photo of the messages on her phone and left the property for good.

CHAPTER 37

Every so often a soft wind would stir, ruffling the placid ocean into a liquid carpet of tiny sparkling jewels, casting agitated light across the water's surface that danced for a fleeting moment before perishing in tandem with the breeze. Rainbird and Georgina sat gazing out to sea on an old wooden bench at the end of the beach house yard. At one time painted a jaunty red, the bench was now faded to a dirty salmon pink, sterilized after decades of sand blasting and exposure to the sun. Rainbird liked it here, it was the perfect place for a morning debrief, where he and Georgina could share their latest findings amid the serenity of the ocean. The surroundings were good for Rainbird, they calmed the overactive thrashings of his mind and helped him formulate a plan. He took a slow sip of milky tea from the mug in his hand and ruminated on the two new text messages in his possession—the one from Lachlan Denoon to Henry Hunt after the discovery of the affair between Patricia Parry-Jones and Professor Aris, and the text Stephanie had photographed on her father's phone that she'd forwarded to Rainbird and Georgina this morning.

"This text from Denoon to his agent, Hunt," said Rainbird, turning to Georgina. "It may or may not be significant to the actual truth of who killed Lachlan Denoon and why, but it gives us a motive to raise with the jury: that maybe Denoon was silenced by Patricia Parry-Jones or Professor Aris to prevent him from revealing their affair. Right now this case is a tangled web and we've got to unravel it. With Mitch recovered though, time is against us, and with him still inside, events have taken a serious turn."

"Everywhere I look there's a link back to Magnus," said Georgina. "Owning the television rights to Stamford Williamson, Audrey Adams, and Lachlan Denoon's work, manufacturing the breaking of Mitch's bail conditions. He's up to his neck in it."

"Maybe. They don't call him *The Pie Man* for nothing. He's connected to a lot of players, no doubt about that, but that goes for many fields with him. Question is, does his involvement here amount to more than a desire to see Mitch out of the way?"

"And then there's Rosina Pavlova being present at the house on the day of the murder," added Georgina. "According to Henry Hunt, police knew about this and yet for some reason it's absent from the discovery."

"Looks like our old friend Detective Bruce may have suppressed it. We'll get him back on the stand after the prosecution has finished making their case. See what he's got to say for himself when it's our chance to adduce evidence." Rainbird pondered for a moment and took another slug of tea. "And what about these cryptic texts from Magnus to *The Commodore*, whoever he is. Sounds to me like Magnus is bringing in something other than seafood."

"Narcotics?"

"It would fit."

"Could Mitch be involved?"

"It's possible."

"And what about that swineherd reference? What even is a swineherd?" asked Georgina.

"A person who looks after pigs," answered Rainbird.

"Police on the take?"

"Could be."

"Detective Bruce?"

"Thought had crossed my mind," said Rainbird, looking now toward a smooth black leather folder on Georgina's lap. "What have you managed to dig up?"

"An intriguing version of Lachlan's second book, *The Audacity of Triumph*," said Georgina, opening up the folder and handing Rainbird a thick ream of bound papers. "It's strange, there are several anomalies in it, the main one being the inclusion of characters who are absent from the version we received in the discovery."

"Is that so strange? Didn't that just happen after discussions with TV producers, so that it matched their planned adaptation?"

"Well, here's the thing, the manuscript is dated as after Lachlan's announcement, and the supposedly cut characters are included."

"Why would he do that?"

"Exactly. Why would he announce they're being chopped and then write them in regardless."

Rainbird mulled this over. "Hunt did say that Lachlan was making announcements before contracts had been finalized, but finalized with whom?"

"And there's more: strange handwritten notes in the margin, but it's the wording, listen to this: '*I don't think so! They are outta here!*' Underlined three times in red whenever the characters he announced were being cut appear in the text. And listen to this: '*I want this character called Mitch and make him a lowly little gardener.*'"

"Maybe Audrey Adams was closer to the mark than she realized—impatient Lachlan, the man who couldn't sit still, he doesn't strike me as the writing type, perhaps not even the reading type," said Rainbird.

"The sort of person who color coordinates their bookshelf," said Georgina, raising an eyebrow.

"Precisely," replied Rainbird. "What if Lachlan Denoon didn't write his books at all, what if he did have a ghost writer who, for whatever reason, didn't like the changes. And what if this is at the heart of his demise?"

CHAPTER 38

Patricia Parry-Jones strutted up to the witness box in a power boss business suit with the sort of cold, hard-faced scowl that had become her trademark during her extensive publicity tour for *Harness the Power of Hate*. How much of it was her genuine persona and how much of it was a media-contrived character to sell her book was hard to tell. She knew the cameras were rolling, that it was being televised across the country and world, and that there were potential book sales to be had off the back of her performance today. Ms. Parry-Jones normally went out of her way to cause as much controversy as she could get away with, typically dropping a pre-planned provocative soundbite or two that was intended to incite, to milk the inevitable publicity that came with it. She didn't mind being disliked, reviled even, so long as she was being talked about and her books were flying off the shelf. Not that any of this bothered Veitch. So long as he could coax a corroborating testimony from her that backed the case against Mitch, then he couldn't care less about the authenticity of her personality or intention to use proceedings for her own self-publicity. What mattered to him were the words and gestures he could elicit from her, the means by which he'd achieve his end of locking away Mitch for the rest of his natural life. That, and his greater overriding objective of beating, humbling and, most of all, humiliating his onetime victim who'd risen to become his nemesis, the only person who'd ever overturned one of Veitch's original convictions—Rainbird.

"I want to take you back to the night of the murder, Ms. Parry-Jones," said Veitch, after the usual preamble of establishing who she was and what her credentials were. "I want to know about your interactions with the accused, Mr. Mitch Owens, and your impressions of him. Could you tell me, did you speak to him during the event?"

"Yes, I did. I spoke to Mitch during the event."

"And what did you make of him?"

"I thought he was generally smart and interesting, although somewhat argumentative."

"In what way?"

"He didn't shy away from confrontation."

"Would you please elaborate?"

"Certainly. I saw him argue on two separate occasions, once with another server and once with Lachlan Denoon."

"Two occasions, you say? Please describe these for the court?"

"On the first night of the event, at around 10:15PM when I was out back of my accommodation smoking a cigarette, I witnessed Mitch Owens and another server, a male of about his age, arguing at the rear of the staff quarters. I'm pretty sure they didn't see me, it was dark and I was there alone, but that they were having a heated argument was plain to see, even from a distance and in the dark."

"What was it they were saying?"

"I'm afraid I couldn't hear the specifics of their argument, although I did catch the occasional expletive."

"What makes you so sure it was an argument then?"

"Mitch Owens's overall tone, his body language, his aggressive finger jabbing in the face of the other server. This went on for about five minutes before Mitch abruptly turned around and stormed off back into the staff quarters, slamming the door behind him."

This was tantalizing news.

To the jury and the court at large.

The argument between Mitch and Lachlan had already been discussed on previous days, but this account of aggressive behavior from Mitch was new.

It was the first time it had surfaced and it spelled bad news for the defense. Veitch lingered on it, savoring the unexpected gift that had come his way, getting Patricia Parry-Jones to reiterate what she'd witnessed and encouraging her to dwell on Mitch's aggressive attitude during this confrontation, before turning to the more widely witnessed altercation between Mitch and Lachlan. She added nothing new here, although she did paint Mitch as the sole antagonist.

"I'd like to ask you about your work that led to you receiving an invitation to the Bucklesby mansion," said Veitch, moving things in a different direction. "Would it be a fair characterization of your latest book to say it is on channeling hatred to achieve positive objectives?"

"Positive or negative, these trite terms are neither here nor there to me. I'm what you might call a moral atheist. I nurture a vast well of personal hatred, but this is simply a tool in my arsenal. Through it comes great power, when correctly applied in a calculated and controlled manner. And that's the key, you need to be in control of your hatred not the other way around. It is like a powerful and dangerous dog that you keep on a leash until you're ready to set it onto an adversary; you don't let it run wild and free, attacking randomly without effective control. You are its master and, if you know how to use it, it will serve you well. Otherwise, it can ultimately kill you."

"Or others," added Veitch with a heavy dose of implication.

"Of course."

"So, when it comes to hatred, it's fair to say you're something of an expert?"

"My clinical research in this area is second to none."

"In your book you talk about individuals with what you term 'DDD,' or 'disempowered detestation disorder,' people who, through suppression of their own detesting or hatred of others, reach a breaking point, where things blow up, often in quite spectacular fashion, during moments of crisis. You also write about your ability to recognize the hallmark characteristics of this in others. From your interactions with Mitch Owens, do you think he may have suffered from this disorder?"

"Objection, Your Honor," said Rainbird, rising to his feet. "This is clearly inadmissible opinion evidence. There is no basis for believing any such disorder exists beyond the fertile imagination of the witness who personally coined the term. It appears nowhere other than her book. Ms. Parry-Jones has not provided credentials with which to establish her as an expert on this hypothetical disorder, or any other. It is evidently wrong for the court to consider an entirely speculative question about an entirely speculative syndrome. If my learned friend intends to pursue this clearly prejudicial line of questioning, then the jury should be sent out."

Veitch was expecting to lose this point and had only raised it in the first place to plant the possibility of Mitch having hatred issues in the jury's minds. And so, no one was more surprised than Veitch when Judge Jenkins sided not with Rainbird but him.

"The witness has demonstrated her expertise in this field, so I shall allow it."

Patricia gave an appreciative nod to Jenkins.

"I have to say, from my interaction with Mitch Owens, I do believe he suffers from DDD—from disempowered detestation disorder. But you have to understand, there's nothing wrong with a bit, or even a lot, of healthy hatred, nothing whatsoever. It's as natural a feeling as hunger or the need to breathe or use the bathroom. I embrace my hatred, I don't shy away from it and therefore it empowers me, not disempowers me. I am proud to say—*I identify as a person of hate.*"

Rainbird rolled his eyes, there was Patricia Parry-Jones's first inevitable controversial soundbite. And she wasn't finished yet.

"It's the great taboo, isn't it? People will admit to affairs, to mental illness, to drug and alcohol abuse, but hatred? There's still a stigma attached to it. I want to end that stigma, so people can take pride in their true self and lead their best life. There is immense fulfillment to be found in seeing the target of your hatred brought to their knees. That fulfillment is open to every one of us, if we just embrace our hatred. Society tells us to deny it, to repress it and pretend it doesn't exist. But like denying your sexuality, it doesn't make it magically go away; to do so only makes it more impulsive. And therein lies the problem. Most people suffer from this to a certain extent, but others, those who are more naturally inclined to hatred, those who are born this way, develop the disorder. I've seen it often over the years and witnessed it with my own eyes at the Bucklesby retreat, in the amateurish hate fueled manner in which Mitch first verbally and then physically attacked Lachlan."

"Why do you say amateurish?"

"To shout and scream is the mark of an amateur. Far better to channel your hatred in a more cold and calculated way, to truly satisfy your inner yearnings for complete and utter revenge. This is not achieved by placing yourself in court, charged with murder. Only a fool behaves in such a manner. Much better to work hard to destroy everything that someone holds dear in this world—professional reputation, personal relationships, even someone's mental health—all the while still remaining within the bounds of the law."

Veitch stared at Patricia Parry-Jones aghast for a second, unsure whether he was repulsed or had finally found a kindred spirit.

"No further questions, Your Honor."

"Your Witness," said the judge to Rainbird.

Rainbird rose to his feet and strode to the lectern.

"You like controversy, don't you?" said Rainbird.

"I like the truth, whatever that may be, which is often unpalatable and therefore controversial. But it is still the truth."

"Ah yes, the truth," replied Rainbird. "That's what we're all after. But what then is the truth of your personal animus with the deceased, Mr. Lachlan Denoon?"

"I had no particular animus with him."

"No grudge? No reason to dislike or, in your case, hate Mr. Denoon?"

"No. I neither liked, disliked, nor hated him. He meant nothing to me. Nothing whatsoever."

"Is that so?" mulled Rainbird. "So, to be clear, there was no instance during the writers retreat when he offended or slighted you in any way?"

"Not to the best of my recollection."

"Not to the best of your *recollection*—ah, that old chestnut! The ol' legal sleight of hand, gives the impression you're saying 'no' but in case I can show otherwise you're putting the onus on your 'recollection' of events, certainly not your honesty pertaining to them."

"Objection," said Veitch. "Badgering the witness."

"Overruled."

"Well, Ms. Parry-Jones, let me try and refresh your memory. I'd like you to think back to the pool house and a particular evening there when the two of you crossed paths. Ring any bells?"

"The pool house, you say?"

She looked flustered but tried to hold it together, her cool exterior visibly cracking.

"The pool house," replied Rainbird, without warmth.

Patricia took a sip of water, the cogs in her head registering as panic on her face, while she struggled to come up with an answer.

"Nothing springs to mind."

"Cute, a variant of 'not to my recollection,' of course, so I'll take that as a fudge too. Lachlan confronted you there, did he not?"

"I really don't recall."

"Your fellow guest Professor Aris was there too, wasn't he?"

"Well, lots of people use the pool room."

"Please tell the court what it was that you and Professor Aris were doing there?"

"I am uncertain as to what you are alluding."

"Your Honor, if it pleases the court, I tender this document as evidence. It is a short text message sent from Lachlan Denoon's phone during the writers retreat detailing, in no uncertain terms, the exact nature of his encounter in the pool house with the witness and Professor Aris."

"I'll allow it," said Judge Jenkins.

As the court clerk quickly assigned it an exhibit number and a copy of the document was provided to the prosecution, Patrica Parry-Jones weighed up her options.

"I shall ask you a second time Ms. Parry-Jones," said Rainbird, getting proceedings underway again. "Did you encounter Lachlan Denoon in the pool house?"

"Actually, thinking about it now, we did have a brief discussion there."

"Well, what a surprise," said Rainbird. "Please tell the court what it was about."

She took a deep breath.

"My relationship with Professor Benjamin Aris."

There was whispering in the public gallery.

"And what was the nature of your relationship with Professor Aris?" asked Rainbird.

"Sexual. We had an intense and unabashed sexual relationship."

There was a collective gasp from the public gallery, followed by giggling.

"Order!" boomed Judge Jenkins, bashing his gavel down hard three times, until an eerie silence pervaded the room.

Rainbird waited, using the silence to accentuate his next question. "How long had you been having a sexual relationship with married father of five, Professor Benjamin Aris?"

"For the last year."

"Let me read you a text Lachlan Denoon sent to his literary agent, Henry Hunt: *'Bro, you're not going to believe this, went for an evening run on the beach and decided to go for a sauna afterward in the pool room, I open the door and there, right in front of me, bobbing up and down like a big wrinkly pudding, was Professor Aris's fat white ass, going at it, on top of none other than... Patricia Parry-Jones!'*"

There was laugher in the court.

"Order! Order!" thundered Jenkins, hitting his gavel again, before restoring calm.

"I shall continue," said Rainbird. *"Talk about caught in the act, you should have seen them both. He was begging me not to tell his wife while she was just laughing at him. She's such a bitch, just like the whore my father cheated on my mother with.'"*

Rainbird fixed her with a stare.

"How do you feel hearing that now?"

"I'm neutral to hearing it. Lachlan Denoon clearly did not approve, but his feelings on the matter were then, and are now, an utter irrelevance to me."

"No, he did not approve. The nature of his text message shows that he thought your intrusion into their marriage and family unit was reprehensible and immoral."

Patricia shrugged in a couldn't care less way.

"Shrug you may, Ms. Parry-Jones," said Rainbird. "But we are dealing with a very serious matter here, someone in that house killed Lachlan Denoon. The reason, well, one has to speculate, but it is not speculation to state the obvious—you had motive to silence Mr. Denoon, to prevent him from revealing your illicit affair. Were it not for the text message in my possession, it would most likely have never seen the light of day, isn't that so?"

"This is ridiculous, just because Lachlan walked in on Benjamin and me is irrelevant. That doesn't mean I would want to kill the man."

Rainbird threw her and then the jury a *maybe, maybe not* look.

"Afterall, what do I lose?" continued Patricia. "I'm not the one who's married."

"Are you suggesting your lover Professor Benjamin Aris was involved?"

"Who said anything about love? Our relationship was physical, not emotional—" Patricia paused, weighing up whether the publicity gained from deliberately implicating Professor Aris was worth the personal fallout from doing so, before concluding that it was. "—And I wasn't the one Lachlan was trying to blackmail," she said, raising a suggestive eyebrow.

The entire court, Rainbird included, was astonished.

"To be clear, you're saying Lachlan Denoon was trying to blackmail Professor Aris?"

"It wasn't stated as such, but that was the implication, yes."

"How so?"

"The morning after he discovered our relationship, Lachlan demanded a glowing blurb endorsement for his next book from Benjamin—wanted the serious academic prestige a recommendation like that would provide."

"What did Professor Aris say?"

"He agreed. And wrote it on the spot."

"No further questions, Your Honor," said Rainbird, sitting down with a barely concealed sense of delight at the unexpected windfall that had come his way.

Things were looking up, but for how long?

CHAPTER 39

The lapping chop of water against the hull of flagship fishing trawler *La Sallette* heralded the arrival of Magnus McLean's wider fleet, a veritable fishing armada coming in to dock at two separate destinations on either side of the vast harbor, under the darkness of a pre-dawn sky. The larger vessels headed off in the distant direction of the old boatyard, the smaller ones taking berths by the wharf, near Magnus's other acquisition, *Clam Palace*. As their collective cargo was brought ashore, the world around the wharf was just beginning to stir. Great bundles of newspapers arrived at a nearby kiosk, while fresh bread and cakes were delivered to a café on the waterfront. Overhead, a squadron of seagulls screeched, agitated by the smell of fish, all hoping to score an opportunistic free meal from one of the trawlers. Other boats offloaded, but none with the military precision or speed of Magnus's army of workers, who lugged huge freezer boxes onto dry land, then into nearby refrigerated trucks. As soon as their rear doors slammed shut, they were off, disappearing into the darkness. By the time they'd all departed, a faint light was visible on the horizon and the morning air was beginning to warm. A few local early risers arrived on the scene: joggers, dog walkers, even a young couple carrying bright green yoga mats, posed in stylistic salutations on the waterfront as they awaited the arrival of the sun.

Nearby, another figure greeted the day, a woman lighting a candle and placing it reverently on a small wooden walkway next to the melted remnants of several other candles, creating a coating of colored wax on the slats. Photos, handwritten notes, flowers—both old and new—and the occasional soft toy stood nearby, creating a makeshift shrine in front of Lachlan Denoon's former yacht, *Billy Doo*.

"I've lit a candle for him every day since his passing," said Rosina Pavlova to Georgina, who stood next to her on the boardwalk, as water sloshed gently underfoot.

Rosina uncrumpled a piece of paper, took a measured breath to composed herself, and began to read aloud:

> Lachlan, my dearest, you are here no more,
> The world is now empty, and my heart feels sore.
> If only our love hadn't been cut so short,
> If only together we could still cavort.
> I hope that you like my brand-new tattoo,
> No prizes for guessing that it is of you.
> I will never forget when we shared a cigar,
> I cry for you now like a budgerigar.

*You know that you always made me feel secure,
Your death is the price our love pays to endure.*

Rosina reached into her pocket and retrieved a single plastic-wrapped cigar. In a manner of thanksgiving, she held it aloft then placed it on the boardwalk by the shrine's other random offerings.

"We shared a cigar after the night we finally became one," said Rosina, turning to Georgina, who was doing her best to look sincere. "Did you like my poem? I wrote it myself."

"It was very heartfelt," said Georgina. "I'm curious about the last line: *Your death is the price our love pays to endure.* What did you mean by that?"

For a fleeting second Georgina thought she saw concern in Rosina's eyes, but then perhaps it was just insanity.

"A poem is but a moment in time, to be interpreted differently by each who hears the words. I wouldn't want to overlay my meaning on top of yours."

"I understand."

"Would you like to see my tattoo?" asked Rosina from out of nowhere.

"Err, sure, why not."

Rosina proudly pulled back her t-shirt sleeve, revealing a horrendously inked depiction of a winged unicorn, only with the mono-horned head of Lachlan Denoon, crying big fat tears from his eyes.

"He was a magical creature, you know. Wherever he went, he left a sparkly glow—" Rosina gasped, her throat tightening. "—I could use that in my next poem!"

She looked skyward and smiled as if inspiration had come from above.

"Come," beckoned Rosina. "I will show you my most sacred item."

Rosina led Georgina toward a nearby apartment building and soon they were walking along a corridor on the second floor, past pictures of seascapes and fishing boats that decorated the space between apartment doors on their way to Rosina's at the end. She reached for her keys, fumbling with the first of four separate locks as Georgina waited. Even from here the smell was noticeable, leaching through the crack between the door and its frame. Rosina opened up and the full force of the smell hit Georgina, an unpleasant mixture of multiple incense sticks, mingling with the combined aromas of several different scented air fresheners. It was overwhelming. Like it was masking something. Georgina felt nauseous. She wanted to turn around and breathe the cool fresh air of the ocean outside, but she pushed on in. A dark hallway led onto a small dark living room. Rosina flicked a light switch and the pictures jumped out of the darkness. Stuck all over the walls were multiple photos of Lachlan Denoon. Some were taken from magazines, others were printouts from his Instagram or publicity shots found online. There were even newspaper cuttings of his death and funeral, all collectively chronicling the multiple faces and evolving images of the man—reality TV star, social media influencer, debonair ladies' man, literary intellectual, corpse.

Beyond the living room was a basic kitchen on one side and a single bedroom on the other.

"This is my favorite one. He looks so intelligent and handsome," said Rosina, gesturing to a photo of Lachlan during his author phase, wearing a diamond patterned cashmere sweater and reading glasses. "I have the same outfit," she gushed.

"I bet it suits you," said Georgina, trying to win Rosina's trust.

"It does. I wore it to the question-and-answer session at the book fair. Lachlan and I conversed."

"What did you discuss?"

For a moment Rosina looked disturbed, triggered by a memory best left forgotten.

"Come," she exclaimed, ignoring the question, leading Georgina into the bedroom, toward another little shrine on top of her bedside cabinet. Here on the wall above the cabinet was a terrible framed oil painting of Lachlan Denoon, his features grotesque and out of proportion with two big, zoned out zombie-like eyes. It was no Audrey Adams portrait, that was for sure. In the bottom right-hand corner was a signature—Rosina. On the cabinet, a signed copy of Lachlan's book lay open on the page bearing his handwritten name. Nearby sat an unopened bottle of Lachlan's onetime fragrance *Bravado*, as did a bottle of the free moisturizer sample that came with it. Next to this was a little mason jar stuffed full of incense sticks and in front of that an antique locket.

"You can hold it if you like," said Rosina, picking up the locket with the reverence of a priest holding a religious relic.

She carefully handed it to Georgina.

"Go on, open it," she beckoned with excited eyes.

Georgina held the locket in her palm and gently opened its tiny metal clasp. Inside was a clump of what looked like human hair.

"I keep a lock of Lachlan's hair in a locket."

Of course you do, thought Georgina, but replied, "It's so beautiful."

"I took it when he was sleeping the night we were together. I will treasure it forever."

"I think you should," said Georgina.

She handed back the locket and glanced around the apartment. There was a clear view from the bedroom window down onto the marina below and of Lachlan's yacht. Along with multiple pictures of Lachlan looking out at Georgina from every angle, the bedroom contained an altogether more interesting genre of photograph—those that Rosina had clearly snapped herself from the window. Mostly of Lachlan on his yacht, unaware he was being watched. Among these random pictures, Georgina spotted something odd. Attached to a pinboard with chunky, colored tacks were several strange photos. One of a white van parked at the marina, another of some unknown men entering Lachlan's yacht and then carrying away what looked like a laptop in a bag. The photos were grainy, taken at nighttime under the glare of the marina's lights.

"What are these?" asked Georgina.

"They think no one saw them," scoffed Rosina. "But I saw everything."

"What was it you saw, Rosina?"

"They broke into my Lachlan's yacht, ransacked his things and stole his possessions. Took them for themselves as treasure."

"When was this?"

"A few months ago, the week after our night of unity."

"Do the police know about this?"

"Yes. They arrived afterward. Look, I have photos of them too."

Rosina opened a drawer and rummaged through the contents, pulling out a pile of photos and handing them to Georgina. There were several pictures of uniformed cops arriving and talking to Lachlan, as well as a photo of a cop dusting for finger prints on the entry hatch of the yacht.

"But do the cops know about *these* photos?" said Georgina, pointing to the ones of the van and the men entering the boat. "Do they know about this evidence of who broke in?"

"I don't like police officers very much," said Rosina, trailing off. "Would you like a drink? I have homemade iced tea."

"Just water, thanks."

As Rosina headed into the kitchen, Georgina seized her moment. With her own phone she photographed the images on the pinboard of the van and the men breaking into Lachlan's yacht, then of the police dusting it for prints.

"Slice of lemon?" called Rosina from the kitchen.

But there was no reply.

Georgina had already slipped out the front door.

CHAPTER 40

She found him in his normal booth at *The Cliffs*, eating a steak that was practically bigger than the plate it sat on, dangling limp over one side, leaving a puddle of oily fat on the table that slowly grew in size.

"Ah, there you are," announced Rainbird through a mouthful of meat on spotting Georgina. "I'm intrigued. Show me what you've got?"

Georgina slid her phone across the table. Open on screen were the photos she'd taken of Rosina's clandestine snaps. She'd mentioned them to Rainbird on the phone when setting up the meeting, but by now she'd done some digging on their significance.

"Scroll through," she said, taking a seat opposite.

She waited while Rainbird stopped chewing and looked at the pictures with increasing curiosity.

"Lachlan's boat was ransacked a month before his death. Nothing unusual about a yacht getting turned over for valuables, but the police report shows that no cash or valuables were taken."

"What did they get?"

"A box of memory cards/USB drives and a couple of computers."

"Huh," said Rainbird, pondering.

"Yeah, and I know who did it too."

Rainbird sat up straight, as an interested look spread across his face.

"I called in some favors with a cop friend who ran a check on the license number of the van in the photos. It's registered to a shell company, JEM Inc, just a PO Box number with no physical address, linked to another shell company, linked to a holding company. It's a tangled web and it took some digging, but it all leads back to a certain Magnus McLean Holdings."

"What exactly was Magnus trying to get his hands on?" said Rainbird.

"What indeed?"

"This case is opening up," said Rainbird, an optimistic bounce in his voice. "That there was an individual present at the scene of Lachlan Denoon's murder who was also involved in the theft of sensitive items from him—well, that's the sort of information that could have a big impact on a trial, if ever it reached the hands of a good attorney that is," said Rainbird with a twinkle in his eye.

"If only we knew one," said Georgina.

"First chink in the armor," smiled Rainbird. "We'll have to work on that. In the meantime, it's about time I had another chat with our old friend Magnus. Let's see what he's got to say for himself this time. But first, there's someone I need to pay a visit to who might just be able to shed some light on what Magnus is really up to."

CHAPTER 41

Rainbird first met Tony Pirelli at the Italian table in Attica Correctional Facility. It was an unusual place for a Scotsman to be invited, but a big honor, an acknowledgment that he was respected among their group of powerful and connected Italian "business men" who ate their meals together, and Tony Pirelli was the main man, practically treated like a god. Rainbird had done one of their own "a solid," a young Italian in Attica awaiting trial whose case Rainbird had examined and discovered a couple of technical errors, loopholes that allowed Rainbird to file a motion to dismiss the man's indictment. It proved successful. The guy got out and, as a major compliment to Rainbird, Tony invited him to eat with the Italians. There were several advantages, not least the food. Tony's crew managed to smuggle little extras inside to liven up the typically bland prison chow served up at Attica—contraband brought in by guards on the payroll and ignored by others, happy to turn a blind eye, for a price. Fresh garlic, prosciutto, real mozzarella, that sort of thing. The joke was that they were working up to getting pizzas delivered from one of their uncle's nearby restaurants. It never happened while Rainbird was in Attica, but he wouldn't have put it past them managing it one day. Another advantage was being seen by other prisoners to be associated with the Italian crew. By association, it meant Rainbird wasn't to be messed with, that he was under their wing and if anyone stepped out of line with him, it would be met with an iron fist from them. But for Rainbird, the biggest advantage was their company. They were a total treat, like something out of *Goodfellas*. They would laugh and joke and hold court at their table, and even had their own version of Joe Pesci—Guilio "Two Toes" Lucantoni—who swore like a trooper and was constantly baiting the guards, much to his and everyone at the table's amusement. There was community among them and a sense of solidarity. When outside in the yard they'd congregate around the bocce ball court, or campo, rolling and throwing heavy leather balls into a rectangular pit to see who could get closest to the white pallino ball, all the time listening to Italian opera or *The Best of Frank Sinatra*.

"Don't be deceived by what on the surface appears a straight forward leisurely game," Tony had told Rainbird. "It is high strategy and can get very intense. Bocce is like chess or checkers but with a ball."

Rainbird and Tony were from different worlds, and it wasn't Rainbird's place to ask too many questions about Tony's one, but the two men enjoyed each other's company. They shared a sharp intellect and had the sort of dangerous charisma that drew people in. Both appreciated these traits in the other, as well as their joint interest in effective strategy. Following Rainbird's acquittal and release, the two had sporadically remained in touch, writing letters to the other. Rainbird knew how much a handwritten letter was appreciated by those incarcerated; he wasn't a fair-weather friend but a real one, and so, even after all these years, made the effort to put pen to paper to people he'd connected with during his own darkest days. Tony had been transferred twice since Rainbird had been released, first to maximum-security prison North Lake in Michigan, then to minimum-security prison, Loretto in Pennsylvania, where he was seeing out the last three years of his sentence, surrounded by a lush woodland just beyond the towers and coils of razor wire.

Normally, former inmates were prohibited from visiting current ones, but with Rainbird's full exoneration and legal accreditation he was permitted to visit old alumni of the US Justice System. And so, he found himself waiting at a table in the packed visitors room of Tony's current Pennsylvania abode, awaiting his arrival amidst a racket of chatter that gushed forth like an open faucet between visitors and the visited.

As Tony spotted Rainbird across the room, a smile tugged at the corner of his lips, then spread into a broad grin.

"Look at you!" he exclaimed, eyes feasting upon Rainbird's attire with impressed approval, all pinstripes and polished shoes. "You scrub up well, old friend."

"It's Italian, tailormade," said Rainbird with a smile.

"Of course, it is," said Tony with a touch of pride. "Only the finest for you, Alfie."

They embraced and settled in. Soon they were chatting away as if it were weeks, not years since they'd seen each other. They had an hour on the clock for visitation and filled it almost entirely with anecdotes and laughter, the craziness of life on either side of their current divide, but Rainbird wasn't here just to chew the cud—there was business to attend too.

"I was wondering what you know of Magnus McLean?" asked Rainbird, lowering his voice.

Tony glanced from side to side, first to the guards, then to the other prisoners and their families, making sure they were all caught up in their own little worlds of intrigue and gossip and that no one was trying to snoop. He leaned in close to Rainbird, eyes gleaming, as if assessing his old comrade's character one final time before he spoke.

"You're a friend, Alfie, but what you ask of me is business, and business doesn't come for free, you know that, and I always collect what I'm owed."

"I wouldn't expect it any other way."

"So long as we understand each other," said Tony.

Rainbird nodded.

"Don't buy the Magnus myth in the financial pages," whispered Tony as he fixed Rainbird with a stare. "He's a wise guy like the rest of us, made his money running dope before diversifying."

"Is he still running it?"

"Magnus is very much in the same line of business, more than ever, one of the biggest players on the East Coast."

"Huh," said Rainbird. "On his boats, right?"

Tony gave a little nod of confirmation.

The shrill ring of a buzzer on the wall rang out, cutting through the chaos of the room with an urgency that truncated conversations mid-sentence and heralded the end of visiting time.

"Finish up!" yelled a guard.

"I'll let you know what you can do for me," said Tony, holding out a palm to Rainbird.

They shook, firm and strong.

The two men were friends, but there were boundaries that had to be observed.

"By the way," said Tony, leaning in close before releasing his grip. "Rumor has it, Magnus pulled strings to get '*The Leach*' the gig opposing you."

Rainbird's eyes registered shock, he hadn't heard that name for a long time. Nicknames were prevalent among the Italians—some were amusing, others menacing—and Tony Pirelli had coined "The Leach" himself, a name he hissed with bad intent after hearing of Rainbird's encounter with the man who'd turned his perfect life upside down—Jon "The Leach" Veitch.

CHAPTER 42

Rainbird stood in a charcoal-colored suit on the Broadway sidewalk in front of *MagNet's* Manhattan headquarters and stared up at the towering glass structure above him with a look of unyielding resolve. He glanced at his watch. Five minutes to go. Five minutes until he confronted Magnus in the heart of his own empire. Rainbird was going into the lions' den, but he was doing so as Daniel, and it was Magnus, not him, who was in need of divine intervention.

An imposing glass door resembling a sheet of frozen ice slid open and Rainbird stepped inside.

"Alfie Rainbird. I have an eleven o'clock with Magnus McLean," he announced at the main reception.

"Thank you, Mr. Rainbird, someone will show you up immediately."

The receptionist gave a member of the security team the sort of prearranged nod that hinted at them having had a prior briefing of his arrival, and Rainbird was whisked by the guard to a private elevator with polished golden doors. He stepped inside the gleaming metal box and with a confident finger pressed the only button on the panel—The Boardroom. Floors began rushing by in a rapid climb as he traveled skyward with surprising speed. Suddenly the motion slowed, then ceased altogether. A crisp *ping* rang out and the doors slid open.

Standing there to meet him was Magnus himself, hands on his hips to emphasize his size, and a steely gaze etched on his furrowed face. His heady aftershave lingered in the air and wafted into the elevator, a formidable fusion of dominance and unabashed masculinity.

"Come in, Mr. Rainbird," he said with an air of seriousness, leading him into a boardroom adorned with opulent furnishings that was part luxury hotel suite, part corporate control center. Floor-to-ceiling windows framed the room, giving a sweeping panorama of the city, and in the center of the room was a long rectangular table topped with a slab of polished black jade that was darker than the night sky.

"What is it that you wanted to discuss?" said Magnus from the opposite side of the table, resting his palms on its surface and spreading his arms wide.

He lowered his head and locked eyes with Rainbird.

Rainbird held his stare unflinching.

"I know how you established your business, what your real business is, and how it operates."

Magnus's eyes widened, his normal impenetrable exterior visibly cracking.

"I'm not a federal agent or an officer of the DEA and neither is Mitch for that matter," continued Rainbird. "What you do is your business. My business is loyalty to my client and my quest is to see justice prevail in his case. Problem is, your business is getting in the way of mine. I know you got Veitch on board as state prosecutor to throw me off my game—ha, some hope—and I know about Denoon's yacht. I know you ordered the burglary and I want to know why."

Magnus didn't answer, silence hung in the room like a presence, while he considered his options, before finally he spoke. "Why should I tell you anything?"

"Because if you don't, I'll call you as a witness. I'll put you on the stand and I'll air all your dirty linen in public for the whole world to see. By the time I'm finished with you your whole kingdom will be shattered into a thousand pieces and I shall scatter them to the wind."

"You wouldn't dare."

Rainbird scoffed. "I've been to the darkest depths of hell and back and I've mapped every level. There's nothing you or any other man can do to me. Never underestimate a man who's lost everything he holds dear; no longer does he have anything to lose."

A flicker of fear danced in Magnus's eyes as he breathed out hard.

"All right," he said with palpable reluctance. "Lachlan Denoon was interfering with one of my assets, sticking his head into a commercial interest of mine where it didn't belong. He got his hands on incriminating footage that could have sunk my investment, before I was ready to cut that investment loose. I couldn't allow that to happen."

"What investment?"

"Stamford Williamson."

"What did he have on him?"

Magnus frowned and began to pace back and forth. His glance darted about the room, desperately trying to maintain control as he searched for a mental escape that didn't exist.

"Weigh it up, Magnus," said Rainbird. "Williamson may have been worth breaking into Lachlan Denoon's yacht for, but he's not worth this. Give me what I want even if it sinks him. You've other pies, and plenty more palatable than Williamson."

Magnus scowled and shook his head in frustration. Being threatened was uncharted territory for him. With a heavy exhalation, he paced to a nearby drawer and wrenched it open, reaching inside. As he returned to the table, he slid a flash drive across its shiny black surface that spun to a halt in front of Rainbird.

"Everything's in here. Watch it. Then we can talk."

"It's all here?"

"Uh huh. And I'd appreciate it if you acquired it *anonymously*."

Rainbird nodded his consent and began to walk toward the elevator but stopped and turned.

"Take a tip from me, Magnus, your best course of action is to cease all action against Mitch. Like me, his interest lies elsewhere, and his motivations are honorable."

CHAPTER 43

"Do you swear to tell the truth, the whole truth and nothing but the truth?"

"I do," said a smug Stamford Bingley Williamson O.B.E., who earlier in the morning had taken the court clerk aside for a discreet word, to make sure that his full name and title would be used for any official pronouncements by the court, thus highlighting his O.B.E. on camera for those watching the televised proceedings.

He was dressed immaculately in a crisp pink shirt with oversized cufflinks and a gentleman's bespoke navy-blue blazer.

As Stamford settled into the witness box, Veitch began the show.

"Mr. Williamson, I'm sure many of us here are familiar with your work, but for those who aren't, would you mind telling the court a little about what you do?"

"Difficult to pin down, but I was recently described in a magazine piece as an explorer from a bygone age, skilled in multiple disciplines: botany, anthropology, geology, zoology and, of course the field where I've really made my name, survival skills. The article referred to me as a polymath, which in Greek means 'having learned much' and in the Latin is simply 'universal man'—obviously."

"Obviously," replied Veitch.

"But perhaps I'm best known by the general public as a travel writer, television presenter and producer, of shows made by my independent television production company *Stampede Films*. My books focus on what might be described as the more extreme end of the travel genre, you know, hitchhiking through conflict zones, epic long-distance treks through the Indian subcontinent or Saharan North Africa, that sort of thing. Sometimes my shows faithfully follow the content of my books, others are contestant driven platforms where members of the public dip their toes into my world and get to experience some of my normal day-to-day derring-do. My most recent project is *Stamford's Survival Stampede*, which sees contestants race their way from one end of an immense wilderness area to another, living survival style as they go—the essential skills of which I teach to them beforehand—with the winner being the first one to complete the trek."

"And it was your work as a writer that saw you as one of the authors in attendance at the Bucklesby residence on the night of Lachlan Denoon's murder?"

"It was. My latest book, '*Williamson's Will to Survive,*' was another bestseller—number one in adventure travel books and number five in the overall nonfiction chart—so it was in recognition of this success that I received, and graciously accepted, the invitation from Mavis Bucklesby."

"Mavis Bucklesby being the owner and organizer of the event?"

"Yes, that's correct."

"Talk me through the basic premise of the event. It's an author retreat, right?"

"Yes, it's an *invitation-only* retreat for *bestselling* authors in the major different genres—fiction, nonfiction, children's, historical, self-help and, of course, travel. A love of literature runs deep in the veins of all of the attendees and we get to share this passion for the written word with each other throughout the retreat, with some really great roundtable discussions taking place."

"Did you speak to Mitch Owens much during the event?"

"Not really. He did bring me a couple of drinks though, as did the other servers present."

"And you had previously met Lachlan Denoon as an early contestant on one of your television shows?"

"Yes, that's correct, although this was only brought to my attention recently. I'm afraid we have so many people trying out for these shows that it's difficult to remember everyone individually."

"Had you heard of his writing before the event?"

"Yes, I had. I mean, he's not what you might refer to as established author, he is—sorry, *was*—a newcomer in the book world, but I like to keep an ear to the ground as to who the new kids on the block are, so to speak, and I first heard murmurings about his work a year or so ago."

"Have you read his book?"

"No," scoffed Stamford, steepling his hands, fingers splayed wide apart, in a classic superior gesture. "I tend to go for the slightly more highbrow end of things, but I understand he's very popular, so well done him."

"Did you have much in the way of interaction with Lachlan Denoon at the retreat?"

"Oh, yes. All the attendees got to interact with each other, some more than others, of course, but I spoke to Lachlan on several occasions and witnessed many of his discussions with others present too."

"Were any of the discussions you witnessed what could be referred to as ill tempered?"

"Not between authors, we always keep it professional."

"What about with others present?"

"I'm afraid to say there was an argument between the server Mitch Owens and Lachlan Denoon. There was no love lost between them, that's for sure."

"When did the argument between them occur?"

"Well, I don't know if it was their only argument, they may well have had others prior to this, but the one I saw was during the afternoon, just after an author discussion about the merits of some book or another, the specifics of which I can't recall, when we were all having some downtime. Most of us were sitting around the pool area enjoying the hospitality when shouting erupted in the courtyard nearby."

"And who was it that was shouting?"

"It was Mitch Owens and Lachlan Denoon. And it got quite personal."

"The defense has tried to paint this as a one-way argument, as if it was Lachlan Denoon inciting Mitch Owens, not the other way around. Is this your recollection of events?"

"Certainly not. From where I was standing, Mitch Owens was very much the antagonist."

Mitch was incensed and leant in to whisper words of protest to Rainbird.

"What happened next?"

"Well, from my point of view, I was monitoring the situation—and situational awareness should not be underestimated, not in my business anyway; in fact, it's the cornerstone. We were currently in what experts refer to as Code Yellow—there's a potential danger for escalation, but I was ready and relaxed. As the argument between Mitch Owens and Lachlan Denoon progressed, we moved to Code Orange—I identified a potential threat and was prepared to act. At the moment Mitch Owens took his aggressive first step toward Lachlan Denoon we entered Code Red—emergency time, I was focused on dealing with the emergency at hand. It all comes back to the OODA Loop: observe, orient, decide and act."

"In what way did you act?"

"Verbally, after Mitch Owens struck Lachlan Denoon in the face, I put my training into action: 'Hey, you two, pack it in!' I said. Luckily, they both seemed to recognize my authority, and, after a few curt words, things seemed to simmer down, although I was ready to pacify them physically if necessary—I'm trained, Cornish wrestling among other combat systems, so it was there if I needed it."

"Mr. Williamson, I want to ask you about slightly later on in the afternoon, when, according to your written statement, you and Professor Aris were on the sand dunes together, is that correct?"

"Yes."

"Could you tell the court what you were doing there and what you saw?"

"Professor Aris and I were sharing a brandy, a nice drop, discussing the earlier chaotic and animated altercation at the house between the server and Lachlan Denoon, when who should come running over the dunes with a great big red stain on their t-shirt, but none other than Mitch Owens."

"You're sure it was Owens?"

"As sure as I am looking at him in this court today," said Stamford, turning to fix Mitch with a stare.

Mitch shook his head in disbelief, but Stamford was only warming up. When Veitch got him to describe the moment Lachlan's body was found, Stamford really got into his stride.

"I was back in my own room when, all of a sudden, I became aware of yelling, someone calling for help. Instinct took over, I sprang to my feet and ran as fast as I could outside toward the sound, by which stage it was clear it was coming from Lachlan Denoon's room."

"And what was it that you saw when you entered the room?"

"Carnage. Sheer bloody carnage. Lachlan Denoon was on the floor, blood seeping profusely from a gaping neck wound. He was unconscious, possibly already dead. It was a hopeless situation really, but I had to try something. Someone had to take control as the others present were in a state of shock, no help to him or themselves."

He turned to the public gallery for the next bit, addressing them as if part of one of his nauseating TED Talks.

"First though, I stopped to assess the situation—first aid 101, you look out for danger, both to yourself and others. You ask the question, is it safe to approach the scene? If not, you've got to make the scene safe before proceeding. I gave it the all clear and moved in. Next up was your classic ABC."

He began counting on his hand.

"A: Airway, you check for obstructions, B: Breathing, is the casualty breathing? C: Circulation, does the casualty have a pulse? His airway was clear, but there was no sign of breathing or a pulse. It was time to activate the next stage in the emergency protocol—call for help, gotta get some pros on the scene. I outsourced this to Henry Hunt, who, like the others, was standing around with a look of helpless bewilderment on his face, but I instructed him to call 911. While he was placing the call, I made a makeshift wound dressing from a flannel in the bathroom and applied this to Lachlan Denoon's throat, after which I attempted resuscitation, but in truth it was already too late. The EMTs arrived soon after but, despite our best efforts, poor Lachlan was pronounced dead at the scene."

Stamford looked wistfully at the jury.

A man jumped to his feet in the public gallery and jabbed a finger in Mitch's direction.

"Murderer!" he yelled, before security grabbed hold of him and dragged him out under a severe reprimand from Judge Jenkins.

"No further questions," said Veitch, when order had finally been established.

"Your witness," announced Judge Jenkins.

Rainbird rose to his feet.

"Stamford Williamson—O.B.E.," said Rainbird, methodically sounding out the letters. "*Order of the British Empire*—is that still a thing?"

"Well, technically no, it's an award for chivalry."

"Bestowed by the monarch of England, I believe."

"Yes, that's correct. It was a great honor to meet the sovereign—for my charitable work in the Scouting movement. I don't normally like to highlight the award, I'm really just regular Stamford."

"Mmm," mulled Rainbird. "Just regular Stamford. Well, I certainly think you're deserving of an award—keeper of the peace, heroic would-be paramedic. Sounds like it was lucky you were on the scene."

"One does what one can."

"Really? You see, I think you've weaved quite a tale here today for the court, isn't that the case?"

"If by 'tale' you mean something factually inaccurate, then I refute that emphatically."

"You're no stranger to accusations of factual inaccuracy, are you? There have been accusations leveled against you recently, claiming that certain elements of your programs are mere fictional dramatization, have there not?"

"Objection, Your Honor," piped up Veitch, rising to his feet with a look of disdain. "The unsubstantiated accusations Mr. Williamson has endured from certain elements of the gutter press are in no way relevant to the proceedings of the court here today. This is clearly a primitive attempt to cast doubt over Mr. Williamson's testimony by introducing a subject to the mix that is without substance or merit."

"This is not the case, Your Honor," said Rainbird. "If you will permit me a little leeway, I will demonstrate for the court that my line of questioning is entirely relevant."

"I'll permit it, but watch yourself, Counsel. This is not a theater production, understood?" said Jenkins.

"Yes, Your Honor," said Rainbird. "I will proceed with the dignity and brevity befitting this court."

Jenkins gave an approving nod.

"Mr. Williamson, are you familiar with the television series *Stamford Stamps Out Street Crime*?"

"Of course," said Stamford, rolling his eyes.

"Would you describe the show for the court?"

"I take a group of hardened young offenders on a wilderness retreat, during which they're shown tough love, and take on tough challenges to rehabilitate them back into society to better serve their communities."

"But there have been accusations leveled against you and the production team, claiming that these supposedly hardened felons were in fact middle-class first-time offenders."

Stamford shook his head.

"There are only two types of people in this world—doers and critics. I tend to ignore the latter."

"Mr. Williamson, are you also familiar with the reality television series *Williamson's Will to Survive*."

"Yes," said Stamford, releasing a frustrated breath.

"Would you tell the court what it is?"

"It's a television series hosted by me, based loosely on my book of the same title, in which I put volunteers through different survival challenges, as well as participating in others myself."

"And recently you have been accused of faking certain scenes in the series for dramatic effect, so as to capture more exciting footage? To take just one example from a long list, it is claimed that several of your life-and-death encounters with wild animals were anything but, with the supposedly dangerous animals in question—a rhino, hippo and a crocodile—actually being heavily sedated."

"The footage speaks for itself, there is no question as to its authenticity. I have a great respect for the strength and power of wild animals. If I seem able to easily control and evade their attacks on screen, then I assure you it is due to skill and a lifetime of experience in the outdoors, not some ill-administered veterinary medication."

Stamford gave a little chuckle to himself, as if this line of questioning was quite ridiculous.

"I'd like to ask you about an expedition you led where one of the participants, a Miss Chloe Brand, tragically died," said Rainbird.

Stamford's eyes widened, perhaps not enough for the jury to notice but it was a clear enough "tell" to Rainbird. Stamford clenched his jaw and momentarily scratched his neck.

"I don't see how this is relevant," said Stamford, glancing over at the judge in a futile hope of intervention. "What happened that day is entirely unrelated to the baseless accusations in the media. It was a tragic freak accident. A thorough investigation was opened into the circumstances of Chloe's fatality, which fully exonerated *Stampede Films*, and, by extension, myself, of any wrongdoing."

Rainbird moved in for the kill.

"I put it to you today, in a court of law where you have taken a solemn oath to tell the truth, the whole truth and nothing but the truth, that something quite different occurred than what you claim. Isn't it the case that you actually strong-armed Chloe Brand into taking part in a faked accident, in which she would fall into a crevasse in a glacier and dangle perilously from her rope until you emerged, her shining savior, to haul her to safety? While cameramen capture the action, of course?"

"Nonsense."

"Only things didn't go according to plan, did they? The faked fall caused her to hit her face with such impact as to cause, what medics later described as, the collapse of her entire facial structure."

"What happened to Chloe, who was a dear friend, was a freak accident. The independent inquiry proved that. There was no fakery involved. Any inference of such is without the remotest basis in reality, and I resent it."

"A dear friend, you say?"

"A dear, dear friend."

"Goodness, she must have been for you to use the double adjective."

Rainbird fixed him with a penetrating stare.

"Let me ask you, are you familiar with the name Reggie Brown?"

"I'm afraid I don't recall."

"Well, let me try and refresh your memory. Mr. Reggie Brown used to be a freelance cameraman, someone your production company hired to work on the series of *Williamson's Will to Survive* that Chloe Brand died on."

By now Stamford was looking nervous, small beads of sweat were forming on his brow and his cheeks were flushed scarlet red.

"If you say so, but I can't be expected to remember all the freelancers who come and go on shows like this—sound, camera, makeup, there's plenty. That sort of thing is dealt with by the production manager. I don't have much to do with those sorts of people."

"*Those sorts of people*," repeated Rainbird, mulling over the phrase. "Well, after finishing a stint on your show, Mr. Brown worked as a cameraman on the series of *The Rookie* where Lachlan Denoon really made a name for himself. Sadly, Mr. Brown can't tell us this in person as he too died recently, in a hit and run."

"Objection, Your Honor," said Veitch. "This has no relevance to the case before the court. Mr. Rainbird was generously given leeway by Your Honor to proceed, but has yet to deliver anything of substance. He is harassing the witness."

"It has every relevance, Your Honor," responded Rainbird. "As I am just about to demonstrate."

"I'll allow it," said the judge. "But tread carefully and do get to the point!"

"You see, unlike you, Mr. Stamford Williamson O.B.E., it seems Lachlan Denoon became close to several of *those sorts of people* on the show when he was a contestant—you know, freelancers, production assistants, runners. In fact, I'd say he became quite close friends with Mr. Brown. And friends talk, you know. And what was it that these friends talked about over a beer one night after the end of filming that is relevant to this case? They talked about the man they'd both met independently, and their experiences on his show—the great Stamford Williamson, O.B.E., that's who they talked about. Specifically, Mr. Brown's experiences on *Williamson's Will to Survive* and how things weren't quite as the viewer was led to believe. But talk, as the old cliché goes, is cheap, what matters, of course, is the evidence, and where's that? Well, unbeknownst to you at the time, Mr. Williamson, was that Mr. Brown had in his possession damning video evidence of your fakery and dramatization, including the moments leading up to Chloe Brand's death, and that he subsequently passed this on to Lachlan Denoon. Although you learned about this, didn't you? And set out to destroy both Mr. Brown and Lachlan Denoon. Isn't that so, Williamson?"

"Codswallop. Absolute codswallop!"

"If it will please the court, I would like to tender a document, a short video now in possession of the defense, a video which shows that Mr. Williamson is lying to the court."

Stamford turned to Veitch for help but before he could utter a word Judge Jenkins spoke.

"I'll allow it."

With no further ado, Rainbird picked up a remote control and clicked "play."

There on a screen in the center of the court began the opening credits of *Williamson's Will to Survive.*

"This is the show in question, ladies and gentlemen," said Rainbird to the jury. "And there's Mr. Williamson."

Dramatic music struck up and on screen appeared a flinty-eyed, sideways-glancing Stamford Williamson, dressed in khaki safari shirt and desert head scarf.

"I'm Stamford Williamson," announced the voice over. "Have you got the will to survive? I've put it on the line in some of the most dangerous environments on the planet and come out alive. Could you?"

A series of crash cuts of Stamford in expedition mode appeared on screen: trekking over sand dunes in the Sahara Desert, scaling a snow-covered peak in the Himalayas, a closeup of him blowing a smoldering ember into a flame, firing a hunting rifle, jumping from a rope bridge into a torrent of water below and taking a ravenous bite of a dead badger.

"This week I'm taking a team of recruits through their paces in the Russian Arctic Far North—a land of extremes where only the toughest of the tough can make it. Join me and a group of hopefuls for—*Williamson's Will to Survive.*"

The title words slammed individually into the center of the screen, one after the other, crashing, rapid fire in place, accompanied by the sound of an explosion for each word— BANG. BANG. BANG. BANG—followed, a beat later, by three further explosions as the text "*With Stamford Williamson*" underscored the title. There was a final momentary pause for effect and then another explosion, as "*O.B.E.*" concluded the opening.

Rainbird paused the video.

"The opening sequence for the latest series. Exciting stuff, I'm sure you'll agree," said Rainbird. "But for our purposes we'll need to watch some footage of outtakes from Series One, video taken that never made it into the show itself. Footage that has, until now, never seen the light of day."

Rainbird pressed play.

There on screen was a nervous looking Chloe Brand, poised above an icy crevasse, rope around her waist. Off screen a voice gave a countdown: "*Three, two, one, rolling.*" At this moment she took a tentative step forward and tumbled into the crevasse, where, a few feet into her fall, she was caught by her rope. "*Haul her up, try again, more rope,*" said the voice off screen. The process repeated, only this time she fell much further.

"I won't play you take number three," said Rainbird. "The one in which this young lady falls all the way to her death, after her length of rope was increased yet again, increased so as to make for a more visually dramatic 'accident.'"

"I had nothing to do with that," protested Stamford. "That's not even my voice you can hear. This is the first time I've seen this footage, and I, more than anyone, am outraged by what I'm seeing."

"Outraged, you say? I wonder then what your reaction will be to the next footage. Ladies and gentlemen of the jury, pay close attention. What you're about to see is the real Stamford Williamson O.B.E., unguarded and unaware he is being recorded, footage taken hours before this deliberate accident took place, in which Mr. Williamson can be seen casually discussing the faking of his own show with the program's production manager, Don Raffles—the man whose voice we heard off camera—and their mutual disregard for the safety and wellbeing of Chloe Brand."

Rainbird pressed play.

On screen was some shaky footage taken from a camera still turned on and recording, as the cameraman carrying it made his way toward a mess tent. Suddenly the angle of the footage shifted as the camera was placed on its side on a table outside the tent, capturing two individuals sitting nearby in opposing travel chairs—Williamson and Raffles. After a couple of minutes of bland and boring chit chat about locations and logistics, Stamford dropped a bomb.

"I've asked the new girl, forget her name, blonde one, quite tasty."

"Chloe."

"Yeah, Chloe, that's it, great ass," said Stamford.

"You're kidding, aren't you? Like the back end of a bus."

"The way I like them," he said with a glint In his eye.

"You don't?"

"Sir Isaac Newton put it best: *the greater the mass, the greater the force of attraction*!"

They both laughed.

"Anyway," continued Stamford, "I've instructed *Big Bottom* to take a tumble when we're making it over the crevasse, you know the drill. She'll dangle from a rope, and then, *BOOM*, the money shot! In comes 'The Stamford' and hauls her big squishy rear end to safety"

"She alright with it?"

"Bit reluctant, but I've told her if she wants to progress in this business, then she'll have to do as she's told."

Rainbird pressed pause.

"Are you or are you not a liar, Mr. Williamson?"

Stamford was speechless.

"I...I..."

"—The truth and you are strangers, sir, are they not? Lies emanate from you like a bad smell. Why is it that you attempted to paint Mitch Owens in the darkest possible way? Why is it that you claimed you saw Mitch coming in over the far side of the dunes, when your distance from there would make such a positive identification utterly impossible? Is it to deflect attention from someone a little closer?"

Rainbird stared hard at Stamford, as if his eyes were cutting into his soul.

"I put it to you, that you were blackmailed by Lachlan Denoon and that you had the motive to kill him. Isn't that so?"

There was a collective gasp from the public gallery.

Stamford went white, the color draining from him like a poorly dyed shirt on a hot wash.

"No, that's not true!"

"It was you who went to his room that afternoon, under some false pretense, and then, when his back was turned, you attacked him, viciously striking him and thrusting the pointed section of his award into his throat, until he was dying on the floor in front of you, when you struck him a final blow—smashing out his two front teeth. You were furious that his career was in its prime while yours was on the turn, and he had the evidence to destroy it completely. You were jealous of his popularity, you were jealous of his acclaim, and I put it to you, that you were jealous of his teeth too, and that is why you smashed them out as a spiteful parting gesture."

"No, that's not what happened. I mean, yes—he did have good dentistry—but look, I'm not a killer, I swear. The first I knew of it was when Professor Aris began shouting from Lachlan's room."

"Lies!" boomed Rainbird. "Lachlan confronted you at the writers retreat and told you he had the footage, he even taunted you about it. It was then you decided to murder him, not in a rush of blood to the head, but in the worst cold and calculated way. You evidently lied with a breath-taking nonchalance about the woman you killed in your television show and you're lying now too. Rather apt title really: *Williamson's Will to Survive*. You knew your career wouldn't survive evidence of your complicity in a young woman's death; your will to survive, *Williamson*, was strong enough for you to kill another human being, wasn't it? Perhaps the third person you have killed. First Miss Chloe Brand, followed by the cameraman, Mr. Brown, killed in a hit and run, and now Lachlan Denoon."

"No. Look, I admit to lying earlier about the stunts in my show, but you've got to understand this is standard practice for these sorts of programs..."

Rainbird cut in. "—No further questions."

"But I want to..."

"—No further questions," insisted Rainbird with authority.

There was pandemonium in the public gallery.

"Order in court! Order in court!" yelled Judge Jenkins, bashing down his gavel again and again before he restored quiet.

With a solemn look he turned to Stamford Williamson.

"Whether it is standard practice or not to lie and deceive viewers by way of a television program is neither here nor there to this court. What is standard practice in a court of law is for those who have committed perjury, and justly been shown to have done so, as you patently have, to pay the price for it. The powers vested in me allow for a sentence of between one and five years' imprisonment for the very serious crime of perjury. Your one saving grace is the nature of the perjury you just admitted to committing, with it concerning your television show rather than events directly related to the case in front of this court today. For this reason, and this alone, you may escape the maximum penalty. However, you should not expect to escape a custodial sentence altogether. Mr. Stamford Williamson O.B.E., henceforth not only will you have letters after your name, but also numbers of the prison system. Your sentencing will occur after this trial has run its course. You shall return in front of me then."

As Stamford stepped down from the stand in tears, cheers erupted from the public gallery and this time Judge Jenkins let them pass. Rainbird couldn't resist a little grin at Veitch, whose face contorted in frustration.

Rainbird turned to an awe-struck Mitch Owens and winked. For the first time in a long while, Mitch smiled, a long-fought smile of relief

Little did he know just how short lived it would be.

CHAPTER 44

Solemn portraits of notable legal figures from yesteryear stared out from the dark wooden panels of the side room just off the main court, where Mitch sat at a small round table with a different expression to those on the wall—a broad and relaxed smile on his face, unaware of the grenade about to blow up in it. As far as he was aware, his masterful attorney had just obliterated the case against him, pointing the finger, and convincingly so, at Stamford Williamson instead. Reasonable doubt had been established and, by the looks of it, he'd be going home.

For a moment Rainbird stood and gazed out the window, watching the branches of a nearby cottonwood tree rustle in the wind, its leaves illuminated an iridescent green by the brilliant sun, while he formulated what to say to Mitch about the bombshell news Georgina had just delivered to him during the afternoon recess.

He turned to Mitch.

"You need to listen to me very carefully, do you understand?" said Rainbird in a manner of grave seriousness that took Mitch by surprise.

"Yes, of course," replied Mitch, a combination of confusion and concern etched on his face.

"As a lawyer, I'm legally bound to tell the truth in court. I'm bound by earnest oath that I cannot lie to the judge. If, for example, a client were to admit a crime to me, I couldn't then claim in court that they didn't commit the crime, as I would be knowingly lying to the judge. Under such circumstances, I would be severely restricted in doing my job, and the job of a good lawyer is to shine a light on all the little holes in the state's case against his client, to highlight the government's failure to conclusively prove that his client carried out a crime. I could and would still do that, after all, I'm also ethically bound to zealously represent my client, but doing so after a client has admitted guilt is no easy matter, do you understand?"

Concern grew greater on Mitch's face as he nodded in silence.

"I mention this as evidence has just arrived in my office which is very unfavorable to our case. I am going to tell you about it and, bearing in mind what I have just told you, I want you to respond accordingly and with great caution."

Again, Mitch nodded.

"Footage from a security camera mounted on a small private boat out fishing in the waters just beyond the Bucklesby mansion has been discovered. Footage from the day of Lachlan Denoon's murder that shows, contrary to your previous claims, that you did, in fact, return to the Bucklesby mansion after your initial departure."

Mitch went white and swayed a little in his chair, panic building in his eyes to the point where he looked like he might puke.

"The boat in question was accidentally rammed when back at the harbor, minor damage, little more than a dent, but enough to prompt the owner to file an insurance claim. The insurance company recently requested the vessel's camera footage to support the claim and in scrawling through the video, this is what they found just 30 minutes before his nautical fender bender," said Rainbird, opening up a laptop on the table and clicking play on a video file.

There, on screen, was footage from a camera mounted on the rear of the boat's cockpit, looking out across a small stretch of water, with sand dunes and the Bucklesby mansion just beyond. The footage rocked from side to side as the boat ebbed with the gentle flow of the waves, but then another movement became apparent, a lone figure walking along the beach and then clandestinely making their way over the sand dunes into the Bucklesby Mansion. Rainbird forwarded the video to the moment the same figure appeared again, this time running over the dunes with a backpack toward the camera. As the figure got closer, Rainbird clicked *pause*. The individual was plain to see—Mitch, wearing a t-shirt now bearing a stain of some sort that had been absent in the previous footage. It was unambiguous. The footage was time and date stamped. Here was Mitch doing exactly as was alleged by the prosecution, entering and exiting the property after his initial fight with Lachlan Denoon.

"It's not what it seems!" exclaimed Mitch, distraught. "I never did it, I promise. You've got to believe me, Mr. Rainbird. I went back to get my bag. After my row with Lachlan, I left the property, got in my car and drove out of there. Only, about five minutes down the road, I realized I'd left my wallet, phone and bag in the staff quarters. So I made a U-turn and went back, but there's no way they'd open up the main gates and let me through after what had just gone down, so I parked up around the corner and got in over the sand dunes. I was still pretty amped up, but I managed to pick up my stuff without anyone seeing me. But as I was heading out near Lachlan's guest cottage, I spotted him, standing in his front door, head rolled back smoking a fat cigar, blowing great clouds of smoke into the air. I wasn't going to do anything, really, I wasn't, but as I tried to walk past on the path outside, he said, 'You should apologize for this,' and touches his swollen lip. I didn't respond and maybe that's what antagonized him as, despite what happened to him earlier, he just couldn't resist having another dig at me. He took a deep draw on his cigar and blew the smoke right into my face, and said, 'You'll never amount to anything, Mitch—anything at all. And that broad of yours will soon lose interest in you and move onto a real man—someone like me.' That's when I snapped and went for him."

"Don't say anything more!" exclaimed Rainbird.

"No, I snapped and hit him. That's all. I didn't snap and kill him. I hit him on the nose, only the once, didn't even knock him down, he just sort of stumbled back into the accommodation holding his face. I know I shouldn't have, but I was incensed, so I went after him, following him inside, where we sort of tussled for a bit then I grabbed him by the neck and raised a fist ready to belt him again, but when I saw him cowering in front of me, nose bleeding all over the place, I came to my senses. That's when I ran out his room. That's what happened. I didn't kill him. You've got to believe me. Please say you believe me, Mr. Rainbird."

"So why didn't you tell me this in the first place? And why didn't you say this in your original statement and interview?"

"I realized it didn't look good. But I didn't see anyone, so figured nobody saw me or needed to know. I denied it on tape before the police said they a had witness, but by that stage I was committed, and knew that if I changed my story then it would look bad."

"Not as bad as it does now! This footage proves you lied." Rainbird, glared at him unconvinced. "I'm not going to lie to you, Mitch. This is catastrophic to our case, almost to the point of being irredeemable. I do not exaggerate when I say that our defense is in tatters. So much for calling the dog walker who failed to pick you out of the lineup—I guess their eyesight actually is as bad as I made the professor's out to be. No case is ever lost until the verdict of the jury is in, but this is as close to it as I can imagine. The prosecution will have a field day. It is highly unlikely that they will accept it, but I can at least attempt a plea deal to—"

"—No," interrupted Mitch with utter conviction. "I won't accept a plea of any sort. Mr. Rainbird, I didn't do it. I know that might seem unlikely right now, and I can understand why you probably don't believe me, but that's the truth. I hit the guy, I'm guilty of assault, not murder."

Mitch took a deep breath, sat up straighter in his chair and looked Rainbird in the eye.

"As my lawyer, I instruct you to under no circumstances pursue a plea deal."

Rainbird was shocked, speechless for a moment.

Mitch's conviction was plain to see. When Rainbird had first met Mitch, he'd believed that he was innocent of murder. Right now, after Mitch's deception Rainbird had to admit it might be the opposite. All the evidence said he was guilty, he could see that. But despite everything and the seeming implausibility of Mitch's story, Rainbird's gut said the kid wasn't lying. Not this time. And Rainbird always trusted his gut.

"All right then," said Rainbird. "If that's the way you want it, then from now on you have to tell me everything. No more lies. I want the truth. The whole truth. And nothing but the truth."

Mitch nodded.

"Have you ever had any involvement in, or do you have any knowledge of, illegal activity associated with Magnus's fishing fleet?"

Mitch breathed out hard.

"I was never involved, but just before the time I started seeing Stephanie, I heard whispers, rumors among the fishing crews, about Magnus's boats meeting up with random vessels far out to sea, and him bringing in strange cargo."

"Drugs?"

"That was the rumor. I made the mistake of asking questions about it after one of the skippers approached me to see if I wanted extra work on the side delivering packages."

"Did you?"

"Work? Yes. Delivering drugs? No. I told him my concerns and that I wasn't interested if that's what was in them. I'm guessing it got back to Magnus that I knew, and then when I started dating Stephanie, he must have been worried that I would tell her, but I never did, nor would I tell her something that would get in the way of her relationship with her dad. It's none of my business. I think Magnus knew about our relationship from the start and wanted me to back off from Stephanie in case I told her what he's up to, only I got arrested for murder first and it was no longer necessary."

Rainbird pondered all this, frustration imprinted across his face. If he didn't come up with something concrete, and fast, then the whole case would be over with the worst possible outcome, and just at the moment when he thought he had it all sewn up. The jury would now conclude Stamford was telling the truth after all, and that although he'd been exposed as a phony, he wasn't the killer of Lachlan Denoon. All the hard-fought ground Rainbird had gained had been thrown away in an instant. He needed answers and he needed then right now.

"Mitch, you need to know that if you're found guilty after changing your story, then the judge will likely give you a much more severe sentence. And if by some miracle you're found not guilty, there's every likelihood you'll still be convicted of perjury. By admitting you returned to the house, you're also admitting your written statement to the court is a lie, and there's now irrefutable evidence to prove this."

An abrupt knock on the door cut through his counsel.

The door swung open and there stood the Court Clerk accompanied by two prison officers.

"Time's up. Back to lock up, Mitch."

CHAPTER 45

The wooden floor creaked beneath Mitch's feet as he walked back toward the witness box for a second time, following his earlier examination by Rainbird before the lunch recess. Now came the difficult bit—Veitch's turn. With every footstep Mitch took, he could almost feel blood leaching from his brain into his legs, leaving him lightheaded yet making each step toward the stand seem heavy. His heart thumped as he sat down and inhaled deeply. This was the moment of truth. He knew how much was riding on what came next, and so did Rainbird. With a tentative glance, Mitch looked out across the courtroom. The eyes of the jury were on him, all eager to witness the drama that would soon inevitably unfold.

They'd heard Mitch speak when Rainbird had questioned him. Mitch had told his side of the story and, crucially, why he'd changed it. It was a hard sell. Under the circumstances there were few softball questions Rainbird could throw at him. Instead, Mitch had to confront his own untruthfulness head on, but he'd spoken from the heart. He told the jury he'd acted out of fear, that he'd been scared because he knew how bad it looked to admit to returning to the property, and how it looked even worse to admit to striking Lachlan again, but that he was innocent of the crime of murder, and telling the truth and the whole truth—this time. That was the nub of it, of course, but he'd been pretty convincing. At one stage he'd welled up on the verge of tears, not crocodile tears, but the real thing. There was an authenticity to Mitch's testimony that matched the raw truthfulness Rainbird had perceived in Mitch when he'd first come clean to him about returning to the Bucklesby mansion. To Rainbird it seemed to play well with the jury, but Rainbird knew more than anyone that this could change, and fast. The second half would be no friendly chit chat with someone on Mitch's side, but a hostile grilling from one of the toughest in the business; he was prepared, as much as he could be, but then no plan survives contact with the enemy.

Putting Mitch on the stand had been a risky strategy, but after the discovery of the video footage contradicting his initial statement, Rainbird felt he had little choice but to take the chance of letting the jury hear Mitch's explanation. Jurors responded to authenticity, they knew people lied all the time both for honorable and less than honorable motives. Rainbird just hoped they could spot the truth in Mitch.

Mitch swallowed with resolve, his throat parched. He was determined to trust his own honesty and prayed that the jury would see it as the truth.

Veitch rose, a cruel glow in his eyes, like he almost felt a sadistic arousal at what lay ahead.

"Good afternoon, Mr. Owens."

"Good afternoon."

"Are you familiar with the fable of *The Boy Who Cried Wolf*?"

"Er, yes. Yes, I am."

"In the story a young shepherd boy lies repeatedly, lie after lie after lie, always lying, fooling villagers into believing that a wolf is attacking the village's flock of sheep. Only when an actual wolf arrives one day and the boy cries out for help, the villagers ignore him, believing it to be yet another lie, delivered by a well-known liar, and then of course the sheep are killed and eaten by the wolf."

Veitch paused, staring hard at Mitch. "This is basically your defense. You want us to believe that you're the boy who cried wolf. That yes, you did lie earlier but now, when it really matters, you're telling the truth."

"I am," replied Mitch softly.

"You see, I think you are the wolf. Wolves kill, mercilessly and without conscience."

He paused and gazed at the jury, giving them time to contemplate his words.

"Actually, you're worse than that," continued Veitch. "You're a wolf in sheep's clothing. Years in this profession have taught me that killers rarely look or sound the way you expect, not like some caricature of a baddie anyway. And that's true of you. Which is why evidence is always more important than the personable appearance or eloquence of the defendant or, I might add, his counsel."

Veitch glanced over at Rainbird.

"Your testimony this morning was quite the performance, it had the tears and the emotion alright. You tried to tug at our heart strings and perhaps you almost succeeded in convincing a few of the more gullible in this room with your little story."

Veitch gazed toward the public gallery not the jury, he didn't want any of them to think he was saying they were gullible enough to believe such nonsense.

"But it is in direct contradiction to your sworn written statement. And that statement is quite explicit. In it you claim that when you left the Bucklesby property after your fight with Lachlan Denoon, that you did not return there. That was a lie, wasn't it?"

"Yes."

"But you're not coming clean because of a pang of conscience, are you?"

"No."

"You're not coming clean as an act of remorse, are you?"

"No."

"Rather, you're 'fessing up now as an act of desperation. After it's become clear you've been caught out as the liar that you are. Isn't that so?"

"Not exactly."

"That is *exactly* so. Thanks to this new video evidence, we can now see with our own eyes the same thing Professor Aris *correctly* saw with his own eyes: that you returned to the Bucklesby residence over the sand dunes after your initial fight with Lachlan Denoon. Yes, we all remember the performance your counsel put in when cross examining poor Professor Aris, claiming his short sightedness and the absence of his glasses brought his testimony into doubt. Made him look pretty silly too. That little number made a mockery of this court. And all over something that we now know Professor Aris was absolutely correct and honest about from the start. Would you like to apologize to him?"

"Objection," said Rainbird rising to his feet. "Badgering the witness."

"Overruled."

Veitch had to proceed with caution here, he wanted to highlight that the professor had been right all along in stating that he'd seen Mitch running away over the sand dunes, and then move on. What he didn't want to do was explicitly state that Stamford Williamson had been right too. If he did, then, by extension, the jury might draw a parallel between Mitch and Stamford. And that would be unhelpful. After all, Stamford had been shown to be a liar in some areas of his testimony while telling the truth in others, which, essentially, was what Mitch was claiming of himself now. Veitch needed the jury to disregard that possibility with Mitch altogether. He needed them to believe that Mitch had not only lied about one bit, but was lying about it all.

"It was Einstein who once said that, 'those who cannot be trusted with the truth in small matters should never be trusted with it in big matters.' I couldn't agree more. Isn't it the truth that when you returned to the property, you did so with the premeditated intention of killing your former friend Lachlan Denoon?"

"No that's not true."

"Not true, like it wasn't true that you came back to the property over the sand dunes?"

"Well no, not like, look, I didn't kill him."

"I want to take this step by step. In your testimony earlier today, you claimed to have returned to the property and retrieved your possessions from inside the main house. And then what happened?"

"I saw Lachlan on my way out. Standing in his doorway smoking a cigar."

"And you decided to go over to him?"

"No."

"But you did go over to him, you told the jury that this morning. Are you now saying something different again?"

"No. Look, I had to go *past* him to leave, the path to the beach went straight past his accommodation."

"Was it the only path from the house to the beach?"

"I'm not sure."

"Not sure, you say? In actual fact, there are three separate paths to the beach. Once you spotted Lachlan you could have avoided him altogether by using a different path, but you decided not to, didn't you?"

"It was the quickest way."

"A second ago you said you weren't sure if there were any other paths from the house to the beach. Now you're telling us it was the quickest path. How can you know it was the quickest path if you didn't already know about the other paths, which presumably you then most have known weren't as quick? Are you lying again?"

"No. It was practically on the dunes, any other route to the beach would have been longer."

"So, you're walking along the path toward Lachlan Denoon. And then what?"

"He sort of glares at me, takes a deep drag on his cigar and blows the smoke in my direction as I get close."

"How close were you when he did this?"

"I don't know, maybe three feet."

"Three feet? That sounds awfully close, like you got up into his personal space."

"I just followed the path."

"You couldn't have walked around to avoid him?"

"I didn't see why I should move on account of him."

"No you did not! You got up in his face, didn't you?"

"No."

"What did you say to him?"

"Nothing. He spoke to me."

"In your testimony this morning, you stated that Lachlan Denoon said to you..." Veitch reached for a piece of paper and read aloud. "'...You'll never amount to anything, Mitch, and that bimbo of yours will soon lose interest in you and move onto a real man—someone like me.' How did that make you feel?"

"Angry."

"More than angry, you were livid, weren't you?"

"Maybe."

"No *maybe* about it. You wanted to hurt him, didn't you?"

"Yes, I did."

"What happened next?"

"I hit him."

"Where did you hit him?"

"On the nose."

"Describe the blow, was it powerful?"

"Yes."

"How did it feel to hit him?"

Mitch paused. "It felt good."

"And then what happened?"

"He stumbled back into the entrance of his accommodation."

"So to be clear, you could have left it at that and departed. But you didn't, did you?"

"No."

"Earlier today you told the jury that you followed Lachlan Denoon inside, grabbed him by the neck, and raised a fist menacingly into the air, to do what?"

"To hit him again. But I stopped."

"You'd like us to believe that wouldn't you?"

"Yes, because it's the truth. When I saw what I'd done to his nose, I came to my senses and ran away."

A male juror let out a loud derisive snort.

"Order in court!" announced Judge Jenkins, hitting his gavel down hard. "Jurors will not express an opinion during proceedings, and that snort was tantamount to doing so. You may believe the defendant's explanation is worthy of ridicule but you will not broadcast it. Your opinion will be consigned to your role in deliberations when this case has run its course. If there are any more outbursts like that you will be charged with contempt. Do you understand?"

"Yes, sir. I mean, yes, Judge,' said the juror, going red.

"Continue, Counsel," said Jenkins, turning to Veitch, who managed to contain his glee at the juror's response under a heavy cloak of indifference.

Veitch knew he had Mitch on the rocks. He sensed blood and went in for the kill. "You struck him in the back of the head like the coward that you are, didn't you?"

"No."

Veitch reached down to a nearby table and from it picked up a replica of the McIntyre Award, golden in hue, all polished and sparkling.

"This is what you used, isn't it?" said Veitch, holding the award aloft.

"No."

"Bash! Bash! Bash!" said Veitch, aggressively striking the award in a downward motion toward a helpless imaginary victim. "Again and again and again. Each time more powerful than the last, but that wasn't enough, was it? No, you wanted absolute revenge, and you made sure you got it. So as Lachlan was reeling on the ground, his head half smashed in, you thrust the pointed end of his McIntyre Award into his throat. And then, as he lay at your feet, gasping, bleeding, dying, you delivered your final vindictive farewell, striking him in the mouth, dislodging his two front teeth for good measure. Isn't that what you did?"

"No. I didn't do it. You have to believe me. I'm an innocent man."

"You've lied before and you're lying now, aren't you?"

"No."

"Tell the truth! You killed him, didn't you?" roared Veitch.

"No."

"You claim you lied because you were scared. Do you know what scares me? It's seeing murderers escape justice. Seeing them set free to kill again, emboldened by the knowledge that they got away with it before. Keeps me up at night, it does. Do you feel any remorse for what you did?"

"Objection," protested Rainbird.

"Sustained. Counsel will stick to the evidential facts of the case not lead the witness with questions relating to emotional remorse for an act the defendant denies."

Veitch gave Judge Jenkins a contrite respectful nod. "There is a stain clearly visible on your t-shirt in the video footage. What is that stain?"

"Blood."

"Whose blood?"

"Lachlan Denoon's," whispered Mitch.

"So the court can hear you."

"It is Lachlan Denoon's blood."

A stunned wave of shock swept through the public gallery.

"No further questions, Your Honor."

"But I want to explain. I have more to say... I thought—"

"—No further questions," boomed Veitch.

"The witness will be quiet," ordered Judge Jenkins.

Mitch looked first toward Rainbird then over to the jury, his eyes hollow as the twelve men and women stared back at him with certainty in theirs. There was no longer any question in their minds as to Mitch's guilt. It was, in that moment, that a part of Mitch's soul seemed to wither and die. The inevitability of it all hit him. It was emotionally like nothing else Mitch had ever experienced.

As Judge Jenkins called a halt to proceedings for the weekend recess and Mitch was taken back into custody, Veitch sauntered over to Rainbird and leaned in close.

"I want to remind you of our discussion in the café, when you had a chance and threw it all away." Veitch grinned. "Beating you a second time is even sweeter than the first. I do look forward to addressing the press after my victory. Godspeed, my friend."

CHAPTER 46

Rainbird gave a quick polite knock before opening the door and sticking his head around to look into the room.

"Morning, Doc, is now a good time? Nicola said I should come straight up."

Dr. Hobart gave a brief laugh, while gesturing to the chair in front of her.

"Yes, Alfie, take a seat. One of the benefits of being the first appointment in the morning, is that I have a clear head unburdened by other clients. The downside is, of course, having to get out of bed!"

Rainbird smiled. "Actually, I like the morning. The earlier the better."

"Oh dear," Dr. Hobart sighed. "You're one of those people. I'm afraid, if I could manage it, I would stay nestled in my bed until at least 10 o'clock, but there are far too many demands on my time to get away with that. So…" Dr. Hobart leafed through a few notes on her desk, "…where shall we begin today?"

Rainbird pondered for a moment. He forced himself to conjure up images of Abigail, of happy times together, of the difficult last few months, trying to work out where to begin. How do you unpack the sorrow of the perfect life unrealized? Then he shook his head with frustration.

"I'm sorry Doc—Anna—I really did decide to come in here today and make the most of this session. I don't know about all this shrink stuff, but if I'm going to be here, I might as well try and get something out of it."

"Thank you, Alfie, I appreciate that."

"Problem is, today I just can't get work out of my head. You know, every fiber of my being wants to march out of here and do what I can for my client."

"And what is that, exactly?"

"Well," Rainbird frowned. "That's the problem, I suppose. It's not looking that great. In fact, it's looking terrible but I believe in my client's innocence. Obviously, I would do my best for him regardless, but this kid… he's a good kid. He's got potential, but the evidence is against him. Maybe there's more to it. I just need to work out what details are relevant and what is just coincidence."

Dr. Hobart nodded.

"These sessions aren't just about working through your issues, directly. There are many benefits to be had, simply by talking through what's on your mind. Why don't you tell me about your client?"

Rainbird hesitated for a moment.

"It's OK," said Dr. Hobart. "I'm bound by patient confidentiality. Anything you say here will go no further. I won't even take notes. Just use me as a sounding board."

Rainbird looked dubious, but then shrugged.

"I suppose you're right. I'd be talking it through with George anyway. Might as well get my thoughts straight first."

Rainbird relaxed deeper into his chair, staring at a blank spot on the wall, before continuing.

"Mitch is not just some layabout trying to get by on other people's hard work. He may not have been born with privilege, but he is determined not to let that hold him back. He has character and ambition, and sometimes that can put people's noses out of joint. I guess I know how that feels. But there are people out there, decent people, who can see that he has more to offer than the same job for the next forty years, in the place he grew up, married to someone 'suitable.' His girlfriend Stephanie, she too wants to break out of the mold she's been cast in since birth. Experience a bit of freedom, life on her own terms. She's lucky to have money behind her, but it has strings attached, and she's ready to throw all that away to be with Mitch."

Rainbird stopped and looked at Dr. Hobart.

"I'm not really sure this is useful. I'm just wasting your time."

Dr. Hobart nodded. "I understand, but I think you should continue."

"As you wish," replied Rainbird with a mock bow and a cheeky smile. "They want to get out and travel more, see the world. Mitch was a bit reluctant, he doesn't have the advantages that Stephanie has, so he felt he needed to get some sort of qualification, something that would lead to a better future. Then, as luck would have it, an opportunity presented itself. Although, it's not luck, is it? It's never really luck. When he was touring as a roadie, he didn't just set up and relax. He stuck around, watching everything that went on and found he was really interested in what the sound engineer was doing. You know, the guy who sets up the microphones and equipment, makes the band sound good. His attention didn't go unnoticed and the engineer offered Mitch an apprenticeship. Mitch helps him lug his gear around and set up, and in return he not only gets paid as a roadie but also gets training in a career he's really interested in. He's supposed to be joining a tour in a couple of months, and Stephanie was going to tag along, traveling all over Europe and North America."

Rainbird broke off.

"Only if I fail to do my job, that's never going to happen."

"Sounds like you're under a lot of pressure with this case. Not just external, but within yourself," said Dr. Hobart.

"The pressure isn't the problem. I thrive under pressure. But I'm frustrated. The evidence looks terrible and, to make matters worse, Mitch has changed his story. Convincing a jury of his innocence with the evidence we have and after he has admitted lying will be difficult, almost impossible. The whole trial has been a struggle, and just when I thought I had it all tied up and knew the guilty party, it fell apart. There are powerful people who've had an interest in making it look as bad as possible for Mitch, people with the power and money to influence witnesses, even the arresting officer. Stephanie's father, Magnus, not only did he disapprove of the relationship, but Mitch discovered he's involved in serious criminality. And from what I hear, he's right. Was Lachlan Denoon involved? Maybe. Maybe Denoon knew something he shouldn't have and tried to blackmail Magnus, however foolish that would be."

Rainbird paused to gather his thoughts.

"If it is Magnus, well, he's a slippery character to say the least. But my gut isn't sure. There was something about the murder that just feels too messy for Magnus. If only I could work out the missing piece…"

"Gut instinct is important to you. Maybe you're trying to force the answers when you actually need to relax and let them come to you."

Rainbird took a deep breath.

"There's also Stamford Williamson. Without a doubt he hated Denoon, and was being blackmailed by him. I had him on the ropes in court, but the idea he could commit that murder without getting any blood on his clothes, or that he had an identical outfit ready to change into, well, it's just not plausible. He certainly was never alone long enough to clean himself up—wash off the blood, dry his clothes again—unless someone is covering for him, and that's just not likely, is it?"

"Is there anything else that comes to mind?"

"Denoon knew Patricia Parry-Jones and Professor Aris were having an affair. He blackmailed Aris into writing him a glowing endorsement, so there's motive. However, I just don't think the professor is capable of murder, and Parry-Jones has made it abundantly clear that she doesn't care enough about the truth getting out to want to kill Denoon to keep him quiet."

Rainbird sat up and leaned forward in his chair, resting his elbows on his knees.

"And then there's the ghost…"

"A supernatural killing? I didn't have you down as a believer in the paranormal, Alfie."

Rainbird laughed. "Well, Anna, I would never claim to understand all the mysteries of heaven and earth, but no, I don't think this was some sort of unnatural vengeance from an otherworldly realm. No, George has a theory that Lachlan Denoon is not the author of his own work. That actually it is all ghost written and he merely approves the end result."

"Ah, interesting," Dr. Hobart replied with a smile. "Why don't you tell me a bit more about George. You have a good working relationship with him, I think."

"Him?" Rainbird sat back with surprise. "Oh, of course, George. Ha, she's a bit of a tomboy to be sure, but she is most definitely a woman. It's short for Georgina. Not that anyone else calls her George, it's a bit of a term of endearment just between us..."

Rainbird pressed his hand to his forehead in a gesture of realization.

"Of course!"

Standing abruptly, Rainbird stuck out his hand to shake Dr. Hobart's.

"I'm sorry, but I'm going to have to go. There's something I need to see to. Time's almost up anyway, isn't it? I'll book another appointment. Thank you, this has been more useful than I imagined it would be..."

CHAPTER 47

Georgina had been waiting by the pool area of Henry Hunt's palatial home for thirty minutes. In that time, she'd tried his phone twice—with a text on arrival and a call that she'd just placed. Both went unanswered. Henry was late and nowhere to be seen. She took a final sip of her cool peach-flavored ice tea and glanced around for Henry's housekeeper who'd delivered the drink and asked her to wait by the pool. Georgina placed the glass down on the table and slowly rose to her feet. She contemplated leaving the property and heading back to her car but then curiosity got the better of her. Quietly she made her way to Henry's office door.

A gentle push and she discovered it was unlocked.

A firmer push and the door opened.

She stepped inside.

As the door closed behind her, she stood motionless for a second and acclimatized. The normal soft drone of the antique fan was absent today, bestowing an unusual and unsettling quiet on the office, to the point where her own breathing and heartbeat seemed amplified. Georgina took a deep breath then her first tentative step toward Henry's desk. Her inclination was to go through Henry's filing cabinet, but then she spotted a dark blue leather-bound diary on the desk and made a beeline for it instead. She opened it up, found today's date, and there she was: *11:00am. Meeting - Gorgeous Georgina!*

She smiled.

Her cell rang, its piercing shrill shattering the silence and making her flinch.

She glanced at the screen—Rainbird.

"I'm in Henry Hunt's office," she whispered into the phone. "He's not here, gotta be quiet."

"Forget that," said Rainbird. "Mavis is the ghost."

"What?"

"Yeah."

"How?"

"I don't have time to explain. Where's Hunt?"

"He's supposed to be here, didn't turn up."

No sooner had the words left her mouth when a scribbled entry in Henry's diary jumped up from the page at her: *10:15. Mavis discussion, Buck House.*

"He was due at Mavis's at 10:15. I'm looking at his diary now, he has an appointment with her. Maybe he never left."

"Get there as soon as you can," said Rainbird. "Hunt's in serious danger. I'm on my way. I'll meet you there!"

Rainbird was at the beach house, closer to the Bucklesby mansion than Georgina, and so would beat her there. He ran to his Avanti, fired up the engine and hit the gas. The wheels squealed as he powered up the road, driving with critical urgency, weaving in and out of traffic, foot to the floor one minute, jumping on the brakes and sounding the horn the next, making up the rules of the road as he went, to get there in half the time it should have taken, until, finally, his car's tires skidded on the crunchy gravel outside Mavis's magnificent property.

He ran from the car, lungs heaving like a bellows as he stormed inside.

"Mavis!" he yelled as he stepped into the hallway, his words echoing in the cavernous room as he looked for her in vain.

He ran to the kitchen. The French doors were open, curtains flapping by their side in the breeze. Through the doors he strode, out into the brilliant light of the courtyard. As Rainbird's squinting eyes adjusted, four figures came into focus in the distance—Mavis, Henry, Cathleen and Stamford, standing near the dunes. He ran toward them and, as he got closer, his worst fears were realized. Henry, Cathleen and Stamford had their arms raised in the air submissively and were staring down the barrel at a gun, a gun pointed at them in a left hand—the hand of Mavis Bucklesby. Not just any gun either, but, by the looks of it, a beautiful antique pistol, all polished wood and gleaming steel: an early six shot Colt from the 1850s used in the civil war.

"Put the gun down, Mavis!" yelled Rainbird, when he got within earshot.

She spun around, her outstretched arm going from those by the dunes to Rainbird.

"Stay where you are! Move and I'll shoot, I tell you!"

Rainbird froze on the spot like a dead man.

She whipped her head and arm back toward the others, her attention flitting rapidly from Rainbird to them with increasing anxiety as she pointed the pistol between the two with deadly intent.

"I'll kill you too, Mr. Rainbird, if you don't back off. This has nothing to do with you. Go away and let me do what needs to be done to restore honor."

"Think it through Mavis. You'll spend the rest of your life in a cell. Let them go."

She scoffed. "That one's not going to work. Not now. You see, I've nothing to lose anymore. I've been given months to live. Pancreatic cancer. Eating away at my insides. There'll be nothing left soon. I'll never see trial. Nor will they see the light of another day!"

She turned to Henry, Cathleen and Stamford, her finger twitching on the trigger as her face hardened.

"Let them go," said Rainbird. "It was Lachlan Denoon who dishonored the memory of Charlie. You got what you wanted. You got your revenge on Lachlan. Let them go. Whatever part they played in this, it's minor."

"It most certainly is not!" retorted Mavis. "It was Henry who set the whole thing up in the first place. He suggested putting it out under Lachlan's name. I wish I'd never mentioned to him that I'd come across that old manuscript of Roger's."

"Only it wasn't Roger's, was it?" interrupted Rainbird. "You wrote *False Gods and Acid Fruits*."

"You're damn right I wrote it. That old fool of a late husband put his name on and took the credit for all my hard work. Most of Roger's success was down to me, not him. I'd come up with a plot that he'd half listen to and then patronizingly dismiss only, lo and behold, a couple of days later, sometimes even hours later, he'd have one of his inspired 'eureka' moments and would pitch almost the same idea straight back to me. Silly old fool didn't realize he was doing it; thought he was a genius. But there was nothing inspired or genius-like about the man. I had to rewrite most of his prose too, practically authored the entirety of his two most popular books. Not that I got any credit, but he got what was coming to him."

"You killed Roger?" asked Rainbird, astounded.

"Think that boat just blew itself up, do you?"

"My father was on that boat," said Henry.

"Meh," shrugged Mavis. "Two birds. One stone. He knew and was complicit. Back in the seventies he told me the market trend was for strong masculine male voices not housewives. Remind you of anyone? What was it you said to me? That the market trend now was for young handsome social influencers not old ladies. Chip off the old block, aren't you? Ready to meet him, are you Henry?"

Henry didn't answer.

"I've one question, Alfie," said Mavis. "How did you know it was me?"

"When I realized Charlie was your nickname for Charlotte, it all fell into place. Then the money to the stillbirth charity and our discussion at the church, I saw in your eyes what she meant to you."

"Charlie was my world," replied Mavis. "My book gave Charlie the life I always dreamed of for her. While I was carrying her, I would whisper to Charlotte in my belly, tender words of all the wonders the future held in store for her, and how I would help her make all her dreams come true. I kept her alive in my writing, giving her the life she should have had. And then Lachlan besmirched her memory forever and *murdered* her in cold blood for money." She turned to Henry. "With your complicity!"

"It's a work of fiction," he protested.

"She was my child!" screamed Mavis, tears in her eyes. "All I have left is that sacred dream for her, now forever tarnished because of Lachlan and because of you!"

"I only set up the deal, and you did well out of it, Mavis. It wasn't easy mediating between you and Lachlan. But that was my job and I did it well—well for the pair of you. But you need to understand, it was Lachlan's suggestion to kill off Charlotte, not mine."

"But you went along with it. You told me if it went out under Lachlan's name that you'd make sure the integrity of my story was honored. That my Charlie was honored. You gave me your word. You said it was a cast iron guarantee. Some guarantee that turned out to be. My beautiful Charlie was torn out of the television adaptation and you even had the audacity to ask me to rewrite the second book to reflect what Lachlan had announced it would be like."

"But none of this has anything to do with me," protested Cathleen. "We both despise Lachlan. We should be allies."

"Zip it, you cheap whore! Think I don't know about your affair with Roger? Think I didn't read all the little sordid handwritten notes and love poems you wrote for him? Well, think again, you Jezebel! I know why he gave you that endorsement as well—and it wasn't for the quality of your writing."

Cathleen's mouth fell open like a stunned trout.

"And just so you know before I put a bullet in you, it wasn't Lachlan who insisted Henry drop you."

Mavis raised her eyebrows with a suggestive smirk.

"You!?" exclaimed Cathleen.

"You better believe it. There was no way I was going to agree to work with Henry unless you got the chop first. I did so delight in your public humiliation when Lachlan made you the butt of all his jokes. He played his part well, I'll give him that. Still, what goes around comes around and your time is finally at an end."

Stamford Williamson seized his opportunity and spoke up.

"But why me? By all means kill them. By the sounds of it you'd be justified, more than justified, in fact, but I'm just an innocent bystander, aren't I? I think it's best I just leave. I've enough on my plate right now."

Stamford made a first cautious step to walk off. Mavis took aim at his chest and pulled the trigger.

There was an almighty explosion, a plume of white smoke, and Mavis recoiled from the pistol's kick, her arm jolting all over the place as she inadvertently shot Stamford in the leg, not body.

"Ahhhhh! Oh, God!" cried Stamford in agony. "Oh, m' knee!"

"What was that?" said Mavis sarcastically. "O.B.E.?"

As Stamford rolled on the ground, Mavis pulled the hammer back for a shot at Henry. In a flash, Rainbird seized his moment and lunged at Mavis's arm. Henry froze and Cathleen hit the deck. Mavis began to squeeze the trigger just as Rainbird hoisted her arm skyward.

Another explosion and a second shot fired into the air.

"No! I need them dead before I'm gone," yelled Mavis distraught, as Rainbird forced the pistol from her hand.

"It's over, Mavis," he said.

She began to sob and threw her arms around him. "I just wanted to kill them before I'm gone."

As she cried and Stamford screamed, a new sound cut through the turmoil—several police sirens. Flashing red and blue lights arrived in the driveway. Three cop cars, as well as Georgina's vehicle close behind, all coming to a skidding halt on the gravel.

"Over here!" yelled Rainbird as the police and Georgina scrambled from their vehicles.

Georgina and four uniformed cops ran toward the group, while a fifth overweight plain clothes officer did his best to waddle up the slight incline to join them. Even from a distance, it was clear that it was none other than Rainbird's old sparring partner, Detective Bruce.

"Move aside, I'm in charge!" barked Detective Bruce, gasping for air after he finally made it over. "Cuff her, men. Mavis Bucklesby, I'm arresting you for the murder of Lachlan Denoon. You have the right to remain silent. Anything you say can and will be used against you in a court of law."

"In which case, *please don't hit me again Detective Bruce*," retorted Mavis, with a mischievous grin.

Rainbird and Georgina laughed.

Detective Bruce scowled.

As the cuffs closed around Mavis's wrists, Rainbird turned to ask her a final question. "But why Williamson? I don't understand. What was his involvement?"

Mavis looked at him as if it was self-evident.

"Nothing," she stated matter-of-factly. "He's just thoroughly obnoxious. Thought I better add him to the list too. Leave the world a better place and all that. Pity I'm not a better shot."

And with that, even Rainbird didn't argue.

CHAPTER 48

Advancing to the steps of the courthouse, Rainbird clapped Mitch on the back before turning to face the crowd of reporters in front of him. The bright sunshine simultaneously warmed their faces and blinded them after the cool corridors of the building they'd just left. The sound of cameras clicking competed with the onslaught of questions from the news correspondents and, even with Rainbird by his side, it was clear Mitch was feeling overwhelmed by the attention.

Raising his hands for quiet, Rainbird began.

"Mitch Owens stands before you a free man, rightfully cleared of the crime he was accused of. Although he did lie, in a desperate attempt to prove his innocence, the judge has fairly sentenced Mitch to time served, leaving him free to move on with his life. Mitch won't be giving any interviews or comments after this statement today, no matter how much money you try to throw at him." Rainbird added his last comment with a purposeful look directed at one reporter in particular. "Mitch would just like to extend his heartfelt thanks to those who stood by him through this difficult time, and especially to Stephanie, his former girlfriend, now fiancée, and I quote: 'Without your support, I don't know how I would have made it through this ordeal. I look forward to our shared future together.'"

Rainbird smiled to Mitch as Stephanie took his hand.

Turning back to the cameras Rainbird announced, "And that's your lot, folks. Time to find a new story."

Ignoring the barrage of questions that followed, Rainbird stretched out an arm to part the crowd and led Mitch and Stephanie down the steps to where Georgina was waiting by his Avanti.

"Congratulations, Mitch, you two certainly deserve a bit of time to yourselves now," said Georgina.

"But not before a celebratory drink. You'll join us, won't you, Mr. Rainbird? Georgina?" asked Mitch.

Georgina flushed an uncharacteristic shade of pink.

"Oh, I kinda have other arrangements, just now. A date, actually..."

Rainbird turned to face the same direction as Georgina just as Henry Hunt pulled up to the curb nearby in a shining silver AC Cobra.

"No, George, really?" Rainbird groaned.

"What? He's handsome, gentlemanly, and taking me to a very nice restaurant in a very nice car. What's not to like?"

Rainbird laughed. "Well, don't do anything I wouldn't do."

"That still leaves plenty of options, doesn't it?" grinned Georgina. "I'll join you for a glass of bubbles after lunch. Henry has squeezed me into a small gap in his busy schedule."

As Georgina hurried off, Rainbird ushered Mitch and Stephanie into the back of his Avanti and was about to get in up front when he caught a glimpse of Veitch descending the steps.

"I'll be with you in a moment," he said, unable to resist one last dig at his opponent.

"Always nice to see justice done, don't you agree, Veitch?"

Veitch scowled. "You got lucky there, Rainbird. Mark my words, that boy will be back in front of the judge before too long, and he won't get away with it next time."

"Yet again, you're proving yourself remarkably cavalier with any sense of justice. Need I remind you of Mitch's innocence, Veitch? It's a shame the State Prosecution are too lazy to do their job properly, or we might not have wasted so much time here—again."

"Well, don't let me waste any more of your time then, will you?"

"Absolutely not. In the words of Patricia Parry-Jones, 'Sail away on your success, but don't forget to poison the waters behind you.'"

Veitch looked both enraged and confused. "Does that even make sense?"

"Of course not," laughed Rainbird, "but for now there are celebratory drinks to be had. Godspeed, my friend."

As Rainbird turned to walk away, he reflected on the result with a bit less bravado than he showed outwardly. Strangely enough, he'd quite liked Mavis, despite her homicidal tendencies, and felt an affinity to her situation. She'd done right by Mitch in the end—leaving him a percentage of her royalties for "his trouble." The rest would go toward a new maternity ward at the local hospital.

It was a funny business this, defending the innocent or sometimes the guilty, but Rainbird couldn't wait for his next case.

Made in the USA
Las Vegas, NV
17 October 2023